2.00

SECRET PASSAGES

A NOVEL

R. D. HATHAWAY

RD Hathaway Books

Secret Passages, Copyright © 2020, Edward D. Opstein

ISBN: 978-0-578-68002-6
eBook ISBN: 978-0-578-69223-4

https://rdHathaway.com
Twitter: @HathawayRd
Facebook: @RD Hathaway

Cover and interior design: Asya Blue

Cast of Major Characters

Present Day:

Rennie Haran . . . . Reporter for the Des Moines
Record newspaper in Des Moines,
Iowa

Bud. . . . . Rennie's Editor

Angie McGrady . . . . Chief Librarian and Archivist for
Simpson College in Indianola,
Iowa

Ms. Knoche . . . . Administrator of records at
Simpson College

Charles Sfumato . . . . Wealthy collector of ancient
artifacts, primarily Christian
documents; lives in California

Seth Galila - . . . . Affluent solicitor in London,
England who is devoted to pro-
tecting conservative perspectives
of Christian history and doctrine

Professor Matthew
MacDonald. . . . . Archeologist specializing in the
Near East retired from teaching
and ad hoc staff at the British
Museum

Mary MacDonald. . . . . Estranged sister of Professor
MacDonald

1920's:

Professor Matthias Justus . . . On sabbatical from Simpson College at the British Museum

Kenneth Warrington. . . . . Supervisor of Professor Justus
at the British Museum and the
receipt and inventory of new artifacts received at the museum

Bishop Worthy. . . . . Noted cleric and facilitator for
influential persons who support
the British Museum

Priscilla Shefford. . . . . Young administrative services
assistant working for Kenneth
Warrington and assigned to
assist Professor Justus

Lady Jane Sotterfeld-Gris . . . Wealthy benefactor to the British
Museum and sponsor supporting
sabbatical of Professor Justus

Reggie MacDonald . . . . Local thug and water-front
conman

PART ONE

Des Moines, Iowa
The Present

I / 1

"What the world needs is a hard slap in the face. What do you think, Balderdash?"

A large grey cat leaped from the arms of Rennie Haran onto the floor. Its long fur dusted the dark wood as the cat scampered down the stairway.

The hard heels of Rennie's boots banged down the oak steps of an old house until she stopped on a landing and stretched, producing a wide-mouthed yawn. She glanced outside to see the morning weather. Another yawn was captured in her hand.

"Uh!" she grunted, shaking her head. "Where's the coffee? Balderdash! Did you make coffee?" She grinned.

Her hand flowed through her long, dark brown hair to lift it from under the strap of her courier bag. Two steps above the last step, she paused and checked her white satin shirt for dribbles of toothpaste. She shrugged, then she saw Balderdash rubbing back and forth against the corner of the last step.

"Hey buddy, good morning. Sorry I've been such a bitch. Do cats have bad days?"

She lifted him up in her arms and walked to the couch in the living room, letting him jump to the cushion and then to the floor. Dropping her bag on the couch, she stabbed her hand in it when a cell phone demanded attention.

"Okay, okay! I'm here! Hold on!"

Searching through the bag, she dumped the contents on the

couch and grabbed the phone.

"Rennie Haran. Yeah, right. I don't know. I'm leaving for the office now. I'll call her when I get there. Thanks."

She studied the phone and pressed the icon for text messages. Squinting as she read, her mouth and face twisted. She peered over the edge of the phone at a bookcase where there were family photos, stacked books, and a wrapped package. One photo shows a woman in her 50's wearing a swimming suit and with a gold medal hanging from a ribbon around her neck. Next to that is one of a man the same age speaking at a lectern on which appears the seal of a university.

She dropped the phone on the bag and saw Balderdash on the sill of a window, studying something in the distance and flicking his tail.

"Hey, if you're not busy today, call my mom and catch up. Also, read dad's new book when you get a chance. You've probably wondered what ideas were shared by Buddha and Jesus."

The cat twitched its tail but didn't look back.

The phone chanted the arrival of another text message. Her nostrils flared as she checked it. She turned to Balderdash.

"Oh, and call scum-bag, and tell him I KNOW he messed up, like all over town! Tell him I'm busy for the next hundred years."

Rennie stuffed the dumped goods from the cushion into the bag, flung the strap over her shoulder, and stuck the phone in her pants pocket. She grabbed her purse from the table and pulled the strap over her other shoulder. The heels of her boots hammered again on the old hardwood flooring as she walked to where Balderdash was viewing the world. She bent down and stoked his fur. His head tilted up as he pretended to meow.

"Hey buddy, you see squirrels out there? Stick with me. We only need each other. Okay? No more people. Just you and me."

Her lips smacked a kiss in his direction as she stood and stormed out the door.

Des Moines, IA
Offices of the *Des Moines Record*

I / 2

The noise in the newsroom of the *Des Moines Record* was a subtle but continuous, tiny clacking of keyboard strokes in the buzz of a dozen conversations. Rennie hesitated next to her cubicle and looked at the scattered newspapers and messages on her desk. *Welcome to Monday,* she thought,

Dropping her purse on the mess, she slumped into her chair and growled. A moment later, her cell phone danced a loud tune, kicking her into action to dig it out of a pocket.

"Rennie Haran, Des Moines Record ... Oh, hi Mrs. Schmidt. Yes, I'll be there a little early to review the beauty pageant schedule. I'm sure the whole county is excited to see who wins ... Okay! Bye!"

A young woman with curly, blonde hair walked by Rennie's cubicle as she laid the phone down. She looked back, "So, Rennie, what's the big news coming out of the county fair? I hear you're on it."

"Susan, if I have to cover one more stupid, local event, the big news will be I've murdered someone."

The woman chuckled and continued down the aisle as Rennie pretended to shoot her phone with an outstretched finger.

Leafing through the messages, she stopped and stared at one scrawled note.

"I've got an investigation for you. See me. Bud."

Rennie jumped up and called out, "Susan, where's Bud?"

Susan pointed across the newsroom at Bud Shuster's office and disappeared into another cubicle as Rennie spun around and hurried toward the office of the News Editor. She cruised through the noise of ringing phones and the rustle of newspaper pages. Leaning to one side as she walked, she tried to see into the glass partition that forms one wall of Bud's office.

"Rennie. I'll be right there," he yelled from a cubicle behind her. Jerking around, she responded, "Jeeze, Bud. Okay."

"What'd I do? Wake you up?"

He laughed as he sauntered into his office. Rennie followed, arms crossed, and eyes wide open, quickly sitting in the guest chair in front of his desk. She didn't notice the worn vinyl covering on the seat.

He looked through a few phone messages, then dropped into his chair.

"What's up?"

"What's up? You left a note for me about some investigation. What is it?"

He ran his fingers through thin grey hair and leaned forward, looking at his desk and drawing in a deep breath.

"I had dinner this weekend with some people, and I met a fellow who does fundraising for Simpson College. He told me about some rich guy he knows on the West Coast who's into ancient relics. The guy on the coast told him of a Simpson professor who went to London to work at the British Museum on a project involving ancient stuff from Egypt. I guess he came home in a box. No one knows how or why he died."

"Now we're talking. And, you want me on it? What do we know?"

"Not much. They say his wife died in childbirth with their first kid, so he needed a break and got a sabbatical to the museum. Let's see. His name is Matthias Justus. Boy, he didn't get much justice."

"So, is there a police report or any leads?

"Huh? Rennie, this was like 90 years ago. It was in the '20's.

There's nothing. Go out to Simpson and see what they might have."

"You're kidding me, right? This guy died 90 years ago. For my first real investigation I get a hundred-year-old murder? Bud, give me something fresh. I don't believe this."

She jumped off her chair and paced the room.

"Okay, so now I have to give up the big county fair beauty pageant story to learn what happened to professor dead guy 90 years ago."

She stopped and glared at Bud. "You must hate me."

"Rennie, damn it. You're always complaining about not having something to dig into. You want to find the truth in everything. Well, here you go. Find the truth in this."

"Fine, okay. I'll take the big case. But you owe me. I get the next lead, and it will involve current dirt, not ancient."

"If it means you won't be in my office, that's great. If you want to find something, find a way to be nice to someone now and then. We'd all appreciate that."

"Yeah, like relationships make people happy."

Bud glanced at a framed picture of his wife on the credenza.

"Bud, I'm sorry. How are the grandkids doing?"

"Great, great. I get to go see them soon. I wish Grace could've been around. I always thought I'd be the first to go. I'm older, out of shape. She wanted me to retire."

"Sorry."

"What are you doing here? I gave you a dream assignment. Get going."

"Okay. If I do this, then I get something with more meat and contemporary. Right?"

Bud grunted, "Maybe, if you don't give me so much trouble."

A smile forced its way through Rennie's lips. "I'll take 'maybe' for 'yes.' So, what's this professor's name? What all do you know? Any family in the area?"

"Mathew, no Matthias, I think. It was Matthias Justus, spelled J-u-s-t-u-s. The school can tell you. They say he was involved in the King Tut discovery or something like that. That's all I got. The guy from Simpson said it might make an interesting story. He said Mr. West Coast has friends everywhere, and in high places. We need to help people like that."

"What? Bud, don't we serve enough people in high places? I'm doing this to please some money man on the West Coast? We're sitting a mile away from the State Capitol, and you know what crazy stuff goes on down there; closed door meetings deciding public policy, laying off social services people while giving special tax deals to hog lot owners to build more waste ponds to screw the environment. Let's risk upsetting a few people and hold their feet to the fire."

"Rennie, I'm glad you're frustrated. It takes people like you to keep us honest. I used to be like that. Just do me a favor and look into this, okay? Then we can all move on."

Bud grabbed some papers and turned away.

Rennie hurried to her cubicle and plucked two new message slips off her chair. Sitting down, she said to her computer screen, "Why do I do this?"

She found the website for Simpson College and called the main number. Working through an unhelpful phone menu, she finally reached a voice.

"Admin. This is Craig" a young voice responded.

"Hi, Craig. My name is Rennie, and I'm looking for some information on a professor who was at Simpson a long time ago. How would I go about that?"

She gave the young man the information about the professor, her direct line number, and asked how long it might take.

"Well, I don't know. I'm here alone right now. It might be in a few minutes or maybe Wednesday, when I come back in." His voice trailed off.

Rennie's face soured and her eyes closed.

"Is there anyone else who can help? I'm a reporter with the *Des Moines Record*, and this is important."

"Well, ma'am, I'll see what I can find and call you back in a little bit. What's your name again? Randy?"

"It's Rennie, R-e-n-n-i-e. Please call me as soon as you can. Thanks."

Her mind raced as she flicked a piece of lint from the slick fabric of her pants.

Pulling a spiral bound notebook from her canvas attaché bag, she opened it to a page with a small, yellow notepaper stuck on it. Near the bottom of the page, she wrote the date and made several dashes followed by brief notes of her conversation with Bud.

The ring of her cell phone startled her.

"Hello, Rennie Haran."

"Hi, this is Craig from Simpson. I looked up what I could on the professor you mentioned. I went all the way back to 1980 and couldn't find any mention of him in our records."

"Thanks, Craig. This professor was with the school much earlier; possibly in the 1920's."

"Oh, we wouldn't have those records here. You'd have to come in and arrange to have someone go through the old files."

She leaned forward as her head fell into her hand. "Okay, and who would have those files."

"Oh, I guess Admin."

"Fine, thanks."

She terminated the call and dropped the phone on her notepad.

"I'm going to get Bud for this," she snarled.

Rennie stabbed her hands into her pants pockets and left the newsroom. Half-way down the hall, she stopped and looked out the office windows at the city. From the fifth floor, the view was good. One could see the mausoleum-looking City Hall and the gold dome of the Capitol in the distance. She studied the other office buildings and wondered about all the decisions being made and the stories developing behind the windows. Watching people in the skywalks, rushing from one building to another, she thought of mice in a laboratory maze.

A middle-aged man with white hair lying over his ears walked by. "Hey Rennie, you must have a good one going."

"Yeah, Carl. A dead guy!" Rennie raised her eyebrows.

"Way to go," he called back as he hurried on.

By noon, she was on track with other stories. Her special report on the City's condemnation of downtown properties whet her appetite for revealing how big money moves among the privileged, facilitated by the City's Legal Department. That one had meat, but it had no priority with Bud.

Dave, a young staff writer, stopped by her cubicle and asked if she had plans for lunch. He enjoyed the moment of opportunity to look at her. Her large eyes, with equally strong and arched eyebrows stood above a straight nose and wide mouth. Her full lips displayed a light red gloss.

"Thanks, Dave. I've got to go check out a story, and it'll take a while," she replied without looking away from her computer screen.

Rennie looked up. "Not this time. Maybe another day?"

"Ok, sounds like you've got a hot one going," Dave responded with a nervous smile.

"Another day. That's a deal." Dave pointed his finger at her and winked.

As he left, she looked back at the screen and whispered, "Out of here."

To Indianola, Iowa

I / 3

Rennie strolled into the warmth of mid-May. Large, white clouds drifted across a bright blue sky. The smell of an Iowa summer was finally in the air. She hurried to her car. The old, dark blue Volvo stood out among the sleek new cars.

In minutes, she was on the road to Indianola, Iowa, home of Simpson College, with windows and sunroof open. Rennie's hair whipped around in the wind. Her head nodded in time to the thumping of a blues tune that filled the car.

The moment she crossed over Army Post Road at the edge of town, she felt a release of tension and fresh freedom. She realized she had not left the city for too many months. The countryside was so close, just minutes away, but rarely enjoyed.

Rolling hills, erupting in deep green and gold, flowed around her car as Rennie quietly planned her strategy for access to the records at Simpson. She grinned.

They don't know I'm coming.

As she arrived in Indianola, her eyes flashed across the street scenes, the houses, and the small businesses. She drove past a few blocks of modest, old two-story homes set back a relaxed distance from the sidewalk and from each other. It was nothing grand, but it was comfortable.

Iowa, modest and never intimate.

That idea of modesty changed when she arrived at the entrance to the campus. Guarding a walkway was a brick wall interrupted by stone pillars with stair step blocks of contrasting color. A building in the distance was a rich balance of form, with wood and deep red brick rising to a black mansard roof accented by a tower rising high above the roofline.

Rennie took inventory of her surroundings. She noticed another building that reminded her of an English castle, with massive red brick walls that held enormous windows.

She easily found a parking place, grabbed her bag and headed for the Administration Building. Her long legs reached out in strong steps as she swung one arm to match her stride.

"Excuse me," she said to a student. "Where is the admin building?"

The student turned without stopping and pointed at the castle-like structure. "There," he said.

Reaching the entrance, she jerked open one of the large wooden doors and stepped into a quiet, cold marble reception area. She scanned the interior for an office to begin her inquiry.

She walked up to a counter where a petite woman who looked about sixteen stood on the other side. She was sorting ledger-sized sheets of paper on the counter and humming.

The girl looked up. "Hi, can I help you?"

"Yes, thanks. I need some information on a professor. He worked here a long time ago. Back in the 1920's, I think. How would I get that information?"

The student's smile drifted away. She turned and looked at a large, older woman wearing a bright blue sweater, a dark brown skirt extending several inches below her knees, and white athletic shoes.

"Mrs. Knoche, this lady needs some information about a professor —" She interrupted herself and turned to Rennie. With confusion on her face she asked, "— in the Twenties?"

Mrs. Knoche looked over her reading glasses and plodded toward the counter. Her ample size and side to side tilting as she moved seemed to make every step an effort. She offered a polite but cool smile.

"How can I help you?"

"Hi, my name is Rennie Haran. I'm with the *Des Moines Record* and I'm doing some research on a professor who was with Simpson back about 1920. His name was Matthias Justus."

"How do you spell that?" the old woman asked with an old coffee-flavored breath.

"Matthias? Well, I ..." Rennie began.

"No, miss, The last name. Is it Justice as in the legal system? J-u-s-t-i-c-e?" The woman slowly removed her reading glasses and folded them.

"I don't recall, but I don't think so," Rennie responded.

"Well, it might be," the woman offered with a hint of sarcasm.

"Then again, it might be J-u-s-t-u-s, for I believe we had a professor with that name."

Rennie's jaw tightened. "Let's go with that Miss, what's your name again?"

"Knoche, and that's Mrs. Knoche."

"What can you tell me regarding Professor Justus?"

"When and what did you need, Miss? We're closing out the semester and there is much to do for our students." A cool smile curled Mrs. Knoche's lips.

"Just the basics would be fine; when he was here, what he taught. That stuff."

"Fine. You can sit on the bench over there while I see what we have."

The woman turned, walked to a microfiche machine and sorted through small pieces of film in a wooden box. She examined one through her glasses and slipped the film into a machine tray. A bright light lit up the screen, and Mrs. Knoche maneuvered the film around the screen.

Rennie stifled a laugh. Easing onto the bench, she checked her phone for calls and messages while glancing to see if dear old Mrs. Knoche had something for her.

After several minutes, Rennie heard her say, "Ah, yes. Here it is."

Rennie hurried to the counter and watched the woman write a few items on a slip of paper.

She returned to the counter and read from her notes.

"Mr. Justus, J-u-s-t-u-s, was with Simpson from July of 1917 until August of 1923. He was chair of the Department of Religious Studies, taught Greek, and he was a guest lecturer at Iowa State University on the languages of ancient Greek, Latin, Aramaic, and Coptic."

Rennie jotted a few notes. "Is that it? Anything about his death or heirs or belongings? Where's he buried?"

"That's what we have. Personal details are not in our records If you would like more information, I recommend you go to the library and ask for Miss McGrady. She's Chief Librarian and responsible for the archives."

Rennie put away her notebook and took a few steps to leave. The words "Oh, miss," hit her in the back of the head. She looked back at the woman and returned to the counter. This time Mrs. Knoche did not attempt to fake a smile.

"Please keep in mind that the stories of our faculty are not the story of this college. This is a good United Methodist school. We don't get involved in such things."

Mrs. Knoche looked to the side to see how close the student was to her. "There's a sort of history understood here regarding questions that were raised about the professor. So, no shall we say 'remembrance' of him is in the college records. Professor Justus may have come in touch with something evil, miss. It should be left alone."

Rennie studied the woman's face, seeking clues to a sudden mystery. "What do you know that I should leave alone?"

Mrs. Knoche shifted some papers around and pursed her lips. "I wasn't here at the time of course, but reports were that two women from England returned with his remains and oversaw a memorial service and his burial. Two women from England. The professor's wife and child had died just months earlier."

Rennie and Mrs. Knoche held direct eye contact for what seemed like a long time.

Finally, Rennie said, "men."

She backed away. "Thanks. If I need to check back with you, should I call or stop by?"

Mrs. Knoche's expression remained serious. "This is where I am."

Rennie exited and stopped after going down a few steps. She looked up at the sky. "Such things?" she said softly. "Two women from England? What the heck —?" her voice trailed away.

She asked a couple of students walking by for directions to the library. "Oh, Dunn? That's my favorite place," the young woman gushed. "It's right down there."

Rennie hurried through the double door entry into the library and paused. Off to the right was a small pool with a fountain spraying softly onto the surface of the water. She walked to a long counter on the left and told the young man behind it that she was looking for Miss McGrady.

"Sure, hold on," he said and turned and walked through a doorway.

Rennie tapped on the counter and adjusted the strap of her bag. She thought about Mrs. Knoche's reference to "something evil."

A woman about thirty came through the doorway and approached the counter. Her blond hair was pulled back in a stereotypical librarian bun. She wore heavy, navy blue framed glasses. She moved with grace but also a sense of determination.

"I'm Angie McGrady. How can I help you?" Rennie introduced herself and explained what she was looking for.

"I'll see what I can find and then call you. May I have your number?"

Rennie took a business card out of her leather case and set it on the counter. "Do you have any idea how long it may take? I could wait a few minutes."

"I'm tied up with something right now, but I can call you tomorrow. May I ask why you need this information?"

Darned good question lady.

"Well, my editor heard that this professor was an interesting story, and he asked me to look into it. I really don't know anything about the guy. If you could help me with a little information, I'd appreciate it. I have more contemporary stories to pursue."

A point of curiosity shot through Rennie's mind. "Angie, has Mrs. Knoche been with Simpson for a while?"

"Oh, my gosh, yes," she said brightly. "She's been here since the sixties. In fact, the woman before her had been here for about fifty years. The two of them handled the whole twentieth century." Angie's eyes widened.

"I'll bet they knew about everybody and everything."

"Maybe so," Angie said. "I'm afraid I need to get back to something. I'll call you soon about those records."

The drive back to Des Moines seemed much longer than the trip to Simpson. Rennie wondered what Mrs. Knoche knew about Professor Justus. She appeared to be worried that something might come out that could harm the college, or even worse. What did this person do, or what did the college do to him? He died or was killed in London. She spoke of something evil.

"Now, what's up with that?" Rennie demanded of her windshield.

Back at the office, she called her friend John in the newspaper's archives section. Rennie told him of the annoying assignment she had received and that she could use a little help with any information the paper might have on the professor. He said he would see what he could find. Rennie hung up and felt a growing rush of energy for other projects.

By five o'clock, she had forgotten about her mystery professor. She was ready to say "goodbye" to Monday. As she lifted her bag, her telephone rang. She looked back at the phone and closed her eyes for a moment. When it rang again, she grabbed it.

"Rennie Haran."

"Miss Haran, this is Angie McGrady. I found a lot of material here on your professor. Newspaper clippings, some old leather files, books. Three good-sized boxes of stuff. It's rather musty, but it does look interesting. For example, did you know that British royalty came here for his burial?"

Rennie stiffened.

She continued. "I've set it all up in a workroom here. It's locked and you can look at it whenever convenient. Just ask at the counter for the key. They have your name."

Rennie's eyes darted with interest. "Okay. Thanks, Angie. I'll be down soon."

British royalty, in Indianola, Iowa?

San Francisco, CA
The Present

I / 4

"**M**r. Sfumato, Michael is on line one."

"Thank you, Tina."

For a man of seventy, Charles Sfumato moved swiftly and with grace across his expansive, walnut-paneled office. The plush carpeting muffled each step. His fingers grasped an ornate, gold telephone receiver, lifting it from the cradle. The movement was reflected off the polished, black marble surface of a large desk.

He eased into the burgundy leather comfort of his chair. His other hand, speckled with brown spots across long hills of veins, reached up to display manicured fingertips. Gently tugging on the cuff of a fine linen sleeve, he appreciated an ancient, silver coin framed in a circle of gold holding the cuff together.

Sfumato placed the telephone against his ear. The silver hair of his sideburn swept back against the gold edge of the phone. A slight smile parted his lips. "Hello, Michael, how are things in London?"

The man on the line expressed his frustrations with working through bureaucracies and unhelpful people.

Sfumato lifted an ivory pen from a notepad made of parchment. "Yes, I understand. I appreciate your recent efforts to find the documents. I'm not surprised there is such disarray in the records of the British Museum. For all the decades we have been searching for this holy treasure, their custodians have probably stacked another undocumented and dusty relic on top of it."

"That would not be a surprise, sir. Finding any consistent

records is a challenge, as well."

"Yes, and the warehouses are as bad. Our people who have been inside were baffled by what they found in the storerooms. We must not give up, though. Nothing in all of history compares with these documents. Nothing is more holy."

Adjusting the reading glasses over his tired eyes, he listened to Michael's continued report on their efforts. Disappointed, he laid down the pen without putting ink on the pad. "It's okay, Michael. We're not the only ones who haven't been successful in this hunt. I'm pursuing another avenue of opportunity. It's here in the States. I've been in contact with a friend in the vicinity of a college in Iowa, where the professor came from. I'm embarrassed I had not thought of it before."

"But, sir," Michael queried, "didn't you have someone go to the college long ago?"

"Yes, very long ago. But the library was being renovated and no one could access the records. It was poor timing. Besides, they could find no family and the few on campus who remembered the professor were either discreet or hostile."

"Might this new inquiry risk disclosure, sir?"

"I'm certain they are unaware of the real story. Only a few of us have that privilege. If anyone else knew of the treasure lying on some shelf or in some old file cabinet, the media would hear of it. There would be a search with the fervor of a reality television show. We, of course, would be characterized as the evil doers, slithering through the dark to destroy the Word of God. Of course, there are some like that."

Michael laughed, "It's interesting how so many people get lost in the drama of an issue and miss the purpose."

"My friend, the emotion of beliefs often gets in the way of pragmatism, but it can also raise the price!"

Sfumato's voice softened to a whisper. "Let's not forget our competition and what they'll do to stop us and anyone else. We need not have any stones thrown in our path or pushed down our throats. That brutality must stop. Seth has demonstrated his ruthless ways from London to Cairo. We must remember that he also has had people placed in the museum. They are dangerous people. You must be safe."

Extending his free arm and turning his wrist, he studied a large, platinum watch, observing the second hand smoothly sweep across the mother-of-pearl face of time. "It's time for the morning fog to reveal the Golden Gate. You must come to San Francisco and see it. Let's look forward to celebrating the addition of the documents to my collection. It will be our little secret, but we will celebrate with enthusiasm. Michael, please be careful. I sense that we may have to finally confront Seth and whoever else interferes. Great harm may be on the horizon for some. Update me on anything new in London. I'll let you know what I hear from Iowa."

London, UK
1923

I / 5

Matthias paused to enjoy the smell of fresh bread before he stepped into the kitchen. It was the beginning of his fourth day in London, and he already felt at home. The owner of the boarding house, Mrs. Whitley, had been helpful in getting settled in.

He watched her shove a stick into the oven and then wipe her hands on her apron. A short, plump woman, she moved with quick precision around the kitchen. He took a deep breath, savoring the fragrance of the fresh, hot bread. "Ah, that smells so good!"

Mrs. Whitley whirled around and placed her fists on her hips. "Professor Justus, is that what they do in America?"

Matthias stammered, "Oh, sorry, ma'am. I didn't mean to startle you. I was just enjoying the fragrance of the bread."

She nodded her approval. "Well then, professor, come in then. What would you like for breakfast? This is a big day for you, your first day on a new job."

Matthias sat at the kitchen table. "Yes, it is, a very big day for me, indeed."

She took out a fresh loaf of bread and began to slice it. "Just you don't let that cousin of mine run you ragged."

"No, ma'am, I won't."

Turning back to the cabinet, she continued with her work. She brought him a plate with two slices of fresh bread and marmalade, a small slab of butter, and an apple.

"Coffee, then?" she asked. "And, I suppose your being from,

where is it —?"

"Iowa."

"Oh, yes, Iowa. Do you drink milk or juice or something more?"

"Yes, ma'am. All those. Thank you."

Matthias felt like a little boy at his grandmother's table.

"Professor, what brought you here to London? It's awful far from America to work for a few months."

"Yes, America is far away, and I wish the work could be for a longer period. This is a rare opportunity for me to work in what might be the most prestigious museum in the world and on a project of historic significance. The documents from Oxyrhynchus could offer profound insights into ancient times."

Deep in thought, he stirred his coffee. "I experienced a tragedy back in Iowa, and the dean of my college thought it might be good for me to have a sabbatical. He learned of the need at the museum for help on this project and made inquiries. With much good fortune, I was accepted."

Mrs. Whitley moved through the kitchen more quietly than before. Finally, she asked, "Do you know how to get to the museum?"

"Yes, I strolled over there yesterday. It's an impressive sight."

Mrs. Whitley cleared vegetables from the counter and wiped it with a small, heavy cloth.

"Mrs. Whitley? I wonder if I may ask you about Mr. Warrington."

She rinsed her hands in the sink. "Of course, but I can't talk about Kenny as 'Mr. Warrington.'"

"I was wondering if you might tell me a little about him. After all, he will be my boss for a few months."

As Mrs. Whitley sliced carrots and celery for a stew, she tilted her head from side to side as though she was trying to decide what to say. "Well, Kenny is a good chap I suppose. But, he's well, —." Mrs. Whitley turned and stuck a fist against her hip. "I guess you might say he's a bit stale."

"How's that?"

"I think he always believed he would be more than what he is, and if he goes much higher, he has to work around blokes who have education and family history, which he doesn't have."

The busy woman ambled across the small kitchen to grab a large pot off a hook on the wall. "Kenny's job is all he's ever had, and it's very important to him. He has no children you know. That job is everything to him, but to many people it's not much."

"But, ma'am, he's the Near Eastern Collections Manager for the Egyptian Bureau of the British Museum. That is quite an accomplishment."

"Well, professor, if you regard him that way, the next few months will be very good for both of you."

Matthias relaxed in his chair. He cut off a piece of an apple and ate it.

"Professor, I don't see why anyone is interested in those things, those dead things."

Professor Justus nearly choked on another bite of apple. "I'm sorry. Those dead things?"

"You know, all those mummies from Egypt. Kenny said their body parts are kept in jars. This Bloomsbury area is right in the middle of all of this, I call it 'witchcraft.' It's too mysterious. I'll just say that. It's mysterious."

Mrs. Whitley's head rocked to punctuate each of her statements.

"Yes ma'am, the Near Eastern Collection is a fascinating array of ancient artifacts, and you are right about the mystery attached to them."

"Well," she interrupted. "It's more than that. The Temple is not far from here you know, and that is about as mysterious a place as can be. And, the Mason's place is not far from here."

Matthias leaned back in his chair. "The Mason's place? You mean a Masonic Lodge?"

She swiveled around and looked at him. "Do you know about that?"

"There's a Mason's organization in Iowa."

"What! In Iowa!" She shook her hands. "You see; they're everywhere. These mystery places are everywhere, even in Iowa, in America."

Matthias chuckled softly. "Please tell me about the Temple. I'm not familiar with that. Is it near here?"

"Oh, no, no. It may be a couple of miles. But you don't want to go there."

"Really, why not?"

"It's an ancient place, full of old things. You know, those knights that were in the Crusades. That was their place, and who knows what's in there. It's mysterious."

"Knights, and the Crusades; do you mean the Knights Templar?"

Mrs. Whitley swung around. She pointed a large knife at Matthias. "Them's the ones. The Knights Templar. What do you know about them?"

"Well, not much, other than they had a devotion to protect Christian artifacts. You say they have a place here, a Temple?"

Mrs. Whitley turned back to the cabinet. She unwrapped a piece of raw meat and chopped off large chunks. She said nothing for a few moments. She laid down the knife and moved to the sink to wash and dry her hands. The determined little woman looked back at Matthias. "Professor, there is good and evil in the world. One often finds them in the same place, especially if it's mysterious."

Matthias swallowed the last bite and put his plate in the sink. When he started to rinse it, Mrs. Whitley grabbed the dish out of his hands.

"Here, now, that's not men's work. So, what time do you have to be at work professor?"

"The information letter said that work hours began at 9 o'clock, but I'd like to be there early. I'm not sure how long it takes on Monday morning to get there. It's only about six blocks or so. Perhaps, if I leave before 8:30 I'll be fine."

"Well, it might only be fifteen minutes," she responded. "But, be careful of those motorcars. They are all over now. They will as soon run you down as they would blast more soot into the air. Did you have a motorcar in Iowa, Professor?"

"I did. It was a Model T Roadster. I got it new in '19."

Mrs. Whitley glared at him.

"Well, it was necessary. You see, Iowa is quite rural, so to go from one place to the next, well, uh, ..."

"And, I suppose a horse isn't good enough."

"Oh, no. I enjoy riding. I grew up on the farm. I'd better get up to my room and get my things together."

Matthias took a few steps toward the stairs and then stopped. He looked back at Mrs. Whitley. "Thank you, ma'am, for breakfast. I enjoyed it, and I appreciated our visit."

Without turning around, Mrs. Whitley raised her right hand and gave a light wave.

As Matthias prepared to leave for his first day at the British Museum, Mrs. Whitley handed him a tin box. It was a few inches deep and big enough to hold a large book.

"What's this?" he asked.

"It's just a little food, dear. A man's first day on a new job, sometimes he'll need a bite, and I don't know if you'll be able to get out for lunch."

"Mrs. Whitley, this is very nice. Thank you."

"Well, get off then, now. You don't want to be late for your first day on the job."

"I will ma'am and thank you for helping me feel so at home in this new place."

"Professor, you're paying me well for it."

Matthias eased his leather attaché bag off a wooden peg in the hallway and swung the strap onto his shoulder. He released a buckle on the bag and lifted the flap to check what was inside. There were two silver pens and a leather writing portfolio with a small stack of writing papers. He placed the metal tin in the bag, looked at the front door of the boarding house, took a deep breath, and headed for his new job.

As he strolled down the wide sidewalk, all of his senses were drinking in the historic city. The roar of the cars and trucks, the chatter of many dialects, the acrid smell of the air, and the dazzling array of clothing styles reminded him he was far from Indianola, Iowa. He was not sure which was real and which was a dream, London or Iowa.

He didn't notice that people stared at him as he strolled down the sidewalk, with his brisk gait, studying everything. He was in the greatest city in the world, and he was on his way to work at the greatest of all museums.

When he came to the corner of Drury and Broad Street, he wanted to run across the street, but decided to enjoy the pause in his adventure. Standing near him was an attractive woman dressed far better than any he had ever seen. The refinement of exquisite cloth, lace trim, and pearl buttons gave her a regal presence. He tried to observe her without her noticing his attention.

He saw her chin turn slightly in his direction and her eye move, perhaps catching him in her peripheral vision. He reached up and touched up the brim of his hat. "Good morning, ma'am."

Her chin quickly turned forward again.

"Oh, sorry ma'am. I'm from America, and this is my first trip to London."

His heart was racing. He turned and looked in another direction. In his peripheral vision, he noticed her chin turn toward him again. The corners of her mouth curled up.

With a break in traffic, he dashed across the street. As he continued down the sidewalk, he looked into the shop windows and then out to the street. He found himself wondering where the woman worked. Was it in one of the shops along the way? Or was she a great lady, and he had committed a serious faux pas?

As he paused at one shop window, he studied the images in the glass to see if she was following down the sidewalk. The street was too busy, and the sidewalk was much too crowded to see her.

At New Oxford Street, he turned left and continued on the path he had charted out the day before. A newsboy ran up to him and paused. "Paper, sir?"

Matthias jabbed his hand into his pocket and pulled out some change. He held it out to the boy. "How much?"

The boy got a sour look on his face. "Why, two pence, sir."

He stared at Matthias' hand full of coins and pulled out two pennies and handed him the paper.

Opening it, he scanned the pages with deep satisfaction. Matthias stood in the middle of the sidewalk, ignorant of the people moving around him like a strong river current around a boulder.

He sighed, "my first *London Times*."

He tucked the paper under his arm and moved into the flow of humanity, picking up speed and quickly passing others. Walking up Great Russell Street, the entrance façade of the British Museum came into view. A long row of Ionic columns guarded the entry with huge sculptures held above them. Matthias' pace slowed to a stop. He gazed at the building, feeling full of hopeful anticipation. As he approached the entrance door, he paused to read the inscription on a pilaster to the right. It acknowledged the staff members of the Museum who died in the

War. He took a deep breath and could not move forward.

A woman's voice hit him from behind. "Can I help you, sir?"

"What? No, thank you." Matthias stuttered. He forced a grin at the attractive, young woman.

She tilted her head and looked at him. "Are you sure, sir? I work here."

"Oh, perhaps you can," he responded. "I am Professor Matthias Justus, and I will also be working here, for the summer, at least."

The young woman squinted and leaned back. She was quiet for a moment. "Well, then, I guess we may be working together."

She turned, went to the door and looked back. "This way, sir," she said, then entered the building.

"Oh, miss," he called.

Matthias ran up the steps and into the building. He saw her say something to a man who did not look at her. The man raised his right arm and pointed down the hall. Without stopping, she made a smooth turn and continued down the corridor. The man looked at Matthias.

"Yes, sir, may I help you?" he asked.

Matthias hurried up to him but watched the woman disappear down the hallway. "Yes, thank you. My name is Justus, Professor Matthias Justus, and I will be working here. I need to find a Mr. Kenneth Warrington. Do you know him?"

"I am he, Professor." The man's voice was crisp, yet soft.

"Oh, I am delighted to meet you, sir."

Without another word, Warrington turned to his right and began walking down the hallway. The men strolled down the hall in what was, for Matthias, an awkward silence. He thought of Mrs. Whitley's comment. Indeed, Mr. Warrington seemed a bit stale.

Warrington gestured in a slow sweeping motion with his right hand. "We are in the Roman Gallery, now."

"On the other side of the Entrance Hall, you will find the Manuscript Saloon, the King's Library and various oriental libraries. That area contains mostly manuscripts. There is an early biblical document there that might interest you; a Pentateuch. There are also a variety of Greek and Latin documents; some are works of Plato, Aristotle and so on."

Matthias' eyes widened. Warrington turned and continued down the hall.

"As you see here, this is mostly architectural sculpture; about the 5th century, B.C. of course. That is the Archaic Room. The lions and figures relate to Apollo's Temple; the one at Didyma." Warrington observed Justus.

Matthias' head swiveled back and forth as they passed each massive display. He quickly studied the forms and the small cards that named and dated each exhibit.

"Over here, this is the Ephesus Room and over there, that is the Elgin Room," Warrington's hand again waved in the direction of another display area.

Matthias stopped for a moment and looked into the room. "Mr. Warrington," he said, without looking at the man.

Warrington had taken two more steps and looked back.

"Mr. Warrington, are these from the Parthenon? I've seen pictures of these." He held his breath as he waited for the answer.

"Of course, Professor. These were a gift from Lord Elgin. They have been in the collection for over a hundred years. Professor, we will arrange a tour for you later." Warrington turned and continued down the hall.

Matthias peeked into the room again, then caught up with Warrington. He walked a little behind the man, partly out of deference but also to more carefully observe him. He appeared about 60, with a pale but slightly red tone to his fleshy face. The black, vested suit he wore may have been of good quality, but up close, it appeared to be thin in areas. The pressed, white collar was faded.

The man moved with a formal, stiff dignity. It did not seem to be a natural gait. His hair was not smoothly cut. They stopped.

"This may be of more interest to you, Professor. The Assyrian Transept has a few interesting items from the palace of Sargon and an obelisk from Nineveh. The winged lions are from Nimroud. Of course, you know all about that."

Warrington seemed to await a reply. He continued, "The Nimroud Gallery is precisely the same size and shape as the original room in the palace from which the pieces were removed."

"Breathtaking," Matthias said. "Simply, breathtaking."

"Yes, well, let's continue, Professor. Over here, we have the Assyrian Saloon."

Matthias stared in amazement at the large, glass-roofed hall. Massive slabs of sculpture were artfully set throughout the room, providing a heavy base to the airy ceiling. He noticed that Warrington had walked away, so he dashed after him.

"These two halls may interest you, considering the find upon which you will be working. On the left is the Northern Egyptian Gallery and on the right is the Southern Egyptian Gallery. We have three halls on the ground floor devoted to the works from Egypt, mostly larger sculptures, and there are six rooms on the upper floor where you will be working. That does not include, of course, the storage and work rooms that you will be in. The mummies and smaller objects are up there. Is there any particular dynasty of interest to you, Professor?"

"Well, that's a good question. By the way, do you prefer to go by 'Mr. Warrington,' or 'Doctor or Professor?'"

The old man stared at Matthias. "'Mister' is fine, thank you." He turned and continued walking.

Matthias again matched his pace. "Very good. I was going to say, the early dynasties are fascinating, such as the fourth, with Khufu, and then there is the twentieth with the Ramses kings. Oh, I'm sorry to digress, but isn't the Rosetta Stone here?"

A cold intensity suddenly filled Matthias. He touched Warrington's sleeve.

Warrington looked down at Matthias' fingertips on his coat and stopped.

"Forgive me," Matthias said. "As one who appreciates ancient texts, the Rosetta Stone is like the Holy Grail. It changed everything. With it, the ancient Egyptian world was opened to all."

"Professor, you are in the most important museum in the world. The greatest historical treasures of all time are within these walls. Not only that, but we are receiving now, and soon, you will be handling artifacts that have not been seen or touched in three thousand years. The Tutankhamun find may be the most prolific of all. It will be important that we maintain our composure as we identify and catalog the items. Yes, we still have the Rosetta."

He turned and began again his slow walk. Matthias quietly followed.

"Mr. Warrington, I assure you that my delight in this opportunity, to serve even briefly here, under your supervision, is a great honor and I will conduct myself in an entirely professional manner."

"Indeed," was all Warrington would offer in response.

After a moment, he added, "I imagine any one room here is more impressive than all of Ohio."

"Yes, Mr. Warrington, it would be. Well, I'm from Iowa, sir."

"Indeed," Warrington responded. "Here we are at the northwest staircase. We can go up to your area."

Matthias held the leather strap of his attaché case with both hands and followed Warrington up the stairs. His eyes nearly filled with tears of happiness. Grief was left behind. Joy was around the corner.

PART TWO

Indianola, Iowa
Simpson College
The Present

II / 1

Rennie hurried across campus toward the library, past students strolling in the sunshine of a warm Spring. She pulled her cell phone from her bag as it blared, and with a twist of her wrist, the screen came alive.

"Hi, Bud. What's up? Yeah, I'm on it. I'm at Simpson now. Yeah, thanks. I'll try to be nice. When I finish this little project of yours, you get me an interview with the Speaker of the House. Hah! No, this will be quick. The bleeding hearts will love it. Bud, I've got to go. I'm at the danged library. Okay, remember you owe me."

Reaching the counter, a student worker on the other side turned toward her. The student had a small chrome ball on the side of her nose and a silver pin pierced through her eyebrow.

"Hi, I'm Rennie Haran from the *Des Moines Record*. Angie McGrady set aside some materials in a work room for me to review. How do I find those?"

The student opened a three-ring binder and turned the pages. Running her finger down a handwritten list, she stopped at one entry. "Yes, here you are. Second floor, room three. I'll get the key."

The young woman turned to the base cabinet behind her and removed a key with a tag attached. "It's just up the stairs on your left side, down a bit."

Rennie took the key and climbed the stairs two steps at a time. She found the room and unlocked the door. She hit the light switch and put her bag on a plastic chair in front of a six-foot table, on which sat three cardboard boxes. The end of each box had a large white label with identity and location information. She peered at one and read, "Archive Permanent. Justus, Professor Matthias. Staff. Sec. 4. 2 of 3."

"Okay, doc, let's get at it. Tell me and tell me quick."

Rennie removed the lids from the boxes and set them against the wall. She leaned over each box to review the contents. One held a small, framed picture. As she turned her head to look at it, the door suddenly opened. Rennie snapped up.

"Oh, sorry to interrupt," the counter student said. "I forgot to give you the gloves. It's necessary to wear these cotton gloves when you handle items from the permanent archives. Sorry."

Rennie let out a deep breath. "Fine, okay, thanks."

Slipping on the gloves, Rennie lifted out the picture frame. It displayed a handsome young couple. The man appeared to be tall with a confident gaze, and the woman was delicate but equally confident. A bouquet of flowers on a short pillar behind them. His right hand held her left. Rennie turned the frame over and looked at the back. There was a handwritten note, "Hope and Matthias, forever." Rennie turned the frame over again and carefully looked at the man. "Yes, you are a hottie, my friend; and, what happened to you miss?"

She put the frame back into the box and carefully moved aside papers, books and folders with her gloved hand. She slid her index finger along the spine of a few books, leather bound and still in good condition. In another box, she noticed that a third of the box was occupied by a black, leather attaché case with a heavy leather strap. She grabbed the handle of the case with one hand and used her other hand to hold back the folders from the case. Rennie lifted the case out of the box and laid it on the table. She looked at the brass clasp that held the top shut.

Someone knocked on the door.

"Come in," Rennie said.

The door opened, and Angie McGrady looked in. "Hi, am I disturbing you? May I come in?"

"Come in, I was just getting started."

"It's a nice case; his attaché," Angie offered.

"Yeah." Rennie looked down at the case. "It's kind of weird. I didn't expect to feel so invasive."

Angie put on a pair of cotton gloves she was carrying and pushed aside some files in one of the boxes. "It's interesting that our lives can come down to a few boxes of stuff. Here at the library, we keep in mind that what we have in storage is not just the item but also the meaning of the item. It's natural to feel something 'deeper' about them. In this case, it's a man's life, or a piece of a life."

She adjusted her glasses. "We don't normally have this much personal stuff on a person. I think in this case, there may not have been any relatives found, and of course, back in the 1920's things were a little less formal in terms of archival science. They might have considered Professor Justus as something of a celebrity, with the royal visitors and all. Did you see the article about the royal woman who attended his burial?"

Rennie was still looking back and forth across the boxes and the leather case. "No, I haven't got there yet."

Angie put her finger on one of the file folders. "It's in here, I think."

Rennie removed the file and laid it on top of the attaché case. She opened the folder and leafed through the yellowed newspaper clippings that had been slipped into clear plastic sheet protectors. She noticed that three were from August of 1923 and one was dated June of 1935.

Angie pointed at one. "This is it."

Lifting up the item, Rennie skimmed the first few paragraphs.

"Wow, this is interesting."

"Also in attendance at the site were two people from England. The gentleman accompanying the woman spoke for them, and he acknowledged the honor and excellence by which Professor Justus had served the British Museum. He referred to the woman as 'her Ladyship' but would not further identify her. He indicated they simply wished to offer their respect to the Professor, his family and colleagues."

Rennie looked up. "Who were they, Angie? There must have been some connection for them to come all the way to Iowa for this guy."

"I don't know. I only looked at a few things. There may be more on them. I've got to get back. Let me know if you need anything." She left the room and closed the door.

Rennie didn't notice her departure. She sat down and began to scan the newspaper articles. She wrote notes on a yellow pad of paper and made an outline of the resources. After a few minutes, she placed the articles back into the file folder and slipped it between other folders in the box. She removed one of the books and looked at the title on the dark leather cover. It read, "Field Notes, British Museum." She opened the cover and leafed through the first pages.

"Boring," she muttered.

Rennie closed the cover and laid the book on top of one box. She removed the framed photo and looked at the two people. "What happened over there?" she asked them.

Sliding the frame back into its place, Rennie looked through each of the boxes.

She grabbed her yellow pad, labeled three sheets of paper as "box 1," "box 2," and "box 3," then inventoried the items of each box. Suddenly, her cell phone began to chime loudly.

"Oh, dang it!" She looked at the door as she ran around the table to her bag. Fumbling through the contents, she grabbed the phone, and hit the "talk" button. "Yes," she said softly but with intensity. "Thanks for calling back."

She was eager to speak with this caller to close in on the key details of her story on the city's condemnation of downtown properties. Ending the call with an appointment to meet, she set the phone to "vibrate."

Now, that's a story.

Nearly an hour later, the door opened and Angie McGrady peeked in. Rennie had both elbows on the table and leaned her cheek into one hand as she flicked her pen in the air with the other hand. "You doing okay?"

Rennie looked up and tugged on her lower lip. She said nothing.

"Sorry, I'll leave you alone."

"Oh, no, it's okay. I was just deep in thought. Come in."

"So, did you find out about the royalty?"

"Not much. They stayed in Des Moines, separate suites, under the name of 'Brown.' Came in and left very quietly."

Rennie looked over at the boxes. "It's really kind of sad. He seems like a nice guy, but something went bad over there in England. His wife, Hope, I guess she died here. There's a note from some guy at the museum. His title is he's the 'Keeper' and he says he would appreciate the Professor's cooperation with the police. That bothers me."

Rennie stared at the boxes. "Then, he died. According to one of the articles, he drowned or was killed. They apparently didn't look into it. They just boxed up him and his stuff."

"So, do you have your story?" Angie leaned against the door jamb.

"I'm not sure what I've got here. This could go in a lot of

directions." Rennie grinned. "It'd be a lot easier to interview the guy; pick him apart."

"Yeah, well, like before, if you need anything, you know..."

As Angie began to withdraw, Rennie asked, "Oh, yes, there is one thing. Where would the cemetery be?"

"Well, it's probably the old one just south of town. It's easy to find, maybe a mile, right side of the road. I don't think there's an office there, so you might want to call the caretaker's office before you go out. It's pretty big. I'll get the number for you."

A few minutes later, Angie returned with a slip of paper with the phone number.

"Thanks. Can I just leave this all out?" Rennie motioned to the boxes.

"Yes, of course. How long do you expect this to last?"

"Oh, not long, a few days, max. I'll be back tomorrow to get at it again."

"No problem. You can lock up and keep the key."

As Angie left, Rennie took her cell phone out of her bag and dialed the number for the cemetery. She gave the person the information on Professor Justus and awaited a return call.

Rennie placed her phone on the table and looked at the boxes. After a quiet moment, she lifted a file folder out of one box. The label read, "Correspondence - Staff." She let it fall open and slid a few pages back and forth with one finger. She stopped at one letter on college letterhead.

In a whisper, she read, "Please accept the heartfelt sorrow of all our staff. The loss of your wife and child has been a tragedy beyond measure. Please know that your well being and presence in this community is of profound value and we support you in the difficult days ahead." Beneath an elegant signature was a reference: "Numbers 6:24-26."

Rennie squinted at the reference. She scanned more memos and letters. She picked up one and looked closely at the short text.

"We highly recommend Professor Matthias Justus for the temporary assignment in the Egyptian Collection. He is a distinguished professor of Greek and Religion at Simpson College, and he has given scholarly presentations on topics relating to ancient Egypt and the Levant. His expertise in ancient languages, his diligent and professional approach to managing a challenging workload, and his collegial regard for fellow staff have made him most valuable to this college. His enthusiasm for assisting The British Museum in properly cataloging and preserving items from the recent discovery in Egypt reflects the sincerity of his regard for the precious qualities of the artifacts and this assignment. Please extend to Lady Sotterfeld-Gris our appreciation for her benevolent underwriting of this opportunity."

Rennie looked at the wall. "Lady?"

Her cell phone vibrated on the table.

"Hello, wait please, I'll get some paper. Okay, go ahead."

She wrote down instructions from the cemetery contact on where to find the gravesite of Professor Justus.

Putting the phone into her bag, she paused for a moment and looked again at the letter in the file. "Maybe, we found our Lady," she said as she locked the room.

The cemetery was just south of town, as Angie had suggested. Rennie turned into the first driveway and slowed to an idle. She looked to her left at the field of upright stone slabs placed in long rows. Turning left, the car coasted forward. Long shadows laid at rest beneath the memory of lives indicated with names and dates.

Her fingers drummed the steering wheel. "There," she exhaled.

She stopped the car and got out without taking her eyes off of a location near an old oak tree. She reached into the car through the open window and grabbed her bag. Rennie walked in slow determination toward the tree.

She counted down three rows, five markers to the right and read the inscription on the small stone. "Hope Felicity Justus, beloved wife and mother. July 30, 1890 – April 20, 1921."

The next stone was identical in size and texture. It read, "Martha Elizabeth Justus, beloved daughter of Hope and Matthias Justus. April 20, 1921."

Rennie crouched down to look at the inscriptions more closely. Then, she stood and took a step to the side and saw another monument. It was a red marble stone, twice the size of the first two.

"Matthias David John Justus, Scholar and Beloved Husband and Father, February 26, 1887 – August 11, 1923."

Rennie covered her mouth. The afternoon sun behind the stone darkened the surface to a dull, sad glaze. She stepped up and brushed her fingertips across the name. "Wife and daughter. Both on the same day," she whispered.

The pressure of tears came to her eyes.

London, UK
The British Museum
1923

II / 2

Kenneth Warrington paused when he reached the top of the staircase on the second floor of the British Museum. Matthias was almost amused with the ceremonial effort of entry.

"This is the Second Northern Gallery. It might interest you. The exhibits are mostly Semitic, with a variety of Phoenician and Hebrew writings. There are also Carthaginian, Sumerian and Assyrian items. At the end there are Coptic antiquities. We also have some Coptic objects of interest, mostly personal items, in the storage area."

When he reached a doorway, Warrington made a sharp left turn and entered another large hall. Professor Justus stopped and did not turn. His arm floated up and he limply pointed across the room.

"Oh, Mr. Warrington, excuse me. Over there, is that, are those the Hammurabi laws?"

Warrington stopped but did not turn. "Not the original, Professor. It is only a cast. The original is at the Louvre."

Warrington slowly, in his rigid form, walked forward with Justus following. "We are now in the Fourth Egyptian Room. Most of what we have here are burial items and personal items such as jewelry, some writing materials, a few frescoes, toys and other ordinary items. Up ahead, this is where you will be working. It is one of our student rooms. Since it is near the lift, we thought it would be a good sorting place."

Another left turn and they entered a large, elegant room in which rows of wooden shelving had been built. The fresh lumber formed long sections of storage space, with each shelf about four feet long by three feet in depth, and two feet separated each of the six levels of structure. Only one quarter of each surface area held any items.

In one corner of the room, two wooden desks faced the wall. A window to another interior space hovered in the wall behind the desks. A young woman sat at one of the desks. She did not turn around.

Matthias turned to Warrington. "Professor, I mean, Mr. Warrington, did all of these items come from the discovery in Egypt?"

Warrington gazed straight ahead with his eyes half shut. "Yes," he said.

"Fabulous. Simply, fabulous," Matthias whispered. He looked again at Warrington. "May I go over and, may I ...?"

Warrington shrugged his shoulders. "Of course. You are now responsible for them."

With a broad smile, Matthias hurried to the shelves. On the nearest platform, there was a stack of four wooden wheels, each about three feet in diameter. Next to the wheels were what appeared to be wooden axels and large, curved sheets of wood with carved figures accented in gold.

Matthias looked back at Warrington. "Are these, or is this a chariot, disassembled?"

He slid a finger along the rough bottom of one wheel.

Warrington stood as lifeless as the artifacts.

"Mr. Warrington," Matthias said breathlessly, "before this was disassembled three thousand years ago, someone, perhaps the Pharaoh, was riding in this chariot. The sand still stuck in the surface of this wheel was put there under his weight."

Warrington said nothing. He turned and slowly walked

toward the desks. Matthias followed but noticed each of the items on the shelves with boyish wonder and scholarly analysis.

Warrington stopped in front of an unoccupied desk. The woman at the adjacent desk continued sorting small, white cards and sheets of paper. She didn't look up.

Warrington gestured to the desk. "This is where you will be, Professor."

"Thank you, Mr. Warrington."

"Glancing at the woman, Matthias stammered, "Oh, we met outside the entry. Thank you so much. I'm sorry you got a bit ahead of me there."

She did not look up nor change her composure. For a moment, she stopped working.

Warrington tilted his hand toward the woman. "This is Miss Shefford. She will assist you, as you need it. She will not bother you."

"I'm certain she will not. I mean I'm sure she will be of great help to me. I'm delighted to meet you Miss Shefford, and I look forward to working with you."

Warrington glared at Matthias. "Professor, you will not be working with Miss Shefford. She is here to assist you and to do her duties."

"Of course, I just assumed that since our desks were here together, ..."

Warrington interrupted him. "We can separate the desks further if that would serve you better, Professor."

"It's no problem, Mr. Warrington. I look forward to proceeding with my work."

Warrington turned and marched away. He stopped and looked back. "Miss Shefford will acquaint you with the room and whatever else you may need. I will be back in one hour."

Matthias sat in an old wood chair at his desk. He placed the palms of his hands on the polished mahogany desktop and said, "yes."

He turned to the young woman. "Miss Shefford, shall I call you 'Miss Shefford?'"

She continued to sort through papers and small note cards with writing and numbers on them. Without looking up, she said, "If you wish, sir."

"Oh, no, it's up to you, really. We aren't as formal where I'm from, so whatever you wish is fine. A first name is also workable. please refer to me as 'Matthias,'"

"Whatever you wish is fine, sir. The first name is 'Priscilla.'"

"I may use that when it's just you and me. I wouldn't want any problems with Mr. Warrington."

"Very well, sir."

Matthias got up and walked to the nearest row of shelves. He looked at the strong timbers that formed the shelving units, and then he noticed a delicate whip, lying alone on bare wood. A small white tag was attached to it with a string. Clasping his hands behind him, he crouched forward to see it more closely. He studied the finely woven leather strands that ran its full length. After a few moments, he looked back at the woman.

"Miss Shefford, these items, what is the protocol for handling them?"

She slid her chair back from the desk, got up and moved toward Matthias as though she was floating across the surface of the floor. Her hands floated down to the great expanse of the black, cotton cloth of her skirt. "Professor, in order to handle them, you simply pick them up."

"Really, we can just, —"

"Yes, Professor, you just pick it up."

She turned, walked back to her desk and sat down.

Matthias reached forward and gently grasped the whip with the fingers of both hands and swiveled away from the shelf. He lifted the artifact as though he was holding a newborn child.

Then, he returned to his desk. "You know Miss Shefford, this is an absolutely amazing moment for me. I don't know if I can ever set this down."

She continued working but turned her head slightly so she could see him. Her mouth revealed a delicate smile. "Well, Professor, that would certainly be an impediment to our progress."

Matthias snorted a laugh. "It certainly would be Miss Shefford. I'm just stunned to think that the hand that previously held this whip may have been the Pharaoh of Egypt!"

"I don't think so Professor. I believe my hand was the last to hold that whip."

She offered a real smile but continued to look at her work.

"Okay, well then, maybe before that."

"Well, Professor, I think that prior to my hand, there would have been the workers at the dig site, and of course Dr. Carter, and then of course, those who placed it in the tomb itself, and who knows how many that would have been, and of course, —"

"Miss Shefford, please allow me to enjoy this moment just a little." He laughed.

"Very well, Professor."

"I imagine, after one takes these in, documents them, sets them on the shelf and handles them in more routine fashion, the wonder of it all may lessen."

The young woman said nothing, but continued sorting.

"Miss Shefford, how many actual items have you taken in so far from this expedition, and how many are yet to arrive?"

"Oh, I can answer that, sir. We have received at this point, except for these that we are itemizing now, 619 thus far, and there are approximately 4,200 total items in the find that we know of."

A breathless sense of shock ran through him. "Miss Shefford, where are all of the items, those that are here now and those that are yet to come? What is the process?"

Justus laid the whip down on his desk, leaned forward and looked intently at his associate.

The woman neatly stacked the index cards on one side of her desk, assembled the paperwork she was working on, moved that to another part of her desk, and turned to face Matthias.

"At the excavation site Professor, there are certain individuals who are trained in excavation procedures, based upon a field notes manual of The British Museum. I shall see that you receive a manual later today."

She continued to explain the process in specific detail; from the moment an item is found until it arrives in London.

"Where does it all go?" he asked in amazement.

"We have a section of the lower level set aside for the preliminary sorting of artifacts from many finds across the world, including the Tutankhamun discovery. Most are from the new find at Oxyrhynchus. We will focus on those. There's another area of the lower level for pre-display storage and for permanent collection storage. From the preliminary sorting in the lower level, the items are brought up here on the lift for us to catalogue and make recommendations as to whether any special maintenance needs may be required or whether the item should be on display. Once that is done, they return on the lift to the permanent storage section in the lower level. The Keeper, Mr. Budge, is currently in Egypt, overseeing the initial documentation of all the artifacts. He has been quite brilliant in assembling much of the Egyptian collection, and he is renowned not only for his expertise in finding and identifying antiquities, but also for his shrewd efforts in obtaining them."

As Matthias listened, intently analyzing the process she described, he studied the young woman's delicate features, watching her lips move and the small, auburn curls of hair at her temples tapping at her ears. He began to wonder how old she was and how she came to this unique and meaningful position.

"Miss Shefford, I'm impressed with everything about The British Museum, and I'm also impressed with you and Mr. Warrington. How did you happen to come here?"

"Well, Professor Justus, I didn't happen to come here."

With that, she turned in her chair and picked up her paperwork.

"Oh, I'm sorry ma'am. I didn't mean anything derisive. I'm simply impressed and, well you are obviously well educated and, of course ..."

She looked at Matthias. "And, of course, I am just a girl."

"Oh, no, not that; but, ..."

"But, what Professor?"

"Well, I don't know. I'm just not acquainted with how things are done here."

"Professor, perhaps when Mr. Warrington has further briefed you, we could proceed with the cataloging process."

"Yes, of course. Thank you."

Matthias got up and hurried over to a different row of wooden shelving. He walked past items of gold, pottery, and jewelry that he could not believe were available to his touch. As he moved, he occasionally looked past the items to see the young woman at her desk. With hands clasped behind him, he moved among the racks, studying every feature of each artifact.

When he reached the end of one row, he found himself face to face with Kenneth Warrington. "Oh, Mr. Warrington. I did not hear you arrive."

"It is all well and good sir, to be appreciating the new collection, but of course, one could do this while we are cataloging them. The work that lies ahead of us is quite substantial, and we will need to get on with it."

"Yes sir, of course. I'm eager to do that."

"Has Miss Shefford advised you as to our processes?"

"Well, yes and she did a fine job. It was something of an"

overview, and we were going to be getting into the details next."

"If you will come with me, Professor, I will introduce you to your benefactor, Lady Jane Sotterfeld-Gris."

Warrington turned and made his way to the door.

For a moment, Matthias could not move. He quickly caught up to Warrington. "Mr. Warrington, I did not expect this, at least so soon. I'm delighted with the opportunity to meet, her ladyship; or, I'm not sure how to address her."

"That's quite all right. She is most sociable and a great benefactor to this institution. By her efforts and her own personal contributions, we've been able to obtain and to secure antiquities that have significantly enhanced the assets of The British Museum."

Matthias removed a white handkerchief from his pocket and dabbed at his temples.

Warrington stopped, looked over Matthias' shoulder and squinted. "What is that, Professor?" Warrington moved past him toward the desks. He stopped a few feet away and looked at the whip lying on the desk. He flexed his fingers, and his cheeks became pink.

Matthias followed and said, "Isn't it wonderful?"

His smile evaporated when Warrington glared at him.

"Professor, there is only one activity we actually have here. We place in security valuable items of the past. Studying them and displaying them, in my opinion, is more frivolity than purpose. Please keep that in mind. Where does this go?"

Matthias grabbed the whip and put it on the shelf where he had found it. He looked back at Warrington. Together, they silently walked to the door and into the hallway. "Mr. Warrington, would it be possible to get a drink of water? It has been a long morning."

Warrington stopped and looked at Matthias. His face softened. "Yes, of course. I regret I did not show you the facilities or our staff comfort area. Come with me."

They entered a small room and Warrington opened the door to what might have been a closet. It was a pantry, in which personal belongings were neatly organized on shelves. At the end, there was a large container and coffee cups of different colors.

"This room is for staff, for meals and refreshment. You may use the cup that is blue, if you need one."

"Thank you, sir. That will be fine."

"In this container, we have drinking water for the staff; and, of course, the men's lavatory is just outside your work room."

"Would there be time for me to make a brief stop there before we meet Lady Sotterfeld-Gris?"

Warrington looked at his watch. "We must never keep the Lady waiting. Fortunately, she is not here at the moment."

Matthias took the blue cup off the shelf, looked into it for a moment, and then filled it with water. He drank it down quickly and then a second cup. He excused himself and hurried to the men's room.

In a few minutes, he returned to the break room and noticed Warrington standing in the hallway. His arms were folded in front of him, and he stared at the opposite wall.

"That was helpful," Matthias awkwardly muttered.

The old man turned and began to walk down the hall. "Indeed."

As they approached another gallery, Warrington's mood lightened. "We normally greet our dignitaries in the Keeper's office and reception area, and not in the collection rooms. The Lady prefers the collection items and is quite a scholar. She has supported a variety of excavations and discoveries, as well as supporting staff needs.

"I'm quite grateful to her for enabling me to come here to do this work. Would it be inappropriate for me to express that?"

"Not at all. Of course, it is not for our words that they do their giving."

"Certainly."

"We'll be meeting the Lady in the Ethnographical Gallery. It's just ahead, on the right. The room we are in, it is our Sixth Egyptian Room. As you see, it is mostly small items. You may have an interest in the books. They are of papyrus and are written in hieratic and hieroglyphics. You can find them over there. This is the Northeast staircase."

Warrington made a broad, sweeping motion with his right arm. "The collections here are an overview of primitives from around the world. This is not one of my areas. Mr. Hobson is Keeper here. I believe you will find examples of some of the native cultures of America, as well. Your 'red man,' I believe."

They walked past exhibits of tools, ornaments, weapons, and apparel from cultures in Africa, Asia, the Pacific islands, and America. Even Warrington appeared to be interested in some items.

"Kenneth, have I kept you?"

A woman's voice echoed through the gallery. The men spun around.

From the far end of the gallery, the most elegant woman Matthias had ever seen was walking briskly toward them. She wore a lightweight, gray wool dress and jacket, and rising out of the jacket was a white silk blouse. Hanging beneath the silk collar was a silver necklace interrupted with small, oval sapphires and holding at its center an oval sapphire the size of the end of a man's thumb. A small, gray hat of the same material as the dress perched slightly off center on her head. The silver pin in her hat held another oval sapphire on a coat of arms design. Her smile was confident, and her walk was graceful, but commanding.

Warrington moved forward with an astonishing smile on his face. Professor Justus was frozen in place. "My Lady, your timing is perfect as usual. It is a great privilege for us that you would visit us."

Warrington looked down as a humble gesture. She extended her hand to him. Embarrassed, he reached out and briefly grasped her fingers.

She glanced over his shoulder at Matthias, and then looked into Warrington's eyes. "How is your wife, Kenneth?"

"Very well, ma'am. Thank you for asking."

Warrington suddenly appeared to be flustered.

"And, Kenneth, is this our new man?" She looked straight at Matthias.

Warrington whirled around and further surprised Matthias with the speed of his movement. "Yes, my Lady. Professor, I present to you Lady Jane Sotterfeld-Gris."

After an awkward moment, Matthias stepped forward. He pressed his hands against his legs and looked at the floor.

Warrington continued. "My Lady, this is Professor Matthias Justus of Simpson College, United States of America."

She extended her arm forward, presenting her hand. Matthias looked up and reached out to take her hand in his.

"How do you do, ma'am?"

They gazed at each other for a moment. She smiled broadly and finally said, "Well, Professor, I do quite well, thank you."

They both blushed and turned to look at Warrington. He appeared to be quite confused.

"Well, Professor, the Lady is a patron of the Museum to the highest order, and we are grateful for her support."

"Ma'am. I too am grateful for your allowing me the privilege to assist in this great project. For me, it is an opportunity of a lifetime."

"Professor, your credentials were most impressive and, Keeper Budge and Kenneth here, were their typically brilliant selves in making this all happen. I am very pleased to see that you were able to accept the offer and that you made the journey. Was it agreeable to you?"

"Yes ma'am, most interesting. And, Mr. Warrington has been of great assistance in the arrangements."

Warrington smiled and looked down.

"Well, he has always been helpful to me, as well."

"Thank you, ma'am." Warrington's cheeks became pink.

"Kenneth, may we see some of the items with which Professor Justus will be working? I assume they are arriving."

"Oh, yes, my Lady. They are indeed. Please, this way."

Warrington nearly bowed as he swept his arm toward the end of the gallery. As the Lady and Warrington moved ahead, Matthias followed, studying her with intensity but discretion. Occasionally, she would pause to look at one of the exhibits.

"Professor, don't you think that people, especially of other cultures, are just the most interesting?"

"Yes, ma'am, I do."

Warrington looked back at Justus, but he was not smiling.

"So, Kenneth, how is the girl doing?"

"Thank you for asking, ma'am. She is adequate. I expect she will be able to assist Professor Justus without inhibiting his progress."

"Let's hope so. Keep me informed. I assume the Archbishop is aware of her performance."

"Yes, ma'am, I have kept him apprised."

Matthias listened carefully to the conversation.

When they reached the workroom, Warrington stopped at the door and bowed briefly as Lady Jane entered the room.

She walked directly to the first row of wooden shelves, gesturing to the artifacts with an open hand and repeatedly saying, "Oh, my." She smoothly turned and nodded to the men. "Yes, Kenneth, you have treasures here, wouldn't you say Professor?"

In unison, both men said, "yes, ma'am."

Matthias noticed that Miss Shefford had stood up and turned to face them, but she looked at the floor. Lady Jane walked past

49

the woman without acknowledging her. When she came to the end of the wooden shelving, she glided up to Matthias.

"Professor, once you have had a chance to get started, I would be most grateful if you could acquaint me with some insights of what we are receiving from Egypt. I am certain these are treasures of the first order."

He couldn't suppress a smile. "Of course, I would be pleased to do so. I am here to serve you."

"How nice, Professor. I look forward to that."

She turned toward Warrington and slipped her arm under his, guiding him toward the door. "If you need anything at all, or if Professor Justus needs anything, just let me know."

With a quick grin at Matthias, and a slight flip of her hand, she left the room.

Matthias heard a noise behind him. Priscilla was slapping her note cards onto the desk as if she was squashing bugs.

Des Moines, Iowa
The Des Moines Record

II - 3

"Rennie, get your butt in here. What? Okay, PLEASE get your butt in here."

Bud Shuster banged down the phone and dropped into his chair. He picked up a sheet of paper, reviewed it quickly, and tossed it onto his desk.

Rennie arrived and sat down in the guest chair. "Yeah, boss, what's up?"

Bud stared at her for a moment. He picked up her story copy. "Do me a favor. That was all I asked. A simple story about some long dead, small town, college professor so I could score some points with a local big shot. And, what do I get? You lay down a screaming headline, 'Simpson Professor Murdered?' Rennie, can't you be nice and fit in a box like everyone else?"

She rested on one arm of the chair.

"Listen," he continued. "Maybe, it's possible, he got killed over there. It's all over and it's too bad. But you raise questions in this."

He picked up her copy and shook it. "Don't raise the questions if there isn't an answer or if you can't get one. I even had a call from upstairs about this stupid story. Upstairs! They never call unless I'm stepping on somebody's turf or they need to crank up the revenues or cut costs. Get rid of this story, and quietly Rennie."

"I'd love to, Bud. You wanted a quick story about this guy, and this is what we've got. Hey, maybe it's King Tut's curse, right here in ol' Iowa."

She waved her arms like a ghost. "Bud, I have other things to do. At the same time, it's a shame that a talented guy like this could be forgotten. Tone it down if you want. You got the red pencil. I'd like this guy to have his day."

Bud fell back in his chair, exhausted, and stared at the ceiling. "I didn't plan on you moving to Indianola. Take another look at it and see if you can find a way to wrap this up. Life goes on, and I'd like my life to go on without calls from upstairs!"

Rennie got up, shaking her head. As she walked toward the door, she looked back. "Bud, I don't know what happened, but I think it was important. There's an important truth lying in this and I want to find it. Is that okay?"

"Yeah, okay. Just do it quickly. We've got living people to take care of."

He waved at her and turned to pick up his phone. He didn't need more trouble.

She walked with determination back to her desk. Opening an expandable file folder, she removed a spiral binder and flipped through the pages. "Ah ha! Here you are Ms. Knoche. You thought I'd forget you, huh?"

Rennie studied the notepad, and then dialed. She asked for Mrs. Knoche.

"Hi, this is Rennie Haran from the *Record*. I'd like to visit with you again, briefly. When would be good for you? I just had a few questions.

"Can't you just leave it be?" the old woman responded.

Rennie heard a click and a dial tone. She stared at the phone. "Okay, lady. Now I'm coming for you."

She pulled two file folders out of the larger one and opened them on her desk. She organized selected pages into one pile.

"What am I missing here?"

Rennie grabbed her notepad and pen. She wrote on separate lines:

Motivation?

Why police at British Museum?

How died?

Who is the Lady?

She drew a line through and changed the last one to, *Who and how connected to the Lady?*

Looking over her notes again, she added a new line - *What happened to everyone -*

She looked at it again. "Naw, that's too much."

Her phone rang. "Metro, this is Rennie."

"Hi, Rennie, this is Will, down in the vault. You called about some Simpson prof, back in the twenties. I've got some info on him.

"Great! What've you got?"

"There's some scattered stuff here, Rennie. There's a notice of him speaking to some organization on Egyptian stuff, and then, there's his wife dying when she has a baby. Man, that sticks it, huh? Oh, and then there's the big hoopla of him going to work in London, and then another on him coming back in a box. Wow, it's like live hard, die hard?"

"I guess so, Will. Can you send me copies of those?"

"Sure, you can take me out to lunch, and we'll talk."

"Will, you shouldn't be chasing old ladies."

"When you work in the vault, you can't be choosy."

They both laughed.

"You know, Will, you could have said something like, 'Rennie, you're not old. You're hot!' Give me a little help here, guy."

"Right, you'll have that stuff tomorrow."

Rennie looked at her watch and put all the paperwork and notepads back into the binder. She slid down in her chair, tapped at her temple with a pen and looked at the ceiling. She wondered how she could catch Mrs. Knoche.

Rennie lurched forward and uncovered a file marked, "City Condemnation." As she looked through the pages, she paused and looked up.

"Dang it," she said as she tossed her pen on the desk. She got up and picked up her bag and the file labeled, "Simpson – Justus."

As she walked past the end cubicle, she said, "Susan, I'll be in Indianola. Back tomorrow."

Coming to a stop sign, she looked right. There were no other vehicles in sight and her route was straight ahead, but she needed a break. A quick stop at her house could be quick and a cold beer would taste just right. It was only Tuesday, but it had already been a long week.

Turning into the driveway, she saw a man sitting on the porch steps. He was leaning back and smiling with his eyes shut. She walked up and stood in front of him, blocking the sunshine.

He opened his eyes. "Hey, girl, did you come home early for me?"

Rennie sat down next to him. "Well, Steve, what brings my ex to town? You must need something."

"Come on, Ren, give me a break. It's springtime. Can't you just enjoy life a little?"

"You know you're out of luck here. So, why the visit? Hmm, could it be you need money or a place to stay? What is it this time, Steve?"

"Come on, can't you ever just enjoy life a little? Can't you get out from between your ears?"

He laughed and turned again into the sunlight. They were quiet for a long time.

Finally, he said, "I miss you, Rennie. We had good times. I know we aren't going to get together again. That doesn't mean we can't still enjoy a little company now and then."

"Steve, I've moved on. I don't want to deal with the past."

He turned again and looked at her. "Hey, I'm just passing through. I just wanted to say 'Hi' and see how you're doing. Nothing heavy. You look good, Rennie. But you're dressing more like a man with this pants and sport coat thing. It is better than the old granola look."

She grinned. "Oh yeah, so men's wear turns you on now?"

Steve feigned a feminine giggle.

"Where's your bike, or don't you have a ride again?"

He stepped off the porch a few steps and pointed at a truck parked in front of the house. "There she is; that's my ride!"

He spun around. "It's great, Rennie. You know, I kind of move now and then, and a pickup is great for that!"

"You working, Steve?"

"Well, you know, I'm working all the time. It's just not at the same thing. I'm too creative to stick with one thing. You know that! That's why we're so great together. Your little head never stops spinning and neither do my wheels. Hey, you wanna go for a ride in my new pick'em up? Come on. We could go out to the lake and get wild and crazy."

Rennie shook her head. "Steve, I'm in another place now. I grew up."

Steve threw his arms in the air. "Boring! Hey, you know what 'grown up' means? It means 'settle' and I won't settle. Life is all about growth and going places and, well, living; and, loving!"

"How about dying, Steve? What about that?"

"Hey, when you got to go, wouldn't it be nice if you had lived once? Man, I'm living. I'm living every day."

"Really, Steve, you're living? So, living is running away from commitments and doing whatever you want to do no matter how it affects others? Is that living? Is that loving? Just what is that?"

He put his hands on his hips and stared at her. "Thank you, mister prosecutor. You've got all the questions and no answers. You're always asking questions and looking for answers, looking for what you call 'truth.' Do you have any idea what it is that you are looking for? God, you might want to answer that question first!"

"Haven't you heard, Steve? God supposedly has all the answers. He just isn't around anymore to tell us what they are."

Rennie got up and brushed off her bottom. "Hey, let's not fight. I hope you find some happiness somewhere; something that lasts more than just the moment, something meaningful. I know it seems like work to you, but when you find it, it's easy. You can get excited about it and you are willing to do whatever needs to be done."

"So, this newspaper thing, is it 'THE thing' for you? Is this what gets you hot on life?"

Rennie picked up her bag and stepped close to Steve. "Thanks, for coming by. Now, leave."

She walked up the steps into the house and closed the door without looking back. As she crossed the old, hardwood floors, a grandfather clock chimed in another room. She took a beer out of the refrigerator and went into the living room.

The roar of an engine lacking a good muffler, sounded through the neighborhood. Tires briefly screeched and the noise disappeared down the street. She held her bottle up. "Here's to you, Steve. Go have your fun, and ... whatever."

She dropped onto the old sofa, kicked off her shoes and put her feet up on the coffee table. Balderdash jumped onto a chair and sat upright, looking at her before saying, "Meow."

"Hi, buddy. How's your day?"

The cat responded again.

"Right. You and me, pal."

She knocked down a few gulps of the drink and trudged upstairs to her bedroom. Rennie looked in the back of her closet and removed a hanger with a long, light cotton skirt. She caressed the cloth for a moment, then slipped off her slacks and put on the skirt. Playfully, she turned to one side and then the other, as she watched herself in the mirror.

She looked at the cat. "What do you think, big guy. Am I hot, or what?"

Walking toward the closet, she noticed her alarm clock and stopped. "Oh, my gosh, it's almost two thirty!"

She changed back into her slacks, brushed her teeth, gargled, and looked in the mirror. "Oh, Ms. Knoche, you and I need to go out and have a few."

By 3:15 she was hurrying across the Simpson campus toward Hillman Hall. Along the way, she passed by a man sitting on a bench and reading a newspaper. He wore a nice suit, and for some reason, he did not seem to belong there. Rennie instinctively slowed her pace and peeked back at him. When she reached the building, she paused. Something felt wrong.

She went into the Administration office and asked the student if Ms. Knoche was in or when she would return. Answers were uncertain so Rennie left the building and walked across to the Chapel. The steps were a good place to watch for the old woman, but she felt out of place there. She had not had time for spiritual matters for a long time.

Rennie noticed Ms. Knoche coming down the walk. "Hey, Ms. Knoche! Nice to see you again."

The old woman looked straight ahead and rumbled forward.

Rennie slowed down and matched her pace. "You know, this story about Professor Justus is fascinating. He was quite a guy. It was pretty sad, though too."

The woman ignored her.

"I've heard you've been here quite awhile. Someone said

your predecessor was here a long time, too."

They continued down the walk.

"Did she ever say anything about Professor Justus?"

Mrs. Knoche suddenly stopped. She turned and looked at Rennie. "Are you investigating me?"

Rennie leaned back. "Of course, not. You're a valued resource here and I appreciate your help. I don't want to get anything wrong."

"Well, there was plenty wrong with that Justus."

The old woman turned to walk again but stopped. Her cheeks flushed with color. "I don't know anything, okay?"

"Ms. Knoche, this isn't about you, but I guarantee you, I will find the truth. You can help me and serve this school, or you can stand back and see what happens."

The woman's eyes grew large and her lips twitched. She wobbled over to a bench and sat down.

Rennie sat next to her.

"I don't know. Evelyn was here before me. She said he was not a good man, your professor. I don't know any details, just the attitude."

"What attitude is that, Ms. Knoche?"

"You know his wife died, in childbirth."

"I read something about that."

"Then, pretty quick, he was off to London and involved with two women. That's what they say."

Ms. Knoche looked around, then whispered, "Some said he was involved in stealing antiquities. That's what got him killed! It was disgraceful. This fine school deserves better."

"Ms. Knoche, from what I learned about him, I have difficulty with that."

"I know, I know. Something obviously snapped. But Evelyn was certain."

"Did Evelyn actually know Professor Justus?"

"Oh, yes," the old woman nodded quickly.

"She was just a young thing at the time, and when she first met him, she thought the world of Professor Justus. He was the most handsome and nicest member of the faculty. He was an expert on the Middle East, and he traveled to give programs on his study of Egypt and the Bible. For Iowa, that's pretty exotic."

Mrs. Knoche relaxed a little. "After his wife died, you can imagine, he couldn't teach for awhile. He could hardly talk to people, according to Evelyn. Then, he heard about all that weird business in Egypt, with King Tut or something. He got focused on that and away he went. He was just supposed to be gone for the summer, but he never came back, alive that is."

Rennie patted her arm. "Ms. Knoche, it seems you've been holding this back, protecting the college from this story for a long time."

The woman straightened out her dress and turned to Rennie. "Evelyn was heartbroken. When those women showed up for the funeral and then again years later, she knew the professor was not who he seemed to be. He must have changed. They can do that you know."

"Who were these women, ma'am."

Ms. Knoche's eyes grew large. "One was a princess they said. Evelyn said she saw her at the funeral, and she was not nice; arrogant, they said. She was stone cold and didn't speak to anyone. But she directed everything, all the arrangements, even his monument."

She took a deep breath. "I'm sorry, dear, it's been a long day."

"Would you like some water or something? We could go for coffee."

"No, it's alright."

"Ms. Knoche, you mentioned two women. Who was the other one? Were they together?"

"Oh, no, that's what set Evelyn off. It was years later. This other English woman showed up, quiet as the first and formal, but not as elegant, and she asked about Professor Justus. I guess she visited the graveyard and a few places. Then she was gone. No one knows who she was. Evelyn thought he had gone wild in England and chased the ladies."

"I can see why that would have bothered Evelyn. Listen, I promise that what you have told me will remain confidential, and if I come across anything that is not good for the image of Simpson, I won't include that in my story. Okay?"

Ms. Knoche's gaze slowly rose to meet with Rennie's eyes. "I have this feeling you may open up something that you might regret. There are dangerous forces out there. You need to know when to step back. Evil is easily disguised. Professor Justus may have run into that. Be careful."

A chill ran up Rennie's spine. The image of the man on the bench, reading the newspaper suddenly came to mind.

A mischievous smile slipped across Mrs. Knoche's mouth. "I'm sorry I can be a crotchety old woman. This is a good school, and I've been here a long time. I guess I think of it as mine."

"Ms. Knoche, could I ask you for some advice? I was talking with someone today, and we got talking about life."

Rennie took a long breath.

"Well, you've probably known a lot of people and you are obviously a very intelligent and thoughtful person. I wondered, what would you say makes life meaningful?"

Ms. Knoche's face beamed. "That's the easiest question, dear. I've not only seen but met many important people. Every four years, even the President comes to Iowa, and I've met most of them!"

She laughed and hit her knee. "To have a meaningful life is based on what you give and not what you get. Our society is devoted to just getting things, and getting them now, when they want them. That's why I think, as rich as this country is, we may have the saddest, most empty people in the world. The people who have given the most are the happiest people. The ones who are just out to get for themselves, they get the headlines, the flashy cars and are popular, but their cup is always empty. They are always trying to fill it up."

Rennie put her fingertips on the old woman's arm. "I'll bet your cup is overflowing, Ms. Knoche."

"Well, I've been lucky to have had the opportunity to help a lot of people here."

She put her handkerchief to her nose.

Rennie sensed she had lost track of her mission. Over the years, she had become good at blocking out tenderness.

"There is one last question. Did Professor Justus have any family here? Is anyone left?"

"Oh, no. I don't think so. I'm not sure where he came from, but it wasn't around here. It's kind of sad, really. He started out alone, had a family, and then was alone again. Now, he's gone and there is no one to remember him."

She squeezed Rennie's hand. "You write whatever you like. I know you'll do the right thing." She smiled. "It's good to finally get it out."

Rennie laughed. "Yes, this ordeal is over. Thank you for sharing and for being a wonderful part of this school."

As they arose, Ms. Knoche placed her hand on Rennie's arm. "Just remember, dear, when you've given your all for what you believe in, your rewards will be greater than anything you could ever imagine."

London, UK
The British Museum
1923

II - 4

"Excuse me, Miss Shefford," Matthias asked.

He looked away, shifted from side to side, and ran his fingers through his hair. "I, uh, Mr. Warrington said I should go to lunch now and, I'm not certain what people do here."

He waited for a moment. He noticed that her face was nearly white, like fresh papyrus. Her lips were pressed together as though she was concentrating very hard, but he worried she may be angry. "Miss Shefford?"

She exhaled a deep sigh. "I'm sorry, Professor Justus. This has been an awkward day."

She turned and looked at him. "I'm sure it is particularly awkward for you."

She relaxed back in her chair. "Our luncheon period is forty-five minutes, but no one keeps track of our time. It is quite a decent system, really. Sometimes, I think they forget I am here."

Matthias sat down and tilted his chair back. "So, do you bring something in or go out to eat?"

"Oh, I cannot afford to eat in this neighborhood. I just bring a few snacks from home. What would you like to do today?"

"I'm not sure. Going for a walk and seeing what's available outside would be nice. We could, oh, wait."

Matthias pulled his attaché across the desk and opened it. He removed the tin box Mrs. Whitley gave to him and set it on top of his bag. "I just remembered. Mrs. Whitley, the host where I stay, sent this along."

Miss Shefford peeked at the box. "My, biscuits, and from Harrods. How nice! Will you be sharing these?"

She suddenly seemed like a delicate and innocent little girl. Matthias was delighted to see her smile.

"Well, let's open this up, Miss Shefford. Hmm. It doesn't seem to have any biscuits in it, just some sliced apple, a pickle, and what appears to be a sandwich."

She grinned. "Mrs. Whitley must be a thoughtful lady, but I would ask her what happened to the sweets!"

She laughed but caught herself. "I'm sorry, sir. That was not appropriate."

She looked down for a moment and straightened out her skirt.

"Not at all, Miss Shefford. So, are biscuits sweets?"

"Yes, Professor, I believe in America you call them cookies."

She looked into his eyes for what felt like a long time. Abruptly, she stood up. "Professor, obviously your linguistic skills will be useful here. As for lunch, it appears yours has been resolved. If you like, we can sit in the staff comfort room. That is where my refreshments are kept."

"I'd be delighted."

Matthias watched her cross the room, her heels clicking on the marble floor. When she reached the door, she stopped and looked back at him. She raised one eyebrow, and then walked across the hall.

Several, slow minutes allowed them to awkwardly open their food tins and find places to sit at a small, rectangular table in positions not too close to one another yet not too distant.

"Miss Shefford, since we will be working nearby one another, and since I am new to England, feel free to advise me if or when you think of any suggestions that might be helpful. I will appreciate it."

"Of course, Professor. How long will you be with us?"

"Only a few months. I must be back in Iowa for the fall semester by mid-August. I'm sure my time here will fly by too quickly. Here it is, only half a day, and I already feel as though I am in the midst of treasure and I'm wasting my time. And, this city! This is such a place of great history. I wouldn't know where to begin."

Matthias got up to get a drink. Priscilla delicately nibbled on crackers and a small piece of cheese. Matthias nervously rearranged the remains in his food tin.

"Miss Shefford, I hope that you might tell me something about yourself sometime; nothing personal, of course, but just to be acquainted. I hope that would be agreeable with you."

Without looking up, she said, "I'm certain Professor, we will become acquainted over the next few months. Tell me about Iowa."

A grin came to his face as his shoulders rose. "You would be amazed with how green it is there. That part of America is considered the heart of the agriculture industry for the country. We have vast fields of corn, and there are cattle and hogs on every farm; and, the people are good."

Matthias looked into the distance and closed his eyes just a little. "It is what one might call good living, simple living. It's a place to build a life."

He stopped and looked away. After a moment, he quickly packed up his food tin and stood up. "Well then, I had better move on. There is much to do."

Priscilla tilted her head and observed Matthias march out of the room. She stopped eating and listened to his footsteps cross the hall. She sensed he carried something that he needed to hide.

When she returned to the work room, he was holding and examining one of the golden boxes from the racks. It made a heavy noise when he set it down. He moved down the aisle, picking each one up and turning them for a quick but total review. After twenty minutes, he returned to his desk. He looked commanding instead of warm.

"Professor, would this time be convenient to review our processes?"

He agreed, and for the next hour and a half, she reviewed in detail the process for inventorying all new relics for the collection. She found for him a new copy of the Field Notes Manual of The British Museum so he would have a better idea of what happens at a dig site. She mentioned the names of other staff persons with whom he might interact when they have newly received antiquities that are received, stored or shipped to another facility.

He made simple and precise notes of her descriptions, asked clarifying questions, and occasionally asked her opinion on certain processes. She had no opinions on how the work was being done.

She noticed when Warrington entered the room. He stopped and discreetly observed them. Matthias was slouched in his chair but looked at her in a way that was suddenly uncomfortable.

Warrington approached and was nearly at their desks when Matthias turned to see him. "Ah, Mr. Warrington," Matthias said as he got up, "Miss Shefford has been explaining your systems here. I'm looking forward to moving ahead with this. Would it be possible to see the storage areas in the lower level?"

Warrington was unresponsive. Finally, he said "follow me."

Warrington noticed a new energy and confidence in Professor Justus. Matthias whistled as he looked with more delight than awe at the display items they passed by. Even in the elevator, Matthias looked relaxed and in control, nodding at Warrington when their eyes met.

The lower level storage area had a lower ceiling and less light than the upper floors. It appeared to be more of a warehouse and had the musty smell of one. Warrington gestured to the right as they exited the elevator.

"Over here, Professor, is the section that holds newly received items from the recent excavation of Dr. Carter. Down there, are the inventoried items organized according to the status Miss Shefford has described."

Warrington strolled down the aisle. "Over in that corner is the freight elevator for the Egyptian section and there is another on the left side of the building, over there. That serves more general collections. When the deliveries from Dr. Carter have concluded, both lifts will serve the convenience of all the collections."

Warrington turned down another aisle and proceeded with his descriptions of various sections of the storage area.

"Ah, here is a section you might like Professor."

Warrington offered a slight smile. "These are the recently documented finds from Egypt, from the site called 'Oxyrhynchus.' Have you heard of it?"

Matthias looked confused. "The name is not familiar. It's a Greek name. I assume Hellenistic Egypt, referring to a nose?"

Warrington displayed a satisfied grin. His chin raised a little. "We've had people working there for nearly twenty years. The site is a series of what we might call garbage mounds from the first century. Most of the findings are papyrus, and quite a bit of it. Flinders Petrie is there right now. It has taken a back seat, of course, to Dr. Carter's find of the Tutankhamun treasures. Gold easily outranks paper."

"Well, I guess it depends what was written on the paper," Matthias quickly added.

Something small and black swiftly crossed their path, nearly touching their shoes. Matthias jumped and looked down the aisle where it went.

"That, Professor, is the 'collections cat,' as we call him. No one is certain how he came to be here, but he doesn't cause any trouble and might help in case any pests may appear. I don't particularly like cats or pets myself, but he seems to be worthwhile."

Matthias crouched down, looking into the shadows. "Does he have a name?"

"Yes, someone named him Tobias Luxor, I imagine because he seems disposed to remain with the Egyptian storage items."

Matthias' eyes sparkled. He went to a storage shelf on which there lay rolls of papyrus and various personal effects such as combs, simple jewelry items and containers.

"All this came from Oxy, what Oxyrhynchus? Fascinating."

He lifted one of the scrolls, then laid it back in its position. He continued down the aisle, occasionally leaning forward to see one of the items more closely. "Mr. Warrington, may I come and examine these? Have they been given any scholarly inspection?"

"Professor, most of what we have here is for preservation and, in a few cases, display. If something stands out, it is given proper consideration for professional review. There is simply too much to read and analyze in depth."

Matthias seemed unable to contain his astonishment. "I would certainly like to read whatever might be available here."

"You may, on your own time, of course."

Warrington stopped. Anger bubbled within him. "But nothing must be displaced, Professor."

"No, of course not."

Matthias gestured toward two nearby study desks. "Perhaps, I could use one of those when I have a moment."

"Yes, when you have your moment."

Warrington turned and continued the tour, satisfied with his leadership.

When he and Warrington returned to the second floor, Matthias noticed that Miss Shefford was standing halfway down one of the rows of storage racks, speaking with a museum worker who was moving collection items from a large cart onto the shelves. He didn't say much but she was relaxed and giggling. Occasionally, her fingers touched his shirt as she gestured.

The moment she saw the two men enter the room, her expression became serious and she returned to her desk.

Matthias shook hands with Warrington. "Thank you. The visit to the lower level was a delightful addition to an amazing day. I am grateful for this opportunity to be here and to work for you."

Warrington looked uncomfortable, but pleased. "Yes, it is good you are here, and I am certain this arrangement will serve us well. We have work to do, now. Your schedule ends at four o'clock. By the way, Archbishop Worthy will be here tomorrow. He shares your interest in documents and is supportive of our Keeper's work. You may wish to meet him. Good evening."

Warrington observed for a moment the man with the cart, then slowly marched away.

Matthias' thoughts tumbled as he watched Warrington leave the room. Then, he was a bit startled to see that Miss Shefford appeared to be staring at the wall behind her desk as though she could burn a hole through it. As he approached, she pushed back in her chair to get up from her desk, nearly running over Matthias' foot. Obviously not seeing the encounter, she exited the room. Her heels clicked down the marble hall to the lady's room.

Puzzled, Matthias shoved his hands into his pockets and strolled over to the man with the cart.

"Hello there," he cheerfully said.

"G'day, sir."

The man continued to move new things from the cart to the shelving and the documented items onto the cart. He didn't look up.

"My name is Justus, Professor Matthias Justus."

There was no answer or eye contact.

"And, what is your name?"

"Mort, sir," he said after a moment.

"Well, Mort, I'm new here, and I wondered what you might be doing."

Mort put his hands on his hips and let out a deep breath.

"I move the items, sir. I get the newly received ones from the lower level and am then directed to bring them up here. Then, when Miss Shefford has done the paperwork, I bring up a new batch and take the old ones down to storage."

He paused and gave Matthias a dull stare.

"Well then, Mort. I guess I'll be seeing you on a regular basis. If you have any suggestions, let me know."

"Suggestions about what, sir?"

"About how we are doing with this. You know."

"I'm sorry, sir. I don't know exactly what you mean. I just do what I'm told, sir."

"I see. Very well. It was nice to meet you, Mort."

When Miss Shefford returned to her desk, Matthias noticed that her eyes appeared to be red. They worked silently at their own desks. As Mort was about to leave, he stopped on his way to the door and said, "Oh, Miss."

Miss Shefford stopped her work but ignored him. Matthias looked at her and then at Mort.

"Yes, Mort?" Matthias asked.

"Nothing, sir. I just thought I'd let you know I was leaving for the day."

Matthias looked again at Miss Shefford. She didn't move. "Fine, Mort, I guess we'll see you tomorrow."

As he pushed his cart down the hallway, Miss Shefford left

her desk. She breezed over to the storage racks, turning and shifting the items with a nervous energy. When she returned to her desk, Matthias noted that her more relaxed and precise processing had returned.

"He seems like a nice fellow," Matthias quietly offered.

She didn't respond.

"Miss Shefford, Mr. Warrington mentioned that Archbishop Worthy was coming tomorrow. That name is new to me. Can you tell me about him?"

Her face slowly turned toward him. Her expression was hard, and her lips had lost their color.

Matthias felt cold. "What can you tell me about Archbishop Worthy," he asked, clearly hitting every consonant.

She responded in a flat, dry voice with a hint of cynicism. "The Archbishop comes on Tuesdays, usually. He is well thought of by Mr. Warrington and Keeper Budge. As yourself, he has an interest in old documents, and he reads Latin of course, but also some Hebrew. I believe he has an added interest in popularizing the museum's collection with officials of the Church and in the community amongst distinguished people."

Her expression remained empty as she looked at Matthias.

"I see, thank you," he said.

He returned to the paperwork on his desk, but his senses where alive to what she was doing. She resumed her work. It was quiet for a long time.

Just before four o'clock, Matthias left the workroom and visited the men's lavatory. When he returned to his desk, he placed the biscuit tin into his attaché case with the Field Notes book. "Miss Shefford, this has been quite a day. Thank you for your assistance. I look forward to working with you over the next few months."

He waited. She glanced at him and a slight smile curled the corners of her lips.

"You're welcome, Professor. I guess we'll be back tomorrow."

As Matthias strolled down the marble halls and then the stairs, he swung his case back and forth along his side. He glanced at the various exhibits and softly blew a faint whistle. When he reached the entry, he waved at the entrance clerk. The man returned a hesitant acknowledgement with a lifted hand.

Matthias walked down the sidewalk as though he owned it. He nodded to everyone. Some paused to look back as he passed them by.

When he arrived at the rooming house, he ran up the porch steps, flung open the door and dashed up the stairs to his room.

He laid his attaché case on the small desk, took off his coat and lay back on his bed. The colorful comforter welcomed him with a soft rise. Closing his eyes, his breathing became deep and resonant.

"Professor Justus, it's seven o'clock," Mrs. Whitley said at the door. "Professor Justus."

His eyes fluttered open. He rubbed them and yawned deeply. "Yes, ma'am, I'll be right there."

"We're about to serve dinner."

He heard her thudding shoes go down the creaking stairway. Getting up, he took a few steps over to a small window and looked at London, bathed in dusk. He pressed his cheek to the window-pane and squinted to see if he could see the British Museum. A few buildings were in the way. A bang sounded from the street and a truck lurched forward with a plume of black smoke behind it.

Stretching his arms up to the low ceiling, he surveyed his room. He put on his coat, removed the biscuit tin from the attaché case, and went downstairs to eat.

He paused on the stairs, thinking about Warrington, Miss

Shefford, and Mort. The treasures of the museum flashed past his eyes. A sly grin emerged.

PART THREE

Indianola, Iowa
Simpson College

III - 1

A ngie McGrady lifted the receiver of her office desk phone and punched the buttons on the base. She leaned back in her chair, looked up at the ceiling, and twirled her hair with a finger. The young woman's glossy red lipstick accented perfect, white teeth. Her pert nose flowed up to large, blue eyes behind her heavy glasses.

"Hi Greg, how's your day?" She waited a moment, fingering her hair. "Well, I just wondered where we're going for dinner tonight."

She sat up and drew hearts on her desk pad. "That sounds great. I'll meet you there. I'm sorry you have to work late all the time."

She carefully examined her nails. "Okay, sweetie, I'll see you then!"

She laid the receiver on the phone base and stretched out her arms.

Tom, a student aide, drifted in and stopped by her desk. "I was wondering if I could take off for a few minutes."

She grinned at him, but her mind was elsewhere.

"Miss McGrady? I was wondering if I could leave for a few minutes?"

"Huh? Oh, yeah. Fine."

She got up and drifted out to the front desk. As Angie approached the counter, she gestured to an assistant who was speaking with Rennie.

"That's okay April, Ms. Haran already has a key to her work room."

Angie greeted Rennie with an energetic smile. "So, how is our project coming along, Ms. Haran?"

Rennie reached across the counter to shake hands with her. "Great, Angie, and it's getting more interesting."

After an awkward pause, Rennie asked, "What's new with you?"

"Oh, nothing, just the same stuff," Angie nearly giggled. "So, what's the latest on the professor?"

"Well, the professor was a nice guy who might have become a bad guy; maybe a womanizer, but with good taste. International intrigue and ...," Rennie leaned over the counter and looked suspiciously to the side. Meeting Angie's eyes, she said, "And, he may have been murdered."

She drew out the last word in a dramatic way.

"Oh, my gosh! That's awful!"

Angie shifted back to a sillier persona, tilting her head from side to side and rolling her eyes.

Rennie asked in a more professional tone, "So, what's the good news? You have something going on?"

Angie looked down at the counter and underlined with her finger a sentence on a form which lay beneath the glass surface.

Rennie whispered, "As a seasoned investigative reporter, I'd have to say I see something important on the horizon."

Angie turned to her assistant who was a few feet away. "April, perhaps you could organize those archive requests at the work desk."

When April left the area, Angie quietly said, "I've been seeing a guy named Greg for a couple of years, and I think he might ask me something tonight."

She blushed and covered her mouth with one hand. She

looked over at where April sat at a distant desk.

Rennie slapped the counter and laid her bag down. "Hey, congratulations. Tell me about him."

"I met him at an event at the Civic Center. I was with a girl friend and we were getting a glass of wine during the intermission. He looked so great; well, he still does! He's a lawyer; deals with bonds and big financing deals, mostly government stuff."

"So, what's with tonight?" Rennie whispered.

A big smile grew across Angie's mouth as she leaned onto the counter. "He said his parents are coming to town in a couple of days. He told me he wanted to tell them something important, but first he needed to ask me something."

Her voice softened. "I asked him what, and he said in this really cute, devilish way that he would save it for dinner tonight. I don't know what else it could be."

"Angie, I'm happy for you. Thanks for sharing the moment with me."

Rennie chuckled, seeing the innocent little girl in the confident, professional woman.

Angie became serious. "Right, I guess I couldn't contain it for a moment."

"Yeah, I'd better get back upstairs. I need to wrap this up. Unless something extraordinary pops up, the mystery of Professor Justus will lie with him."

Angie couldn't concentrate. "Okay then," she said and strolled back into her office.

Rennie ran up the stairs and unlocked the work room. Flipping on the light, she laid her bag on a chair, took off her jacket, and surveyed the documents spread out on the table. She removed a file from her bag and reviewed her notes.

"Okay, Doc, let's finish this up," she said to an old memo

lying on a stack of papers.

After a couple of hours, Rennie left the work room and went downstairs to get some coffee and fresh air. As she was leaving, she met Angie on her way out.

Rennie walked her to the door. "Be sure to tell him you'll accept nothing less than two carats."

Angie gave her a thumbs-up sign. "Anything new with the professor?"

"Nope. I've got to move on to the real world. At least this century."

Rennie watched her turn the corner and run lightly to the parking lot.

In a low voice, Rennie said, "Good luck."

Minutes later, she was refreshed and sitting again in front of the boxes of paperwork and personal items of Professor Justus. She covered her face with both hands, then drew her fingertips through her hair. She got up and walked slowly around the table.

"What's the angle? Bud always wants an angle," she muttered.

At the other end of the table, she noticed the leather-bound book with "Field Notes" engraved on the spine. She looked through a few pages of text and photos and tossed it into one of the boxes. She opened a file folder labeled "Staff - Professional Background" and spread the papers on the table.

Rennie read the list of contributions he had made to various journals including titles, "Ephraimitic Sources of Hebrew Wisdom," "Abram and other Semite Wanderers," "The Role of Aramaic in a Roman / Greek Near East," and "The Christian Church of Alexandria – Christ Comes to Egypt."

Rennie snorted. "Boy, I'll bet those knocked'em dead."

She sat down, put on the gloves, and placed all the papers back into the appropriate folders, briefly scanning each one to make sure she hadn't missed anything important.

Another hour and a half of review passed by. She called her office for messages, then checked those on her cell phone. As the messages played, she wrote notes from the callers on her tablet. She looked at her watch. It was twenty minutes after seven. "Oh, jeeze," she whined. "I've got to finish this tonight. This is not going on another day."

She jerked the gloves off her hands, grabbed her bag and left the room, locking the door. When she reached the counter, she asked the student on the other side, "Where can I get a quick meal?"

The student was helpful, with directions to a nearby café. Forty minutes later, Rennie returned to the library with an increased sense of urgency. As she dashed through the entry, she nearly ran into a well-dressed man standing near the door.

She hurried up the stairs and settled into her work room. As she was about to sit down, she noticed the "Field Notes" book lying open. The pages in the back of the book were not printed but were lined and filled with handwritten notes. She moved closer to the box.

She lifted the book both hands, as though it were a delicate piece of glass. Rennie studied each word and the artful style of the handwriting. The ink on the page was still sharp. She brought the text close to her face and smelled the page.

She sank into the chair. *It's his journal.*

Laying it on the table, she put on the cotton gloves she was supposed to have been wearing. Feathering the front pages of the book, she discovered the printed text and photos only filled the first third of the book. The remainder was left open for a diary or for ... Rennie gazed at the wall. "For field notes," she whispered with a smile.

She turned to the first page of handwriting and read,

"America's Independence Day is not celebrated in England. I guess I am not surprised."

"Wait," she said. "That's July. He arrived in May!"

She set the book down and stood up again. Looking into the boxes, she found two more books with the same leather covers. Her heart was thumping. Her mouth was dry. Her gloved fingers opened one of the books. Her breathing slowed to a shallow drifting of air through her nostrils. She quickly fanned the pages to find the written text.

"I'm using this fine guide to archeology dig management" wrote Professor Justus, "to document not an historic find, but rather, the treasure of this journey abroad. I shall begin with my notes of the journey from the goodness of Iowa to the grandeur of England."

Rennie's eyes widened. Again, she smelled the pages. Turning to the last page, she read the last paragraph.

"The Princess and the Pope have actually become quite enjoyable company. I know they are not liked by many, but for the brief time that I am here, I intend to celebrate the intrigue of their characters rather than judge them. They are brilliant, attractive people and I don't mind if I am a curiosity to them. I intend to have some fun."

A mischievous grin grew across Rennie's face. "We just may have a story," she said as she leaned back in her chair. "Okay, Bud, this is for you."

She flipped the pages back to the beginning of the writing and set the book down. She removed her jacket, pushed her chair away from the table, and picked up the book. She sat down and rested her feet on the table surface.

An hour later, she heard a door slam in the lower level of the library. She snapped to attention and laid the book on the table. She looked at her watch. It was nearly ten o'clock. Rennie listened with intensity as she stared at the door. She placed a piece of paper into the "Field Notes" book where she had been reading.

Removing the cotton gloves, she took her cell phone from her purse and pushed the buttons for "9" and for "1." She held her finger over the number "1." Slowly, she opened the door to the work room and looked into the dark library building.

The only lights on in the library were a few security lights and what came in through the windows. However, there were no windows in her room. She thought that if she turned out the light, she would be in total darkness. If she left it on and went out the door, it might draw the attention of whoever was downstairs. She took a deep breath and turned off the light.

She heard someone yell. It sounded like an angry woman. There was shouting. Something crashed to the floor.

Rennie opened the door and gripped her phone. Her eyes, adjusted to the darkness, helped her tiptoe to the stairway. Moving without a sound, she was on high alert to everything around her. Stepping down the stairs, she peered over the railing. Another crashing sound came from the offices behind the counter. She stopped and crouched down.

"You bastard!" screamed the woman.

Rennie recognized the voice of Angie McGrady. She quickly and lightly descended the last few steps. When she reached the counter, she looked for something that could serve as a weapon, just in case. The counter was clear of everything and the cabinets behind it were locked.

"Oh, no," the woman's voice moaned. "How could you do this to me?"

Rennie clenched her teeth. She focused on the door to Angie's office. A sliver of light came through a slight gap of the door in the frame. It had not been fully closed. With fearsome energy, Rennie lunged at the door.

"Stop," she yelled as she jumped into the office.

Angie stood frozen in shock as she stared at Rennie. Her

mouth dropped open and she trembled.

Rennie glanced around and saw no one else in the room. She looked down at her own clenched fist then back at Angie.

"What the heck is going on here?" she yelled.

Angie slowly sank down to the floor and put one hand over her eyes.

Again, Rennie surveyed the room. A metal folding chair was flat on the floor and several large books were nearby. A wastebasket was on its side under a table. She looked at the young librarian. Her tears had washed her makeup down her cheeks. Her bright red lipstick was smeared, and there appeared to be a streak of it along one arm.

Rennie sat down next to her. "Angie, what's up?"

Her voice was soft.

Angie removed her hand from her eyes and turned away from Rennie.

"What are you doing here?" She bit her lip and gazed at the floor.

"I guess I lost track of time. I was upstairs, in the work room, and I heard something. It sounded like a fight or something. I thought someone was being hurt. Angie, are you okay?"

She took a deep breath. "Greg broke up with me."

Her tears poured out again.

Rennie put her hand on the shaking shoulder of the young woman.

"Oh God, what am I going to do? I thought this was the night, our night. I am so stupid."

She looked up at Rennie, tears flooding her cheeks. "I lost it right there in the restaurant. You know what he wanted to ask me?"

She turned away again and clenched her fist.

"Tell me. What did he say?"

Angie got up and grabbed some tissues from a box on her

desk. She dabbed at her eyes and blew her nose. After a deep breath, she turned around.

"The love of my life, my big hero, that jerk, told me that he was being made a partner at his law firm. He's never looked so happy. He couldn't stop talking. He's going to be working more and traveling to Washington, dealing with big hotshots."

Wiping her eyes again, she marched up to Rennie. "So, my mister big shot said that it was best if I understood that we might not see each other as much for awhile. His big question was whether that was okay for me! In a year or two, when he made his mark, then he could concentrate on us."

She held herself and quietly cried.

"Listen, kiddo, you're not stupid." Rennie got up. "You are terrific. I've been through crap like this before, and I know it's no fun. Give it a rest and you'll see it in a new way."

Rennie laid her hand on Angie's shoulder. "Maybe you two have a great future together. Guys can be stupid. You can't figure it out tonight. Just wait a day and give him a call or wait for his call. Then get together and talk about it."

Angie looked up at Rennie. "It really stinks."

"Yeah, it does. Relationships can be the worst and they can be the best."

Rennie set up the folding chair and picked up the waste basket from under the table. She lifted the books from the floor and put them on the desk as Angie wiped her eyes with tissues.

"I am so embarrassed," she said. Then she laughed. "What were you going to do when you burst in here? Start fighting with someone?"

"Hey baby, I've got a mean right hook. You don't want to get in my way at the wrong time."

They both laughed as Rennie shook her fist.

"Hey, my ex has seen these knuckles up close."

Angie was so amused she snorted.

Rennie began to relax. "I think we both could use a drink. What do you say?"

"I don't know. It's kind of late."

"I'm not talking about an all-night binge. Let's just go out, get a drink, and get out of here. We need a change of perspective. I'll go upstairs and lock up, then I'll meet you back down here. Okay?"

Angie dabbed at her nose. "Okay, I can use that."

Rennie ran upstairs to the work room. She put on her jacket, dropped her cell phone into her bag, and returned downstairs.

As the two women walked out of the library, Rennie asked, "Where should we go?"

"I don't know. I've heard some students talk about a place in Indianola called Lucky's Place. It's not far away."

"Okay, I'll follow you."

Fifteen minutes later, they were sitting on tall stools at a small round table. Country music rolled through the beer-scented atmosphere. Two young men in T-shirts and jeans, with baseball caps worn backwards stared at them from across the room. One of them lifted his long-neck beer bottle and took a drink. He pointed it at the other guy and made a few comments. They laughed.

"What are you going to have?" Rennie asked Angie.

"I don't know; maybe wine. Do you think they have a shiraz?"

"Girl, if they've got wine here, you don't want it. It's either going to be beer or something hard."

Angie rubbed her eyes. "My dad used to like a brandy old fashioned, sweet. They're pretty good."

Rennie gave her a shocked look.

"Okay, brandy old fashioned it is."

Rennie went to the bar and came back with a beer and Angie's drink.

Rennie held out her bottle. "Angie, here's to men and to the women who can live without them."

"Amen," Angie said as she clinked her glass against the beer bottle.

"You want to talk about it?"

Angie stirred her drink. "No, I'm exhausted right now. Maybe later."

"A break is good," Rennie responded.

A few moments of quiet passed between them. Angie cleared her throat. "So, what happened with you and your ex? I just wondered. You know, this situation with me and Greg."

Rennie picked at the label on her beer bottle. "I don't know. It just wasn't right from the beginning. The heat of the relationship blinded us. We didn't look at who we were and how we were. We just looked at what we wanted."

"Everyone does that, and it's easy to throw blame around; boyfriends, job, parents."

Rennie raised her beer, "I'll drink to that. We underestimate the power of our earliest years in forming us. My dad, Walter, is a professor of religious studies at Iowa State and big questions were always on his mind. My mother, Kirstin, was and still is in her 50's a competitive athlete. She was also a local beauty queen. So, now I'm stuck with competing for answers to big questions. It's all their fault."

Angie touched her glass against Rennie's bottle. "Now, I'll drink to that. I guess I'm stuck with being mellow because of my hippie parents."

"Hmm, hippies. So, is Angie short for something, or is that the real name?"

"No, that's not the 'formal' name. It's just better than what I got from my parents."

"Really. Tell me more."

Angie blushed. "If I tell you this, you can't tell anyone, and you have to tell me a secret about you."

"Okay, deal."

"Like I said, my parents were from the '60's, and they were into the flower power thing. They named me Angel. Can you believe that? Do you know how much kidding I got in school when kids found out? 'Hey, Angel, fly over here!' So, I use 'Angie.'"

Rennie studied the label on her bottle. "Names are something. You wouldn't believe how many times I get messages for Mister Rennie Haran."

Angie tilted her drink toward Rennie. "Okay, your turn."

"Between us, right?"

Angie leaned in for the secret.

"Well, it's not a big thing. I almost went right here to Simpson College out of high school."

"Really?"

"Yeah, my parents were big in the United Methodist Church, at least our church. This was the only place I was supposed to go. When I was in high school, I even thought about going to seminary and being a minister, but that wasn't too cool for girls back then. I actually enjoyed studying Scripture. There's so much history and intrigue in it. I kept wondering what God was trying to tell us."

Angie sat back and gave Rennie a serious look. "Now wait a minute, that's no big thing! I want real trash, girl."

Rennie chuckled. "Okay, give me a minute. Back at the library, I mentioned my ex. I really did deck him once. I found out he was cheating on me. We were at the house and he came toward me in the hallway. He opened his arms up like, 'oh, baby girl.' I was so hot, I just reared back and decked him."

"No! What did he do?"

"Not much. After he hit the wall and grabbed his face, he just looked at me in shock. I was afraid he'd hit me back. He muttered something through his hand covering his bleeding mouth and turned around and walked away."

"So, what was it like? Did your hand hurt?"

"Yeah, my hand hurt. I had to run it under cold water for a while."

"I could never do that. I could never hit Greg, even if he cheated on me. Besides," she laughed, "he'd sue me. So, you really thought about being a pastor? Were you into the Bible and all that?"

Rennie swiveled her beer bottle again. "Yeah, I was pretty much into that, but from an analytical perspective. That probably came from my dad. It was long ago, and I'm not into that anymore."

"How did you get into reporting?"

"Like everybody else, I went to college, and didn't know what I wanted to do. I got a degree in history of all things and had no idea what to do with that. I got a job at the paper, and this drive inside me for answering deep questions, truth-and-justice came out. I found I was able to use my reporting as a way of satisfying that drive. It gets pretty frustrating, though, because the powers-that-be don't really want answers, at least to the dark questions. Otherwise, they wouldn't be the powers-that-be! We can only do so much."

"At least you're doing something meaningful. I'm just pushing books around and helping people look stuff up."

"You've been a big help to me."

Angie swirled the ice around in her glass. "By the way, what's the latest with your professor? Are you done with that?"

"No, in fact, I just hit the gold mine. I came across these books that I had ignored. I was looking at paperwork and trying to piece everything together. Then I came across his journals from when he was in England. It's like him writing to me. It's incredible."

Angie sat up straight. "Did you find out how he died?"

"No. He couldn't have told about it. But the end isn't the story. Somebody killed him, and that's the story. I can only find out by reading the whole thing. Bud, my editor, constantly told me to get the whole story, and then, tell it."

Rennie looked away. Her eyes narrowed. "From what I've read so far, I'm wondering who did it. There's this rich gal he seems interested in and a creepy guy who's some church official. Heck, maybe he just said the wrong thing in a bar. I don't know what happened, but I intend to find out. He deserves to have his story told. From what I've seen in the world, the bigger the story, the more closely it is kept."

Rennie took another drink of her beer and pointed the bottle at Angie. "Okay, your turn again. Just what did you say in that restaurant?"

They chuckled.

"It wasn't so much what I said, but that I stood up and looked down at him when I said it. He's not accustomed to that."

"Details, I want details, I'm a reporter."

"It wasn't much. In fact, it was pretty tame. I said something like, 'you jerk, I hope you and your career are happy together.' He's not used to people talking to him like that, especially me. I suppose I'd better call him tomorrow."

"You might want to give it a day or two. He's a lawyer and probably into playing tactical games. If you call him right back, then you're in a subordinate position."

"Yeah, I can't stand all that game stuff."

"You may have to with this guy. You might be better off taking a rest from him. Have you got any hobbies or anything?"

"Nothing much. I help students set up Web sites. It's kind of fun. I also got into digital photography a year ago. That's really satisfying for my creative side. You know, modern library work is heavily computer based."

Rennie leaned back, "Whoa, I've got a techie here!"

Angie laughed, "Hardly. It's easy once you get into it. Hey, it's getting late. I'd better take off. Thanks Rennie. I appreciate your being there tonight. Your entrance was pretty special, too!"

"It would have been more interesting if there had been a bad guy in there."

"So, would you have decked him?"

"I don't know. I don't like trouble, but I'll deal with it."

London, UK
The British Museum

III - 2

Matthias jogged up the entry steps to the British Museum and entered the hall. He greeted the stoic security guard with a wave and stopped.

He pointed at an imposing marble statue. "Is that William Shakespeare?"

The guard looked at the statue, then returned his dull gaze to the energetic newcomer. "Yes sir. I believe it is."

"Wonderful! How far is it from here to Stratford?"

The guard studied the statue. "Actually sir, I don't know."

Matthias grinned broadly. "We haven't met. I am Professor Matthias Justus and I'll be working here for the summer. I thought you should know."

"I believe we do know, sir."

"Very good. I'll see you later."

Matthias breezed down the hallway and ran up the stairs to the second level. As he entered the work room, he noticed that Miss Shefford was already at her desk shuffling the inventory cards and paperwork. "Good morning, Miss Shefford!" he shouted across the room.

The cards in her hand spilled to the desk, and she turned to look at him. When he reached his desk she responded, "Good morning, Professor. Is all well this morning?"

"Excellent, and how are you Miss Shefford? I've never seen such a beautiful day!"

"Professor, are all Americans this energetic in the morning?"

"My students certainly are not. When they enter my morning

classes, they nearly crawl through the door."

He laid his black leather attaché case on his desk and removed his suit coat, arranging it on the back of his chair. "Is it acceptable to not wear a coat in the office? I don't want to appear inappropriate."

"I don't know, Professor. Your situation here is unique."

He paused for a moment and tilted his head. "Hmm, unique. That's interesting."

As he sat down, she organized her cards. "I don't mean that in a negative way, sir."

"Of course not, Miss Shefford. In fact, I like unique. Perhaps, that's why I am in this profession. I look for what is unique. Say, am I supposed to report to Mr. Warrington, or do I just come here and get at it?"

"I believe Mr. Warrington would prefer the latter. He comes by now and then to see if there are any particular problems or if anything is needed. But, he tends to, ... well, he appreciates the distance I believe, between himself and staff. Then again, your situation is ... "

"Yes, unique!"

They laughed.

Matthias was delighted that the young woman appeared to be more relaxed today. He looked through several inventory sheets in a neat stack on his desk. "Yesterday, Mr. Warrington mentioned that Archbishop, what was his name, would be stopping by to meet me. What can you tell me about him?"

She stopped handling her paperwork and became still for a moment. "Archbishop Worthy is an influential person. His promotion of the Museum's interests is appreciated by Keeper Budge."

She turned to Matthias. Her face had lost its color. "He is a determined person. You should be ..."

She suddenly looked back at her work.

"I must be what?"

"I understand things may be different in America. Here, people of my class do their jobs and do their best to remain invisible unless they are called upon by others. I imagine America may be more open to all people."

"Yes, it is. Of course, all societies have social strata. America has less history to create the traditions or perceptions of class, but it is definitely there. Wealth, of course, does not need time to create influence."

For the first time, he felt an anxiety that was more than simple nervousness. He removed from his attaché case the biscuit tin in which Mrs. Whitley had again placed his lunch. "I think I'll put this in the staff room. Please excuse me."

He left their work area and placed his food tin in the cupboard where others had left their items. He leaned back against the counter and studied the floor. His eyes followed the pattern in the marble, but his inner vision was looking for something else. He realized he had found an exceptional work opportunity at the Museum, but he had also joined an intense and conflicted group of people. He worried how their tensions might affect him.

When he returned to the work room, he removed his coat from the back of his chair and put it on. They worked quietly next to each other for nearly an hour.

Matthias noticed that Miss Shefford had stopped working. She was sitting still and looking straight ahead at the wall. He realized that someone was quietly approaching them. He turned to look just as Mr. Warrington arrived at their desk area.

"How are we doing today?" Warrington asked.

"Very good, sir." Matthias attempted a smile. He stood up, awkwardly close to the old man and looked down at him. They both stepped back a bit in a polite dance of comfortable distance.

Warrington cleared his throat. "Well then, as I mentioned yesterday, Archbishop Worthy will be visiting you today. I am sure two scholars of the ancient Bible will have much to talk about. He said he is quite pleased that you are here. I've indicated to Miss Shefford that any time he needs you, do not hesitate to accommodate him. He has spoken highly of the assistance Miss Shefford offered to him in getting to know the collections."

Warrington nodded in her direction.

She looked at her hands in her lap.

"On another matter, there has been a slow down in the delivery of new shipments." Warrington allowed a smile to begin on his face. "I imagine you may not have noticed that, but for the next few days to a week perhaps, we will await the clearing of some delay at the docks. Keep busy as you can. Very good, then."

Warrington turned and began his procession across the room and down the hall.

Matthias peered out the door at the outer hall for a moment, then noticed Miss Shefford. She was busy with paperwork again. Scratching his head in this moment of uncertainty, he looked over at the racks of artifacts from yesterday's delivery and walked in their direction.

For a few minutes, he examined a tiny wooden boat with accents of color and gems. His morning joy returned. His wide eyes darted across the precious object that he carefully turned in his hands. He gently laid the boat on the heavy wooden shelf and shifted his attention to a small gold box. In his peripheral vision, he noticed that Miss Shefford was walking out of the room. He listened for her footsteps in the hall, trying to determine where she was going.

After looking at two more items, Matthias realized she had not returned. He decided to go into the hall to see where she was. He found her on the far side of the Fourth Egyptian Room. She was slowly moving through the collection, looking studiously at each exhibit description card. When he came up behind her, she spun around with shock on her face.

"Sorry. I didn't mean to surprise you."

"Oh, Professor, I was just taking a short break. I enjoy going through the collection."

"I certainly understand. It is marvelous. We stand in the midst of history and treasure. Have you always been interested in the ancient world?"

"Perhaps, we choose that which interests us. I don't know why. For me, these things represent something wonderful and everlasting."

She returned to her review of the exhibit descriptions as they came upon them. Her lips slightly moved as she read them.

"Did you study history or archeology in college, Miss Shefford? I would assume there are some excellent opportunities for that, considering the treasures that England has."

She did not answer but continued to review the exhibit descriptions.

"Miss Shefford, I can't help but observe your study of these exhibits. May I ask why?"

Still, she did not answer. After a few more moments, she finally stopped and looked straight into Matthias' eyes.

"Professor Justus, I was able, or I'm not sure how to put it, but I have been quite fortunate to secure the position I have here as a result of knowing the collection, the Egyptian Collection. My knowledge of these things came as a result of self-study. I have not been to college. My entire schooling opportunity lasted six years. That is considered more than sufficient for someone of my place in society; especially for a girl. I am here, at the British Museum, as a result of my hopes and hard work. It is a concept not limited to men."

Her beautiful eyes grew bright and she tilted her head. "Perhaps you would like a demonstration, sir. Please go there, to the entry to the Third Egyptian Room, and look into the room. Please, go ahead."

Matthias was puzzled and intrigued. He walked to the entry

of the next room and as he moved, he occasionally looked back at Miss Shefford. When he got to the entry he looked into the room, then looked back again at the young woman. He shrugged his shoulders.

From far away, still in the Fourth Egyptian Room, she began. "Professor, you will see that this room contains primarily coffin lids, cartonnages, and mummies. Most of the artifacts in the room are from the period of the 26ᵗʰ Dynasty to the Roman occupation. That would be from what is called the Late Period, about 650 B.C. to 30 B.C. In perspective, the find of Tutankhamun is currently dated at around 1300 B.C. in the 18ᵗʰ Dynasty."

Matthias looked in disbelief at Miss Shefford, far away in the long Fourth Egyptian Room. He hardly breathed. He looked back into the other room.

"Professor," she continued. "you will see located in the room, there are several children's mummies, as well as the mummy of one Artemidorus, who was thought to be Greek. Continuing around the room, there are several gilded masks and plaster heads, the mummy of Ankh-Pa-Khart from around 600 B.C., some painted wooden chests for canopic jars, and a large floor case containing the mummy of Arit-Heru-ru. Please note the porcelain beadwork."

Matthias looked back at the young woman. She was not looking in his direction but seemed to gaze at some distant object in the air.

"Miss Shefford, you need not continue. I am more than impressed."

As he returned to her, her chin eased downward, and her distant gaze turned to hardened determination. She crossed her arms in front of herself.

"Professor, if you wish, I can describe for you every display item in the collection."

"You need not do that," he said. "I could not do that myself if I worked here for the rest of my career. You have a remarkable mind, Miss Shefford, and I am delighted to be able to work with you."

Her arms loosened and slid down until she had one hand on top of the other.

"However, you came to work here, it is a credit to your resolve and to your vision. As far as ..."

"Priscilla, my dear!"

A man's voice startled him.

Entering the room was a short, stocky man in a black, three-piece suit with a clergy collar. He had broad shoulders and a thick chest which seemed to cause him to lean forward as he walked. His thin, black hair was combed straight back. His eyes darted from Matthias to Miss Shefford.

Matthias noticed a slight pink color flushed into Priscilla's cheeks. She closed her eyes.

As the man reached them, he grabbed her hands and gently shook them both.

"Ah Priscilla, what a delight to see you again." Releasing her hands, he turned to Matthias and offered his hand. "You must be Professor Justus. Another delight!"

Matthias took his hand and felt a vigorous response. The man held his hand for just a moment longer than what Matthias was used to.

"Welcome to the British Museum and to England, sir. I am Robert Worthy, Archbishop, Canon, Reverend and all that title folderol. Please call me Robert. I look forward to getting to know you. We must get together during the short time you are here."

Before Matthias could respond, Worthy leaned toward Miss Shefford. "Priscilla, I hope you don't plan to keep him to yourself."

She looked down but did not respond.

Worthy quickly turned back to Matthias. "Professor, are you free for lunch? I can't wait to hear about your travels here. Lady

Jane and I were immediately delighted to see your application for this assistantship. I told Keeper Budge this is the man. Please get him here!"

He threw his hands wide and kept his arms up for a moment. "Well then, I'm very sorry. I've done all the talking, and it seems I have interrupted something you were both doing."

He squinted as he looked back and forth at Matthias and Miss Shefford. There was something ominous about his look.

"Not at all, sir," she whispered. "The Professor and I were discussing the collection. He is beginning to become familiar with what is here."

"Well, Professor, there is no one better to tell you about the collection. Priscilla has a phenomenal mind. Watch this, Professor. Priscilla, please tell us what is in the Nimroud Central Saloon."

He folded his arms across his chest and beamed at her. The young woman gazed into the distance.

"The Nimroud Central Saloon displays sculptures from the palace of Esarhaddon, dating from the seventh century B.C. and earlier. There is the 'Black Obelisk,' recording on five rows of reliefs the campaigns of Shalmaneser II. Beyond that, two statues of ..."

This is not necessary," Matthias interjected. He looked with concern at her.

Her chin lowered again.

Matthias stepped forward. "Archbishop Worthy, I would be delighted to join you for lunch or at whatever time is convenient for you."

He looked into the small, brown eyes of the cleric.

"I see, well then," the Archbishop hesitated as he looked at Matthias and Priscilla. "Very good, we shall have lunch. What do you say, one thirty today? Will that work for you?"

He leaned toward Matthias as though pointing with his nose.

"Well, today sir, today is good."

The cleric displayed a wide grin with crooked, yellow teeth. "Wonderful. I shall return and collect you at that time. Good day, Professor!"

He turned to Miss Shefford. "Priscilla, I am so delighted to also see you again," he said. "If there is anything you need, please do not hesitate to let me know." He reached out and slid his fingers under her hand.

"Thank you, Archbishop. I appreciate your courtesies," she whispered.

Matthias' nostrils flared slightly. As he watched the man march away, he felt a hint of disgust and intimidation. For an awkward moment, he didn't know what to say. Then, he said. "So, who gets to call you 'Priscilla?'"

She took a deep breath and looked at the entry where the Archbishop departed. She then looked at Matthias with a sly grin. "We shall see, Professor."

She quickly left the hall and went to their work room.

At 11:30, Priscilla excused herself to go to lunch. Matthias offered to share with her the modest meal in his biscuit tin, but she declined. After she had gone, he got up and walked along the rows of shelving, looking for something new to examine.

Hearing a rumbling sound, he looked through the shelves and saw Mort pushing an empty storage cart across the room. "Hi Mort," he called out.

The cart stopped. Mort bent down to see him. "Oh hello, sir," came a flat reply.

"It looks like you have nothing new for us today."

"No, sir, we were winding down a bit just before you came, and it might be a few days to get the next shipment. It goes like that."

Mort shrugged his shoulders and moved the cart to a shelf in the back row. He picked two relics off the shelves, checked their inventory tags, and placed them carefully on the cart.

Matthias stuck his hands in his pockets and strolled into the hallway. He checked his watch and saw it was nearly noon. He wondered what he would do for the hour before he had lunch with the Archbishop. He noticed the elevator. Returning to the work room, he asked Mort if he could use it to access the storage area.

"Yes, sir, just take the lift to the LL level. The lights are on. I was just there."

"Great," Matthias said as he headed for the lift. "Oxyrhynchus here I come."

As he stepped from the elevator doorway into the storage area, Matthias rubbed his hands together with delight. He began his expedition through the maze of documents, large boxes, and stone sculptures. He ventured far from the elevators without concern for where he was. Occasionally, he would stop at a shelf and pick up an item or open and review a document. He felt compelled to touch nearly everything he passed by. He looked again at his pocket watch. It was nearly one o'clock.

Reaching the end of the aisle, he realized he was lost. He took a few steps in one direction, then stopped and went the other way. Everything looked the same. He hurried down another aisle. As he turned a corner, something jumped past his leg and screeched. Matthias leaped backward and shouted.

He laughed when he realized it was the cat he had seen during his visit to the area with Mr. Warrington.

"Hey, Tobias," he called. He crouched and made a clicking sound with his tongue. "Come here, buddy."

Hearing a sound behind him and, still kneeling, Matthias turned and looked directly at a man's legs and boots. A large knife hung down the side of one leg. He shouted again as he jumped away. Looking up, he realized it was Mort.

"Is there something wrong, sir? I heard you yell."

"Oh my gosh, Mort, you startled me. No, everything is fine. I was surprised with that cat. It jumped past me."

Matthias got up and brushed off his trousers. "Mort, do you happen to know where the Oxyrhynchus documents are? I thought I'd take a look at them."

"They're over here, near the lift."

The men walked around one section of shelving and down a few more rows. As they walked, Matthias took a deep breath to calm down. He noticed that occasionally, Mort rested his muscular hand on the handle of the long knife strapped to his belt. They stopped.

"Here it is, sir, and over there is the lift."

"Thank you, Mort. I appreciate your assistance."

Mort just stood and looked at the Professor. "May I say something, sir?"

"Of course."

"Well, I'm not sure how to put this."

Mort flexed his hairy arms. "I guess sir, I'd just like to mention that I think Miss Shefford is a lady."

Matthias nodded. "I agree."

"I think she's a lady and, it's hard for a lady to be in a man's world. They can be influenced in bad ways, sir. I wouldn't want to see Miss Shefford influenced, if you know what I mean, sir."

"Mort, I couldn't agree with you more. I think Miss Shefford is one of the treasures of this Museum."

"So do I, sir."

For a moment, they stood almost toe to toe. Mort turned and walked into the soft light of the storage area.

Matthias relaxed and checked his pocket watch. As he took a few steps toward the elevator, he noticed a wooden box on a shelf. He stopped and lifted it up. Although this was in the Egyptian section of storage, the box design and markings did not appear to fit that cultural style. It was about a foot square and six inches deep.

Unlatching and raising the lid revealed a variety of personal jewelry items in a shallow tray. Setting aside the tray, he found beneath it another section with jewelry, a comb, and a small, leather bag. In the bag were three coins.

Matthias' eyes grew large and he looked around for a light to examine the markings on the coins. He noticed a small reading desk at the end of the row with a lamp on it. He checked the time. It was ten minutes after one. He placed everything back where it had been and hurried upstairs.

London, UK
The British Museum

III - 3

"**P**rofessor! You are here!"

A shock hit Matthias.

"I was concerned with your absence," Worthy exclaimed as he seemed to come at Matthias. He looked hungry.

"I'm sorry. I went downstairs to see if I could find something. I hope I have not kept you waiting."

"Not at all. It gave me another chance to visit with Priscilla. Brilliant, isn't she?"

Matthias looked over the Archbishop's shoulder into the work room. He felt like going in to see if the woman was alright. "Yes, she is very sharp. I wonder if I should let her know that I am leaving."

"Well professor, you know Priscilla. She works no matter what goes on around her."

Worthy swung his arm through that of Matthias. "Let's go old boy, we must not be late for lunch."

As the man whisked him down the hall, Matthias glanced again to see if he could see Miss Shefford through the doorway. But they moved too quickly.

The dull-faced guard at the entry hardly moved his head as they went out the front doors.

Reverend Worthy stopped on the top step and squinted at the street. Waving his hand above his head, he hurried down the steps and yelled, "Let's go, Professor!"

Matthias held back, perplexed. Worthy joyfully signaled for him to join him at the street. Matthias jogged down the stairs. A long, black automobile with sparkling chrome accents came to a stop in front of the two men.

Matthias was amazed with the size of the vehicle. A uniformed man got out of the open cab area. His dark blue coat had gold buttons and the bill of his cap looked like a black mirror.

"What is this?" Matthias asked.

The Archbishop breathed heavily through his mouth. His small eyes turned to Matthias. "This, Professor, is our carriage and our company."

He grabbed at the door handle, startling the chauffeur. With a quick twist, he opened the door and gestured inside, offering a modest bow. "Professor, after you."

Matthias hesitated, then jumped into the large compartment. As he landed on the deep, cushioned leather, he realized he was sitting across from Lady Sotterfeld-Gris.

Her white face, red lips and golden hair appeared to hover in the midst of the black leather upholstery. Her black satin dress and jacket, and the black ebony buttons on her white silk blouse beckoned the eyes of a breathless young man. He suddenly realized where he was looking.

Reverend Worthy climbed into the cabin with a heavy bump against Matthias that allowed a polite moment of distraction.

"Well then," Worthy seemed to shout, "isn't this fun?" He looked quickly at his two companions.

Lady Jane's confident gaze softened into a smile. "Professor, I am so pleased that you could join us today." She looked at the Archbishop, who was panting with an occasional, soft hiss as air passed over his lower lip.

He patted Matthias on the leg and said, "This is going to be fun. Any moments with Lady Jane are special!"

Matthias grinned. "I don't know what to say, but I am delighted to be with you both. These first days have been a bit overwhelming. I would like to say again that I am most grateful for this privilege to be at the Museum. It is an honor."

As the limousine eased into London traffic, Reverend Worthy softly hissed in a more relaxed rhythm. The attention of Lady Jane discreetly shifted to the passing street scenes but often returned to Matthias. He nervously looked out the window. The fragrances of the woman and the leather, his lack of food thus far, and his uncertainties made him feel a little faint. He hoped they would soon arrive at their destination, and he was eager to get out of the car when it finally stopped.

"Ah, here we are!" Worthy suddenly exclaimed.

He seized the door handle and quickly pushed his way out of the vehicle. Matthias looked at the Lady and she nodded to the door. He moved through the opening and onto the street. Worthy reached up to take her hand, as she glided from the car to the ground.

Matthias looked around, somewhat confused. He saw no restaurant.

"What's wrong, old boy?" Worthy asked. "We are here."

Worthy offered his arm to the Lady, and placing hers through his, they walked up a few marble steps to a building with four levels of classic façade. It appeared to be a residence.

Inside, Lady Jane removed a long, silver pin from her black hat and gave them to an awaiting young woman in a starched, light blue uniform. Reverend Worthy strode into a room of luxury. Crystal vases held fresh flower arrangements, the red fabrics of cushioned couches and chairs were contained by ornately carved and highly polished walnut, and oil paintings were suspended in heavy, gold frames.

Matthias placed his hand against the entryway molding to steady himself.

"Professor, please come in," offered Lady Jane. "Robert thought it might be more comfortable if we ate here rather than in some distracting old restaurant."

With that invitation, she went into a dining area, in which an elegant table awaited them.

As Matthias followed into the dining area, he shook his head in disbelief. "My Lady, I simply do not know what to say. This is quite overwhelming." He began to laugh as he spoke. "You and Reverend Worthy have been more than kind, and this is well beyond what I am accustomed to!"

She strolled to the head of a long mahogany table, lined with four chairs on each side, and a higher-backed chair on each end. The table was covered with a bright white cloth inlaid with lace. On it were tiny crystal vases each holding a fresh rose. The dishes displayed a pearl-like finish.

"Professor, please come and sit, over here. Let's get to know one another. Robert and I are both eager to hear about your journey here, what it is like in America, and much more. I hope it was acceptable that we came to my home for lunch."

"Yes, ma'am," Matthias said as he sat where she gestured at the table. "Your home is simply wonderful. I have never seen anything like it. Royalty is not very common where I am from."

He looked into the eyes of Lady Jane for the first time. She seemed to enjoy the moment.

"What's that you were saying?" Worthy asked as he entered the dining room.

"I said that this is a wonderful home, and you all are most gracious."

Worthy stuck his hands to his hips and looked at Lady Jane with a broad smile. "Yes, she is, most gracious. I think we will all get along famously. Don't you think?"

His eyes darted at each of them.

"Robert, is there anyone with whom you do not get along?" she asked.

"Ha!" he said, picking up a fork in his left hand and setting its end upright on the table. "I try, my Lady, I try!"

He looked at the small layering of plates in front of him as if his stare could create food.

Matthias began to relax and leaned into the back of his chair. He noticed Lady Jane's left hand as it lay on the crisp tablecloth. Her skin was a creamy white. The index finger lightly and almost imperceptibly stroked the sculpted end of the heavy, silver fork handle. On that finger she wore a gold ring, delicate in size and texture, with an embossed coat of arms, accented with a sapphire at each side. It was the only ring on the hand.

As household help moved in and out of the room, presenting the meal, Matthias felt compelled to initiate conversation.

"I didn't know that you lived near the Museum," he offered.

Worthy laughed. "This is only our Lady's town home. Her home is in Hampstead. But one needs a place in the city."

He eagerly began to eat his salad.

"It is a convenient location," she said lightly. "The city demands so much, and yet offers so much, that one must really have a place to rest or change."

After a brief silence, Reverend Worthy laid down his fork and knife. He looked across the table at the young American. "Professor," he blurted out, "do you consider yourself to be a man of faith first or a man of science?"

Lady Jane's delicate application of fork to food continued. She discreetly looked at each of the men, and then sipped some water.

Matthias paused from eating and sat back for a moment. "That's an interesting question. I don't know if I've thought about it. I'm not sure one needs to be in conflict with the other. As with yourself, we are guided through this world according to some inner compass. Those of us who are blessed with faith have the challenge of applying the gifts God has given us in ways that would please Him."

Matthias peered at the Archbishop. "You honor me with the

idea that I'm a man of science. I have an interest in certain things that bore most people. Thus, they call it a science."

"Professor," Lady Jane added, "you are too modest about your skills. Your credentials indicated you have obviously applied yourself to a noble effort and succeeded handsomely."

"Thank you, ma'am, I find real delight in unlocking ancient texts. Language and how people have chosen to express their thinking through it has always been fascinating to me."

Matthias tilted forward and placed his elbows on the table, resting his chin on his folded hands. "When we consider the great minds and the great people of the ancient world, reading their words can at times unlock one of the thousand little doors that contain our spirit. Insight is, I think, a hint of the step from this world in the other; through that door and into the realm of the divine."

He sat back. "I'm sorry. I just rambled on and in the company of people whose learning has certainly far exceeded me in all ways. It is dangerous to ask a small college professor an open-ended question."

Lady Jane sat quietly, listening and observing. "Professor, I think the depth of your skills may have been much disguised. You need not be modest. During this short time you will be with us, we look forward to your enlightening us on the wisdom you have gleaned from the ancient world."

Worthy observed his companions. "Professor, if I may, I remain curious as to where faith enters into your understanding of things. Wisdom or insight come to us in rare moments, and we may all agree that for me, the timing is indeed rare."

Everyone chuckled.

"I can only place such new awareness in the structure of what I already know. How then can I become acquainted with God if He is not an Anglican?"

Lady Jane looked at him with a shrewd smile. "Perhaps

Robert," she said slowly, "that is precisely why your insights are so rare!"

Now, everyone laughed, with Worthy's being the loudest.

"Well done, my Lady; well done!" he responded.

"If I may Reverend," Matthias interjected, "your point is well taken. How do we, as people of faith, come to know anything as truth if it is not within a framework of what we consider to be externally given wisdom? Then, how do we allow that truth, which we may attribute to God, to be used to serve Him without being constrained by that very structure in which our learning came to us?"

"Professor, I believe it is my duty to weigh in on God's behalf for His people the church, on the relative merits of what men say is truth. One way the church is cared for is to decide for it what is truth. Is that not how you see it?"

Worthy's demeanor grew more serious.

Matthias studied one of the flowers on the table then looked at Lady Jane. Her eyes flickered with intensity.

"Well sir, you have touched upon yet another of the great challenges of our understanding of God. Can we come to know what He has to say to us if the church does not tell us? A few hundred years ago, devout men argued that the church may actually get in the way of such truth."

Worthy's his face became red.

Matthias sipped from the crystal water glass. "Truth, of course, may be more relevant to knowledge than to faith, which is more like the channel down which truth may plummet. While many yearn for faith, not everyone hopes for truth. Truth can be quite unwelcome to some."

He felt satisfaction with his comments.

"Bravo Professor," Lady Jane declared. "It is not often that our dear archbishop is left on the periphery of an argument."

She raised her water glass and tilted it in the direction of

Matthias. Reverend Worthy's eyes darted at her and held fixed.
She sipped from the crystal glass and placed it on the table with
confident grace.

"Professor," Reverend Worthy said slowly, "holy Scripture
calls us to come to God as children, innocent and without guile.
Children need to know little other than they are to trust and obey
their parents. Truth is of no use to them. Thus, the Church, as
the shepherd of the flock holds the true authority. Truth is sec-
ondary to that. Above all else, we must protect the Church and
remove these arguments over truth."

"Reverend Worthy, I would not debate with you about matters of faith or the church. It is interesting, though, that for one
to grow in faith, which is certainly a hope of the Church, a person
must challenge what they believe and know. In that way, they
question what they consider to be the truth that has been given
to them by the Church, and hopefully, enrich that knowledge."

Worthy squinted at Matthias.

Matthias continued with confidence. "I'm a small-town college professor. My study of old texts has given a flavorful taste
to my understanding of who God calls us to be. But I must admit
I have not lived up to that obedience to which you refer. I do
not know who can fully obey the totality of rules in any system,
especially religious ones. They focus on the failings of the people
who are expected to abide by them. If it were not for grace, perhaps the ultimate gift, it would be easier to just give it all up and
devote oneself to the world, as so many do."

Worthy finally relaxed against the back of his chair.

"If I may just add one thing to my stumbling thoughts,"
Matthias said. "We can become excessively complex in how we
approach God. Jesus said what He said, and if we allow that to
enter our hearts and minds, I'm not sure what else we really
need."

"Well said," Worthy responded.

Matthias nodded in appreciation. "My dereliction of faith is to have become complacent in learning Scripture, and to have become focused on the so-called meaning of the individual words. It is easy for one to get into the facts of the words and to lose sight of the intention of the text. I admire those whose faith is personal versus simply intellectual, as mine may be."

Lady Jane tilted toward Matthias. "Professor, the record of your scholarship is impressive. Complacency would have led you down an indifferent and unfertile path."

Archbishop Worthy stroked his forehead. "My Lady, once again you offer the generous and considerate view most appropriate for our discussion. Thank you for your most generous hosting of this luncheon."

"I thank you as well," Matthias added with an eager look.

Her nod of approval to the men was greeted by another comment from Reverend Worthy.

"Professor," he hissed, "a thought has just struck me. You mentioned the personal relationship of faith. What if you allowed yourself to more fully experience that personal relationship versus what you described as a presumptuous knowledge of faith? How would your life change if you had an encounter with God and not simply with the mechanics of His Word?"

Matthias felt bewildered. He looked at Worthy. "Your question is both marvelous and frightening. I can only imagine that the meaning of my life would be clearer and everything else would be less important. I'm not sure what I would do, but I know that little else would have value than the message I receive from Him."

Worthy responded, "History has demonstrated that people who have what you call a personal faith become dangerous to themselves and maybe even to the Church. We must protect the Church at all costs."

PART FOUR

Indianola, Iowa
Simpson College

IV - 1

Mrs. Knoche rumbled into the Simpson College library and made her way to the counter. Dabbing at her temples and cheeks with a handkerchief, she waved at a student worker who came to the counter from the room behind.

"Excuse me, is Miss McGrady here?"

"No, ma'am, she won't be in until about 9:30. She had other business this morning."

"Is that reporter from the *Record* working here today? Have you seen her recently?"

"I don't know. Do you know what she's researching?"

"I think she's working on some archival materials relating to Professor Justus."

The student removed a three-ring binder from the shelf. She looked through a few pages, ran her finger down the list, and looked up at Mrs. Knoche. "Would that be a Ms. Haran? H-A-R-A-N? *Des Moines Record?*"

"Yes, that's it. Is there contact information for her?"

"No ma'am. There is no phone number."

"Would you leave a note for Ms. McGrady, please? Just tell her that Mrs. Knoche was here, K-N-O-C-H-E, from Administration, and that I have the last name of the woman who was here in 1935. She will understand. Tell her there was another woman from England who came years later."

The student made a quick note. "Okay, anything else?"

"Yes. Please ask Miss McGrady to call me. Do you know when Miss Haran will return to the work room?"

"No, but she has a key to the room."

Mrs. Knoche was lighter on her feet as she left the library. Her arms swung smoothly as she strolled across campus. She felt refreshed. Her life had a purpose again.

Angie marched into the library, turned past the end of the counter and entered her office. She opened a drawer of her desk and set her purse inside. Standing behind her desk, she looked through a stack of memos, letters, and file folders.

A student worker peeked into the room. "Miss McGrady, Mrs. Knoche from Administration was here to see you. She said something about knowing the name of a lady from 1935 and another one sometime later. She also asked about the woman from the *Des Moines Record*. She asked you to call her."

"Were there any calls for me?"

"Yes, a man called. He said he was with the library association. He wanted to talk to you about a committee meeting."

Dropping the slips of paper on her desk, Angie dialed the extension for Mrs. Knoche and left a message. She then called Rennie's office and got her voice mail.

"Hi, Rennie, thanks again for last night. Mrs. Knoche from Administration stopped by this morning and left a message. It was about some woman from 1935. There was also information on a woman who came later. I'm not sure what it's all about, but good luck."

A few minutes later, Mrs. Knoche was on the phone with Angie. She told her she had found some of the distant family of Professor Justus and wanted to get the information to Ms. Haran. The family found a note in an old bible that was from the woman who visited in 1935. Her name was Mrs. MacDonald.

Mrs. Knoche wondered if Angie was helping research the case.

Angie offered to forward the information.

Mrs. Knoche's tone was upbeat.

"Also tell her that another woman from England came here years later and asked about Professor Justus. Evelyn, my predecessor, had mentioned it. She said the woman didn't seem to know much about him but did ask about his letters, for some reason. I remember it like it was yesterday. Evelyn thought she'd never have to hear about him again. Miss McGrady, I don't know if you're interested in helping Miss Haran, but I thought some of your library contacts in London might be able to assist her with the research."

"That's a nice thought Mrs. Knoche. I'll consider that and I'll pass along this information to Rennie."

Angie was bewildered with the old woman's eagerness to assist and her cheerful attitude. She gathered the file folders from her desk and noticed the message from her library association contact. She set it in front of her and stared at it, then dialed the number.

"Hi, Bob. Angie McGrady from Simpson. Yeah, it's been a long time. So, what's happening? Yeah, that date for the next meeting will work for me. Can you e-mail an agenda to me? Good, we'll see you then. Oh, would you happen to know if we have any association members in London, at any of the local colleges or universities? Something came up here, an old research issue, and I wondered if someone in London would be available to check out a missing piece of it. Thanks, I appreciate it. I'll talk to you later."

Twenty minutes later Rennie called. They joked about the previous night. Then, Rennie asked about Mrs. Knoche's message.

"Yes," Angie said, "she had a name. It was a Mrs. Mac-Donald."

"That's not a name I've read before," Rennie responded. "Are you sure it was MacDonald?"

"Exactly, at least that's what some distant family member told Mrs. Knoche. It was on a note or a letter in an old family bible. Also, she said that another woman came here to ask about him years later. Your professor was some lover boy, huh?"

"Well," Rennie paused, "he got something going over there. I guess I'd better get back to the work room and finish things up. By the way, has your boyfriend called?"

"No, and that's okay with me. See you later."

About an hour later, Angie spun around as Rennie yelled "hey!" Rennie gave her a thumb's up signal then hurried up the stairs.

Opening the door to the work room, she turned on the light and saw that everything remained as she had left it the night before. She had begun to develop a personal sense about the mystery professor and felt a strong but subtle drive to find his story. He seemed so close and yet, far away.

Rennie approached his black, leather attaché case lying at the end of the table. She realized she had been looking through the files but never examined his case. Tentatively, she put her index finger on the brass clasp that held the strap to the case and gave it a flip. The end jerked a little and slipped out of its retainer.

She pressed on the case and realized for the first time that there was something hard inside. Lifting the strap and the cover of the case, she looked in. She reached in and removed a decorative, tin box.

The metal box was wrapped many times with a strong, string-like cord, and beneath the cords was a handwritten note that simply said, "letters home." She lifted it and gave it a slight shake. It felt heavy. As she set it down, she looked at the imprinted name of "Harrods."

Further in the case, she found two silver pens, an envelope and some writing papers. Rennie put on the cotton gloves and removed the envelope. Inside it was a folded sheet of paper. It read, "Thank you Holy God, for this incredible gift of your amazing love. No other discovery in all of human history will ever compare with this."

Rennie looked up at the wall. "What the ...?"

She studied the paper. It was unfinished. Assuming it was the beginning of a love letter, she slipped the letter into the envelope and returned it to the case. Then, she replaced the box back in the attaché case.

As she was about to close the cover on the case, she noticed something in a bottom corner. Delicately, her fingers removed a small, white linen handkerchief on which the letter "S" had been stitched in purple thread. She lifted the handkerchief to her nose and took in a breath. A heavy fragrance was on the handkerchief of leather, musk and something feminine as well. She made a clicking sound in her mouth and winked as she put the handkerchief into the case. "Alright, Professor!"

She latched the strap and sat down in front of her notes, two file folders from the archives, and the journal she had been reading the night before.

IV - 2

Nearly three hours later, there was a tap at the door. Rennie looked up.

"Come in."

The door opened a little, and Angie looked in. "So, how are you doing? Did you find that name?"

"Come in. No, I haven't found it, yet. It's a bit of a mystery, but this is good stuff!"

Angie stepped in and placed her hands on the back of one of the chairs. "Really?"

Rennie removed her gloves, placed a paper marker in the journal and closed it. She pushed away from the table and leaned back in the chair. "I don't know where to begin. He truly was on an adventure. I just don't see how he got into trouble. Everyone seemed to like him, and he got along alright with the powers that be."

She looked at the cover of the journal. "He's pretty hot on two women, and they seem to be hot on him. There's a young woman that he works with, her name is Priscilla Shefford, oh wait, that's an 'S.' She's kind of an assistant, and their relationship has developed very nicely, thank you."

Angie tilted her head. "Like what?"

"Let me read this for you."

"Priscilla and I have had several opportunities to have lunch together. She is a truly amazing young woman. I must admit, I have grown fond of her. I struggle with the emotion since it seems it so recently that my own darling wife, my Hope left me to be with God. Priscilla is, in a way, a new hope but with a small H."

Rennie looked up at Angie and said, "Isn't that cool?" She looked back at the journal and continued to read.

"I will also admit that Lady Jane intrigues me as well. She is quite a tease and yet, she remains aloof. I am not quite sure what to read from her behavior. It is only on rare occasions that I get to see her alone for a few moments. Most of the time when I see her, Reverend Worthy is with us. He is an interesting fellow, but he could be described, as my mother might say, as a feisty one. He is prone to argument, but even that is delightful since our topics are of scholarship and of faith. It has been very rare for me to have another with whom I can engage in such targeted 'mental gymnastics,' as my dad used to say. Besides, there is no need to get serious on matters when I am only here for a few months."

Rennie gave Angie a big grin. "Oh my gosh, you know what? Lady Jane's last name is Sotterfeld-Gris. That begins with an S, also! I found a woman's handkerchief in his attaché case, and it has an 'S' on it."

Angie saw the black case at the end of the table. Rennie followed her look with an eager anticipation.

"Don't you get it?" Rennie asked. "One of those ladies became his, well we don't know what she became, but considering the close quarters they all were in, there could have been sparks flying. That could have created the sort of tensions that might get someone killed."

Angie's skeptical look did not please Rennie. "Since you're doing the research and I haven't read the journals, I'll have to leave the intrigue to you, the reporter."

Rennie slouched in her chair and took a deep breath. "Maybe, I got a little ahead of myself. There's probably more to it than a simple love triangle. The Museum does sound a little creepy for me, full of so-called treasures they dig up. Hey, maybe it's the curse of the mummy."

They both laughed.

"I need to push on," Rennie said. "Bud, my boss, is on my tail about this. For some reason, our editor keeps calling him about this story. Maybe, she wants me to get back to the local issues. It's the usual municipal power play stuff. The public is such a flock of sheep. If they knew what was going on, we'd probably have public stoning become acceptable again; and it would start with the attorneys!"

"I have one in mind," Angie offered. "By the way, it's funny you should say 'stoning.' I recall hearing a weird news story about the British Museum. Someone was killed with a stone. It was gruesome. A clerk or someone who worked at the museum was murdered with a stone jammed down his throat. They thought it was a cult thing. There had been reports over the years of people at the Vatican Library and some museum in Germany dying the same way. Pretty ugly, huh? I noticed it because of my connection with archives people."

Rennie's face wrinkled in disgust. "Gross! So, how's it going with you and the lawyer? Are you planning a stoning?"

Angie stared at a blank space on the table. "Well right now, I'd like to say no news is good news, but I'm not sure."

She looked up at Rennie. "But, I'm not necessarily against that stoning thing. Let me know if you need anything."

"Will do."

Rennie opened the journal and found her place.

"Oh, by the way," Angie added, "I'd appreciate it if you would wear the gloves. We have a certain protocol to follow. I'm responsible for these things."

"Right. Sorry."

The moment the door closed, Rennie slipped on the gloves and proceeded through the pages. She often stopped to write a comment in her notebook. She set aside her pen when she came to his commentary in late July.

"Although I have been intrigued by Lady Jane, I find that I have little remaining energy for her elusive enchantment. She flutters through life as a butterfly in a breeze, and I never know whether her intentions demonstrate an interest or if they come from some momentary gust of indifferent fancy.

Her advanced degree from Oxford, in ancient Near Eastern peoples, though extraordinary and having required exceptional focus and dedication, is considered by her as simply another dalliance. Her heart is unmistakably good and generous, yet it is generous and good for every new thing that strikes her interest. It would seem that commitment is not a part of her world, except for her momentary fascination.

In no way does this impugn the quality of her soul; it is simply a lifestyle to which I am not accustomed. Perhaps, it befits her class and not my own. She would probably be a good friend, and I hope that is the path on which we are proceeding. There is great value in that.

I wonder if that is how things have worked out between her and Reverend Worthy. Their relationship may be the model to which she aspires. It is interesting, lacks intimacy, respectful, yet engaging. As we have come to know one another, she has not been shy about sharing with me her amusement about the good Archbishop. She is amused with what he calls his dreadful life in a 30 year marriage with a woman whom Lady Jane says is youthful and delightful.

She said rumors have it they only share a dedication to a daughter that is being raised in a most strict manner.

Lady Jane has hinted that this cleric's interests may be more directed to a certain gentleman with whom he has traveled. Although I offer no judgment on that, the number of awkward moments he and I have shared prompted me to such suspicion before Lady Jane teased the thought.

Worthy is a complex man with great energy for the world and all that is in it. It is actually quite a gift that he has, to give all his attention to whatever is in his presence for the moment. That can also be most awkward for those who cannot tolerate that level of interest.

I have observed on many occasions how Priscilla nearly shuts down when Reverend Worthy enters her environment. More than once I have asked her about my observation, and she is clear that it is not a matter for discussion. I have the impression that the Archbishop was instrumental in her being at the British Museum, yet she holds something akin to fear in her heart whenever he is present."

Rennie sat up, staring for a moment at the page. She turned to the next blank page of her notepad and wrote at its top, "Key Players." She wrote "Priscilla" and drew a line beneath it. Then, she resumed reading.

"There have been times when, in a competitive discourse on some issue of faith, I sensed something ominous in the intensity of his passion. I'm not sure if he has always controlled it. Some people of authority can escape irresponsible behavior.

The power of the church can be a great gift of God or a tool of those who hold the office, and his views tend to suggest the latter is what captures his interest. For him, it is almost as though God's very presence on Earth exists as the church, and that the good reverend is most ready to assume a divine role in putting heavenly law into effect.

I told him once that I agreed with him on the role of obedience among the faithful but suggested that this is true when the church lives in accordance with Scripture. I was quite surprised when he suddenly tensed. He quickly posited that God's Holy Spirit flows through the church and its authority, and therefore it cannot be questioned.

I then asked if he considered that he and I were reasonably well schooled in not only the Holy Scripture but its source and surrounding documents. He immediately agreed, lifting his chin high. I asked him if he thought we may disagree on what certain passages may say or mean. He laughed with glee. "Of course!" he exclaimed. So, I quickly followed with the idea that real truth can only rest with the Word and not with those who interpret it.

He was so stunned his eyes seemed to bulge slightly. He turned and walked out of the room without a sound.

I offer no judgment on him, of course, and I accept with humility the many ways God chooses to bring His will into the world. Not only is the harvest great and the workers few, but we need many different skills to bring that harvest in. I am sure God has chosen Reverend Worthy for some special purpose."

Rennie set the journal aside and turned to her notes. She wrote "Reverend Worthy" on a line, underlined it, and returned to the text.

"A difficult question for all of us is to ask, what was the purpose that God chose us for, and will we honor it or invent one of our own? Sometimes, I wonder if I was created for some little thing, some comment to another in need, or some insignificant duty that later has great portent."

Rennie sat up and shook her head. "Oh man, not this purpose thing again," she muttered.

"Men look to great deeds or high office to justify their existence, but Jesus needed neither. That is not to say that healing the blind and lepers and raising the dead are not magnificent beyond what any mortal has ever done. Rather, he did them out of love and to glorify God, not himself. If I, or any of us, know our mission in life, how easy it would be and how well defined our energy would be expressed! So, why am I here?"

Rennie picked up her pen and wrote "Purpose?" in her notebook. She circled it twice. She tapped the pen point on the underlined names and then wrote "Why?" in a margin. Releasing the pen onto the notebook, she looked down at the journal.

"Priscilla is undoubtedly a woman with a mission, and she lives it with gentle goodness, yet focus. I find that to be one of countless admirable traits in her. I am occasionally amused if not shocked with my own hopeful prospect each morning, not for the ancient treasures that I get to examine, but for the mere presence of Priscilla at a nearby desk and for our moments together at lunch.

There is a joyful tension between us. I believe our hopes are not indifferent to where this could ultimately lead. This journey far from Iowa has been restorative to every aspect of my being, and I am grateful beyond measure. What lies ahead can only be good. I feel as though God is preparing me for something wonderful. I am appreciative of the incremental and deliberative way in which God has removed the shroud from my soul and allowed the light of Priscilla and this place to refresh me.

As though nibbling at the crumbs of the most delicious

pastry, I have come to learn of Priscilla's origins and her presence with me at the British Museum. It is a story that we Americans would call true grit. It is astonishing how someone born in poverty, actually living on the grounds of Bethlem, a simple girl as she calls herself and given no encouragement or opportunity, lifts herself up to such a respectable place in society.

She succeeds on attitude and vision. Her intelligence and her manner indicate nothing less than the finest of families as the garden from which she grew. Her delicacy, charm, awareness, and strength, create a purity that leaves all else a mere shadow of being. It would be a grave error for anyone to underestimate her dedication to her vision of a better life for herself and, I am sure, for those she loves.

Our mutual attention to discretion at the museum recently permitted us to take the step of having dinner together on several evenings after work. Here am I, a small town college professor from Iowa walking the streets of London with a most beautiful and enchanting young woman on a summer evening. This is truly what the heart hopes for but can never fully imagine in its glory.

On those evenings, my senses are so heightened that every sound, every taste, every fragrance seemed new and exciting. Even the breeze on my face felt like a caress. I take note of the finest details of her hands and face when I can in discreet ways.

Even at rest, the corners of her mouth appear to be slightly curved up as though a smile was about to break loose. Her nose makes a subtle twitching motion when we are discussing some issue and her mind becomes particularly focused. Her hands and her arms express her ideas in the way a ballerina defines the spirit of the composer. When she sits down at the table and rises again, and when

I hear her walk through our work room, the mere sound of her clothing rustling against itself raises within me feelings that I thought were long gone."

Rennie took a deep breath. "Wow. Matthias, chill out baby." She grabbed a water bottle from her bag for a quick sip. Rennie stood up, removed the gloves, and walked to the end of the table. She looked back at the journal and gazed across the files and Matthias' black, leather case. "Things are cooking,' huh Professor?"

She stretched her arms up high, reaching for the ceiling, then slowly turned her head in a circle. She got her phone and checked to see if she had any messages. After half a dozen return calls, she put the phone away and left for a break.

Rennie strolled through the library, occasionally looking at a book on the rack and for the first time simply allowing herself to enjoy being on campus without a mission. She observed students studying, visiting, and doing their research. She thought about Professor Justus and how different his time and his students were from those who are there now.

She realized that even those contemporary differences with the past are just a different coating on the same people; people who wondered what the world held for them, who they were going to be with, what they were going to do, optimistic or sad, embarrassed or prideful. Asking in different ways why they were here.

Rennie looked out at the campus through the large windows and observed what a beautiful place of peace this campus offered for all that self-questioning. Long shadows flowed across the lawn and soft light filled the air. As she took a deep, relaxing breath, Rennie noticed a man sitting on a bench.

Something about him seemed out of place. He wore a suit, but he had no briefcase or papers with him. She squinted. He just sat there, as though he waited for someone. She sensed a threat.

She hurried back to see if she had closed the door to her room. Finding it locked, she felt the need to return and see the man, again.

She paused and thought, *This is ridiculous.*

She returned to the room, settled into her chair. "Okay Professor, let's please finish this up."

She found where she had been reading, put on the cotton gloves, and read the next passage. Matthias's journal notes were easy to follow because after each entry he drew a delicate line beneath the last sentence. Some entries consisted of just a short sentence, and others continued for a page or two.

Then, she came upon an entry filled with exclamation points.

"Amazing! Amazing! Amazing! An extraordinary find! I cannot believe it. I cannot write fast enough to put down my excitement. Things were a little slow today, so I went down to the lower level again to read some documents on the shelves and see what other marvels might be lying about. I returned to the Oxyrhynchus section and found the box that I discovered so long ago. I took it to the study desk and opened it again, looking through the personal items, and once again found the small bag of coins.

As I examined them, I noticed some writing in the corner of the box. I lifted up and tilted the box to the desk light and then became breathless upon reading the Aramaic inscription. It said, "Matthias of Antioch."

I cannot believe it; my name written from that great, ancient city of earliest Christendom. It may have been the box maker or the owner of the box; I do not know which. But in any case, it led me to examine the box further. I had known when I first saw it that it was of the Damascus or New Babylon style.

After removing all the loose items from the box and placing them on the desk, I noticed that the interior was unusually shallow, given the depth of the box. Suspecting that there was in fact a hidden compartment, I lifted the box up high and rotated it, looking for evidence of how one might open such a compartment.

Just then, Mort walked by. He surprised me greatly. He is quiet and has a suspicious nature that presents itself in a bold way. He has made it clear that he does not like my growing relationship with Priscilla. I am certain he admires her but knows that she aspires to someone and something much more than what is in his corner of the world.

My efforts to befriend him have not been successful thus far. In those moments when I stop to chat, he removes the long knife from the sheath at his side, and he uses it to clean beneath his fingernails.

With him hovering in the near distance, it was necessary to return the items to the box and place it on the shelf. I continued my stroll through the lower level as though his presence had meant nothing to me.

At a later, selected time, I went to the lower level again, eager to find that box. First, I checked to see where Mort was so I would not be interrupted. He must have previously told Mr. Warrington something cautionary, because the old man paid me a visit just yesterday. He asked if I would like other assignments in our quiet times. He seemed to be more suspicious than helpful. He reminded me again of the importance of keeping artifacts in their appropriate places and not disturbing them. I think his ultimate wish is to be frozen in time along with everything in the collections.

Finding the box again, I quickly removed the items and began my search for the secret compartment release. It is maddening. I am sure it is quite simple, but I cannot find it. I gave the box a quick shake and felt a heavy movement inside it. The movement was very brief, but it confirmed that something was in there. I must try again tomorrow.

Joy! Excitement! Frustration! Oh, what a day this has

been. I only have a moment to jot a few notes on two wonderful events. First, it is Friday evening, and Priscilla has agreed to have dinner again. I have found a special place for us to eat. Second, I was able to go to the lower level and found the release on the box. It allows the entire bottom of the box to slide, revealing an open space beneath. Unfortunately, it has not been open for such a long time that I can only move the base an inch or so. But I know there is something inside.

I must be very cautious. I believe that Mort is tracking my movements, perhaps at the direction of Mr. Warrington.

Neither of them likes my respect for and growing relationship with Priscilla. If noticed, my activities in the lower level with the box can only add to their concerns. I know not what will come from either discovery, the beauty of Priscilla or the mysterious box from Antioch, but I know I must move forward (I wonder if my casual and indiscreet comment to Mrs. Whitley about Priscilla was conveyed to her cousin Warrington. I hope not.)"

Rennie sat to attention and glared at the blank wall. Her mind raced and her breathing was shallow. She knew the outcome of the story she was reading but could do nothing about it.

She grabbed her phone and called Angie.

"Hey, are you still here at the library? I'm in the work room. I was wondering if you could do your research magic and find the name of an investigative reporter in London. No one in particular, just an investigative reporter. I came across information in his journal, and it occurred to me that we do not have any cause of death report. I wondered if the London police might have such a thing."

"I can get some names for you. I also asked a fellow with the library association to connect us with people in London who might do background research on any of this for you."

"Great, you're a step ahead of me. According to his journal, events are becoming intense. I think I might be on to who did it. It's too bad. Everything in his life was coming together in a wonderful way."

"How sad. My little life in the library doesn't seem too bad."

"Yep, life is tough and then you die. One other thing, what time would it be over there? In fact, what time is it here?"

Rennie glanced at her watch.

"Oh, my gosh, it's six o'clock, already. It's probably midnight over there. I guess we've got awhile to chill out here before we contact anyone there. Did I tell you I found what I think is his lunch pail in his attaché case?"

"Yuck! Did you open it?"

"Heck, no. It's all bound up, and there's a note on it that says it's filled with letters he wrote home. He's a pretty good writer; of course, I might now be in love with him."

Angie chuckled. "Now, that's what you call a safe relationship!"

"Yeah, let me know what you find. I'm going home to start writing this up. I've got to finish it or my boss won't let me write the obit notices!"

"Say, did you call Mrs. Knoche. She was eager to give you some information. I'm a little surprised with her interest in this."

"Oh, I forgot to call dear ol' Mrs. Knoche. What do you think is up with her? She was so cold to me at first, and now she wants to help. Maybe, she likes the idea that this thing of defending Simpson from some big mystery might get solved, and that looks good to her. Who knows! I'll check in with her in the morning. Maybe, she can get more than just Mrs. MacDonald. I also need to ask her about the other woman she said came later. Thanks for your help. Have a good night."

Rennie sat back and removed her gloves, slid the journal away, and looked at the boxes and folders. "So, Professor, just what was your purpose? Why did God put you here? And, is that why you were killed?"

She stared at the journal and sighed again. "And, what is mine?"

Rubbing her eyes, she collected her things, turned off the light, and headed for her car.

As she walked away, a man watched her. When she was gone, he took a phone from his suit coat pocket and made a short call.

London, UK
1923

IV - 3

Traffic was jammed down Drury Lane. Matthias's anxieties grew as his taxi lurched forward and then stopped every ten feet. Extending from Broad Street, just south of New Oxford Street, Drury conveniently connects to Strand via Aldwych.

The privileged citizens of the West End of London leisurely motor in long lines down the street to be seen and to get to the theaters along Strand. On this pleasant Friday evening, Matthias wanted to leap out and push them out of the way for his first visit to Priscilla's home.

He thought of their lunches and dinners over the past two months at restaurants in the vicinity of the British Museum. They were convenient and informal outings. But this evening, he was on his way to the home address she reluctantly provided to him so he could take her out for a magical evening.

She said her home was in the City, not across the Thames, and "it is just East End, nothing grand," she said. He had toured as far to the east as the Tower, visiting St. Paul's and The Temple along the way. He thought about those treks and wondered if he had walked past her door.

Matthias leaned forward. "Are we there?"

"Just ahead, sir," came the bored reply.

When they stopped, Matthias looked around. "Where, where is it?"

"Right there. That building. The one with the fat cat on the step."

Matthias paid the man and stepped out of the cab, then he turned around and knocked on the window of the cab.

"Can you wait for us?" he yelled at the window. "Or, can you come back in a few minutes?"

"How long?" the cabbie shouted back.

"Come back in ten minutes, no fifteen!"

He flashed a broad grin that made the driver smile. The cabbie gave a quick salute with a hand to his cap and drove off.

Matthias turned to look at the building. It was beautiful. It didn't matter what anyone else thought. He approached the steps.

"Hey, big guy," he said to the cat. "Are you in charge here?"

Matthias knelt down and cautiously stroked the furry head. The cat leaned into his hand, and then rolled onto its back. Matthias laughed. He stood up, straightened his tie, wiped his hands on his suit coat, and lightly banged on the door three times with the heavy iron door knocker.

He heard footsteps approaching from the other side. The latch clicked, and the door creaked as it slowly opened. An old man appeared in the early evening light.

"Who are you?" his gravelly voice scratched into the air.

"Sir, Matthias is my name. Matthias Justus. I am here to see Miss Shefford. Is she here?"

"What's that?" the old man's toothless mouth smacked. He took an awkward step forward. "What do you want?"

"Miss Shefford. Is this where she lives?"

Matthias looked at the outside wall to see if the number matched the one he had been given.

The man turned around and waved Matthias to follow him. Cautiously, he entered the building and removed his hat. The air smelled dark and old. Matthias was certain Priscilla could not live in this place.

As he turned to leave, she stepped into the hallway from an

adjoining room. She attempted to display her usual confidence, but her nervous hands defied her. They smoothed and pulled at her skirt. They touched her hair and her hat.

Awkwardly, she extended her hand to Matthias. He attempted to conceal his uncertainty with a nervous smile. Then, realizing her hand had been hanging for a moment too long, he quickly grabbed it and didn't know what to do next. Luckily, they laughed at the same time.

"Did you find this place agreeably?" she asked.

"Yes, very well. The cabbie seemed quite comfortable in knowing where to go." Matthias turned around. "So, this is where you live; very nice. Yes, it's nice."

"Professor, would you —"

"Matthias," he interrupted. "Remember, we agreed that on our private time it would be first names only."

"I know, this is just so different. Special." Her cheeks flushed with pink. "Would you like to go now?"

She turned to the old man. "Arthur, thank you, I'll be leaving now."

He appeared to be confused.

Matthias hurried to open the door as she smoothly slipped into the evening.

"Priscilla, Arthur is an interesting fellow. I expect we will see him at the museum some day?"

Priscilla gave him a sly grin and lightly slapped his forearm. He laughed and offered his arm to her. Her back straightened a little as she reached forward and cupped her hand onto his upper arm. They both took a deep breath.

After a few more steps, she asked, "And, what were the plans for this evening?"

He stopped with a shocked look on his face. "Well, the first item was to take a cab from your place. I hope he comes."

"Quick, there he is."

He put his arm behind her and hurried her down the sidewalk to where they had begun.

As they settled in the back of the cab, Matthias leaned forward and said to the driver, "the Waldorf, please."

Priscilla's eyebrows raised a little, and then she subtly braced herself as the vehicle leaped forward. She looked out of the window with some concern.

"Priscilla," Matthias began hesitantly, "we have had lunch or dinner together nearly twenty times."

"Twenty-one, actually," she replied. "Fifteen lunches and six dinners after work."

He grinned. "Well, I was going to say that for me, this feels like our first, real dinner engagement. I mean, it seems more special."

She peeked at him with a sly look.

Matthias sat forward and watched the traffic go by the cab. "I don't know if I could get used to driving on the wrong side of the road."

"Wrong side?"

"Yes, in America, we drive on the other side of the street, in the other direction."

A perplexed look eased into her face. "Then, might it be you who is motoring on the wrong side."

They shared a laugh.

"Priscilla, what do you think of them?"

"Of what?"

"Of automobiles. Do you like to ride in them? I think they are wonderful. I miss the one I had in Iowa. They will change everything, just like the chariot. Oh, here we are!"

The driver eased to a stop in front of the imposing entry of the Waldorf Hotel. Priscilla's eyes could not become larger.

Matthias paid the driver and helped Priscilla out of the vehicle. His chest seemed to swell up as he again offered his arm. He walked into the building feeling that all eyes were on them.

He said, "This is a wonderful night, so we had to go to a wonderful place. I asked around and I heard that if we are to go to the theater, we must first have dinner at the Waldorf."

He gestured in a broad, sweep of his arm.

"The theater? I didn't know we were going to the theater or the Waldorf. I'm not sure I'm dressed for the theater and the Waldorf."

"Priscilla, if you were dressed any better, they would think the royal family had just arrived, and I'm not sure they could take that shock."

His arm squeezed her hand against his body.

"I wouldn't be surprised if one of the royals were here at this moment," she responded with particularly precise diction.

Matthias stopped walking, briefly startling her. Concern filled his eyes. "If you would rather go somewhere else or do something else, let's do it. I wouldn't want you to be uncomfortable for even a moment."

"And, which theater did you plan to attend, and what is the show?"

He leaned a little closer to her. Reaching forward slowly and delicately, he touched her hair. It was just a moment, but it was a shock to both of them. Priscilla adjusted her hat and looked around the cavernous entry.

Matthias recovered. "The show; yes, it seems there are two that might work for us."

She turned to him and their eyes met. "I'm sorry, I'm not accustomed to this."

"Neither am I," he whispered.

She looked down and noticed she still held his arm. Releasing it, she grabbed her purse with both hands.

To ease the tension, Matthias suggested they find the restaurant. They strolled to the front desk and were directed up the grand stairway.

London, UK
The Waldorf
1923

IV - 4

The buzz of elegant patrons in the main dining room couldn't cushion the impact on Priscilla and Matthias of the aristocratic moment into which they walked. Four massive chandeliers hung from a ceiling painted with cherubim and winged creatures scattered through four gardens of flowers separated by heavy beams accented in gold. Green, marbled granite columns stood in silent rows along the edge of the main salon. Hints of light from lantern-like electric fixtures on the walls brought attention to ornate, Victorian damask wallpaper in deep purple.

A stoic man in a tuxedo greeted them with deference yet less than subtle arrogance. Confirming the reservation, he turned in silence and strolled into the dining room, apparently assuming they would follow, which they did with innocence.

A waiter brought them menus and bowed as he departed. Priscilla took a deep breath and placed her napkin upon her dress. She looked across at Matthias whose head slowly swiveled as he absorbed the wonder of this alternate society. "I heard you say to him that you wanted a quiet table. Does that mean we should not speak while we eat?"

"On the contrary, I want only to hear your voice and nothing from anyone else."

She reviewed their surroundings with a discerning gaze, studying in detail the people and the place. With discretion, she looked at the glass accents in the ceiling and the crystal globes on the lamp posts.

Matthias could only study her. The candlelight flickering in her eyes was hypnotic. As if she moved in slow-motion, he could feel the impression of her flesh when she placed her lips on the glass as she sipped a drink of water.

"You were saying there were two shows we might see?" she asked brightly.

"Yes, there are. Depending on your preference, I thought we might see either *The Rainbow* which is set to Gershwin's music and is at the Empire or *Dover Street to Dixie* which they say is a fun revue and is playing at the Pavilion. Does either sound better to you?"

Priscilla tilted her head a little. "I'm not familiar with Gershwin. Is he a composer?"

"Yes, yes he writes some wonderful tunes." Matthias exclaimed. "He is modern but classical at once. And, he has this gift of writing for a certain theme."

He held his breath as he waited for her response. "Do you have any favorite music?"

"I don't know what is current. I probably don't know much about music."

She adjusted the silver at her place setting then asked, "Do you like any other music?"

"Pretty much everything. There's a lot of music in America. We get people from all over the world and they bring their music. I do like opera, though."

"You do? Is there one that you prefer?"

"I used to be a Verdi fan, but I have come to like Puccini. He writes with more of a passionate understanding of people."

Matthias stared across the table. "I'm sorry. I'm just babbling on."

He picked up his menu and quickly looked through it.

"I'm not too familiar with Verdi, but like you, I do enjoy Puccini," Priscilla said with confidence. "There was a rumor that he was considering coming to London. I would love to attend if he does."

Matthias looked at her with delight. "Tell me how a poor and uneducated girl, as you call yourself, has come to enjoy opera, much less all the marvelous and civilized things you prefer. It just astounds me."

Her lips slid into a delicate smile as her eyes wandered away from him. "I think there may be simple reasons behind every action we take. It's easy to dramatize how we end up in a particular place or doing certain things. But, doesn't it all come down to choices? You may honor my appreciation of opera, but I'm sure old man Warrington doesn't care."

Her eyebrows suddenly rose, and she put her hand to her mouth. "Oh, my goodness. I shouldn't have said that."

Her serious look melted into a laugh as Matthias joined her silliness. "I think I'll take him out and get him roaring drunk some night."

Priscilla covered her laughter with both hands. She caught her breath. "*Butterfly*," she said. "I guess everyone likes that one. I heard it when it first came out. Everyone hated it, but then Puccini rewrote it."

"It's a beautiful piece," he added. "I'm always drawn to *Tosca*. The intrigue, the music, the characters, and the integrity which they express when everything is at stake. Do you know *e lucevan le stelle*? It's Cavaradossi's aria when he's in jail."

Matthias leaned back and looked past Priscilla into nothingness.

"So, are you listening to it right now?" she asked.

"I'm a little concerned you know me too well. There are words and ideas expressed in that aria that feel meaningful to me. At the end, when he is facing death, he says something like '*and never have I loved life so much; so much.*' He didn't love the situation he was in, but he had known a great love, and that meant he had really lived."

The wine steward arrived and discussed with Matthias a variety of choices for the evening. Matthias interrupted the steward and asked Priscilla if she would enjoy some wine. She nodded her approval.

When the steward left, Matthias noticed that she looked pensive, stroking her cheek with her hand. "Okay," he said, "now you remind me of a line from Shakespeare. It's is from *Romeo and Juliet*. Romeo says, '*Oh, that I were a glove upon that hand that I might touch that cheek.*'"

He felt a moment of panic. "I'm sorry. I do apologize. That was forward."

He quickly looked for the wine steward or waiter, to distract from his breach of good manners.

"I suppose I should be in some shock," she finally said. She looked away but quickly laid her eyes on him. "I will be so bold as to say that I am flattered. If you have any other lovely quotes from the bard, please offer them."

They remained quiet and drank in their rich surroundings.

Priscilla cheerfully changed the mood. "Matthias, you have been somewhat, shall I say daring, this evening. I would like to be so as well. May I ask a question of you?"

"Yes, of course, what would you like to know?"

"I have shared with you some of my past, my early years, but I know so little of you. Please tell me of your family, your parents, and," she paused, "and of your wife."

He scratched lightly at his temple and pulled on his right ear lobe. He sipped more water. "Well, my family came from a small town in central Iowa, which is in the center of America. I guess you could say we were well-centered! Anyway, my father was a self-taught engineer, and he was well respected for his ability to see and anticipate how things should be built or how they should be rebuilt. Like most people in Iowa, he had a hand in farming."

He became thoughtful for a moment.

"I think one reason why he so much wanted me to become a college professor was his appreciation for learning and the fact that he did not get much of an education. Hey, you are a little like that aren't you? So, he would get calls to work on all sorts of interesting things."

Matthias paused with a troubled look.

"One day, he got a call from the man who managed a coal mine east and south of Indianola; that's where I lived. Anyway, there are many coal mines in Iowa, and the man that called him was from a big mine in Buxton, Iowa. It's an interesting place, or at least it was. I think every person in the town was an African person. They brought them in to work the mine until the disaster."

Matthias took another drink of water.

The wine steward arrived and offered a respite from the obvious tension in Matthias' story. When the steward left, Matthias raised his glass.

"This is to you Priscilla, for reminding me," he paused, "for reminding me that life can be good."

She nodded and raised her glass.

They sipped the wine with appreciation, and he continued. "So, one day the manager of the mine called my father and asked him to help them with some structural problems. He offered some very attractive wages for the work. My father accepted. He worked out there for several weeks, but he became increasingly disturbed by how the Negro men who worked the mine were being treated."

"You know Priscilla, we Methodists can be troublesome now and then when it comes to social issues. Well, he said some things to the management about treating the men better, and they did not like that. I think they considered him disruptive. It ultimately didn't matter."

Matthias stopped and studied his wine glass.

"Why didn't it matter?" Priscilla finally asked.

He set the glass down. "There was an accident in the mine. My father was killed when a part of the mine structure collapsed. Since then, the situation has deteriorated. People are leaving the town. It's slowly dying."

"How long ago was that? Were you a child?"

"Oh, no, it was only about ten years ago. It was pretty hard on my mom. She and he were a great couple, and she was not someone to mess with either. I admired her determination. She is also gone. You probably are aware of the influenza pandemic that hit America about five years ago. I don't know if it reached Europe or England, but it took my mother."

He poured more wine into his glass and asked her if she wanted more. She declined.

Their waiter arrived and took their orders. They both seemed unsure of what to do but had fun figuring it out.

When the waiter left, Priscilla again leaned forward and gazed directly into Matthias's eyes. "You've had a lot of loss in your life, Matthias. I'm sorry for you. You don't deserve it."

"Well, I am not sure if good fortune or bad is ever deserved. There are consequences to our actions, but it seems that much of what happens to us is not deserved, whether good or bad. I'm not sure that I've deserved the pleasure of this dinner with you."

Her cute smile reappeared. "Well, you certainly have worked to get here!"

She grew serious again. "Matthias, I understand there is another loss. Will you someday share that story with me?"

He breathed in deeply. "Yes, I will someday. Ah, here is the food!"

For the first few minutes after being served, they ate quietly. Matthias looked at Priscilla to see if she enjoyed the dinner, and he noticed that she made quick peeks at other tables, as though she was picking up cues on what to do.

"Are you enjoying the meal?" he asked her.

She offered a respectful nod as she chewed.

She raised her wine glass in salute to Matthias. He followed with the same.

After a few more minutes, she asked him, "Have you ever come here with Lady Jane?"

Matthias immediately answered. "No, not at all, Reverend Worthy and I have eaten at her town home a few times and at a restaurant she prefers. We've also been to her country home for a weekend."

He sat up straight. "It was amazing; really quite grand!"

The home is in the area called, oh what was it again, either Hampstead or Highgate. I am not sure which. It seems every street and place in London is deserving of multiple names."

Priscilla did not seem to be amused.

"I don't believe I've been out there, Matthias. What's it like?"

He stopped eating and touched his mouth with his napkin.

"Well it's wonderful, as I said. Hmm, it is Fitz something. Fitzjohns, yes that's it. The road her estate or country house is on is called Fitzjohns Avenue. There is a small public library out there that has a collection of letters from Keats. The scope of classic literature that is lying around London is simply phenomenal."

He eagerly ate more.

"Have you ever been to Stratford, Priscilla? I would love to go there someday. Could we do that together? It would be marvelous to walk the streets where William Shakespeare walked."

"Yes, it would be marvelous. You probably make every journey an interesting adventure. What else have you seen here?"

His eyes widened and looked into the distance. "Well, there have been so many things. One place stands out. I had quite an odd experience there, actually."

He relaxed onto one arm of his chair. "I finally got around

to visiting the Temple. It was a pleasant Saturday afternoon, so I walked over there. A fellow let me in and offered to show me around. I told him my name and why I was in London. He was intrigued."

Matthias laughed. "It's clear that someone from Iowa is an oddity here. Anyway, he later introduced me to an elderly gentleman who warmly shook my hand."

Matthias held up his hand and looked at it with some concern. When his gaze drifted up to Priscilla's eyes, he became serious. "The old man greeted me as though he was expecting me. Then, he said, and I'm certain this is what he said, he told me that it was unfortunate my work will not be completed, but all will be well."

Priscilla's hand stopped as she raised her fork to her mouth. It slowly lowered to the table. "What did he mean?"

"I'm not sure. He didn't say it in a threatening way. He was quite friendly, almost happy to see me."

Matthias paused as though uncertain of what to say next. "All will be well," he added.

"If all will be well, then we should be grateful."

Thoughtful attention to the story ran through his mind.

"Have you traveled elsewhere, Matthias?"

"Just a little. I've been to a few conferences; to Chicago, Kansas City, and to Minneapolis. But they are only a couple of days from Des Moines; quicker if you can go by train. My trip here was fascinating because I got to go beyond Chicago to Philadelphia and to New York."

He felt a surge of energy.

"Those are amazing cities. Priscilla, you simply must come to America, not only to see Iowa, but also to see New York, Philadelphia, and Chicago. Those cities tell people that whatever their view is of life, it should be bigger."

"It would be wonderful to come to America some day. Does

this mean I'm invited?"

She added the question without looking up.

"Are you invited? Young lady, do not toy with me!"

She pointed her fork at him and arched one eyebrow. Then, she became serious. "So, what time do we need to be at the theater?"

He looked at his pocket watch and exclaimed, "Oh, no. We're already late."

He slid his chair back a few inches from the table and appeared to be ready to leap up. Then, he relaxed. "Priscilla, would you please forgive me? I've been so delighted with our conversation, and the time has flown by, so that we can't make it to the show. I'm so sorry. Can we try it again some time?"

She appeared to be content. "Of course, let's plan to go some other time. I wouldn't have traded this evening for any other. I think our conversation is wonderful entertainment."

"Excellent. Then, we might as well slow down and plan for dessert."

He watched her with delight as she giggled and finished her meal. He thought of asking her about her family, her work preceding the museum, and much more, but he decided to let go of the details for this evening.

She stopped for a moment and studied him through the candlelight. "Now Matthias, what is on your mind? You seem to be having much too much fun just sitting there. Is that acceptable to a professor of religious studies? Tell me, is it proper for religious people such as you to indulge the world?"

"You raise a good question. Actually, I'm not what you might call a religious person. I'm more of a scholar of religion than a real man of faith."

Matthias noticed the flowers in the small vase on the table. "I've often been cynical of people who say they have a personal relationship with God. I just don't see it. I'm burdened with more of an intellectual understanding of God."

Feeling her eyes on him, he felt encouraged. "Scripture is the most intriguing writing in the world. It's in some ways, a means for discussing with oneself the meaning of life, of relationships, of truth and mystery. Do you read Priscilla; I mean have you ever studied the Bible?"

She rested her elbows on the table, clasped her hands, and nestled her chin on top of them. "I am able to say that I first learned to read using the Bible. Our family was not keen on books, but we did have a Bible. My mother read a little, but the rest of them didn't much care."

"I was fascinated by the relationships in the stories. I often asked myself why someone did what they did and how the other person felt. I did not understand what God intended, because it seemed that people went through so much trouble. They trusted Him to give them a better life, but they often got into much more trouble. Why is that?"

That's a good question. Some say that Scripture was written to keep you wondering about God. I don't like that because it suggests that the Bible is merely a contrivance, and I don't believe that. I like the idea that the words are inspired, because that word 'inspired' feels like a bridge between the world we live in and the place where God is, or at least where something more wonderful dwells."

"Perhaps, that may be where hope and love dwell," she said softly.

"What, what do you mean?" Matthias suddenly shot back.

Priscilla was stunned and quiet. Neither of them moved. His eyes began to wander and blinked several times.

"I'm sorry. I'm so sorry, Priscilla."

His chin dropped and he breathed deeply. He looked again at her. "A little earlier this evening, you discretely asked about my wife. Her name was Hope. When you suggested that hope and love may dwell in heaven, I thought you may have referred to her. I am sorry. You could not have known."

"Matthias, I'm the one who is sorry. I wouldn't bring pain to you for anything."

"I know you wouldn't. She," he glanced away, "she died in childbirth. Our daughter was lost with her. I lost two great loves in one moment; one that I knew and one I only hoped for. Since then, I have just been going through the motions of living."

He slid the fork around on his plate. "It's odd. As much of a scholar as I am supposed to be about what God says about things, at least as written by ancient people, I still do not understand the misery we know in the world. That's probably something that separates me from God and that personal relationship one might ideally have."

They were quiet again and seemed to be alone in the restaurant.

The waiter interrupted their isolation. "May I remove these, sir? Will there be anything else?"

Matthias motioned to the plates. As the server collected a few and was about to leave, Matthias said, "Wait, we will need dessert before we go."

"Matthias, I don't need dessert," Priscilla laughed. "The meal was generous and wonderful enough."

"Very well, then we're finished."

"Would you care for a liqueur, sir? A brandy or something?"

Matthias nodded toward Priscilla, and she shook her head to decline the offer.

"I guess not. Thank you."

When the man departed, Priscilla said to Matthias, "This was most extravagant. This meal would cost me half a year's wages. May I help in some way?"

"Not at all but thank you. It would be extravagant for me as well, but the funds provided in the grant for my work here are remarkably generous. They cover my travel, lodging, food, and much more. I'd like to think that this wonderful evening out was compliments of the British Museum."

They raised their glasses in a toast to the museum. With glasses raised, they stopped for a moment and looked at each other.

As they left the restaurant, Priscilla took Matthias's arm with both hands without him offering it. Together, they moved as one down the open, curved stairway to the lobby, Matthias's chest expanded to fill his shirt. He gazed at Priscilla. He sensed peace in seeing her appear so confident, enriched, and happy.

"Would it be alright with you Priscilla if we walked past the theaters for a few minutes? I must admit I feel a little guilty about not getting us to one of them, and it is a pleasant evening."

She gripped his arm more firmly. When they reached the sidewalk, Priscilla paused and looked back into the hotel. Matthias watched her with loving attention. Then, they turned and walked along the busy, Friday night streets of the theater district.

"I must say, this is a magical night for me," Matthias said to the air in front of him.

"Oh, so this is all about you, then!" she countered.

Matthias enjoyed the idea that their silly attitudes were obvious to and envied by those who passed by.

"Priscilla," Matthias began, "I have an awkward question to ask of you."

"And, what might that be?"

"I just wondered, and I may be completely inappropriate with this, but I wondered if you and Arthur, the man I met at your residence, are involved?"

She let out a full laugh. She put her hand on her belly and stopped walking, continuing to laugh without restraint. Matthias looked around briefly to see if anyone was looking at them. Then, he began to laugh with her. They stood face to face, holding hands.

As if in slow motion, they drifted together in a gentle but firm embrace. Her head rested against his chest. All he cared about was in his arms.

He leaned his face toward hers, until their noses almost touched. Then, his arms dropped slowly to his sides, releasing her. "I feel I've kept you out very late. This has been, it has been a most wonderful evening."

Priscilla clasped her hands in front of her. She turned to look around. "Yes, this has been most wonderful. Thank you. Shall we return to the hotel to catch a cab or can we get one here?"

"Priscilla, I'd like this night to never end. Could we talk, tomorrow?"

"I'm not sure of my plans for tomorrow. I'm sure we can find some time to chat."

He took a small step forward and whispered, "I'm not sure what to do. Please be patient."

She sighed, took his arm, and led them down the sidewalk. "I must warn you, professor, Arthur has a nasty temper when it comes to any gentlemen coming near."

She laughed, but weakly.

"Then, I must prepare for battle!" Matthias responded with glee, putting up his hands in a fighting pose.

He waved at an approaching cab. It turned to the curb and they hurried to climb aboard. As they fell together in the seat, Priscilla slipped her arm through his and held him tightly. He leaned against her and patted her hand on his arm.

London, UK
1923

IV - 5

Matthias asked the driver to wait for a few minutes while he walked "the lady" to her door. A few steps from the cab, three men approached them, two walking a pace behind the first. The men swaggered, smelling of alcohol and sweat. The lead man looked at the cab driver and flipped his hand, motioning the driver to leave. Matthias noticed concern on the cabbie's face as he pulled away.

"Hey, wait!" Matthias shouted.

He felt a rush of adrenalin. Firmly holding Priscilla's arm with one hand, he moved her to his other side, away from the men.

The man in front displayed a smile of twisted and broken teeth and leered at Priscilla.

"Don't you look pretty tonight? Been out on the town?"

He didn't look at Matthias.

Priscilla suddenly looked fierce. "Reggie, you can be on your way." She gave a pull to Matthias's hand with her arm and turned toward the house.

"Oh, sweet one! Is that any way to talk to an old friend?" He followed closely behind. "And, good evening to you, sir. I'm an old friend of this fine girl. What's your name?"

"Leave him, Reggie," Priscilla barked. "Come on, professor."

"Ah! A professor! Oh, Priscilla you may have struck it rich this time!"

Reggie laughed loudly. "Well professor, you'd better be good to my girl." He caught up to Matthias and looked into his eyes.

"And, if you want to get frisky, you may not like what comes next."

Matthias gently but firmly pushed Priscilla toward the door but turned to face the man and his friends. His nostrils flared.

Priscilla swiveled, reached past Matthias, and jabbed the man in the chest. "Reggie, you get out of here. You have no right to speak that way. Now, get out."

She opened the door and pulled Matthias into the building. His focus was intense and ready for a fight. Outside, the voices of the men could be heard laughing and yelling as they moved down the street.

"Who was that?" Matthias asked in a dry, hot breath.

"Reggie MacDonald. He's a local troublemaker. We've known each other since we were kids, but he never grew up. He comes from a bad lot. I thought he'd stay on the other side of the river but he's unpredictable. Matthias, he means nothing to me, and he never has."

Jerking the door open, he stepped out into the darkness. He could hear them far down the street. Returning inside, he closed the door. Priscilla was sitting on a plain, wooden chair.

He snarled, "They obviously wanted trouble, and I will deal with that if I have to. I was afraid you might be threatened."

She stood up and put her arms around him. They held each other. Letting go, she took his hand and led him to the end of the hall. She opened a door that revealed a narrow, dark stairway going down.

He hesitated, unsure.

"It's alright," she sweetly encouraged him.

Matthias had to crouch to make his way down the staircase. Each step on the old wooden boards caused a creaking sound that suggested his foot might break through. A damp odor contrasted with a sweet fragrance. When he reached the bottom, he looked around the small, basement room wondering what it was for. Then, he realized that this was Priscilla's place.

The walls were rough stone, which had been decorated in various places with hanging ribbons, a poster, a brightly colored cloth remnant, and shelving. The shelves were wrapped with fabric and on them were short stacks of clothing. A single electric bulb hung from the ceiling in the middle of the room. It was covered with an Asian looking shade. In one corner, two dresses were laid out on a small bed. Priscilla took off her hat and set it on a small dresser. When she turned, her eyes revealed sadness.

"I'm sorry that you must see this. This is where I live. No one else has ever been here."

Matthias didn't know what to say. He put his hands in his pockets and looked around.

"Well," he finally said, "I guess I should consider this an honor, being the first visitor. I think you've done some nice things with it." He grinned. "I particularly like the light shade!"

Her expression warmed from embarrassment to determination. "I like to think that Puccini would consider it a tribute to the characters of *La Boheme*. Matthias, I would have liked you to think of my surroundings in a more comfortable setting."

He took her hand in his. "Actually, this only accentuates the wonder that you are. One's surroundings can hide the nature of those who enjoy it. You must admit, the mummies at the museum look better there than they would here!"

Priscilla gave a snort of laughter, putting her hand to her mouth. "Must you always find the good in everything?"

"It seems my lady, that we are often starting over tonight. I think you and I have had to start over in some ways rather frequently in our lives. That's what has gotten us to this place and time. I'm pleased with the results. So, where do you entertain your guests?"

Priscilla gracefully gestured across the short room. "Well, many choose to enjoy viewing the local works of art on the walls, while others prefer to retire to the drawing room, which of course also serves as the bedroom and the dressing room. Oh dear, I forgot I had laid these out."

She rushed to the bed and gathered up the dresses. "Please feel free to sit there. I'm sorry. I have no chair. The comforter is clean."

Matthias smoothed the bed covering with his hand and sat down. He realized he was still wearing his hat and quickly removed it, setting it on the end of the bed.

As Priscilla folded her dresses and put them on a shelf, he said, "May I ask you a question? It's about Arthur, again."

"If you must."

"Would you tell me about him? He seemed to be somewhat protective when I first arrived."

She sat next to him. "Your instincts are good. He is protective of me, and I like that." She paused. "Girls, and especially poor girls, are in a vulnerable place in this world. As I grew up, and as I matured, there were many times when my integrity was at risk."

She turned away. "Sometimes it comes from one's own family, and other times, from those you know. Arthur is my mother's oldest brother. When I was fifteen, I left home, and mother said this would be a safe place for me."

Priscilla took his hands. "It's been good; modest, but safe. Arthur is an odd duck but a caring one. They say every place is a step up for someone."

"I agree, but only people with your vision of a better life and a willingness to make it happen can create good things out of a difficult situation."

"You're very kind. I think if you look at your own life, you will see a dedication to what one must describe as noble."

Priscilla rose and went to a short wooden shelf. She picked up a heart-shaped, silver picture frame holding her mother's picture. "My mother's life was more difficult than mine has been, yet she was determined to be true to her good values."

Her fingers drifted across the face on the photo. Her thoughts seemed to renew her spirit as she returned the picture to the shelf. "Matthias, I'd like to ask you, if you're willing, to share with me how you and your wife met."

He sighed.

"You may remember that I mentioned my father's passing occurred in a mining accident. Hope was in her last year at Grinnell. It's a wonderful college in Iowa. She was doing some research in Buxton, where the mine was."

Matthias stared at his hands in his lap. "After the accident, I made a few trips to the mine. Hope was interviewing the management people and I was in touch with them, too. We ran into each other a few times. It seemed perfect, and it was, except life isn't."

Matthias ran his fingers through his hair. He stood up and turned to face a brightly colored poster of leaping ballerinas. His heart struggled with sorrow as his mind grasped for understanding.

"God probably vexes people of faith and even scholars of faith as much as those who are indifferent to faith. Intellectually, I understand that the world is a broken place, a place of sadness. I know it's faith and a relationship with God that can lift us out of that darkness."

He looked at Priscilla. "I just wish He would not take so long in bringing the light. Speaking of long, I should be leaving soon. Do you know how I can get a cab from here? Another question, and a bit awkward, is there a, well a —"

"Oh, I'm sorry. The toilet is up the stairs, the first door on the left as you go toward the entry door."

When he returned, Priscilla excused herself and went up the stairs.

He drifted over to the bed and sat down. He put his face in his hands, closed his eyes, and let his thoughts return to his life in Iowa. He realized how little he had thought of his home since he arrived in London.

Priscilla came down the stairs and sat next to him. "I went to see if Arthur was up. He could get a cab for you, but unfortunately, he's had a little of the bottle and cannot awaken."

"That's okay. It's a pleasant evening, and I can walk until I find one. I'm a big boy."

They were quiet for a moment.

"I was just thinking about their grave sites, where Hope and Martha are. I just realized that when you stand to view their markers, in fact all the markers in the cemetery, you are looking to the West. You stand and face the direction where the sun goes down. It's very sad."

"It does sound sad."

She put her hand on his. "I wonder if it could be looked at another way."

"How's that?"

"From the perspective of the markers, they would be looking to the East, to where the sun comes up. They see the coming light."

"That's a beautiful thought."

A big smile grew across his face. "Yes, thank you. It might even be a perspective for those of us who live on; to look to the coming light in our lives, especially when it has been darkness."

He turned his hand so their fingers embraced. They sat holding hands for what felt like was a long time. He listened to their breathing.

"Would you do me a favor, Matthias, before you must leave? It is a bit embarrassing, but with Arthur the way he is, I must call on you, as a friend."

"Of course."

"To be quite frank, I need your help with the buttons on the back of this dress. The styles are so tight, and the buttons are small and remote. There are many I simply cannot reach."

"Certainly, I understand. It's not as though I haven't had to help before. I often helped Hope. Just turn a little."

With careful precision, Matthias slowly applied his thick fingertips to the tiny buttons, pushing them through the little slits in the material.

As he did so, Priscilla reached up to remove the combs holding her hair in place. It fell in soft, brown waves upon his hands. She turned her head, meeting his eyes over her shoulder.

As the back of the dress spread open, Matthias' hands stopped. He couldn't move.

"Matthias," she whispered, "will you also help with the strings?"

Enclosing her back, Matthias observed the tightly strung, white corset. The upper edge pressed into her flesh. Slowly, his fingers pulled the end of one cord. He watched it slide through the tied bow and suddenly release its pressure. With both hands he carefully drew the strings apart, allowing the corset to open and reveal her back.

Priscilla sighed.

He loosened more strings from their bonds, further releasing and separating the garment.

In one smooth motion, Priscilla reached up to her shoulders and slowly drew down the top of the dress so it fell into her lap.

A few hours later, Matthias was awakened by a distant thumping sound. It was a slow hammering that resonated through the walls. He turned to look at Priscilla and discovered that she was awake and also listening to the noise.

"What is that?" he asked.

"I'm not sure. I think someone is banging on the entry door."

"I should go see what it is."

He sat up.

"No, stay here with me. They will go away."

"Who will go away?"

"I don't know. At this hour, it's no one in their sane mind. Lie down here."

He took her tenderly in his arms.

"I don't think I've ever been so happy, Priscilla. I was destined to be with you, forever."

She smoothed his hair with her fingers.

"I guess that will require mummification!" she laughed. "Can't you just see us on exhibit at the museum?"

"As long as we're together, my darling."

He kissed her forehead. "Now, sleep my perfect love."

Matthias heard Priscilla turn over. He stood beneath a small window, high on the wall, reaching as far as he could to move the curtain. Priscilla covered her eyes with one hand as morning light sneaked past the window shade.

"Sorry," he said. "I didn't want to wake you. It's a beautiful day."

She leaned up on one arm, still covering her eyes. "What are you doing? You're dressed. Get back here."

He returned to sit on the bed. He stroked her hair. "Please, don't be upset. I must go back to my place. I'm sure Mrs. Whitley has the police looking for me. I've never been gone all night. Let's talk for a moment about meeting this afternoon for lunch."

Priscilla fell into her pillow. "No! I don't want you to go."

"I'm not leaving. Let's just say I'm going to freshen up; and, there is much truth to that."

He leaned over and kissed her. "When shall I pick you up? I was thinking, there are many places that I've wanted to visit, but doing so alone held me back. Can we tour some places outside of

London?"

"Oh, I would love to!" she said and sat up. "Oh, Matthias, what shall I wear? Will we go far? Wherever it is, I simply want to be there with you."

"And, I with you my love." He realized what he said. They gazed into each other's eyes. He gently kissed her.

Matthias rose up and went to the stairs, looking back at her several times in the short distance. Blowing a kiss, he looked up the stairway and marched up.

Entering the hall, he noticed Arthur was sitting in the chair by the door. As Matthias approached, Arthur stood up, appearing unsteady.

"Hello, Arthur. Are you okay? I heard you were a bit under the weather last night."

Matthias grinned at the old man.

Arthur looked angry and confused. "You're the gentleman that came to meet Miss Priscilla last evening! How did you get in here?"

He tilted toward Matthias.

"Priscilla let me in."

"What? She let you in? When? I've not seen her yet this morning. Say, are you the professor? The one they were asking about?"

"Who was asking, Arthur?"

"Reggie did. Reggie MacDonald was at the door in the middle of the night! That boy is a troublemaker. He was banging on the door demanding to see Miss Priscilla. He said some professor was here. You'd better watch yourself. He doesn't know right from wrong."

Arthur steadied himself with his hand on the back of the chair. He staggered down the hall and turned around. "You be good to that girl. She deserves the best."

He waved his hand in a dismissive way and disappeared

through a doorway.

Matthias waited for a moment, watching for Arthur. Then, he jerked open the heavy, wood entry door. The morning light flashed into his eyes. He stepped into it and felt the sun warm his face. Closing his eyes, he savored the moment.

Matthias remembered the men he had met in this same place last night. His heart raced, and he glanced around. Seeing no one, he turned in the direction of his home and hurried away. Occasionally, he looked across the street and behind him. Nearing the corner, he spotted a cab, waved his arm, and sprinted to where it stopped. Settling into the comfort of the seat, he thought of Reggie and what Arthur had said. He would have to deal with him. It would be ugly.

PART FIVE

Des Moines, Iowa
Des Moines Record

V - 1

Hi Rennie, this is Angie. I'm sorry to call so early in the morning."

"It's okay. What happened?"

"Nothing, I think I have a lead for you on the professor story. I found someone in London who may help you with background information."

"What do you mean? Who is this person? I'm sorry Angie, I've only had one cup of coffee so far and my circuits are not firing yet."

"It's okay. I mentioned that someone in the library association I belong to might be able to help. You know, that whole six degrees thing. I sent out some inquiries by e-mail and someone in London responded. What's cool is it's from someone at the University of London. They work in the library at the Institute of Advanced Legal Studies, so they have connections with police records. Not only that," Angie's voice quickly rose in volume, "but it's right next to the British Museum."

"Angie, I'm a little annoyed. What ticks me off is I should have had that idea and been running with it. Who's the so-called investigative reporter here?" she laughed.

"Thanks, it's nothing. It's so easy with e-mail. So, here's the scoop. Is that what you reporters say? Anyway, my contact in London has two summer interns, and they were eager to dig up what they could for you. It beats helping grad students with research papers, I guess. They'll need a little more info than what I had. I'll forward the e-mail to you."

"What do you know about them?"

"One of the interns is pre-law, so that one wants to go after the police information. The other is more library science oriented, so they will pursue British Museum info and anything personal you want to track down."

"Wow," Rennie whispered. "How quickly can we get at this? Can you send me that message now?"

"It's on the way. Oh, and I e-mailed the *London Times,* but I've not received anything back. You had wanted to connect with a reporter there. I can give you phone numbers."

"Thanks. I'll see you at the library. I'm near the end of his last journal. Maybe I can wrap this up and move on. Since I've got you on the line, what's new with you and your guy?"

"It's okay. We talked, but just on the phone. He wants things to be the way they were before. He doesn't understand why I feel hurt. I told him I need to think about things, and he seems to like that."

"I hope it works out for you. You deserve a good guy."

"Don't we all?" Angie nearly shouted.

Rennie went into the kitchen and dumped her coffee into the sink. She hesitated as she poured another cup. She put down the pot and cup and hurried to her computer. She found the message Angie forwarded and sent a brief response to introduce herself. She saved the addresses of the sender and "cc's" in her address book. Then, she composed a new message to those contacts.

"Hello. I appreciate your help in resolving this 'cold case.' I only need a few details – some are personal to the victim and some are 'crime' related. Crime related: the victim's name was Matthias Justus; he apparently died on 8-11-23; cause unknown – are there police records and what do they say? Who was interviewed, what was done? There is some information that Professor Justus, who was working at the British Museum to assist with documenting Egyptian relics, may have been investigated himself – why? On the personal side – we need to know what happened to the following people who were associated with Professor Justus or the Museum – Kenneth Warrington was the Professor's supervisor at the Museum, Priscilla Shefford worked with Justus, an Archbishop named Worthy (Robert?), a woman referred to as 'Lady' Jane Sotterfeld-Gris, and a fellow who worked at the Museum delivering freight by the name of Mort. I realize this was 90 years ago but solving it will mean a lot to people here and to the college he came from. Thanks, Rennie."

She fell back in her chair and hit "Send." When a message box appeared that read "Message Sent," she folded her arms on her chest. Suddenly, her cat jumped onto the desk.

"Jeeze Balderdash, you scared the heck out of me. So, what do you think? Can we wrap this up today?"

The cat purred.

An hour later, Rennie was in her office cubicle looking through a thick file of paperwork when someone touched her shoulder and said "boo."

"Bud, you're going to have to stop that huffing and puffing as you walk if you want to sneak around."

He fell into the guest chair.

"How you doing? We contacted the Des Moines Police to find you since you've been gone so long."

"Really? How long were you on 'hold' before you spoke to someone. Wait, that's only for 911 service."

"Rennie, you have so much respect for public officials. Maybe you should try to do their job, or even your own."

"Ha. Did you miss me? It's been a whole, what three days? I'm nailing that story on the condemnation games the City plays, and I'm pushing ahead on other leads. And, your Simpson professor is about done. Or, is this a personal visit?"

"Hey, give me a break kid. I've got problems, too."

Bud tried to stick his hands in his pants pockets but couldn't. His eyes wandered around.

"I don't know. I get fed up, too. Everything is done for the short term, now. Cut costs, boost revenues, and oh, by the way, do some good journalism without taking any risks."

"Bud, why don't you go visit your grandkids? When are you going to take a break? After Grace passed, you came right back to work. It's been two years."

Rennie leaned forward and put her hand on his arm.

"Listen, there's more to life than this big filing cabinet we work in. You have a purpose Bud."

Bud looked confused. "What? I have a purpose? What are you talking about?"

"Sorry, I don't know where I was going with that. It just came out."

He rubbed his face and got up.

"You've changed. You're deeper or something. Are you okay?"

"Yeah, fine. I've been reading about that professor and some of the things he wrote. It was quite a situation. I'm close to the end."

"Well, wrap it up. I had another call from our dear publisher last night. She has this story on her radar screen. I can't figure it out."

He looked out across the dozens of cubicles and sighed. Without another word, he trudged back to his office.

Rennie reopened the file she had been studying, but she couldn't focus on the pages. She closed it and checked her e-mail. She sorted through the spam, the administrative notices from the *Record*, and other messages when she saw one from London. Holding her breath, she clicked on the message and read the reply:

"Miss Haran. Pleased to get the additional information. We are acting on it immediately. A good project. Should not be a problem with the BM nearby and our contacts with the police authorities. Thank you for this assignment. Brilliant opportunity. Tiffini Gibson and Josh Ramsey, Summer Interns."

Rennie logged off, grabbed her notebook, and hurried out of her cubicle.

Indianola, Iowa
Simpson College

V - 2

Eager to get to the library and finish the story, Rennie thought ahead to her other assignments. She parked in a familiar spot near the Simpson mall, grabbed her bag off the seat, and flipped open the door. Jumping out she slammed the door shut and leaped back against the car to avoid a truck that just missed hitting her.

"Hey" she yelled.

The truck slid to a quick stop. A man got out and leaned forward as he stomped toward her. He wore jeans, work boots, and a rumpled shirt. His name could be "road rage."

Rennie fumbled to find her phone.

"Man, you almost hit me."

Fear charged through her. He didn't slow his pace and seemed to gain energy as he approached.

"Back off, man," she demanded. "Let's not cause trouble and move on."

He continued his approach and glanced around. Finally, he stopped but too close for her comfort. She stepped back.

"You said you want trouble? Is that what I heard?" He snarled, "I can help with that."

"What the hell? You almost hit me as I got out of my car. I'm okay, so let's move on."

"You're okay now miss nosey reporter, but you might not be later if you don't stop looking into private things. In your business they say that losers do the obituaries, but the real losers are the people they write about. You don't want to be a real loser, right?"

"What? You're threatening my life. What story? Damn it! Back off, right now. I'll have you tracked down and you can sit in a cell while the cops build a story on you!"

"Lady, you're way out of your league. You don't know who you're dealing with. Get back to writing about cheerleaders and recipes. That's where you belong."

He spun around and went back to his truck.

"Who are you? What do you mean? Which story?"

He jumped in without responding and screeched his tires in leaving.

Rennie tried to see the license plate number, but it was obscured with a slab of mud.

She dropped her keys twice trying to get back into her car. Inside, she couldn't find her phone. She realized she was in panic mode and took a deep breath, then another.

"Who the —?"

Rennie looked out the windshield and nothing was in focus. She shook her head and closed her eyes. More deep breaths followed.

Which story, flowed through her thoughts.

It had to be the one on the city's condemnation practices in the downtown area. Too many important people and too much money was involved. Lawyers for the city, lawyers for the property owners, the property owners themselves, city administrators; no one gave her straight answers on what they did and why each case was settled the way they were. No other assignment involved anything important.

She could let that one go and come back to it at a less intense time. The paper had little interest in it, anyway. Of course, that lack of support could mean it was too sensitive for some important people.

Anger boiled in her gut. Once again, the powerful would get their way. She hated that.

Rennie decided to back off on that assignment and finish the unimportant ones. That felt good, and she nodded a sharp confirmation of the plan.

She grabbed the door handle to get out but paused and looked around the car. Firmly holding her phone in one hand, she pushed open the door, closed it as she kept watch, and locked the door. She thought it might be time to get a more modern car, one with a key fob, but she loved that old Volvo.

Rennie's pace to the library was faster than usual, and her senses were on high alert. She didn't slow down at the counter but dashed up the stairs. Unlocking the door to the study room, she waited for a moment before going in. She felt as though she was about to say good-bye to someone, someone she had come to care for. She closed the door and went to her chair.

Rennie examined the boxes, the attaché case, file folders, books, journals, the sheets of paper where she wrote her notes, diagrams, and reminders. She removed her linen sport coat and hung it over the back of another chair. Sitting down, she studied the cover of the closed journal in front of her. She hesitated to open it. Rennie worried about what she would find in the final pages.

Without putting on the gloves, she opened the journal to the marker and began to read Matthias's next entry.

"I must write a quick note! New life! What a night of joy and love! I am new again, and I think so is she. Priscilla, a gift of love. There, I've said it again. Love! Oh, if I only dared to write about it. The pages themselves would catch afire. Dinner at the Waldorf, a walk past the theaters, and a night with her; most wondrous of women! I must make plans for this incredible new day. Who knows what will be? A new life."

Rennie sat back. "What the —?" was all she could say. She

re-read the entry again.

Very nice, professor, she thought. She found the next entry.

"It is late, Sunday evening, and I must rest for a new day. Nothing is the same. How will I keep from holding her as she sits just a few feet away???? These last few days have been profoundly good in every way – love, adventure... I even asked her if she would come to Iowa. I can't believe it. I nearly proposed. And, I am certain she would say 'yes' if I asked.

In Stratford, she held my arm as we strolled through the streets where Shakespeare walked. I don't know what was better, being there or being with her. Priscilla, I thank God for you!"

Rennie could hardly breathe. "Whoa, professor," she whispered.

"We did our best to conceal our feelings, but I doubt we were successful. Old Warrington may be crusty, but he is not lifeless or stupid. I, on the other hand, was apparently quite stupid. I don't know how I could have been so careless. He handed me the bag of coins I had found in the box. He said they were found on the study desk, and he looked as though I had been caught stealing the entire collection. I'm sure my apologies and embarrassment were insufficient.

I must be most careful in opening the contents of the box from Antioch. What JOY! My love for Priscilla and an ancient discovery in one place. I may have to see if I can extend my stay here and ask Simpson for a release from teaching next month. How can I leave here now? I must get to sleep."

A strong line separated the last paragraph from the next. The text of the following section was written in a more precise and less fluid manner than his previous entry.

"It has been a few days since I offered my last thoughts. These have been most awkward times. Priscilla and I do our best to conceal our love, but our eyes cannot keep it hidden. Mort is coming into the room more often, and at one point, he looked at me as though he might explode. Even Reverend Worthy has come by and acted quite strangely. I have wondered if I should simply make an announcement of our love and clear the air. Priscilla objects to the idea.

Oh, and my box from Antioch. I immediately returned the coin bag to it, with Mort suspiciously drifting in the background. Later, I was able to return to it and force the opening half an inch further. It may be nothing, but who knows? Rest, I need rest."

Rennie found her notebook and added a few comments on Mort and Reverend Worthy. She circled both names and then continued her reading of the journal.

"This was not a good day. Reverend Worthy was unexpectedly harsh, particularly on Priscilla. Despite her high standards and precise work, he suggested she might be inappropriate for the position she occupies. He suggested he might speak with Keeper Budge about her when he returns from Egypt. Worthy loves to speak of rules and ideals. Compassion is the heart of living in faith but it has no part of his life. It was all I could do to not get up and confront him. I sensed he was baiting me. Warrington seems to approve of his behavior.

To make matters worse, that troublemaker Reggie stopped her on the way home from work. He demanded to know where she was this past weekend. She told me he frightened her. I replied that if this MacDonald character ever ..."

Rennie gasped. She said "MacDonald," with the air remaining in her. She glanced around as if searching for something. Questions raced through her mind.

Who is Mrs. MacDonald? Who is this guy confronting Priscilla?

She returned to reading.

"I told her if this MacDonald character ever bothers her again, I will seek him out. She said I shouldn't be so silly. We must be careful. She is too precious to be at risk."

Another strong line separated the text.

"This day has been most odd. Lady Jane stopped in to see me. I cannot believe I am writing this, but she flirted with me. I am certain of it. Never before has she been so forward, and she did it in front of Priscilla. Priscilla wasn't pleased.

On the side of great fortune, I was able to add another inch to my efforts to open the panel on my box from Antioch. Soon it will open. A mass of folded papyrus lies within and contributes to the difficulty in opening the panel.

I am torn as to whether I should tell Warrington, or even Priscilla of this discovery. I don't want her to get into trouble if my activities were to cause a problem. Warrington would probably ban me from the lower level and nail the box shut! I don't know what to do. But! I am driven to see what the mysterious document might be.

Priscilla and I had dinner again this evening. It is so wonderful to be with her. There is something distant in her behavior. She is less engaging when we talk. When I accompanied her to her home, she said it was best if I didn't come in. I reassured her of my love, but she seems to be more cautious."

Rennie placed the marker on the page and stood up. She stared at the journal.

"What's going on here?" she asked the air.

She put her hands on her hips and shoved the chair with her foot.

"Dang it!"

She walked around the table and occasionally paused to move a box or a file folder. But her mind was on what was going on in Matthias's life. She stopped across the table from where she was sitting. She gazed at the journal.

Is THIS what got you killed? Some darned flirtation?

Rennie fell back into her chair and read the next journal entry.

"I almost did it. I nearly proposed to her. Priscilla said she wanted me to know that her behavior last weekend was new to her and she shocked herself. She was quite embarrassed. I see her as more perfect every day. Even her modesty is a tribute to her.

This weekend, now our second and just like the first. We dined at a restaurant on the West End to which I was introduced by Lady Jane and Rev. Worthy. Priscilla loved it. She was a bit unsettled when I mentioned how I learned of it. I don't know why she so dislikes those two. Until recently, they were most kind to her. Soon after I came to London, she referred to them as the Princess and the Pope. I thought she had meant it as flattery.

Priscilla does not know much about the better parts of London. She said she had been to the West side only a few times. I am SO glad I could discover it with her.

I think Arthur is warming to me. That bully Mac-Donald —,"

Rennie gasped, but she continued to read,

"— observed us as we departed in a taxi. He must be dealt with, I fear. It is clear I need to remove Priscilla from here. Perhaps, I should leave for Iowa early and take her with me. I cannot believe what I am saying! What joy. Thank you, Holy God for this great gift of love."

Rennie stopped reading and looked at the attaché case. "Great gift of love," she said. She got up and opened his leather case, finding the envelope and folded paper. On it were the words, "Thank you Holy God, for this incredible gift of your amazing love. No other discovery in all of human history will ever compare with this."

She placed the note and envelope back in the case. Noticing the bound-up tin that was his lunch box, she touched it. *I guess I could open you, sometime*, she thought.

Rennie found the next journal entry.

"In the last few days, the road I walk has become a tight rope. The box from Antioch has revealed its treasure – an ancient manuscript. I still have told no one and I don't know what I should do. If I tell Warrington, the old man will dispose of me in an instant for 'tampering' with the relics. Whatever is on the papyrus will never be revealed.

I must review the document. Then, I can decide whether or whom to tell. It has become so difficult. That blasted Mort is almost tracking me now. Even my darling Priscilla acts in such an awkward way. I have neglected her. I will change that immediately! I must stop now. I'm exhausted with tension."

Three strong lines separated the journal entries.

"I don't know where to begin. I sobbed when I got back here to my room."

Rennie's eyes widened and she held her breath. A knock on the door interrupted the moment.

Angie peeked in. Her smile was followed by a perplexed look.

"What happened to you? Oh, my gosh! Did you find out?"

"Find out what?"

"You know, how he died. Your face says you found out."

"No, I don't know yet, but things are happening fast. I'm near the end of the journal. Something big is about to happen."

Angie held out a piece of paper.

"I'm sorry to interrupt. I just read this e-mail that was sent to you with a copy for me from the interns in London. They discovered something important."

She handed a print of the message to Rennie.

Rennie scanned it.

"Oh, my — Oh, no!" she exclaimed. "He got pulled from the river, from the Thames? Cause of death may have been drowning. He also had a stab wound? Oh, no."

"Yeah, it's pretty sad."

Rennie tossed the print aside. Her eyes filled with tears.

"I'm sorry. I didn't expect this, I mean this reaction. I know he died over there. It's just, I didn't know the details."

She looked up at Angie.

"Why? He was just a nice guy in love."

The corner of her mouth quivered.

"Rennie, how about a break for lunch? You've been at it pretty hard this morning, and it's way past lunch time."

Rennie took some tissue from her bag. She blew her nose.

"Okay. Good idea. Let's get out of here."

Standing, she turned to see the journal and the black, leather attaché case. She sighed and shook her head.

"I'm sorry. I can't leave now. I'm near the end."

Angie saw the red eyes of someone in distress.

"Rennie, a little fresh air, some nonsense gossip, and food

are just what you need right now. They'll refresh you and give you a better perspective when you come back to this. It's not going anywhere. Twenty minutes. That's all. Let's go."

"Girl, you get bossy, you know?"

She slipped off the cotton gloves and pushed her chair back. Her eyes didn't leave the journal.

"Rennie, I'm hungry. Let's go. I have a quick errand to do and will meet you there. I'll leave a note at the front desk with the place info."

"There's something else. Angie, when I arrived on campus, a guy tried to hit me with his truck. He got out and came at me. He threatened my life and said I had to stop work on an assignment. He didn't say which one. Angie, he threatened my life."

"No, no."

Angie slid out a chair and sat down as if all the energy had suddenly left her body.

"Rennie, are you certain that it was a personal threat? It's so extreme."

"Absolutely. I've gone over every moment of the incident. I don't know what to do. Should I call the cops? I could give a good description. But Angie, he said I don't know who I'm dealing with. That suggests some real power-players are involved."

"Is it this story, about the professor?"

"I can't imagine it's that. I mean, who cares? What's in it for anyone? It's got to be about my investigation into the city's condemnation practices in the downtown urban renewal projects. There's a lot of big money and some important people involved. And, the top brass at the paper seem to not want the story told, too. You know who they talk to. It's not the common man."

"Rennie, whatever story it is, the number one issue is your safety. Did you report it to anyone at the paper? What's the procedure for this?"

"Who knows? This isn't an everyday thing in sleepy old Des

Moines, Iowa. I might call my editor, Bud. In fact, I should. Our professor here got killed and no one investigated it. He was distinguished, and I'm not. If someone whacks me, too bad."

"Stop it. Don't think that way. You've gotten the attention of some big shots because you ARE important. Now, what we need to do is plan how to proceed."

"Well, listen to you. Angie the Avenger!"

Rennie sat back and grinned.

Angie laughed. "Let's get out of here and eat. I'll meet you there. Look out world, there's a librarian on the team!"

Indianola, Iowa

V - 3

The incident with the jerk in the street didn't leave her. Rennie sat in her car outside the restaurant. She had to tell Bud.

"Bud, it's Rennie. Call me as soon as you get this message. Someone threatened me. It's about a story I'm working on. Call me."

She felt a burst of energy.

As Angie reached the door to the restaurant, Rennie yelled.

"Hey, what's good in there?" She displayed a smile full of teeth.

Angie waited and held the door. "You doing okay?

"Let's get a table, food, and then talk."

They went to the counter, reviewed the menu on a large board on the wall, and placed their orders. Finding a table in a quiet corner wasn't difficult.

"Angie, I'm a fighter. I don't know why. My folks are so, I don't know, intelligent and calm. I guess I'm the other side of the coin. Sometimes, it has worked against me. You know, like Don Quixote, tilting at the windmills as if they were demons. I'm not sure I know who to fight with, anymore."

"Why do you feel a need to fight? I don't get it."

"I think it's not so much the fight. It's some inner drive to make things right. You know? That's probably part of my zeal to find so-called truth. What's the real story?"

"Rennie, I don't know the people in your business, but what you describe seems to be a common trait. I see on TV the reporters in war zones and think they are so brave. You're not different from them. The world is a war zone. Every neighborhood is a war zone. Consider the gun violence and child abuse and problems with drugs. You're reporting on it just like those people on TV."

"So, you think I should stick with all my assignments and forget what happened?"

"No, not at all. The war zone reporters take appropriate precautions. They don't go running into combat. The stay safe and tell the stories. I imagine their editors control a lot of what they can do."

"True, and I do have a rebellious side my editor has trouble controlling. Some would portray that more negatively. Oh, they called our numbers. Let's eat."

As they ate, Rennie felt the need to change the subject away from her situation.

"So, what's the latest with your lawyer?"

"I don't know. He's probably consumed with his big career step and has given me no thought. I'm coming around to the idea that I need to live my life and pursue my goals regardless of his plans. It's unfamiliar territory for me. I've thought in terms of us for so long it's not easy to think only of my interests and goals."

"Yeah, why do we do that? Love shouldn't be a sacrifice of a life. My gosh, that makes me think of dear old professor Justus. I need to get back and finish this ..."

Rennie's phone declared a call coming in. "Oops, sorry. It's my editor. I'll take it outside. Hey Bud, hold on a moment."

"Okay, I'm outside. I was in a restaurant with Angie. The librarian at Simpson."

She described the incident in quick, stark detail. "So, what do you think? What should I do? Bud, I don't know what assignment he was concerned with. You know what I've got. What do you think? No Bud, I don't want to clean the whole slate. That's not needed. Other than the city condemnation story, I see no threats to any special interests in anything else I'm working on."

She shook her head and frowned. "Okay, for now, I'll drop the city story, but only for now. There's activity there that needs to be exposed. Do I need or do we need to report this to law enforcement? It was pretty damned threatening from my perspective. Fine, you talk to the big shots upstairs. If my body is found somewhere, you might have another story. Bye."

Returning inside, she found Angie had finished her sandwich and cleared the table except for Rennie's food. "Well, I guess I'm off the only story that I think has real teeth. I'll focus on our professor, get that done, and hope nobody knocks me off so I can finish it. Bureaucracy!"

"The main thing is that you stay safe. Maybe a better story will come your way."

"That's a nice thought Angie, but it doesn't get my juices pumping. Let's get back to the library."

Rennie dropped the bag with the remains of her sandwich on the passenger seat of her car and started the engine. She checked the rear-view mirrors for traffic and began to move ahead when she saw it. The truck that nearly hit her. It slowly passed by in the opposite direction. The man inside stared at her as he went by.

Fury again rose in her. She pulled on the steering wheel to make a sharp turn to follow him and nearly accelerated into cars that were passing by. She slammed a hand on the steering wheel and looked back. Cars continued to come as the truck turned a corner and disappeared. She hit the wheel again and pushed back into the seat.

Indianola, Iowa
Simpson College

V - 4

Rennie settled into her chair in the study room. Angie strolled by the table and scanned the boxes and files.

"I need to get this professor thing off my back so I can take on the big boys. Angie, I'll let you know when I'm done, and we can go over everything."

Rennie put on the gloves and nervously flipped through the pages of the journal she had been reading.

When Angie left, Rennie picked up the e-mail message. She read again the introductory sentence.

"This is what I have learned thus far, based on a few phone calls. I'll be over at the records office in the morning to see the actual file. Professor Matthias Justus was observed in the River Thames ..."

She set the paper on the table removed the gloves and decided to visit the rest room. Looking in the mirror, her face revealed a quiet, deep pain within. She stepped into the hallway and appreciated the peaceful view of the campus through a wall of windows. Her vision drifted up to the tops of the trees outside. Leaves flickered in the sun and an occasional breeze brushed small branches aside.

She thought, *Why can't the good guys win?*

Then, she saw a man sitting on a bench outside. It was the same man on the same bench she had seen the other day. She shivered when he tilted his head up and saw her. Their eyes met despite the distance. His face expressed nothing. Hers was intense. She felt her temples harden. Slowly, he stood up, turned, and walked away.

She pressed a fist against the glass as her mind raced with questions. She felt like running down the stairs to go find him. She waited for a moment to see if he stopped and looked back at her. He didn't.

Rennie breathed hard. She hurried back to the work room. She reached behind her and flipped the door shut as she crashed into her chair. Her teeth were clenched.

"Maybe, it's time for the good guys."

She resumed her position with the journal, put on the gloves, and began to read the next entry.

"I don't know where to begin. I sobbed when I got back to my room. I can only write for a moment. This is all too overwhelming. I feel I am at risk of losing my love, my Priscilla, and at the same time I have placed in my hands a precious writing that caused my knees to buckle. It exceeds all the treasures from the crypt of the Egyptian king.

Priscilla, my darling, fears what is going on around her. Everyone is so intense. I don't know what to do. Our love remains but is so fragile and subject to the threats of Warrington and Worthy, not to mention Reggie. I want what is noble and good for all, but I don't know what to do. AND, now I can examine the hidden prize from the box from Antioch.

Mort was not at work today and Priscilla was distant, so I had a chance to return to the lower level. The box opens smoothly, now. But, I knew not what to do with the contents. Although I feared I would be discovered at any moment, I carefully lifted and peeled back the top layer of the document, and then the next wrapping layer. Under these was the first page of the document – a letter! AND! The opening words, in Aramaic, could easily be read – 'Brother Mark, my dear friend and blessed disciple...' Could it be? Could this be a letter to the Apostle Mark?

I heard a noise and panicked, replacing the package into the box and returning it to the shelf. I cannot leave it alone! I must recover it and transcribe it. What am I to do?"

Rennie stared at the page. She took a water bottle from her bag and drank half of the bottle. Her breathing was shallow. She refocused on the page and continued with the next entry.

"Oh, joy comes again. Priscilla has agreed to leave with me! At dinner tonight, she said she has been confused with my behavior and fearful of what Warrington and Worthy could do to her and to us. I affirmed my love and devotion to her, and we agreed to go away again this weekend to plan our new lives together – in America."

Rennie put a hand over her mouth. She glanced at the message of Matthias' death. She leaned back in the chair and breathed deeply. A few moments passed by before she could begin to read the last pages of his journal.

"It occurred to me that I could never properly open and translate my secret discovery if I continued to play hide and seek games with Mort and old Warrington. Either I needed to trust what good would happen if I revealed my discovery, or I must remove it and perform the work away from the Museum.

I have taken the manuscript and brought it to my room. If only Mrs. Whitley knew what treasure was up the stairs. Tomorrow, I can return to work without the pressures of fearing for my love and sneaking into the lower level. All is good again. Praise God."

Rennie jotted the words "took manuscript" into her notebook. She sat up and continued to read.

"This has been a good day, of rest and peace and a return to hope. I still think of my Hope. She was my warmth in a cold world, my light in its darkness. I am more and more beginning to see the many gifts that God has put into my life. I have too often seen them one at a time instead of as the vast blanket of goodness with which He wraps me up. Now, he has woven Priscilla into the texture; another thread of love.

Tonight, in the privacy of my room, I have the additional delight of further opening the hidden manuscript. When fully revealed and transcribed, I am not certain how I will disclose it to Warrington or to the world. Yet, it will be. For now, I will enjoy this special privilege."

A gap but no line separated the journal entries.

"I'm barely able to hold my pen. I can hardly breathe. This first page, at least as far as I have gotten this evening, and it is now late, cannot be what I think it is. It may truly be a letter to the Apostle Mark. The writer says that this Mark is a blessed disciple of the risen Christ! AND, dear, Holy God, he speaks of the many days they shared writing down their memories of the Lord. Who and what is this??? Am I holding a personal letter from the time of Christ? from and to His followers, His disciples??? What else is said in the remainder? I must give it time and scholarly distance. I must not rush ahead! I need to sleep. Tomorrow is a fresh day."

A knock on the work room door broke her focus. Rennie's eyes flashed to the door. Slowly, the door opened, and a man stepped in. He awkwardly apologized and looked at the number on the door.

"Oh, sorry. Wrong one," he said as he gave a light wave of

his hand and softly closed the door.

"No problem," Rennie answered.

She studied the doorknob. Sliding her chair back, she stood up. He seemed harmless. In fact, she thought he was attractive. He wasn't the man from the bench, but her instincts connected the two. She removed the cotton gloves and slipped her fingers through her hair. Then, another knock startled her.

Angie looked in.

"Hi! Is this an okay time?"

Rennie stared at her.

"I thought you might be someone else. Was there a guy out there?"

Angie turned and surveyed the area.

"What guy?"

Rennie leaned a little to see out the door.

"It's nothing."

She rubbed her eyes.

"I'm sorry. I guess I'm a little gun shy."

She sank into her chair and turned a page in the Field Notes volume. She noticed her hands and put down the journal.

"Sorry. I took the gloves off for a moment. I'm not too good with procedures, but I try."

She tried to grin, but it was forced.

Angie didn't move.

"Rennie, we recently talked about faith issues. When I think of God, I think of one who established order out of chaos. For me, that is what is needed in life, order."

Angie's voice grew in strength. "Procedures are part of that. They generally have a purpose and a good one. Our procedures in the library have reasons. I need you to follow them."

She turned and was quickly out the door.

Rennie followed her into the hall.

"Angie, I'm sorry. I don't know why, but events have made

me scattered. I'll pay attention to the gloves."

Rennie glanced into the study room. "I need to learn the whole story. There's energy to it. It's like, it's become my purpose."

"Your what? What do mean your purpose?"

"I don't know. I only know I'm consumed with his story. I'm off the case that meant something to me, but this one has taken on special meaning. This assignment and reading can't be little incidents in life. There must be more meaning to it. It leads somewhere I wasn't planning to go but must go."

"Since this thing with Greg happened, I sometimes wonder about that. Maybe, the whole purpose of my life has been to do some simple thing that seems meaningless to me but is important on a bigger scale. My profession, and my relationships, and my hobbies are no big deal to the universe. There must be something about my being here that has a bigger meaning."

"So, what are you going to do about Greg? You said you would focus on yourself, but the change isn't easy."

"It's hard to think about starting over. Have you been through that?"

"Yeah, I've even been through the big split, divorce. That's really starting over. In marriage, you take on all these roles of wife and housekeeper and partner, and you question whether you should work. You think about what your babies will look like and whether you will be a good mom, or at least as good as you think your own mother was. Then, it ends. You are none of those things. You are back to aloneness. That's your only role. Then, you wonder. I mean, I'm glad he's gone. But I'd like there to be someone."

"Rennie, you're such an independent person. It's not easy to think of you as relationship-oriented."

"I know. I guess I retreated to my old rebellious self. Being tough feels safe. Speaking of relationships, is there anything else relating to the prof? Any other boxes or files?"

"No. Why?"

"Well, Matthias found some important document just before he died. It's not here, and I wondered if there was anything else. It might actually be why he got whacked."

"I'll check the records again, but I don't think so. Let me know if you need anything."

"Wait, who else is using these study rooms?"

"You're the only person who has a room right now. Things are quiet. Why?"

"You mean no one is using another room?"

She set her jaw and became tense.

"Rennie, what's up?"

"Angie, what study rooms are available? Tell me."

"There's the one you're in, one down at the end of that stack, and two at that end over there. What's going on?"

"Some guy stepped into my room a little while ago and acted like he just made a mistake, as if he picked the wrong room. I was suspicious but let it go. Something didn't feel right. Now, you tell me I'm the only person with a reserved room. So, who was that guy, and what was he doing?"

"I don't know. Maybe, he was just looking for somebody. Did he seem threatening or anything?"

"No, he was fine. I don't know. I've got to finish this. Sorry."

"It's okay. You've really done Matthias a service. Maybe, he's returning the favor by introducing you to some nice guy."

Returning to the study room, she slipped on the gloves and found her place in the journal.

"Another good day at the Museum, except Mort has been uncooperative and almost hostile. He's most nettlesome when Priscilla and I speak with one another. Priscilla's spirit is light, and she's eager for our weekend. Now, I will investigate the precious letter from Antioch."

Rennie found a page in her notebook on which she had written and circled Mort's name. Behind it, she added a large "plus" sign. She checked a few other pages, and then returned to her reading.

"It's nearly two o'clock in the morning, and it is a new day in so many ways. Christ and the Saints are alive. They are here with me. Next to this simple journal, on this humble desk, and near the hand of an even more humble man lies folded papyrus. On those sheets are the living hand strokes of ink from Matthew, a disciple of Jesus. It is in truth a letter from Matthew to Mark. I simply cannot believe it. Here in my room. I have touched the same parchment that they touched.

Even more astounding, he describes another letter within it from the Lord's mother, Mary. I can hardly write these words, but possibly folded within all this are letters from Jesus Himself. Here on my desk! I have decided to send a message to the museum tomorrow that I am unable to work due to illness. That will allow me the time I need to open this treasure. It must be done with utmost care and patience. I am exhausted. I am humbled beyond measure. How has this happened?"

Angie knocked on the door and opened it.

"Sorry to interrupt again. We got another e-mail. This is from the other intern; the one that was checking out the British Museum people. Should I just leave it or what?"

"What do they say? Is it useful?"

"I don't know, but it sounds promising. Some Lady something was married in a big wedding in 1928. I guess that was after your guy's incident. Her husband was a wealthy business tycoon who also funded archeology hunts or whatever they call them. The museum had no record of someone named Warrington after he retired in 1931. A woman named Priscilla Shefford left the museum in 1924, but her name then was MacDonald."

"What?" Rennie shouted. "What did you say? Priscilla married? She married that jerk? Let me see that."

Rennie grabbed the paper from Angie's hand. Her eyes flashed across the words.

"This can't be! It doesn't make any sense! Just months after she finds her greatest love, she runs off with some bum? Everyone lives happily ever after, except for Matthias who gets buried. Damn it. I'm sorry, Angie. This is awful."

Rennie fell into her chair. She tapped her gloved finger on the journal page.

"You will not believe what he discovered! I mean, aside from finding real love, he discovers handwritten letters from Matthew, Jesus' disciple and maybe from Mary, Jesus' mother. So, he gets killed and everyone lives."

Angie's eyes grew large. "He discovered what?"

"That's what Matthias wrote in his journal."

Angie blinked as though trying to awaken herself. "I've never heard of that. Where are these letters?"

"Probably at the British Museum. Heck, I would've figured they would be in a Vatican library. We have got to check that out. Who knows about this? I also need more information about what happened to Priscilla. Can you get that intern back on it? This, Angie, is where we make our final push. I need to know this."

Angie saluted and said, "Okay, chief, and hey, I want to know more about those letters. Now, we're talking library business!"

Angie checked her watch. "It's kind of late over there, so I'll send an urgent e-mail and ask them to get back to us ASAP. Now, I'll leave you alone. Are you okay?"

"Yeah, I'm sorry I snapped, earlier. I appreciate your help. It's just lousy news to hear about Priscilla marrying that jerk."

Rennie covered her eyes with her hands. "Why?" She shook

her head and looked again at the journal as Angie departed.

"Mrs. Whitley was very kind this morning. I did my best to appear sick and she did her best to tell me to rest and not allow 'Kenny' to work me so hard. She had a boy deliver my absence note to the museum. I hope Priscilla is not overly concerned. It would be delightful if she were to come here. I'm certain she wouldn't, though. It would be highly inappropriate in the eyes of many."

Another wide gap in the journal separates the text without the break lines used before.

"Yes, I am now certain the letter is from the Apostle Matthew to Mark. He refers to others in Antioch whom we know (Theophilus and even Matthias!). Mark is apparently on the way to Alexandria. Dear holy God, he even mentions a woman Priscilla, who was going to Ephesus. How glorious that her name and mine are written by the hand of a disciple of Jesus, and here am I reading it. I have fully transcribed this first letter and now am beginning the next. More later!"

This time, a line of curves separates the text.

"For this entire day, I have been reading simple, beautiful Aramaic words written by Mary, the mother of Jesus. This is a holy piece of history. No, it is beyond that. It is also remarkable that a woman in that era could write. But then, she was remarkable, or even more."

Rennie stood up and stared down at the page. She shook her hands as though she had touched something sacred. She took a deep breath. "This is just too incredible," she whispered. "People have got to know about this. Why haven't they told anyone?"

Maybe, those letters would upset everything. The authority of

the church could be questioned. They've been hidden away.
She sat down to continue reading.

"Mary described what is going on in Jerusalem and how she plans to come to Antioch. She says she is meeting with Luke. She is telling him her story and the story of Jesus as she has witnessed it. LUKE. Another of the gospel writers. She mentions Thomas and Peter and Miriam. What more treasure is within this papyrus?

Mary said that she is sending for safekeeping certain letters that Jesus wrote. He wrote them "when he was away," whatever that means.

Once again, I can hardly breathe. I'm looking at the remaining folded papyrus and wondering if letters from the Son of God, are lying on my desk. I have paced the room for many minutes, unable to proceed. I must take a break and get something to eat. Mrs. Whitley has offered to bring food to my room. I need the break. What am I to do with this?"

PART SIX

Indianola, Iowa
Simpson College Library

VI - 1

Rennie leaned back in her chair and took a deep breath. She was limp, but a wry smile formed in her lips. as she read the next entry in Matthias's journal.

"I am refreshed. Mrs. Whitley is a good cook. I allowed myself a mental break by watching the traffic of people and vehicles in the street from my window. The world looks very different now. My hand has touched the same writings as those who walked with Jesus, even His mother! This has given me a perspective of the world that feels more present and more caring. I don't understand. It is profound. Now, with trepidation, I will attempt to unfold the next letter. I am frightened to think who the author may be.

It is time to recover so that I may add some notation, even if brief, of this moment in my life. I am so insignificant, even lowly. I am not deserving of this honor. For many minutes, I have been lying on the floor, arms outstretched. I prayed and cried. I cowered against the wall. It is real, and I have no doubt of it.

My fingers, even my breath, brushed lightly across the same fabric as His did. He put His words onto the material, and I have read them. Me. Insignificant me. I am ill with the endeavor; this awesome presence and the responsibility I have assumed. I do not know what to do with this. The next letter in this astounding packet is from Jesus!"

Rennie shot up, knocking her chair backwards against the wall. Her heart raced. She was dizzy for a moment. She pulled off her gloves, grabbed her water bottle, and quickly swallowed all that was in it. Then she hurried to the door and went out to the railing again. She held it tightly and steadied herself. She glanced back at the work room. She was frightened. Looking down the stairway, she noticed that the student behind the checkout desk was watching her. She took some deep breaths and sat on the floor.

In another moment, Angie was standing in front of her. "What happened? Are you okay?" Angie kneeled next to her.

"Rennie, are you sick. Can I get you something?"

Rennie could see Angie's mouth moving but no words were coming out.

"Get her some water," Angie said to a student standing nearby. "Rennie, do you want to lie down? It's okay. What happened?"

Rennie shook her head and said, "No, I just can't do this. I don't know what to do. What do I do with this?"

"What?"

The student returned with a plastic cup full of water. Angie helped Rennie stand up.

Rennie took the cup and drank from it, her hand shaking. "Angie, I can't tell you about this. You have to read it for yourself."

She went into the work room and pointed at the journal.

Angie walked around the table and scanned the text. "Which entry?"

Rennie placed her finger above the text.

Angie bent over the table and without touching the journal, she began to read. At the end of the passage, she jerked her hand to her mouth. She looked down again at the book, then collapsed into the chair. Rennie slid down the wall and sat on the floor.

The student appeared in the doorway. "Miss McGrady, is there, is there anything I should do?"

Angie waved her away. The door closed behind her. "Does anyone know of this? Rennie, where are these letters?"

Rennie wrapped her arms around her legs and rested her chin on her knees. "I don't know. I've never heard of a letter written by Jesus."

She looked up at Angie. "Why couldn't this be a simple story? Professor goes abroad and gets killed by angry husband! Professor slips on banana and falls off bridge. Anything but this. Angie, Professor Justus knows his stuff. He wouldn't write a bunch of baloney in his own journal."

Rennie stood up and pointed at the book. "He discovered the most incredible treasure known to humanity. He must have told someone about it, and they killed him for it! That letter is in the hands of the killer of Matthias Justus. Well, now in the hands of the heir of the killer at this point. I can't stand it. What do we do?"

Angie arose with a determined, almost angry look. "Rarely in life is there a defining moment. There are two ways one can go, back to what we call the normal life, or in the opposite direction, toward something unknown and possibly incredible. Maybe, this is that purpose you have mentioned."

"Oh, thanks! I wanted to be dicing up the secrets at the Iowa legislature, but oh no! I get to what? I don't even know how to describe this."

Now, Angie was smiling. "You know, it just occurred to me. You are the right person at just the right time for this. Rennie, we've got to go over there. We've got to go to the scene and get the facts. Hey, you said I'd make a good reporter. So, let's go."

"What are you talking about?"

"You just asked me what we should do about this. I say, let's get our butts over there, find out what happened, and find that letter. Do you have something better to do?"

"You know, you are one crazy, wild librarian. You want to go to London and break into the British Museum?"

Rennie pointed at the journal. "You see that? There are a couple of pages left. Maybe he says what happened, at least to the letter. Obviously, he couldn't make note of how he got killed, but maybe there is something important in there. After that, we can talk about jetting across the pond."

Angie nodded. "I'm getting online and seeing what I can get for airfare, and I'm going to set a fire under those two interns."

She nearly jumped for the door. She stopped and turned back. "I don't know about you, but I feel as though I've got a purpose."

Rennie got up and turned to close the door. At the far end of the library, she saw a man on the opposite side of one of the book racks. He seemed to be watching her between the shelves. She stopped and stared. He removed a book from the shelf and opened it, briefly. Replacing it, he quickly paced down the aisle and out of sight. She thought he might be the man from the bench.

Her heart raced. She stepped out of the room and started toward where he had been. She stopped and glanced at the open door to her work room. Rennie ran back inside, found the key to the room, and locked the door as she left.

She ran down the hall to find the mysterious observer. When she arrived at the location, she discovered another stairway and hurried down it. At the bottom, she could only see a few students. She ran to the front desk.

"Excuse me, miss," she said to the intern. "Did you see a man; a man in a suit come by here?"

"Who? A man in a suit?" stammered the young woman.

Her eyes squinted and nose wrinkled as if she smelled something unpleasant. "I don't think so. I don't think I saw anyone in a suit."

She blinked quickly. "Well, he might not have been wearing a suit. I just, I saw this guy who, and he—," It was Rennie's turn to fumble for words. "Never mind."

With heavy legs, Rennie climbed the stairs to the work room. She paused before opening the door, scanning the area for anyone she might consider to be suspicious. She returned to the table and surveyed the room. Everything was as she had left it. She found the gloves, put them on, and then sat down to read.

"It unfolded so easily. I'm not an expert in the art of document preservation, but I would imagine the tightly sealed cedar box and the damp lower level of the museum must have been good for these precious letters.

I laid onto my bed a fresh, linen sheet and have with utmost delicacy placed on it each of the three letters I have examined. The third and most precious of all, is without question from Him. It is to his brother James. The words are loving, guiding, and full of authority. He speaks of His Father, and it is clear he is not speaking of Joseph but of God. The letter is short, and it has a friendly, even brotherly tone.

My transcription is complete, but I have no idea what I will do with this. For now, I must attend to the other, folded documents that remain.

It is now three o'clock in the morning. My body is exhausted, and my mind is vibrating with the reality of what I have just done. The documents in the box from Antioch comprised eight letters. One from Matthew to Mark, one from Mary to the Church in Antioch, and six, SIX! from Him. I cannot even write His name at this point. Six letters from Jesus! Four short ones and two longer ones. All to his brother James. No question. No question at all. They are from Him."

A breath puffed out of Rennie's mouth. Her hands gripped the edge of the table as though it might lunge into her. She glared at the text of the journal. She closed her eyes and took a deep breath. Then, she relaxed and found her place in the journal.

"I have not fully transcribed them all but only opened them, so preciously carefully! I reviewed each of them for authorship and a sense of meaning. Here, next to me are letters from the Savior of the world! He is suddenly real and personal to me. Faith, for me was an intellectual exercise, but is now so simple. Knowing Jesus. That says it all. Nothing more is necessary. I'm at peace. I have touched the hand of the Almighty. As Job wrote, "Now my eye beholds thee." He lives and is personal to me, now and forever. Praise God.

What do I do now? In a few hours, I must sit quietly next to the woman I love in a place that is devoted only to maintaining the past. I have been thrust out of the old and into the new. Nothing needs to be done right now. I shall act as though nothing has happened until I decide how to proceed."

Several, flowing lines underlined the text in the journal. The next writing was more rigid.

"This has been a strange day at the museum; a day of peace for me amidst chaos. My body was most tired, but my perspective was so unique. It is as though I was an observer and not a participant. Everyone senses it, and Priscilla is angry. She asks me why I am so distant. I held her when I could and told her of my love. She just looked into my eyes as though searching for hidden meaning. She knows my heart and mind are consumed with something.

Warrington and Mort are hovering like vultures. My

composure seems to irritate them even more. I noticed them whispering to each other and was amused. Warrington would not even speak to Mort when I first arrived, and now they stick their noses into each other's ears. It didn't matter to me. My future holds the revelation of the words of God. Now that I've had a brief rest, it is time to transcribe the remaining letters."

Rennie again found the page in her notebook where she had written about Mort. She added another plus sign behind his name. Then she returned to the last page of writing in the journal.

"Tears have freely flowed down my cheeks in humility, in awe, and in gratefulness. My soul is on its knees before God. I fear that my enlightenment has filled this room with light that poured out the window into the dark world outside.

In His last letter, Jesus plainly said what was to be. He would show the power of God as it was shown at creation. And, He would sacrifice Himself for His love of all and overcome death itself. I read this. Me, here. Holy words."

Rennie's mouth slightly opened, and tears ran down her cheeks.

Angie knocked on the work room door and opened it. She went to Rennie and knelt down.

"Hey," she said. "That's it for now, my friend."

"No, I have to finish this. It is glorious beyond words."

Rennie put her hand on Angie's shoulder. "For the first time, I feel connected, really connected with God. Deep down, I thought I was a person of faith. You know, I studied scripture when I was young. But it was more of an intellectual thing. Now, I'm so clear, so happy, so hopeful. I knew the facts but missed the person. You must read this, just the last couple of pages. It is a miracle. Right here, these pages are a living miracle. He's real."

Angie seemed to be confused.

Rennie's enthusiasm grew. She sat upright with renewed energy. "You were right. We have to go to London. I don't know what we'll find, but I must go there."

"Okay, but first you need to take a few deep breaths. Okay? Are you alright?"

Rennie nodded.

"Good. The reason I came up here was that I found some smokin' deals on the Net. We can go right away. I need the break anyway. It'll be a 'girls take London' trip."

"Do it, Angie. I'll tell my boss. Do it now. I've got to find those letters. Angie, I've never been so happy in my entire life!"

"Okay, will you be alright? Can I make the arrangements?"

Rennie nodded again, and then continued to read the journal. She hardly noticed Angie's departure. The last entries were in front of her.

"All the letters are now transcribed and are safely folded into the delicate bundle from which they came. I look at it and marvel. It is more blessed than any Scripture, any church, any artifact in all the museums in all the world. Here in my room and held in my hands. It is truly the living Word. Thank you again, holy God. His words in my hands.

How incredible, to catch a glimpse of the missing years of Jesus and to read His own prediction of where His ministry would carry Him. He knew it would be to the cross and then triumph. Now, I must devise a way for these precious texts to be discovered and revealed for the world to see. I will pray for that and then sleep. Hopefully, I will awaken with a plan."

A hard, solid line separated the text from a few, final paragraphs.

"I only have a moment. Warrington has called the police. He must suspect I have taken things, or so he told them. I slipped away from the office to get the letters into the hands of someone to safeguard them. But who? I will go to Lady Jane or even to Worthy. Perhaps, the newspaper. Maybe I should secret them to the Temple. They would treasure them, but would they reveal them? The letters must be made known. Jesus must be revealed as only these letters can.

I left the museum without saying anything to Priscilla. I didn't have enough time to explain. When I see her, I'll tell her everything. I'll ask her forgiveness for my secrecy. I'll assure her of my undying love. We'll go home to Iowa and live in joy. Warrington may know I'm gone. I must leave Mrs. Whitley's, or they'll find me before I can act. Here it is, the 11th. In just a week, I'll be going home. My darling will follow. I must accomplish this sacred mission."

Rennie flipped over the page to look for another entry. There was none. She again read his last entry. Digging through papers, files, and boxes, she hunted for another journal and found none.

She jumped from the chair and searched through his attaché case, discovering nothing more.

"That's it. That was it," she whispered. "The 11th. What happened?"

She fell into the chair.

Angie knocked and entered the room. "You seem spent. Are you done?"

"What do you mean?"

"Did you finish his journals? Is there anything else?"

"That's a good question. My emotion tank has run dry. I feel finished." Rennie sighed. "I don't know what to do next."

"Any more entries I should read?"

Rennie lightly brushed the surface of the closed journal with her fingertips. "It's all in here. The most important part is at the very end."

She opened the book to the last two pages and laid it in front of Angie.

After a few moments of reading, Angie gasped and glanced at Rennie. "Oh, dear," she sighed. "Oh!" she nearly shouted. "Oh, no. Can it be? I didn't understand. How can this be?" Angie muttered. "Does anyone know about this? I've never heard of these letters."

"The last entry was the 11th. Was that when he died? What happened? Did someone kill him to get the letters?"

Rennie pressed her fingertips into her temples. "I'm on overload. I cannot process another question. It's too overwhelming."

Angie snorted a teary laugh. "If you think this is overwhelming, I just booked us on a flight to London the day after tomorrow. We got a four-day package; flight and hotel. I can't afford it, but after reading this, it doesn't matter."

Rennie stared at her. She blinked as she tried to comprehend what her friend just said.

Angie got up. "Well, we had better start putting this stuff away."

She moved a few things, and then stopped and looked at her hands. "I guess I need gloves. Besides, I don't know what's yours and what goes in the archives. I'll leave it to you."

She snorted another laugh. "We'd better start packing for London."

With that, Angie flipped the journal closed and left the room.

Rennie rose up and began to organize her files, notes and materials. When they were collected at one end of the table, she returned the archived files to the boxes. She laid her hand on his attaché case. Flipping open the strap, she reached in and removed the old tin, bound with cord.

"I didn't get to his letters."

She glanced at the door. Then she took the tin, put it in her bag, and placed a few files on top of it.

The door opened, surprising her. Angie entered with a small, cardboard box.

"I thought you might need this to carry your ..." Angie stopped. "Are you okay? You're pale. Rennie, you need to rest up. We've got a big trip ahead of us. Do you need water or something?"

"No, I'm fine, thanks. I can take care of this. I'll pack up his things. You should put his journals in a very safe place. I'm especially concerned for them in particular."

"Sure, I'll take care of that right now."

Angie put on an extra pair of gloves and collected Matthias's journals. "I'll put these in a special envelope and lock them in a safe. Just lock up when you've boxed up the rest of the materials. Rennie, we've got a lot of planning to do and quickly. I'll send the travel details to you. What do you think?"

"I think I need a break from thinking. Let's talk tomorrow. I need to get myself together. This is all pretty fast."

"Sure, we'll talk tomorrow. Remember, start packing."

Angie stepped up to Rennie and grinned. "Can you believe it? In two days, we'll be in London!"

"Pretty wild, huh?"

When Angie left, Rennie placed her bag in the box with her remaining files and materials on top of it. She put his attaché case in another box and rested her hand on it. "Professor, we're coming to help."

Des Moines, Iowa

VI - 2

On the road to her office, Rennie felt a need to go home. There was much she needed to do at the office, but she didn't want more stress.

At the next intersection, she swerved into the turn lane that she hoped would bring some peace. She stared at the green arrow indicating a left turn until the car behind her sounded its horn. The world passed by in slow motion. She thought she could hear her own breathing.

Rennie parked in her driveway and sat in the car, enjoying its warm, quiet seclusion. She laid her arms on the steering wheel and rested her head on her hands. She felt a need to cry, but she wasn't sad or relieved. A new dynamic was happening. She saw her neighbor Cathy examining the lilac bushes that separated their yards. Cathy always had a cheery expression despite her advanced age and illnesses.

Rennie waved and offered a weak, "Hello" as she opened her back door to retrieve the box of files.

"Hello, dear," Cathy called out. "How have you been?"

"Fine, thanks, and you?"

Rennie lifted the box out of the car and swung the door shut with her knee. She stood for a few moments, listening to Cathy's comments about the weather and the yard. Rennie looked into her neighbor's eyes and face as if for the first time. She noticed subtleties of expression and a depth of feeling that she had never seen. Rennie realized that for six years she had lived next to someone she didn't know.

Here before her was a living person, who had been a little

girl, a wife, and a mother. She had known joys and sorrow, pleasure and pain, hope and despair. Rennie could hardly hear what Cathy was saying, but she was completely connected with the woman's depths of feeling. When Cathy paused to watch a car go down the street, Rennie moved closer.

"Cathy, could I tell you something?"

"Why, of course." Cathy smiled.

"I just want you to know that God loves you."

Cathy's eyelids fluttered briefly, and her smile broadened.

"Thank you, dear. He loves you too."

Confused with what just happened, Rennie wanted to put down the box and give the old woman a hug. Instead, she just offered a relaxed smile and said, "Thanks."

She hurried with awkward steps to her front porch, perplexed with her bold comment. She glanced back and noticed Cathy was holding a large lilac blossom. The old woman leaned into it and took a deep breath. Quiet contentment filled the moment.

Stepping inside, she latched a small hook on the screen door into a metal loop on the door frame. She hummed as she entered the dining room and put down the box. When she returned to close the front door, her gaze drifted up to the large, soft clouds in the distance. The world was new and fresh.

She heard a "meow" from the dining room and turned to see Balderdash standing on top of the files in the box.

"Oh, no you don't buster," she said with loving firmness. "That's not your box."

He jumped out of it and flopped down on the tabletop, rolling onto his back. Rennie walked up and rubbed his belly.

"Are you a happy cat?" she asked.

With unprecedented serenity, Rennie unloaded the files onto the table. She set Matthias's lunch tin on a shelf in her bookcase near photos of her parents. She repacked the files that were to go to her office, took off her jacket, and kicked off her shoes.

Hours later, Rennie awoke on the couch. The faint light of early evening colored her dining room in gray. Balderdash rested on her forearm. As she gently moved him out of the way, he jumped down and ran into the kitchen. She tried to get up but fell back onto the pillows.

"What happened?" she said, trying to sit up.

She looked at her watch. It was nearly eight o'clock. Determined to get going, she stumbled into the kitchen. Balderdash sat in the corner in front of his empty dish. "Yeah, I know. We've got eat."

Rennie fed him and then herself. She hurried to her computer, read news items from several sites, and checked her e-mail. When she found Angie's message with their travel schedule, Rennie became fully awake. She moved to the dining room table and made a list of the key activities she had to do in the twenty-four hours before she left for London.

When her list reached the bottom of the sheet, she dropped the pad on the table and held her head. "How am I going to do all this?" she yelled at the list.

She drew lines through some of the entries. In front of others, she put numbers.

Rennie threw her pen onto the notepad and ran up the creaking stairway to the spare bedroom. Removing a suitcase from the closet, she paused, and then removed another one. She put them on the bed and hurried into her closet. After several trips between the bedrooms, Rennie closed her eyes and rubbed her temples. "That's it for now," she whispered.

Her phone rang. It was Angie.

"Are you packed? I was thinking that you need to brief me on what happened and who was who. I didn't read all that you did. Be sure to bring your notes with you, okay?"

"Yeah, fine. This is happening pretty fast. I haven't even talked with my boss, yet."

"Do you think he'll object?"

"It doesn't matter, now. We're going."

"Right on, girl. Rennie, I've got some great news. Guess who's going to help fund our little adventure."

"I don't know; the library?"

"No, I didn't think of that. Greg is putting some money into the pot!"

"Greg? Your lawyer boyfriend?"

"Greg was my boyfriend. I'm not sure where that's at. I called him and told him about our trip. I told him I needed a break to think things over. I said a girlfriend and I decided to do a girl trip. It's a little getaway to refresh ourselves. He thought it was a great idea. I mentioned some concern about finances, and he offered me a thousand bucks! I'll see him tomorrow to pick up a check. It will go to the total trip costs so we both benefit."

Rennie shook her head in disbelief. "You're amazing. But I think you should use it all. I'll handle my expenses."

"No. You spent all those days doing the research, and when we get to London, you have to take the lead there. I sure hope the interns get us more info before we get there."

"Angie, I don't know what to say. 'Thanks' seems too little."

"Have you stopped to think about what is in those journals? What happened to the letters?"

"I have some ideas on that, but nothing about this story has been predictable. Could we meet early tomorrow afternoon, instead of late morning? I've got so much to do, especially at my office. I've got to talk to my boss."

"Sure, no problem. See you tomorrow."

Rennie went into the spare bedroom and stared at the suitcases. A sly grin grew across her face. She started to giggle. "Balderdash," she yelled. "It's time for the wine!" Her smile vanished when she heard her doorbell ring. She froze and quietly listened.

The doorbell rang again, quickly followed by a knock. Rennie's eyes flashed with intensity. She took a few hesitant steps, then hurried down to the entry.

A stranger stood about four feet from the door. He checked his pockets and nervously looked around. He was mid-40's and his protruding gut stretched apart his shirt buttons. His suit coat didn't match the pants. Rennie glanced at the weak and primitive hook on the screen door that provided her only security.

She marched up to the door and said in an assertive voice, "Hi, what do you need?"

She slid one finger through the small, brass hoop that served as a handle to the screen door.

"Oh," he said with nervous surprise. "Are you Miss Haran? I'm sorry if I don't pronounce that right. Miss Haran of the *Des Moines Record*."

"And, who are you?"

"Are you Miss Haran? I'm Dennis Cook of *DC Bonding*. I need to talk with you about an urgent matter. Do you have a few minutes? Could I come in?"

He stepped closer to the door.

"What's this about, Mr. Cook?"

"I have a client who has expressed some interest in you. Well, not interest in you but about your welfare. Do you have a minute, Miss Haran?"

She studied him for a moment. His awkward composure and unimpressive presence bolstered her courage.

"Mr. Cook, we obviously don't know one another, so it might be best if we continue this conversation right here. As an alternative, you could come to my office tomorrow."

"Oh, no, ma'am, that might be too late," he blurted out. He blinked his eyes as though he was wondering if he should not have said that.

"Just exactly what do you mean by that?"

"I'm sorry. That was probably not accurate," he said as he quickly looked to the side and behind himself. "Miss Haran, I'm a friend and just need to speak with you for a moment."

"Okay, friend," Rennie said in a softer tone as her eyes surveyed the neighborhood. "Let's talk now and right here."

Dennis stepped toward the door. "I don't do much private investigation work; mostly, just bail bonds. But I got a call from a fellow who lives, well far away. He said he is aware you are checking into some disappearance and an old mystery. He hired me to tell you that he suspects that people who might be interested in what you are doing, might, I don't know how to put this, might be harmful."

The man turned around again and for a moment studied Rennie's neighbor Cathy as she walked across her lawn.

"Miss Haran, I don't know what this is about. All I know is this fellow somehow found me and paid me to warn you about something. He seemed legit."

Rennie realized she was pulling so hard on the screen door handle that her finger was hurting. She changed it to two other fingers. "I don't get it," she began. "Who is this guy who called you and who are these other people? What's the issue?"

"Ma'am, I don't know. I've told you everything. He just said you should be careful. I'll leave my card here on the porch and you can call me if you like."

He stuck both hands into his pants pockets and pulled out business cards, receipts, and dollar bills. Fumbling with it all, he placed a business card on the wicker chair by the door, nervously smiled and hurried off the porch to a car parked in the street. Reaching the car, he paused, looked back at Rennie as he opened the driver's door, and drove away.

Rennie peered through the screen door to see the card on the chair. She released the door handle and briefly shook her fingers. As she stepped onto the porch to get the card, she noticed

Cathy approaching the house. The old woman swung her arms with strength as she crossed the driveway and came up the porch steps.

"Could I ask maybe a nosey question, dear?" Cathy said with a smile.

"Of course," Rennie answered, glancing past her and down the street.

"Well, it's none of my business. I wondered if you might be selling your house. I certainly hope not."

"I'm not selling my house. Why do you ask?" Rennie felt her teeth grinding.

"Oh, I must be an old busy-body. It seemed as though that man who visited you, and the others I've seen stop in front of the house and look at your place, they must have been interested in buying it. Really, dear I'm sorry I even asked."

As Cathy turned to walk away, Rennie reached and touched her on the arm.

"Wait," she said. "What do you mean those who came here and looked at my house? I'm not selling my house. Who were these people and when did they come here?"

"I'm sure it was nothing." Cathy said with a worried look. "Earlier today, a man parked in front of your house and just looked at the house for awhile. He drove away very slowly, looking at your house all the time. He was talking on a phone, so I thought he must be a appraiser or something."

Rennie couldn't respond.

As Cathy began to walk away, Rennie went with her and said, "Thanks. I appreciate your mentioning it. The good news is that I'm not selling, and I plan to continue to live next to you."

Rennie put her arm across the woman's shoulders and escorted her to the driveway. "Thanks again, Cathy. Let me know if you see anyone else watching the house. You never know who's out there. I'm sure it's nothing."

"Me, too. I doubt a nice person like you could have any trouble. Besides," she quickly added, "this is Iowa."

As they parted and Rennie returned to the porch, her gaze drifted across all the parked cars on the street. She watched as a young man came out of a house and casually jogged to a car. A young woman leaned out the door and yelled something to him in a cheerful voice. He looked back and responded, laughing.

Once inside the house, Rennie locked the screen door and closed the front door. She studied for a moment the old skeleton key sticking out of the keyhole. With a quick grab and twist, the lock slammed into place.

She leaned against the door. Anger warmed her face. She hurried to grab her cell phone from the table and hit Angie's phone number.

"Angie, Rennie here. This might sound paranoid, but have you had the feeling that someone might be watching you?"

Rennie held still without breathing.

"Not really. I haven't sensed that. What do you mean? Is someone following you?"

"I'm not sure. I had a strange visitor a little bit ago, at my house. He said he was an investigator; you know, a private eye. Also, there have been some moments at the library when I felt there were men watching me. Angie, something is up."

Her mind was racing. "I don't think I've felt that anyone's watching me," Angie replied. "Of course, I might like that as a change of pace. I'm sorry. That was stupid."

"No, it's okay. Listen, just be a little careful right now. I don't know if this is real or not. This whole thing with the professor and what he found may be bigger than what we thought. After all, somebody killed him."

"I'll be careful," Angie said. "You be careful, too."

"Yeah. See you tomorrow."

Rennie laid her phone on the table. She listened for any

sounds that seemed out of place. Through windows set in heavy dark wood frames, she watched what had been an ordinary, neighborly world. There was something out there, and it was not going to be kind to her.

With a firm and methodical precision, Rennie slammed and locked every window and door. Upon latching the last one, she stepped back and reviewed the accessibility of the house. She realized that none of the curtains were drawn shut. She couldn't remember ever closing out the world like this.

Soon, she was enclosed by the familiar and hidden from something evil. Yet, she didn't feel safer than before. Rennie looked at Balderdash, who appeared to be interested in her strange actions. "Hey, listen buddy," she growled at him. "Don't look at me like that."

She pointed at him.

The cat stretched out on the floor and licked its paw.

Rennie knelt beside him, stroked his fur, and scratched his head. "So, do you think I'm going a little far with this?"

Rennie got up fast, scaring the cat. She took the cell phone off the table and ran up the stairs. She packed the suitcases with new energy. Decisively, she selected wardrobe items, shoes, accessories, and her reference materials. Occasionally, when a car or truck could be heard driving by, she paused and listened.

By ten o'clock, she realized she was exhausted. She turned out the light in her bedroom but left the lights on in the other rooms upstairs. She laid on her bed next to her suitcases and went to sleep.

Des Moines, Iowa

VI - 3

Rennie's alarm clock chimed at 6:30 a.m., but it didn't awaken her. She was already on the move, planning her day. She had showered, dressed, and made coffee. As she ate a muffin wrapped in a napkin, she checked her e-mail. There was nothing new except spam.

By 7:20, she was at her office organizing her files and notes on Professor Justus. A red file folder held two days' worth of phone messages and notes from co-workers and from Bud. She casually looked through them and tossed most of them. One note made her stop. She stood up and looked across the network of cubicles toward Bud's office. With a relaxing breath and smile, she went to see him.

Arriving at his glass wall, she paused for a moment. He looked like he'd already had a long day. His shirt was wrinkled, his sleeves were turned up to his elbows, and his desk was a mess. He seemed to search frantically for something.

"Hey, big guy. What's this about?" Rennie held the note out.

"Come in, sit down," Bud said without looking up. He continued to open and close files and check slips of paper.

"I need you to take care of something, It's very important to me. You need to drop whatever you are doing."

He sat back in his chair. He studied her for a moment. "What's with you?"

"What do you mean?"

"You look like —, I don't know. You look happy. You got a guy?"

She said nothing.

"Well, whatever it is, or whoever it is, it's got to wait. I need your help on this."

"Bud, something has come up. I came in to ask you for a little time off. I need to go somewhere."

"What? What happened? You're not running off with some guy are you? You can't do that."

His neck became red and he pursed his lips.

"No, nothing like that. I am going away but it's with a girl-friend, not a guy. We leave tomorrow."

Bud jumped up as Rennie had never seen before. "You've got to be kidding me! You can't go anywhere."

She leaned against his desk and stood quietly. "Bud, what's going on?"

"This could be it. There are new rumors running. It's like all other industries. Cut out the middle management people. Bring in more material off the wires and syndicates. Put in a few local stories to make it look like a local paper but fill it with pulp from around the industry. To do that, you don't need people like me."

He stared at his desk. "Or, maybe you."

She sat down in the chair in front of his desk. She wondered if he or she had been fired.

"Rennie, I thought if you could take on some stories with real meat in them, you could save us both. Maybe there's no time left."

He fell into his chair.

"Bud, whatever happens, it could be a good thing. Look at you right now. Is this living? I'd like to see you happy for more than a quick laugh."

He squinted at her as though she was speaking a foreign language. "What? This is my career, here. What are you talking about? I'd die without this place."

"Maybe, you'd really live without this place. When is the last time you spent a few days with the grandkids? You deserve better."

"You're not helping me, and you're not helping yourself,"

Rennie spoke in such a soft, confident manner that he listened to her. "We leave tomorrow morning. We're going to London to find out how Professor Justus died and why. It's big, Bud, very big. Will the paper help with costs? It is about the story."

He sat silently for a long time. "My authority goes up to five hundred bucks. Will that help?"

"That would be wonderful. Bud, things are going to work out for the good. The bad guys don't always have to win."

"Maybe, you're right. You'd better come back with a story, and it better be good! Our publisher, Miss Revenue Maximizer, has asked about your professor story."

"How's that?"

"I don't know. Her secretary called me a few times to see where you were. I told her I figured you were out at Simpson."

Rennie got up and walked around his desk and gave him a hug. As she headed for his door, she said, "I'll see you in five days, and I'll have the story of a lifetime. It'll save more than a few jobs."

"You'd better!" he shouted after her.

Rennie made some calls, left a few messages, and organized the paperwork on her desk. As she reflected on what she was doing, she sensed a joyful peace instead of her usual intensity. She was working and being productive, but it flowed in a current of grace.

At 10:30 a.m., a clerk from Finance stopped by her cubicle and gave her an envelope. Inside, she found a check for $500, payable to her with "Feature Research" in the description section. A photocopied letter enclosed with the check explained the requirements for documenting work-related expenses. She called Angie with the good news and left a message.

Rennie reviewed her notes from the library and selected what she would take with her to London. Then, she reviewed her calendar for the next two weeks, looked over her checklist, and logged off her computer. She pushed back in her chair and sat quietly, looking at the black screen of the monitor.

"Everything will be different," she said.

She left her cubicle and went through the department like a warm breeze. Getting into her car, she realized she wasn't going to Simpson College to review the professor's journals and files. She was going to London to see where he worked, where he lived, and where he died. She hoped it would bring her closure, as a journalist and as a person.

As she turned into her driveway, she felt a rush of energy for all the things she wanted to do. She was on a mission and had a purpose. It created energy. It didn't drain it. The tasks did not matter. Only the end did.

Rennie asked her neighbor Roger to see he would care for Balderdash while she was gone. He still had an extra set of keys to the house from the last time he watched the cat and was happy to help.

She quickly finished packing and fixed a sandwich for lunch. Rennie then sat down at her computer to check her e-mail messages. She had one from Angie and two from the interns in London. Angie's message was brief.

"Are you ready!!?? Tomorrow, 2:00, we fly out of here. I'll pick you up at 12. Arrive in London at 7:30 a.m. next day. How about getting together at 2:30 today to coord? Call me."

Rennie enjoyed Angie's energy and eager anticipation. Next, she opened the first e-mail from one of the interns in London.

"Cheers. More news from the police and my research. At the time of the Professor's death, there was some jurisdictional dispute between two local police authorities, the 'red's' and the 'blue's". The 'blue's' were the forerunners of Scotland Yard and were the Metropolitan Police. The 'red's' were the City of London Police. Apparently, their lack of coordination and perhaps the desire to not deal with the professor's death left the case to neglect."

Rennie sighed with frustration and read on.

"The Metro Police were called to the British Museum to investigate and question some people about possible missing shipments or other property. One memo indicates Mort was questioned about the issue and later about the professor's death. Nothing came of it. Authorities arranged for boxing the professor's belongings and sending them to America with his remains. That's all for now on legal issues."

"By the way, when I chatted with someone at the BM about your questions, a fellow who worked there stepped up and listened to my inquiry. He then questioned me about my interest in these matters. It was quite odd. Tiffini Gibson."

Rennie reviewed Tiffini's last comments and then the section about the police investigation. "Mort," she snarled as she opened the next e-mail.

"Good day, ma'am. A friend who has a genealogy hobby assisted me with finding some of the information you requested. Mrs. Priscilla MacDonald had two children, Mary and Matthew. She died in 1978. No record of death for her husband Reggie MacDonald. Mary was in a nursing home in London. Matthew is a retired professor, also in London. He served here at the University of London in the Department of Languages and Cultures of the Near and Middle East. He was also adjunct staff with the British Museum and an Associate Professor of Judeo-Christian Studies from 1951 to 1993. Last word is that he lived in London. Can't find much on Rev. Worthy other than his grandson who's a prominent lawyer here. Will keep trying. Josh Ramsey."

Rennie hit the "reply" button and let Josh know she would be there in two days and wanted to meet.

Angie called. Rennie told Angie about the messages and her disappointment in Priscilla's marriage to Reggie. "It makes me sick. Priscilla had two kids. One is a son named Matthew; not far from Matthias, huh? Get this. He grew up to be a professor at the University of London as a professor in the language department specializing in Judeo-Christian studies and was also connected with the British Museum. It's like Priscilla took her son and molded him into the man she lost. How sad."

"Well, I guess we try to make people into who we want them to be. Are we going to be able to meet Matthew?"

"I'd sure like to. I asked the intern to get us contact info on Matthew and his sister Mary. They may be able to fill in some useful details." Rennie paused. "I wonder if Matthew knows anything about the letters Matthias found. It seems so odd that he became a professor of languages and Middle East religion."

"Yeah, I guess we'll find out. Do you still want to get together this afternoon?"

"I'm on a roll now and I don't feel the intensity of what we're doing as I did yesterday."

"Rennie, do you still want to go? You seem to have lost that edge you've had."

"I definitely want to go. But, you're right. I've thought about what Matthias found and I feel so much peace. My drive is still there, but it's in a more confident place. But there is something very serious going on behind the scenes. I feel like shaking my fist and saying, 'bring it on!'"

"We've stumbled into an amazing story. Rennie, just be careful, okay? I'll talk at you later."

Rennie hung up, put her feet on her desk, and closed her eyes. A warm, soothing summer breeze came through the one window she opened. Soon, she was asleep.

An hour later, she was back on the computer, checking her e-mail messages. She researched maps of London, the locations of well-known places, information on the British Museum, and did a few name searches. Finding nothing helpful, she ran upstairs and repacked her suitcase while making last minute phone calls.

By ten o'clock, she had cleaned the house and felt ready for the trip. Her eyes burned and exhaustion filled her body. Trudging up the stairs, she was eager for bed. Balderdash jumped onto the comforter and slowly walked across it to where Rennie was lying. "Hey, buddy. I'm going away for a few days, but you'll be okay. You get to stay with your buddy, Roger."

Balderdash bumped his head against her. As she stroked his coat, he purred loudly. Hearing a noise downstairs, she sat up. Her breathing stopped. She focused on the sound, comparing it with the common noises in the neighborhood. Her memory raced through her actions to determine if the windows and doors were locked. She remembered the open window where she dozed off.

Rennie slipped off her bed. Every sound she made sounded amplified. She scanned her bedroom for her cell phone. Then, she realized her bedroom light was on and her window shades were open.

Rennie grabbed a string on one shade. Jerking it downward, she pulled the curtain off the window frame. The moment it crashed to the floor, there was another noise downstairs. Then, she heard a louder, tearing sound.

Her face twisted in anger. Rennie grabbed an antique brass candlestick and took a canister of pepper spray from her purse. She ran to the top of the stairway and looked into the darkness.

"Get out of my house!" she screamed.

Rennie flipped a light switch on the wall and winced in the sudden, bright light. She ran back into the bedroom and called 9-1-1 on her cell phone. In a loud voice, she informed the dispatch person of her fears. Carrying the phone and candlestick, she cautiously stepped back to the stair railing.

Minutes later, she saw through a back-window beams of colored lights flapping across the lawn. Rennie firmed her grip on the candlestick and carefully descended the stairs when she heard a hard knocking on her door.

Feeling fierce, she flicked open the lock and jerked the door open. A police officer holding a flashlight stood a few feet from the door. His other hand rested on the revolver attached to his belt.

"Hello, ma'am." His fingers grasped the handle of his weapon when he saw a flash of light reflect off the candlestick in Rennie's hand. He realized what it was and took a deep breath.

"Ma'am, I'm Officer Samuelson. Are you okay?"

"I am now, officer," she replied. "Did you see anyone out there?"

"I've got another officer looking around out back. We haven't seen anyone, yet. Would you like us to come in and check the house for you?"

"Inside?" Rennie asked, and then looked behind herself.

"Do you think someone might be inside? Yeah, come in."

The police officer turned off his flashlight and entered the house with careful steps. He seemed to be as cautious of Rennie as of what might be in the house. "Ma'am, please put down the candlestick. Is there anyone else in the house with you?"

"No, I'm alone, except for my cat."

"Where were you when you heard the noise?"

"I was upstairs. The noise was down here."

The officer scanned the living room, and then checked the dining area. His big body seemed to fill the room.

"I see your computer is on. Were you working on it?"

"No. I was down here some time ago, but I thought I turned it off."

Rennie noticed the screensaver image floating across the screen. "Wait a minute," she said. "I know I turned that off.

Besides, it goes into a sleep mode if I'm away from it for more than six minutes. Even if I didn't turn it off, I haven't been down here for at least twenty minutes."

"So, what are you saying?" Samuelson asked.

Rennie realized she was still holding the candlestick. She put it on the table.

"What I'm saying is that some intruder must have gotten in here and turned on my laptop."

His face contorted as though he tasted something bitter. "Lady, we don't have a lot of cases where somebody breaks into a house and checks their e-mail."

His grimace turned into a grin.

"Officer, there's more value on people's computers than there is in their wallets. Not only that, I happen to be a reporter for the *Record*, and there may be a story I'm working on that is of concern for someone. In fact, maybe you'd like to be in my next story. On the other hand, you could go through my house and do your job. The jerk that broke in might still be here. What do you think?"

"Ma'am, please sit down over there and I'll look around. If my partner comes to the door, please let him in."

He set his flashlight on the dining table and placed his fingers around the stock of his pistol. As he walked around the downstairs area, he often looked back to see if Rennie had moved. His partner came to the door and entered after Rennie motioned him in.

The men examined each room and the basement. One of them noticed the open window and inspected it. He looked back at the other man and tipped his head in the direction of the window.

After a brief review of the window screen, they turned toward her. "Ma'am, we're going to have another look around."

Together, they inspected every closet and room more diligently than before. One of them tilted his chin toward a small microphone attached to his shirt and said something. They returned to the living room to speak with Rennie.

"Well, someone was apparently here," Samuelson said.

He pointed at the open window. "Over there, the screen on that window has been cut along the frame. It was done very precisely. They got through there and must have left through there. We'll go outside to see if they might have dropped anything coming in or going out. You might want to check your computer to see if you can figure out what they were looking for."

Rennie stared in silence.

He continued. "We've checked the whole house, again. You're alone, now. I'd close and lock the windows down here."

"There's something else you need to know," Rennie said, interrupting the man. "Someone came here today and told me to be careful. He said some guy hired him to tell me that."

She got up, found the visitor's business card, and gave it to the police officer. He squinted at the card and handed it to his partner.

"What did he say? I know Dennis. He's kind of a loser, but he's straight up."

Rennie waited, as though more information would be offered. "Your buddy Dennis," she finally said, "told me that someone hired him to tell me that certain people might be interested in harming me. He said the person who called him wanted me to be careful. It was like a friendly warning, I guess. He wouldn't say who this person was or who the others are."

"Ma'am," the other officer said. "Sorry, I didn't introduce myself. I'm Officer Clark. I checked the exterior and looked into surrounding yards. There's nothing out there of any concern. Here's my card. Could you stop by our station in the next day or two?"

"Sure. Wait, no I can't. I'm leaving for England tomorrow. I won't be back for about five days."

Officer Clark looked again at the visitor's business card. "That's probably a good idea. That will give us a chance to visit with ol' Dennis and sort this out. He shouldn't be telling folks stuff like that. If he knows something about people in danger, he'd better let us know first. Ma'am, you have a good night, now. We'll drive by once in awhile and let it be known that we're looking out for you. Let us know when you're back in town. You've got my card."

Rennie escorted them to the front door. She locked it behind them and then closed and locked the open window. As she did, she observed the police officers shining their lights around the side yard and inspecting the area under the window.

When they returned to their cars, Rennie checked the locks on the other windows and closed each shade or curtain as she came to them. She grabbed the candlestick again, turned off the lights, and went upstairs.

At eight o'clock in the morning, she suddenly awakened. "Holy smoke!" she yelled as she threw back the comforter and jumped out of bed. "I forgot to set my alarm!"

She dashed down the stairs to make coffee and feed Balderdash. She hurried back up the stairs to shower, get ready, and bring her bags downstairs. She ran to the computer and turned it on. Opening the front door, she picked up the newspaper and realized she hadn't stopped delivery.

She noticed that her neighbor Cathy was in her front yard. She walked onto the front porch and called to her. "Good morning, Cathy! How are you today?"

"Oh, fine dear. How are you? Do you have the day off?"

Rennie strolled down the steps. "No, I'm going away for a few days; on a business trip. Say, would you mind picking up my mail and the paper? I completely forgot to have them held for me."

"Of course, dear. Do you have someone to watch Balderdash?"

"Yes, thanks. Do you know Roger? His house is right behind mine. He's watched over things before. He and Balderdash have a guy-thing going. Thanks for your help, Cathy. I'll see you in about four days."

Rennie jogged back to the porch and into the house. She sat down at her computer and checked for new e-mail. There was another message from Joshua. It said that Mary was still alive and lived in a nursing home in Southwark, on Copperfield Street. He spoke with the nursing staff assistant by phone and she could take visitors. Matthew was tracked to a house on Cromer Street in St. Pancras. There was no answer to calls to the telephone number listed for him.

Rennie printed the message and sent a quick response of thanks. She then hurried into the kitchen to eat and pack a small bag of snacks to take on the plane.

When Angie arrived at 10:15 a.m., she found Rennie sticking files and a laptop into a briefcase. "Come on in!" Rennie called to her.

Angie opened the screen door and looked around. "Wow, nice place. I like the old houses. They feel so homey. I love the wood-work."

"Thanks, me too. I have a lot to tell you about last night. It was pretty scary. We can catch up on the plane. Are you okay?"

"Fine. It's amazing what comes up though, at the last minute. Can I take your bag?"

Angie took one suitcase and rolled it to the front door. She stopped and grinned at Rennie. "I can tell there's more than four days of outfits in here."

"Right, I'm sure you packed for the primitive look. How many pairs of shoes do you have?"

"Don't ask."

Rennie locked the door and stepped onto the porch. She

scanned the neighborhood, focusing on every parked car. As a dark sedan cruised down the street, she watched it closely. Going by, she recognized the old man from a few houses away. Sighing relief, she got in the car.

"Leaving Iowa for an adventure in London," she muttered. "Just like Matthias. Let's go."

A few hours later, they were in the air. On the plane, Rennie summarized the visit to her home of the private investigator who warned her and the apparent break-in followed by the police investigation. Angie was speechless.

"It's okay," Rennie said. "I'll deal with it when we return. No matter what it is, I will deal with it. Now, let's see what happens in London."

London, UK

VI - 4

"Angie, wake up. We're about to land."

"Gosh, I hardly slept a wink." Angie sat forward and rubbed her eyes. "I'm going to wash up. Can we still do that?"

"Yeah, I gave you fair warning. I was up a few minutes ago."

When Angie returned, they reviewed their notes and maps. As the aircraft banked into slow turns approaching the runway, the women gazed out the window at the sights below. They gathered their belongings and tried to wake up. Angie removed a map from her purse and pointed out key locations in London. Names, addresses, and phone numbers were written on the margins of the map.

"This is good. It'll be fun so see what things really look like after studying them in print," Rennie said.

Walking down the concourse and through Terminal Three to get their luggage, they paused to see unique displays in the shops and observe the people going by. They giggled and pointed at everything new.

The other passengers were an international fashion show. Men, women, and children from all over the world reminded them that Iowa was far away. Rennie clasped her hands in delight.

"Angie, I'll bet Matthias was amazed with his travel experience."

"Yeah, but it took him a little longer to arrive. We got into a silver bullet, closed our eyes, and here we are. That's a shock!"

They stopped at a bank and exchanged some money. With luggage in hand, they asked for directions to the "tube" for transit into London. Soon, they were on the train to the city.

"I hope we have a nice hotel," Angie mused. "It's small, near the British Museum, in an area called Bloomsbury."

"No kidding. That's the area where Matthias lived while he was there. Way to go!"

"We need to get off at the Holborn Station, and then I don't know how far it is to the hotel. On the map, it's about two inches. It might be longer on foot."

Arriving at the station, they rode the long escalator up to ground level. In a few minutes they were at the hotel. Rennie got out of the cab and gasped. The British Museum was across the street.

"This feels so weird. Matthias may have walked down this same street on his way to work or while he was out for a walk."

"Rennie, did it ever occur to you that you could have said the same thing at Simpson?"

"Oh, my gosh. No, it never occurred to me. He wasn't real to me except now, here in London."

They admired the Georgian exteriors of the well-kept row of houses, inns, and shops.

"Angie, I can't believe we're here," Rennie said. "Let's get checked in. I need to level out for a few minutes."

They struggled to enter the building with their luggage and rang a bell on a small counter in the lobby of what must have once been a large home. The building had been updated but maintained a dignified, old-world quality. A garden terrace in the back of the home provided a tranquil retreat from the busy streets.

A man who appeared to be in his sixties, approached from an alcove behind the counter. He wore reading glasses perched near the end of his nose. He checked them in and showed them to their rooms.

After some preliminary unpacking, Rennie visited Angie's room and suggested they take a short break before starting out.

She readily agreed.

Forty-five minutes later, Angie knocked on Rennie's door. Rennie welcomed her in and struggled to wake up.

"Let's start easy, like go across the street and check out the museum," Angie suggested.

"Sounds good. I need to go slowly. After that, let's find the University of London. I need to meet those interns and see what they've got. Did you see that last e-mail with the info on Mary and Matthew?"

"Yeah, I got cc'd. I guess before we do any tourist stuff, we've got to do your research."

Rennie laughed. "You really thought of this trip as a little escape time, didn't you?"

"Maybe a little, but why not? Sometimes, you have to run with an idea. You didn't exactly give the professor a two-hour review and a ten-inch story."

"That's true. I don't know how I got so involved in this. But I know I've got to finish it. I hope this trip resolves what happened to Matthias and to the letters."

Rennie's mind drifted away, wondering how such precious documents remained unknown to the world.

"Okay," Angie broke the silence. "Let's get going. I need to stop at some point and get food."

Like kids hurrying off to school, they closed the doors to their rooms and dashed down the stairway. When they arrived at the curb, Angie grabbed Rennie's arm to stop her from stepping into the street and an approaching car.

"Oh, my gosh!" Rennie exclaimed. "I forgot to look the other way. How do they drive like this?"

On the other side of the street, they checked their maps and headed to the museum entrance on Great Russell Street.

Looking at the imposing columns and entry steps, Rennie asked herself what he was thinking on his first day at the museum.

They proceeded into the building. Angie purchased a map of the collections, and Rennie suggested they first find the Egyptian rooms on the upper level.

Before moving on, Rennie touched Angie's arm. "My heart is racing. After reading his journals, I almost expect him or Priscilla or Warrington to walk down this hallway."

Amazed with the impressive displays, Angie whispered, "I've got to read those journals."

For nearly an hour, they strolled through the extensive first floor exhibits. When they arrived on the second floor, Rennie's eyes darted around, as if she was remembering where to go. Reaching the point where a hallway intersected to the left, her steps slowed, and she cautiously glanced in that direction.

Rennie was on guard, listening and watching. Entering a room on Coptic Egypt, she felt confusion and betrayal. She turned to Angie. "This was it. This was the work room where they sorted the artifacts. Over there is where their desks were."

Rennie pointed to the end of the gallery. "Angie, this is where they were."

Angie slipped an arm around her. "They're gone. It was a long time ago."

"I know. I'm sorry. His words were so personal and current. I'm so confused. This is the place, but it's not."

Rennie glanced over Angie's shoulder and out the door. She hurried into the corridor and approached another doorway. A sign read "Staff only."

She grabbed the handle with a strong hand and jerked it. It was locked. Rennie grit her teeth and pulled again. A docent at the end of the hallway noticed the women and briskly moved in their direction.

Angie appeared to be confused. "What are you doing? Someone's coming."

The docent was an elderly, pleasant man. "Can I help you, ma'am?"

"Is this a staff room? I mean, is it for lunch or breaks?"

"Lunch? Oh no, ma'am. It's a storage room. It's not available to the public. Is there something I can help you with, ma'am? Perhaps, directions to the restaurant?"

He smiled pleasantly.

"Thank you, but no. Come on, Angie. It's this way."

Rennie took Angie's arm, turned and went down the hall, turning right at the first corridor.

She stopped and put her hand over her mouth. "I don't know what I'm doing. I feel so frantic."

"Why don't we get something to eat? We're both exhausted."

Angie took Rennie's hand and escorted her away.

After a satisfying meal, a server in the upper-floor restaurant brought a check for their meals.

Rennie looked at it. "Thanks for your patience with me. I also want you to know that I'm beginning to remember what year it is."

"Good. I didn't want to have to tackle you as you raced down the hallways yelling 'Matthias! Professor Justus!'"

Rennie snickered. "I deserved that." She relaxed into the back of her chair. "This has been good. Now, let's see if we can find Mary and then Matthew. I guess Mary is in a nursing home, but we don't know about connecting with Matthew. Is that okay with you?"

"Let's do it. By the way, do they live in this century?"

Rennie picked a piece of parsley off her plate and tossed it at Angie.

They hailed a cab in front of the British Museum and discovered the congestion of central London streets. They rode quietly, watching the traffic, people, and sights of London pass by. Across the Thames, the locations became more industrial than where they had been. The cab stopped in front of the nursing home where Mary MacDonald lived. It had the appearance of a cheap hotel. Litter was scattered on the street and windows in an adjacent building were boarded up.

As they entered, they immediately noticed a smell of cleanser and humid, human presence. The old woman at the reception desk didn't ask for identification or show any interest in the two women from America when she gave directions to Mary's room.

Climbing an old stairway to the third floor, they discreetly glanced into the rooms. Occasionally, a moan or cry could be heard down the hall. The women held hands when they reached the third floor and proceeded down the dimly lit corridor.

Another visitor directed them to room 309. Finding it, they peeked in and saw four hospital beds, one in each corner of the modest room. A television was on, but no one was watching it. The four residents lay quietly in their beds.

Rennie observed the details in the room. Her intensity grew in anticipation of meeting a living connection with a great mystery. Angie walked to one bed and then another, looking at a small note cards at the ends of each of the beds. She stopped at the second bed, and then motioned to Rennie to come.

As Rennie approached, she reached into her bag and removed a notepad and pen. She stepped up to the head of the bed and looked at the old woman. Her white hair was matted in a few places and her sunken lips suggested she had no teeth. Her breathing was shallow and quick.

Rennie leaned over her. "Miss MacDonald? Can you hear me?"

She waited. Just as she was about to speak again, the old woman's eyelids opened.

"Who are you? What do you want?"

Rennie quickly leaned back. "Well I just wanted to see you for a moment. I wondered if you were the daughter of someone I knew once. I mean someone I read about once, long ago."

"And, who's that dear?" The old woman had a mischievous smile. Her brown eyes were clear.

"Her name was Priscilla Shefford. Her name became Mac-Donald. She worked at the British Museum. Was she related to you? Was she your mother?"

The old woman tried to see Angie, and then looked back at Rennie. Her eyes shut, as though a bright light hit her. "What's this about? Who are you?"

"I'm sorry, ma'am. I'm from America. I came here to meet you. I read about Priscilla Shefford, and I wanted to meet her family. Are you her family?"

The old woman nodded. After a few breaths, she said, "Yes, she's my mother."

Her eyes closed and she seemed to rest. Rennie and Angie pulled a couple of chairs up to the bed.

"Miss MacDonald?" Rennie asked. "Can you hear me alright?"

"Did you bring anything for me?" the old woman asked.

Rennie looked at Angie and shrugged her shoulders. "I'm sorry, ma'am. We don't have anything. If we can visit you again, we'd be delighted to bring you something." Rennie smiled and added, "We could bring you chocolate."

Mary's eyes opened again, and she said, "How about some cigarettes? I like the unfiltered ones."

Rennie looked at Angie's shocked face. She leaned closer to the old woman. "I'm sorry, but neither of us smoke. I'm not sure that would be alright in this facility."

"Oh, they don't care," Mary said with energy. "What's your name?"

"My name is Rennie, and this is my friend Angie. May we call you Mary or do you prefer Miss MacDonald?"

Mary turned to get a better look at each of her visitors. "You can call me Mary, girls. You know what the boys used to call me?"

She grinned with satisfaction. "They called me 'Happy Time.' Do you know why?"

Rennie looked at Angie in surprise.

Angie chuckled. "Hi Mary, my name is Angie. Could tell us a little about your mother? It seems she was quite a woman."

Mary motioned to a glass of water. Angie took it with some hesitation and glanced at Rennie.

Rennie slipped her hand under the woman's pillow and gently lifted her head so she could drink. When she removed her hand, Rennie felt sickened when she noticed the old hair and grime on her hand and sleeve. She discreetly shook her arm.

"My mother was quite a woman. She would have nothing to do with me, though. I was my daddy's princess." Mary grinned again. "He wouldn't have nothing to do with my brother or nobody else. I was his little princess. That's what he said all the time."

"Mary," Rennie asked, "who was your father?"

"He was the Duke!" Mary exclaimed. "They called him the Duke of the Riverfront. He ran the river, some said. I was his little princess."

"Mary, that's impressive." Angie added. "You must have been proud of him. What was his name?"

"Yes, I was. I was very proud of him. I was his little princess."

Rennie and Angie shared a glance of concern.

"Mary, did your father also work at the British Museum?"

"Oh, no. Only my mother worked there. But that was long before I came along. My daddy, he never did nothing but do business along the river. People used to say that nothing happened on the river unless Reggie MacDonald had a piece of it."

Rennie fell back in her chair and stared at the old woman. "Mary, tell us a little about Priscilla and Reggie," Angie urged. "And, also about you and your brother."

"Do I get some ciggies?" Mary smiled.

Angie grinned. "We'll see Mary. We'll have to check with staff, and it will depend on how much you can tell us."

"Okay girls, we've got a deal." Mary responded. "Well, life was never too kind to me. My mother used to say I was my daddy's daughter. You've got to fight for life, you know. Mother was all prissy-like, trying to be some upper-class person. We were just common folks. My daddy didn't try to be classy. He was tough, 'cause we lived in a tough place. My brother was like my mother. She wanted him to be smart and like a gentleman. When he got old enough, my daddy let him know how men really behave. That's when he left."

Mary's eyes closed and she rested for a moment.

Rennie sat up again. "Mary, this is Rennie. Who left and what happened?"

Mary's expression became serious. "My daddy boxed my brother around once too often, I guess. I heard my mother and my daddy get into a big fight. She always favored the boy. I was my daddy's little princess. He said the boy should get out and start making his way like a man."

"How old was your brother?" Angie asked.

"I don't know. Maybe thirteen. People didn't expect him to make it. My mother cried and yelled. Then it got quiet. It always got quiet after they would fight."

Mary turned her gaze to the window. "Matt didn't leave that time, but he did later. He went to some school, I think. That's when my daddy ..." Mary stopped and stared at the ceiling.

"Your daddy what, Mary?" Rennie whispered.

A tear slipped from Mary's eye. "Oh, nothing. They're dead, you know. Both of them."

Rennie's instincts urged her on. "Mary, do you remember how or when your parents passed on?"

Mary's lips quivered.

Angie noticed several pillows stacked on a corner table and

got one that looked fresh. "Mary, would you like a sip of water and an extra pillow?"

The old woman's face beamed. After she was tilted up and had a drink, she spoke with more comfort. "What were we talking about? Oh yes, my parents. My daddy died one night. I don't know how or why. Some say it was a business deal gone wrong. I was no longer home, so I don't know. My mother died of some sickness, not long ago. Maybe old age. Just like me."

"Mary, tell us a little about your life," Angie asked.

Mary gave a mischievous grin. "It was quite a time. I was real popular with the boys. Say, are you Americans? Your American boys liked me when they were here for the big war."

Mary's face hardened. "I married a couple of blokes, but they weren't gentle. I was my daddy's little princess, but not to those men."

Mary snorted a puff of determination. "My daddy taught me to look out for myself."

Rennie tilted her head. "Mary, how did your daddy teach you?"

The old woman's face became dark, almost fierce looking. Her nostrils flared. Her breathing became stronger. "I'm not going to talk about that. I told my mother, and that's when everything happened. I left and lived on my own after that."

"Mary," Angie asked, "Did you and your brother stay in touch?"

"No, he wouldn't have nothing to do with me. He got all educated and upper class, just like his mother wanted. Then, after that trip, he didn't have much interest in me again. He'd give me money now and then. That's what older brothers do, I told him. A few times, he got me out of the jail."

"Mary, what trip?" Rennie asked with a strong voice.

"The one my mother and brother took to America. Can you imagine? Is that how you learned about my mother?"

Mary lifted her head off the pillow and looked at both women. Rennie was breathless and couldn't answer.

Angie helped with a response. "We were actually looking into something else, and we came across your mother's name. Did you ever hear of a man by the name of Matthias Justus? He was a professor from the town in America where we are from."

Mary squinted and nodded her head slowly. "I heard that name. Once, my mother and my daddy got loud in another fight. My mother said that name. That was it! Daddy knocked her down and went out the door so fast he nearly took the wall down. Then, mother and I got into a big fight. I told her she should treat my father better. He was the Duke. I told her he loved me more than her. So, she should be careful or she would be out, just like my brother."

Mary paused again with a hard look. "He loved me more," she whispered. "I left not long after that."

Mary closed her eyes and seemed to rest. Rennie quietly struggled to understand Mary's story as Angie drifted over to the window.

Rennie got up and looked down at the old woman. "Thank you, Mary. We appreciate your time and sharing your thoughts with us."

Rennie paused and smiled. "Your daddy would still think of you as his little princess. God loves you," she whispered."

Without opening her eyes, Mary smiled and lifted her hand to wave goodbye.

As they walked away from the bed, Angie stopped and went back. She removed several bills from her purse, rolled them up, and slipped the money into Mary's hand. The old woman clenched them tightly.

Out in the hallway, they looked back at Mary.

"Poor thing," Angie murmured.

They walked quietly for two blocks and then waved down a

taxi. Safely in the backseat, Rennie said, "I think I need to rest for awhile. Is that okay with you?"

"Yeah, we need a break. Let's meet up for dinner later."

Rennie couldn't respond. She had not expected how emotionally confusing this trip would be. As a reporter, she had believed that more facts revealed more truth. That wasn't working in this case. She felt more determined to find Matthew and hear his story.

As she looked around, she saw short distance behind their cab a black sedan following them from the nursing home to their hotel.

PART SEVEN

London, UK

VII - 1

Rennie awoke, confused with the sound of a ringing telephone. The clock indicated 8:04 a.m. She grabbed the phone.

"Hello, this is Rennie."

"Hello, Ms. Haran, this is Joshua Ramsey, one of your researchers from the University of London. I must apologize to you for this early call."

"No, it's alright." Rennie stifled a yawn. "What happened? I mean, what can I do for you Joshua?"

"Shall I call back in a little while? I imagine this early in your trip you may be a bit tired."

"No, I'm fine. I appreciate your calling. I need to see you and Tiffini."

"Yes, we would like that, as well. This has turned out to be quite an interesting project."

"How about this morning? We don't have much time."

"We can do that. It appears your hotel is close to us at the University. Miss McGrady had provided the number where you would be staying, and the hotel switchboard offered your lodging name and location. It is most convenient."

"Well, how about nine o'clock?"

"Brilliant. I shall contact Tiffini and see if that works for her. At the very least, I will meet with you and share the latest information I have obtained over the last few days. I apologize if this is intrusive, but I would be interested in knowing the purpose of your investigation. Its disparate elements are most intriguing."

"Sure, Joshua, I'll fill you in. It's innocent really. We're just stumbling forward, and you're helping cushion the fall."

"Thank you, ma'am. There's a coffee shop a short walk from your hotel. Perhaps, we could meet there."

"Great. Just hearing the word 'coffee' has got me going."

After discussing the arrangements and hanging up, Rennie swung her legs out of bed and ran her fingers through her hair. Eager to get into the day, she called Angie's room.

"Hey, I got a call from Joshua, one of the researchers. He's going to meet us at nine o'clock at a coffee shop near here. He's got more info for us. Tiffini might be able to make it, too. We've got to move fast. Can we meet downstairs in forty minutes? He said it was nearby."

"Yeah, I guess I can do that." Angie replied with a yawn.

At 8:45, Rennie paced the small, hotel reception area. She set down a light travel bag filled with her notes and wandered about, admiring the courtyard in the back of the hotel. The furnishings and structure fit well with the classic Georgian facade of the building, combining rich wood trim, floral wallpapers, deep carpets, and flowers in vases. For Rennie, it felt like England. The cool, quiet breeze of conditioned air was the only indication of the modern era.

She thought about Matthias living in London. It didn't seem so long ago. Her thoughts drifted to meeting Mary and what seemed to be her tragic and lonely life. Mary tried to be tough but was so fragile. Rennie felt sadness that Mary had nothing left but wounded memories.

Angie stepped off the stairs with energy. Her hair floated in the air behind her as she quickly crossed the room. She appeared to be a little frantic as she struggled to fasten her watchband.

"Okay, let's get at it. Rennie, did you order room service? I did, and it was not only slow, but the servings were small. These people need to come to Iowa to see how to serve food portions."

She stopped and sensed Rennie's thoughtful mood. "Are you okay?"

"I was just thinking about Matthias and Mary."

"I thought about her, too. I'm glad we went to see her. She probably doesn't get many visitors. I hope she knows we care and we're not just there to interrogate her."

Rennie walked a few steps to the back wall of windows and quietly let her thoughts go into the courtyard. She touched the curtain lace and slid her finger along the curve of stitching.

"I feel like I'm setting the world aside. I look at Mary, and no matter what she has done or who she is, I just have so much compassion for her."

"I know the feeling you're talking about. There's been a change. I don't know what to do with it. I'm still me, but there are little moments of interruption now when I feel centered or something. I have to admit, I like it."

"Me, too. I guess we'd better get going. Who knows what's next."

Strolling down the busy street, Rennie felt unusually self-conscious. She had a renewed sense of focus. There was grace and power in her stride. This came to a quick end when a young, well-dressed man dashed across the street and confronted them.

"Go back to where you came from!" he bellowed.

Recoiling, the women were speechless.

He stepped forward. "Stop meddling or you'll pay a heavy price!"

He pulled several rocks out of his pocket and dropped them at Rennie's feet.

Another man, who had been walking behind them, suddenly moved in front of the intruder. "Leave them alone or you'll deal with me," he barked.

His huge frame hid the other man from Rennie and Angie,

and his hands became fists. "Get away and don't think about coming back!"

The young man backed up and glanced past the defender. "Consider yourselves warned!"

The big man moved forward, prompting the other to run across the street, get in a car, and drive off.

As he did, the defender turned to the women and calmly addressed them. "Ladies, I'm sorry for this rude behavior. England is a tolerant land, but we have our crazies. This fellow apparently doesn't like Americans. Please know that the rest of us are delighted you are here."

Rennie was stunned. "Thank you, Mr. uh —"

"Just Peter is fine, ma'am. Please enjoy your day." He gave a slight bow and strolled away.

Rennie realized she was holding tightly to Angie's arm and released it. "My gosh, what was that all about?"

Angie looked as stunned as Rennie felt. "I don't know but I'm glad that big guy was around. Crazies have been unleashed in the world."

They hurried to the coffee shop, which was only fifty feet away. It was about the size of a school room with a coffee bar along one side. Three tables were occupied. Joshua and Tiffini waved from one of the tables.

Rennie suggested, "Let's not say anything about what just happened. We need to finish what we came for."

They greeted one another at the table, then Rennie and Angie went to the coffee bar to order their drinks. The moment helped Rennie calm down. When they returned, Joshua and Tiffini placed file folders and reference materials on the table.

"Well, here we all are," Joshua began. "It's a delight to finally meet you. Tiffini and I have enjoyed working on this little project."

"From the legal perspective here," Tiffini added, "I wondered if you were resolving anything that may have arisen from dispute or claim. Not that it matters for us, but it has been raised by the authorities with whom I've spoken."

Rennie set down her coffee.

"Not at all, Tiffini. I'm a reporter for a newspaper in Iowa. I was asked to write a story about Professor Justus. Angie here is the librarian and chief archivist at the college where the professor worked. We're just trying to find out what happened to him as part of our work."

"I see," said Tiffini. "That makes sense. We were just cautioned to be wary of whom we may be assisting, particularly since the university is involved. If it were a personal matter, that may be inappropriate."

Her face brightened. "For a college, I imagine it is quite proper. Well then, here are some photocopies of a few old records I have been able to retrieve. There is little more than what I mentioned previously. With Joshua's assistance in tracking down a few of the other parties, I have done some research on them but found nothing relevant to the police records. Mary MacDonald has a bit of a sorry record here and there, but it did not relate to your professor."

"We had a chance to visit with Mary yesterday," Angie said. "She shared with us a bit of her life and memories. Joshua, is there anything else we can learn?"

"Yes, I have found a few tidbits over the last few days. In particular, I've definitely located the son, Professor Matthew MacDonald. He is here in London and not far away. His home is perhaps twenty minutes by taxi. There's an odd wrinkle, though. There are some conflicting records."

"Oh, no," Rennie responded. "Did he also have a difficult life?"

Joshua looked at his notes. "Not at all. His life seems to have been quite, hmm, dignified shall we say. But there are apparent differences in surname that I cannot clarify."

Angie asked, "But, he is the son of Priscilla MacDonald? Did we find a different person?"

"I'm certain he is the son of Priscilla. It's just an odd conflict in name usage. Regarding other information, I have a few things on Lady Sotterfeld-Gris and on the Archbishop that I did not have earlier. The Lady's story is fairly well available, given her social status. The Reverend's was more difficult since he was not particularly important and apparently, at the end, somewhat in disgrace."

"Really?" Rennie asked with energy. "Tell me about that. From what I read, he thought rather well of himself."

"Yes, that is not to be unexpected I suppose," Joshua said cynically.

"The people to whom I was referred did not say anything directly, but there was that clear implication in their tone and in what was not said that pointed toward something important and not positive."

"What do you mean something important?" Rennie asked.

"It sounded like something personal with regard to what the good Reverend may have done. Something improper may be an expression that fits. For Reverend Worthy, it sounded to me like a sex scandal. It seems he may have gone on holiday with a gentleman friend. Those relationships can become quite complicated, especially if one is married and has a child. Differences apparently arose between the Reverend and the church, and he was asked to take a position that might have been considered more modest than what he held previously. It all did not go well after that. They say he did himself in."

Rennie thought of the letters.

"Was there any mention of any change in Reverend Worthy's fortunes around the time of Professor Justus' presence here?"

"In what way, Miss Haran?"

"I wondered if Worthy achieved any special status or even affluence after his contacts with Professor Justus."

"Do you mean resulting from his connection with the professor?"

"For any reasons."

Rennie's gaze at Joshua was cool and professional.

Joshua looked into his file folder and quickly flipped through a few pages of notes and photocopied materials.

"I cannot say there was any notable change in the Reverend's situation from that time, except what may be due to some personal matters. One cannot actually know much with a lack of documentation. I found little information about his wife and daughter. His daughter's son, Seth Galila, became a prominent solicitor. There have been some newspaper stories noting his legal services to the church."

Joshua nodded to Tiffini for her to comment.

She added, "My review of files of the authorities and from my contacts with legal news groups, there is no mention of Reverend Worthy. As Josh said, only the grandson is mentioned, Solicitor Galila. You mentioned in your request that Reverend Worthy played some role at the British Museum, but we could find nothing in their records. His influence, if there was any, may have been through personal associations or style. He may simply have been what some call a 'social climber.'"

"How about the Lady?" Angie asked. "She sounds pretty cool. We had hoped to stop by her house today."

Joshua looked again into his file. "She was indeed an interesting person. About two years after Professor Justus was here, she married a fellow of substantial means who was quite a bit older than she."

"You mean he was rich?" Rennie asked.

"Yes," Joshua said with delight. "He was something of an adventurer, interested in Middle Eastern relics and the like.

From the notices in the papers, they apparently traveled often and did the usual sort of receptions and endowments. About ten years later, he died in some odd way, in Egypt I believe. He apparently ingested a stone, of all things. Quite odd. His wife returned to England and led a much quieter life, not traveling from what I could find. She began an endowment for providing education opportunities for children who have an interest in the arts, culture, and particularly languages and history."

Rennie and Angie looked at each other with concern.

Angie asked, "Did you say he ingested a stone?"

"Yes," Joshua answered. "There was a brief reference to that effect, and it may not have been accurate."

Angie turned to Rennie. "That's just like what happened to those library people here at the British Museum and in the other countries. Joshua, when you have a chance, I'd appreciate your adding another item to your research list. We need to know of any deaths caused by stones in people's throats, beginning with any related to the British Museum. It sounds odd, but we've come across that now and then."

"Will do, ma'am. I'll ask the fellow I contacted at the museum. He seemed to be interested in your venture. Lastly," Joshua continued, "the Lady died in 1968, in her country home. There was no listing of cause of death."

"Wait a moment, Joshua." Rennie studied the young man as if there was a puzzle on his face. "You were in contact with someone at the British Museum?"

"Yes, ma'am, for your original inquiry. I also thought Professor MacDonald may be known to them given his unique expertise."

"I understand," Rennie responded. "Did you happen to mention to this person my name or contact information?"

Joshua shifted uneasily in his chair. "Well, I felt it was necessary to note who needed the information. You did say it was for a newspaper story, right?"

"That's correct."

Angie interrupted. "The endowment, do you know anything about that? Who manages it or how it works?"

"No, it's a private foundation, and frankly, I did not go that far. Is it important?"

Disappointment seemed to spread across Joshua's face.

Rennie folded her arms and leaned back in her chair. "Probably not. Angie, what do you think?"

"I don't see anything vital about that. Joshua, you've done a great job. Both of you have done wonders. given the time you've worked on this and the information you had to go on. Thank you for your efforts."

"I agree," Rennie chimed in.

"As a reporter, I know how difficult it can be to get information and get it quickly. Your work will help me put this story to bed. Thank you."

Joshua seemed pleased. "The address and contact information for Professor Matthew MacDonald is in the file I'll give you. He may be available soon. He's been in the Mideast on some sort of dig."

"Tell us about that." Rennie eagerly said.

"I guess he has continued his interest in the Near East since his retirement from university and the museum by participating in various archeological digs and occasional Mideast peace activities. He's probably 80 or more. He's quite remarkable, really. I'd like to meet him myself. He was expected to return earlier this week."

Rennie took the files from Joshua.

"If we can do anything else on this, please let us know." Tiffini said in a cheery voice. "We would be delighted to see your story when it is published. That will provide a satisfying conclusion to this enterprise."

"Oh," Joshua interjected. "I mentioned a wrinkle with Professor MacDonald's surname. It's a bit odd. There are references to his last name as 'Justus,' as in the name of the professor in your query. I thought it must be a mistake or overlap. A bit unusual, though."

Rennie and Angie shared a suspicious look.

Rennie thought it was time to end the meeting.

"I'll get a copy of the story to each of you as well as letters highlighting your research assistance. If you discover any other information, please let us know immediately. This has been quite an adventure."

The four arose from the table to leave, shook hands and promised to keep in touch.

Rennie and Angie took the file folders and left the coffee shop, returning to their hotel with renewed spirit in their steps.

"Rennie, I know this project isn't about us, but I feel like I'm getting all the benefits. I think we should call Professor Justus. I mean Professor MacDonald. Isn't it freaky, how he ended up in a similar line of work? And, what's with the name mix up?"

"Yeah, a lot of mysteries in this family. You would think that Priscilla molded him as a remake of the guy she lost. I'm looking forward to meeting him. I just hope he's here."

As they approached the hotel, Angie paused and glanced back down the street.

Rennie noticed the look and asked, "What's up?"

Angie squinted. "I'm not sure. For a moment, I felt like someone was watching us."

Rennie scanned the area. "Was it the guy who confronted us? Did you see him again?"

"No, I don't know. It's probably nothing."

"Angie, I told you on the plane about my experience with the break-in at my house and that guy who warned me of people who might want to cause trouble. We've got to take seriously any indication that someone is a threat, even here in London. Did you hear Joshua say he told some fellow at the British Museum about me looking into this case? Who was that person and who was the guy that harangued us on the street? In fact, who was the man who suddenly came to our aid?"

She swiveled around to see if anyone of concern was around. "Rennie, I don't know. I didn't connect with what you've experienced. It's seemed like you've been under a lot of pressure and all this is so strange. But your concerns are real."

"Angie, I'm a professional fact-finder who's handled a lot of strange stories, and I've never run into this type of thing before. It has me unsettled, too. I wonder if that guy in the truck who threatened me at Simpson is related to this?"

Angie pointed at a man across the street. He was speaking into a cell phone. When he noticed her motion toward him, he put the phone away and got into a car. The driver of the car sped off.

Rennie became furious. "What the heck is going on!" she shouted.

"Was that the person you thought was watching us?"

"It was only a feeling."

"Let's get inside," Rennie said.

They hurried to a quiet sitting area in the back, near the windows.

Rennie laid on the table her travel bag of reference material with the file folders.

"Okay, here's what I suggest. We've got to pay attention to what's going on around us. We must be careful. It's too strange. Now, we call Matthew's place and see if he's there or leave a message. Then, we take a cab and go by the addresses we have for where Matthias, Priscilla, and Lady Jane lived. If we don't hear back from Matthias, or I mean Matthew, we go back to the British Museum for whatever other questions we may have. If all else fails, we hit the tourist circuit. What do you think?"

"Great plan. Do you want to call him or should I?"

"Good question. I feel anxious about talking with him. He is so close to the people I've gotten to know but have never met."

"I understand. I feel a little of the same, and you're the one who read all the journals. Do you want me to call?"

Rennie laughed. "No, I'll do it."

She got up and went to the front desk, folder in hand. A few minutes later, Rennie returned, dropping onto the couch.

"No luck. The number Josh had was apparently for Matthew's landlady or somebody. She sounded old and we couldn't understand each other."

"What did she say?"

"She said she thought he was back in town, but she had a lot of questions about who I was and what I wanted. I finally told her I was an old friend of the family, in town visiting from America, and we wanted to stop by. I left her our number here and asked her to be sure he got the message."

Rennie breathed a deep sigh. "I hope we see him, Angie."

"Yeah, me too."

Angie studied her friend. Then, she slapped the arm of the chair. "Okay girl, we need to get going. Grab your stuff and let's get a cab."

The desk clerk approached them with a thick, mailing envelope. On it was a label with a name typed in bold letters. "Ladies, which of you is Miss Haran?"

"That would be me," Rennie replied.

He handed her the envelope and departed to a back room. Rennie felt that something was not right. She set the envelope on the table but asked Angie to open it.

Angie ripped the top fold open and looked inside. Her face became pale and her mouth opened. "Rennie," she whispered. "It's a stone."

Rennie leaped out of her chair and ran to the front desk.

"Hey, you," she yelled to the clerk, barely visible in a back room. "Who delivered this?"

The man approached the desk.

"Who delivered this?" Rennie demanded as she shook the envelope in the air.

"I'm sorry, ma'am. I didn't see anyone. I heard the door open, and when I came up front, the envelope was lying on the desk. I saw no one. It only had a name on it."

"When? When did this happen?" she replied.

"It was about 30 minutes ago," he stammered.

Rennie glanced back at Angie. "That's when we were down the street. They are watching us. Angie, I'm so sorry I got you into this."

Angie motioned for Rennie to return to the table.

"We've got to call the police," she whispered.

"And, what do we tell them? I've been around cops most of my career. They are reactive only. I can hear it now. 'Ladies, let us know when you've been attacked, and we'll find the guys who did it.' No, we have got to stay on track. Let's stay alert, get our job done, and get the heck out of town."

London, UK

VII - 2

Seated at a table in a dark, well-appointed restaurant, Seth Galila's aristocratic style and expensive suit blended well with the clientele and the aloof service personnel. In a whisper, he asked for tea, and with a flick of his finger he dismissed the server.

The trim figure and graceful movements of Galila suggested a younger man than his 65 years. As a successful, influential in London, his appearance demanded recognition from those who saw him.

Another man, whose attire and bearing were far less appropriate for the arrogance of the setting, strolled in an uncertain manner past the tables and stopped near Galila.

Looking above his reading glasses, Galila observed the man. "Sit, Daniel," he said.

"Thank you," the man mumbled. "They're definitely after something," he earnestly reported as he sat down.

Galila's nostrils flared. "Might we begin with something more circumspect?" he sneered.

"Yes, sir. I've been looking into the matter that we've discussed over the last few days. It seems things are proceeding despite our suggestions to the contrary."

Removing and slowly folding his glasses, Galila laid them on the table. Tilting his head slightly, he commanded the full attention of the other man. "Daniel, what is your assessment of these ladies? Do you think they know what they are doing?"

"Sir," Daniel began with hesitation, "they are all over the place. They've visited some of the old sights in the city, where the professor and the lady lived. So, they definitely have some of the history. It seems more of a tour though, rather than a hunt." The man grinned. "Maybe they don't know they are the hunted ones."

Galila's eyes swiveled with the comment as he checked to see who might be within hearing distance.

Daniel squirmed in his chair. "Since our source at the museum heard of their inquiry, nothing further has been pursued there. We know that one of them is a reporter at a paper in the city near Simpson College, and the other is apparently a librarian. Hardly threats to us."

"We shall see, won't we Daniel," Galila said with care. "If they have not been dissuaded by any warnings or activities at this point, why are they not a threat to our mission? Could they be allies with our vile acquaintance in California?"

"I cannot imagine it. He operates at a much higher level. They must be stumbling forward, not knowing what they are dealing with and must also be ignorant of our messages to them. I don't see their motivation in knowingly putting themselves at risk."

Daniel finally relaxed in his chair and looked straight at Galila. "I left a little gift at their hotel. I don't know if they have any idea of its meaning, but it might give them pause."

The muscles in Galila's face hardened. "What do you mean you left a gift? You had better not mean a stone."

The color in Daniel's face drained away.

Galila folded his hands on the table and lowered his voice. "Daniel, our goal is to keep anyone from finding the documents. We don't know where they are, and it is our duty to be sure no one else discovers them. The risks to the glory of the Holy One falling into the hands of man are simply outrageous. It would be desecration of the highest order."

As the server approached, Galila raised a finger and indicated "no" with a quick nod of the head.

"Daniel," he continued, "we must remain men of and protect the law. People of our faith somehow came to perceive the Pharisees wrongly. They don't realize that Jesus loved them and argued with them because of His bond with them. We have taken on the mission of keeping the law to honor our Lord. Anyone who tries to touch His person must be struck down, just as Uzzah was condemned when he touched the Ark. The church must return to being the enforcer of the law. If those documents are ever found, it could unleash the destruction of the church."

Daniel became tense as Galila's nose and mouth began to twitch into a snarl. "That apostate in California," Galila hissed. "Sfumato cares nothing about the holiness of what he pursues. Gold is his god."

A bead of perspiration arose on his temple. "If I ever get the chance, I have a special stone just for him," Galila said with a twisted smile.

He rested back into his chair. "As for the ladies, you've given enough warnings. Simply observe them for now. If you can access their records, do so. The moment you sense they are onto the scent of the treasure, immediately notify me. But, if they can be dissuaded with impunity, act quickly. We must erase this and all future attempts to find what the mischievous Professor Justus uncovered."

Daniel slid his chair back from the table. "I'll take care of it, sir."

"Thank you, my friend. As you know, my dear mother began this holy crusade to protect the church. I must pursue it with all I have. You are a noble warrior in this cause. My grandfather, the Archbishop, would anoint you with his blessing if he were here. There was a reason God gave him the name 'Worthy.' It was a great loss to the church that he was taken to the holy realm much too soon."

As the distinguished fellow drifted into thought, Daniel

stood and took one step away from the table. After a moment, he said, "Sir, I'll be leaving now."

Seth Galila didn't look up. The fingers of his right hand flicked up to dismiss the man.

London, UK

VII - 3

Rennie and Angie looked down the street in front of the hotel waving at every cab that passed by.

"How do you know which ones are available?" Angie said in frustration. "There, there. That one saw us."

The cab made a tight turn in the middle of the street and stopped. They hurried aboard and gave the driver the address. The house where Matthias had lived was not far. When the taxi reached the corner of Bloomsbury Way, Rennie studied the people on the sidewalks and the surroundings.

"I'll bet this is what he walked past every day, on the way to work," she said to the window.

Past High Holborn Street, they continued down Drury Lane. Recognizing the name, Rennie became more anxious. Just beyond Great Queen Street, the taxi turned onto Broad Court. Rennie asked the driver to slow down as he approached the address she had for Matthias' boarding house. When they arrived, Rennie could not move. She just stared at the front door.

The building appeared to be a "boutique" hotel. The exterior was much like the adjacent buildings, but the door and windows appeared to be modern versions of an older time. It reminded her of their hotel.

Rennie asked the driver to wait. Leaving the taxi, she approached the hotel. She studied the door then grasped the heavy bronze handle. She stopped. For a moment, Rennie felt she might step back into time. She gave it a pull and went in. Angie waited briefly in the taxi before going in.

A young man in a white shirt and blue tie came down the

stairway, greeted them, and went behind a short counter as Angie arrived. "Hello, my name is Dale. How can I assist you ladies?"

Rennie felt confused and not sure of what to say.

"We just stopped in to see the place. We've been doing some research on a family friend who lived at this address long ago, back when it was a boarding house."

"When was that, ma'am?"

"It was in the nineteen twenties."

"Well, the hotel is certainly much different now. After the war, this property was joined with an adjacent one. Then, in the 1980's there was a major renovation. I doubt there's much that resembles what was here in the twenties. Was there anything in particular that interested you?"

Rennie glanced around. "I'm not sure. Are any of the sleeping rooms as they were then?"

"I'm sorry, ma'am. It's doubtful. The only room that may have any connection with the old building is what we call the Hearth Room. It's apparently where the old kitchen used to be. In fact, the display table in the room supposedly was the kitchen table. Rather quaint, wouldn't you say?"

"Really?" Rennie gasped. "May we see it?"

"Of course. It's right over here."

Dale led them across the lobby and through a doorway. He gestured to a comfortable sitting room.

"This is it, and over there is the table."

Rennie felt drawn across the room to the simple oak dining set. She brushed her fingertips across the table surface and sat in one of the chairs. She rested her arms on the tabletop and closed her eyes. The question, *Matthias, what happened?* filled her thoughts. She wanted to warn him. Angie came to her and rested her hand on Rennie's shoulder.

Dale cleared his throat. "Ladies, is there anything else?"

"No, thank you, this is fine," Angie responded. "We'll go now.

We appreciate your time."

They said nothing as they got into the taxi. When the driver asked where they wanted to go, Angie read the address from a circled note in Rennie's file. The cab moved into traffic.

"Thanks, Angie. When I sat at that table, I felt so close to him while having a great sense of loss. I had hoped for some connection."

A few minutes later, they made a hard left from Bow Street onto Aldwych and drove by the Waldorf Hilton Hotel.

"Look, Angie. That's where Matthias and Priscilla ate on the night of their big date. I'm so happy for them."

The cab continued to Strand and then Fleet Street. They passed through Ludgate Circus and continued a few blocks, then turning right again. The taxi slowed as it approached Queen Victoria Street.

"Nearly there, ma'am," the driver said. He continued down the block for the listed address until he was at St. Andrews, just a block from the Blackfriar's Underpass. In a jerking moment, he turned right at the church and stopped.

"Ladies, we cabbies need to know this city but I'm not sure about the address you provided. It doesn't appear to be on the properties here on Queen Victoria. Did you say it was a residence?"

Rennie shifted nearer the partition. "Yes, this is the address we had, and it was for a house. It was a very long time ago. Have there been many changes to the properties here?"

"Yes, ma'am. Considering the war, the fires, just your normal development interests, it's not likely that a house would still be there. From the address, it was probably located where the park swimming pool is now. Much of that park and recreation area was built long ago. I'm sorry ladies."

Rennie fell back in the seat. She had enough disappointment.

Angie asked the driver to wait for a few minutes.

Angie opened the door and stepped out. "Rennie, let's walk down the street and get some fresh air. Come on. Let's go."

Rennie pressed her fingers to her temples. "Okay, let's do this, but I'm getting really ticked off."

They walked to the corner and then down the street one block. They said nothing, but simply observed buildings and traffic. They crossed the street to the pool facility.

"I don't know why I'm surprised or disappointed that everything has changed." Rennie blurted out. "It's just hard to let them go."

Angie hooked her arm through Rennie's. "It seems you're still trying to find them, as you did at the museum. Maybe this is how Matthias felt when he realized he was holding handwritten letters from Jesus. For the first time, he realized the present, living essence of someone he had studied but who had not been real flesh and blood to him."

Rennie looked away. "Matthias is a real person to us because we held his words in our hands."

Rennie turned to face her friend. "We've got to find those letters or learn what happened to them. This trip isn't about Matthias anymore, it's about the letters. At this moment, I am realizing that this is my purpose. It's all coming together. Those letters were safeguarded from the Romans or from the Jewish authorities and sent to Egypt. Then they came here, to London, where Matthias found them. He told us about them, so it's now our job to find and reveal them."

Rennie's thoughts were clear and determined.

"Wow," Angie whispered. "It's a little overwhelming. Should we forget about going over to Lady Jane's house?"

"No. She is the one person who might have ended up with the letters. He trusted her, or at least liked her. She seemed harmless but resourceful. Angie, consider the fact that she married some guy who traveled to the Middle East and was involved in antiquities. There are just too many connections. Tiffini and Joshua need to get back into this."

"Rennie, what if Matthias put them back into that box, from where he got them?"

"I don't think he had time. He wouldn't go back to the museum because he thought they were after him. He wanted to get them to someone who would value them and do the right thing, reveal them to the world."

Angie nodded. "What about Professor MacDonald? He might be able to help in some way."

"I forgot about him. We have so little time. Let's find out if he called our hotel." Rennie turned to cross the street. Angie pulled her back just as a car raced by and nearly hit them.

"Dang it!" Rennie yelled. "Can't they drive on the right side of the road?" She glared at the car as it disappeared around a corner. "We've got to keep going, Angie. Nothing must stop us."

"Rennie, listen to me. You've got to be careful or something bad could happen. Remember, there might be people out there who could cause us trouble."

They hurried back to the taxi. Getting in, they realized the driver was turned in his seat and looking at them.

"Ladies, as I waited for you, a car stopped behind me about a hundred feet. The driver seemed to be waiting, as I was waiting for you. When you stopped to cross the street, he suddenly raced forward. That's when you were nearly hit. His brake lights never flashed. Maybe, it was just a coincidence. Everyone drives crazy, today."

Angie pointed at Rennie. "That's it. We've got to tell someone about this."

"Not yet. We must press on. We don't have time for any distractions."

Angie told the driver to return to their hotel.

As they drove away, Rennie shifted to see out the back window, imagining where Priscilla had lived. She realized they were all gone. Those times were gone.

When they arrived at the hotel, Angie ran in to see if they had any calls.

Angie's complexion was pale when she returned to the cab.

"Angie, what happened?"

Finally, Angie grinned.

"I'm so nervous. Professor MacDonald left a message that he will be pleased to share a few minutes with us in his home this evening at seven o'clock. Can you believe it? The clerk said he sounded distinguished. At last, we get to meet him."

"Let's make it count. We have to get over to Lady Jane's townhouse, return here, and check our notes. Then, we'll meet Matthew."

Rennie gave the driver the address.

After half an hour of traffic, the taxi eased to a stop in front of 47 Berkeley Square. The driver turned and looked at his passengers.

"Here you are, ladies. That house right next door was the home of Clive of India. Is this where you wanted to be?"

Rennie peered out the window at the elegant home. Its white trimmed windows glistened against light blue walls, accented with window boxes overflowing with multi-colored flowers.

Angie checked her notes. "This is the right address," she said. "Driver, who was this Clive of India fellow?"

"He was a controversial chap. He served the British government in India and came back quite wealthy. Questions arose from his activities and there were investigations, of course. Mayfair is all about prominence and influence. Even Handel lived here, you know. Was your person someone like that?"

Rennie thought about the subtle power that Lady Jane must have wielded. "Oh, yes she was," she said firmly. "I've got a quick question. If it was 1923 and I needed to get from that first stop on Broad Court to this place, how long would that have taken?"

The driver studied her in his rear-view mirror. "Times have changed things a lot. There probably were plenty of taxis for someone to catch back then. Traffic may have been a bit different, but I'd say half an hour would be an easy time frame."

"Okay," Rennie said, "And, what if one then wanted to go from here in Mayfair to that location on Queen Victoria Street?"

The driver stroked his cheek. "That might be a little longer, perhaps close to an hour. I don't know what traffic might have been like that day, and the time of day, just as now, plays a strong role in the timing."

"What are you thinking?" Angie asked.

Rennie tilted toward her and said in a low voice, "When he left his house, the boarding house, what did he do? What could he do? He either had to take the letters to Priscilla, to Lady Jane, or to Reverend Worthy. Priscilla was probably still at work. Even if she wasn't, giving the letters to her would have shifted the risk to her, and he would not do that. Besides, what would she do with them? He must have planned to take them to Lady Jane or to Worthy. I think Jane is the more likely of the two choices. We have to focus on her now."

Angie's mouth dropped open. "Oh, my gosh, what if Lady Jane got them, and in her crafty way, she was able to get them back into the museum? Her benefactor role would have made that a possibility! The letters could be on a shelf back where they started. She could have even gotten them into the collection through her husband's activities. He might have not known about it."

"You're right," Rennie whispered. "How do we track that down and do it discreetly? We can't just go to the British Museum and ask, 'Do you happen to have in your collection some handwritten letters from Jesus, the Son of God?' Let's get back and prepare to meet Matthew."

Arriving at the hotel, they quickly surveyed the area for anyone suspicious. Rennie got out and hurried to the hotel entrance. Angie paid and thanked the driver. She asked him for a receipt.

He prepared the form and handed it to her. "Miss," he said, "I'd like to offer a thought." He hesitated. "I see a lot of people, and I don't know what it is that you and the other lady are here for. It seems you are on a quest of sorts. If it involves the high and mighty of Mayfair, or something with the British Museum and their like, you need to be careful. There are good people in both places. There are also strong but quiet forces you may not see coming until they are there. They don't like intruders in their world. I just hope you're careful."

Rennie stood at the door, holding it open. She studied who was out on the street. As Angie approached, Rennie said, "hurry, get in."

They stopped in the lobby. "Angie, I think someone was watching us. There was a guy down the street who seemed to be just standing there doing nothing. When we got out of the cab, he turned and walked away."

"Should I go out and look?" Angie replied.

"No, don't do that."

"What are we going to do? They seem to be everywhere."

"Let's do this. We'll freshen up for a few minutes, then I'll meet you down here. We'll find some place to eat, review our notes for our meeting with Matthew, and then we'll go see him. All the time, with every step, we need to be extra careful."

"Sounds like a plan. I don't know how to say this, but that taxi driver used the word 'quest' and that's what this feels like." Angie took a deep breath.

"I feel the same way. The neat thing is that we didn't choose this. Maybe more interesting, we might not be in charge. Do you feel that? It's strange and sometimes ominous. Events are pushing us forward. Okay, let's meet in fifteen minutes."

PART EIGHT

London, UK

VIII - 1

Rennie and Angie left a small restaurant just north of the University of London campus. They strolled in silence through the light of the late day, but they were on guard for who might be watching them.

"That's a nice place. I'm glad we went there," Rennie said, trying to lighten the moment.

"Yeah, it was. The hotel was right; decent food, nice atmosphere. I'm looking forward to our meeting with Professor MacDonald. It'll be interesting to see if he even knows about Professor Justus. There's no telling if Priscilla even mentioned him."

Rennie laughed. "I'm beginning to think there is no point to our planning anything here. It's just one surprise after another. Of course, some surprises are not welcome."

She stopped, suddenly intense. "Angie, in some ways I'm sorry you're involved in this because of the risks. I didn't expect it would turn out like this. I don't know who wants to cause me or us harm."

"That's alright. Neither of us expected something sinister. I think the main reason I'm on this journey is my experiencing a renewal of faith. The story of Matthias and what he found made me aware of a new, personal connection we have with God."

"That's what hit me, too. I'm determined to see this through, wherever it goes. At some point, we need to take a stand. If those letters can be found, I'll get them and make them known to the world."

Rennie noticed a taxi coming and stepped toward the street, waving at the vehicle. She held back at the curb and looked for the direction of traffic. Glancing at Angie, she said, "I'll never figure out what direction cars are coming from. Let's go!"

They dashed across the empty street to the awaiting cab and gave the driver the address for Professor MacDonald.

Once settled in the back seat, Angie said, "I'm excited about meeting Matthew. I hope it works for his benefit as well as ours. From what Mary told us, he's had a rough life."

Rennie was energized. "Besides finding out what happened to Matthias, we've got to track down the letters. Matthew's knowledge of the museum and expertise in the ancient Middle East might be useful."

Although light outside, the sun slipped behind the buildings, casting blocks of darkness. The taxi quietly rolled along the narrow road flanked with flat-fronted buildings rising a uniform three stories high. The evening light and gentle ride provided the calm they needed to prepare for their encounter.

Torrington Place continued on as Tavistock Place when they crossed Woburn Place. Fifteen minutes later, the taxi turned left onto Gray's Inn Road and then another left on Cromer Street. The driver stopped and turned on the interior lights of the vehicle.

"Here we are, ladies. Enjoy your evening."

Angie paid the driver. She stepped onto the sidewalk where Rennie was waiting. "Are you ready?"

Rennie took a deep breath. "This will be interesting."

They checked the address against their notes and then stepped up to the door. Rennie gently placed her fingertip against the doorbell button. Her thoughts filled with questions about Matthew and whether he would help them. She pressed the button, took another breath, and then saw a light go on through a small pane of glass at the top of the door.

The lock on the door snapped open. A light next to the door

went on, surprising them. As the door opened, they stepped back.

"Good evening, ladies," the old man said crisply. "Please come in." He stepped to the side and gestured down the hall.

Rennie stepped forward and extended her hand to the man. "Professor MacDonald? I'm Rennie Haran, and this is Angie McGrady. We're very pleased to meet you. Thank you for taking this time to see us."

Standing so close to him gave her a chance to see his face clearly. She was pleasantly surprised with the idea that he looked a little like Santa Claus. His short beard was white. The top of his head was bald but the hair on the sides of his head was thick and also white. He had a gentle smile, and his eyes truly seemed to have a twinkle in them. She motioned to Angie to step forward.

Professor MacDonald shook their hands and offered a slight bow to each.

"Please come in, ladies. I'll get the door and we can visit as you may need. I'm not clear as to why I may be honored with your effort. Please follow me to my study."

As they proceeded down the dimly lit hallway, they glanced at photos on the walls. There were shots of people from different eras, drawings of ancient places and maps, and small artwork.

The professor walked with a slow grace, his shoulders slightly forward, as though he had carried many burdens in his life. Although the temperature was comfortable, he wore a sweater. On his feet were woolen stockings and sandals.

In the study, he gestured to a small couch. He eased himself into a wingback leather chair that looked as old as he was. Music played at a low level in the background.

Rennie cleared her throat. "Professor, I'd like to thank you again. It's a delight to meet you. I don't know exactly where to begin."

"Sometimes there is no beginning and no ending," he said with a smile.

Rennie chuckled. "Well said, sir. That seems to be the case with this adventure. I'm not sure when it began, and I don't have a clue when it might end."

"Who is it again that you ladies are with?"

"I'm a reporter with a newspaper in Des Moines, Iowa, in the central part of the United States. Miss McGrady here is with a small college just south of Des Moines, called Simpson College. She's the librarian and director of the archives there. I'm doing a story on a professor from Simpson who came to work at the British Museum in the 1920's. His name was Matthias Justus."

The professor nodded and clasped his hands together in his lap.

"Angie helped gather materials from the library archives. I researched old information indicating he had known various people while he worked at the museum. One of them was a young woman by the name of Priscilla Shefford."

The old man's gaze didn't flinch.

Rennie continued. "We thought that she and you might have been related." She waited again. He said nothing.

Angie slipped forward on the couch. "Professor, we wondered if you could share any information about Miss Shefford or Professor Justus. There are some gaps in the story about him, and we hoped you might be able to help us fill them in."

He listened intently and smiled warmly. "I will do what I can, ladies. I'm not sure how to ask this, but I wonder what lies beneath your interest. You have come a very long distance to check an employment record."

"Professor," Angie continued, "I don't know if we can tell you why we're here. It's not a secret. I think we've become so involved in the story of this man we need to learn more. Anything you can tell us will help."

"I'll do what I can."

He became quiet for a few moments and tugged lightly on

his beard. His eyes focused on a distant point across the room. "Before we proceed, can you tell me something of this professor you mentioned. What sort of chap was he?"

With a slight motion of her hand, Angie indicated to Rennie that she should respond.

"My research and my interpretation of what he wrote in his journals, demonstrated that he was a respected scholar, skilled in ancient languages. He had an innocent, positive energy, and was a good man, as well as a man of faith. He had a very strong faith at the end."

"I see," Matthew said. "How is it that you see him as a good man? People see good in many ways. Some men are good at what they do but their acts are abhorrent in the perspective of others. What made this man good, at least as you see him?"

Rennie grinned. "I have a feeling we're not going to leave here without a few lessons."

"That's not my intention. I am simply inquisitive. When one studies other people, whether it is an entire culture or just one person, it's important to know of the culture from which they arose."

Rennie studied the old man. He appeared weary on the exterior, but he thought quickly and deeply. She liked him. "Professor, I believe Professor Justus was a man who tried to do the right thing. He loved from his heart, he worked with diligence, and he died far too soon."

"You mentioned something about journals. Were these personal diaries or records of his work?"

"The ones I came across were like personal diaries from his work at the British Museum. He used some books that were apparently intended for documenting archeological work. His entries said little about his work and were mostly devoted to commentary on the people he worked with."

"What did he say about them?" Professor MacDonald asked.

Rennie felt a sudden chill spread through her shoulders. She blinked for a moment and then swallowed. She realized she was sitting with Priscilla's son, talking about Matthias.

"There were a few key people: his boss, a Mr. Warrington, his co-worker Miss Shefford, Lady Jane Sotterfeld-Gris, and a church official, Reverend Worthy. Of these, Priscilla, or Miss Shefford was most important."

Rennie swallowed again. "I'm so sorry. I don't know what's wrong with me. I must be tired." She took a deep breath. "I can simply say, Professor Justus was deeply in love with Miss Shefford. He wrote wonderful things about her. There is no question how he felt. Then he died. It's quite sad. I guess that's why I feel some emotion about it all."

Professor MacDonald smiled with loving compassion. "And what happened, according to your information?"

"He was nearing the end of his work here and was about to return to Iowa. He came across something in his work that was profoundly important, and it distracted him. He wanted Priscilla to return to Iowa with him, but he died before he could ask her. I guess she then left the museum and got married. That's all we know and why we are here with you this evening."

"Miss Haran, did he indicate in these journals whether she was so inclined to go with him? I also heard you say something about him discovering something. Can you tell me about that?"

Rennie looked at Angie, but she offered no help. "Well, based on what he wrote, her feelings were similar to his. She was quite a remarkable woman. He was very impressed with her strength and her values."

A wide smile became visible in Professor MacDonald's whiskers.

Rennie cleared her throat again. "Professor, one of our early questions and why we are here with you this evening relates to Priscilla. Our research suggests she may have been your mother.

Forgive me for being so direct. I guess that's the reporter in me."

"I'm certain you're a very good reporter Miss Haran, and on that point, you are quite correct. I am her first born."

Rennie stared at him without breathing, then realized what she was doing and looked at Angie.

"Was Mary her second, and your sister?" Angie eagerly asked.

A full smile grew in the old man's face. "You have done your research well, ladies."

Rennie sat back and took a breath. "Professor, this is one of the points where we are confused. Priscilla was clearly in love with Professor Justus, and shortly after his death, she left the museum and married your father. I mean no disrespect sir, but it doesn't make any sense to me."

Professor MacDonald nodded slowly. His expression became serious.

Angie spoke up. "Professor, we visited with Mary yesterday. We went to her care facility and talked with her for a few minutes. She's led a life that's, uh, interesting. She told us life was hard for you in those early years. Your father did not sound like a supportive or even kind person. That's Mary's perspective of course. This is all a little off the topic, but it relates to Priscilla."

Professor MacDonald breathed what looked like a sad sigh. He slowly rose from his chair and walked around to its back. Placing both hands on top of the chair he said, "Ladies, this might last longer than we expected. Would you like some tea?"

"Yes, thank you," they replied.

He casually walked out of the room and could be heard in the kitchen, running water and placing a pot on the stove.

Rennie's thoughts drifted through Matthias's journals as she surveyed the room.

Angie whispered, "Is that opera playing in the background?"

Rennie listened for a moment. "I think so." She smiled. "In

his journal, Matthias spoke of how he and Priscilla enjoyed opera and a particular composer. The coincidences just don't stop."

Professor MacDonald returned with a wicker tray holding a teapot, three cups on saucers, milk, sugar, spoons, and napkins.

"I hope you don't mind. I selected a brew for us. I picked it up in Beirut on a recent trip through there to Turkey."

"What's of interest in Turkey, Professor?" Rennie asked. "It sounds terribly dangerous."

"Well, one of the great mysteries of Christendom and of archeologists is what happened to one of the earliest of churches, the one in Antioch. I have joined with others to make inquiries about continuing the efforts to pursue that sort of expedition."

He set the tray on the coffee table and asked them to partake in a refreshment.

Rennie poured tea into two cups and handed one to Angie. "I was just thinking about what you said about Antioch. What has been discovered from there? Are there any relics or documents of any kind?"

Matthew eased back into his chair with a cup of tea. "Well, I am impressed with your interest. Unfortunately, nothing has ever been found from that early church period. The city was ultimately devastated in 713. All we have are a few early maps or renderings from educated guesses. That is why getting another dig started there would be so beneficial to history, to the church, and to our understanding of the era. Some excavations were begun in 1979, but hardly 10 percent of the area has been worked. Although the site is in Turkey, it is very close to Syria, and working near borders in this part of the world can cause unnecessary tensions. The recent events in Syria and Iraq have raised new problems with the finding of antiquities. Frankly, it's rather dangerous and our visit had to be brief." He sipped his tea.

Angie and Rennie tried their tea. Angie added some milk to hers and said, "This is yummy."

Rennie was deep in thought about the box from Antioch that Matthias had found. He found the letters from Jesus in it. "Professor, could there be items from Antioch in museums that haven't been identified?"

"There certainly are. Over the last one hundred years or so, there have been many expeditions by the French, the Italians, the Germans, and of course, us Brits. Those who led the efforts were originally indifferent to and ignorant of the modern concerns that archeologists have now. They simply dug things up and took them away. In the twenties, the craft took on a much more technical approach, to the benefit of our understanding of those items that were found. If one considers the millions of items held in museums and libraries all over the world, and if we consider the fact that only a small portion them have been examined, it is likely that a treasure from Antioch or elsewhere is sitting on a shelf." He sipped more tea.

Rennie's tea remained untouched since her first taste. She felt weak, knowing that finding the letters from Jesus is reasonable if not probable. "Professor, what would happen if some treasure was found in a collection? Would it be announced?"

He leaned his head back against the leather. "It would depend upon how it is found and what it was. In this discipline, it is important for new discoveries to be related to the context in which they were found. For example, if a sealed jar is found within some ruins, it must be evaluated in that environment, amidst other things or simply in the strata of the ruins. That context tells of the nature and authenticity of the find. If one were to have happened upon what are called the Dead Sea Scrolls on a shelf in the Israel Antiquities Authority without knowing how they got there, the full understanding of their origins would be less than finding them in the cave. Their intrinsic truth would not change but whether the world recognizes that truth is an open question."

He set down his teacup and used a remote control to turn off the background music. "Ladies, I appreciate your interest in this topic. There is an ongoing and sometimes rather bitter debate in the field regarding items that seemingly pop up from the collector world. The recent controversies over the James ossuary are a fine example. What is disappointing is the lack of civil discussion and review on these matters."

As the professor refreshed his tea, Angie set her cup down. "From my work with library archival material, I understand what you're saying. That work involves documents rather than jars. Wouldn't the legitimacy of a document stand on its own, regardless of how it's found? It would seem that one could date it and read it and discern some reasonable truths about it."

"You are quite right. For example, the 'Damascus Rule Document' was found in this way, in a synagogue storeroom in Cairo. That was fifty years prior to the Qumran discoveries. Finding those synagogue scrolls was a watershed in scroll research. While the documents themselves can be fairly well placed in history, one dilemma that is difficult to establish is their authorship. For example, did a priest, some lowly scribe, or someone with historical weight write them? This returns us to the issue of context. The more surrounding evidence of a find, the better it will be regarded. I've gotten a bit off track, haven't I?"

Rennie chuckled. "You won't believe how on target we are right now regarding our agenda. I've just realized how big our agenda really is!"

They all laughed. When quiet returned, Rennie continued. "Would you share with us some insights about your parents and yourself. We have a sincere interest in you as a result of reading the journals of Professor Justus."

Professor MacDonald set down his cup and saucer. His eyes flickered and he stroked his beard. He appeared to sigh. "Ladies, I'm an old man, and maybe with age I'm less concerned with the details of the life I've lived than I am with its truth. As an arrow is sent from the bow, we begin a course in life that we can do little about. How one sees that path will vary depending upon one's perspective. I think your coming here affords me an opportunity to look at that perspective in a fresh and honest way."

Professor MacDonald rose from the chair and ambled to the door. "Would you join me please? I would like to share with you something special I have shared with no one before. Please follow me." He appeared more tired and frail than before.

Rennie and Angie followed him down the hallway to a small bedroom. He eased into a simple wooden chair next to the bed and gestured for his guests to sit in the chairs at a small table. He rested one hand on the bed and stroked the quilt.

"Ladies, this is the second of two bedrooms in our home. This room is where our children Sarah and John grew up. When they became six or eight years old, I renovated a room in the basement for John's room. He became a fine fellow, gentle and smart. Sarah is simply wonderful."

"Both brought grandchildren into our lives. David and Elizabeth are Sarah's children and John has Dawn, Richard, and Christine. Sarah was the rock I needed when my wife, Ruth, passed on in 1983. How can it be so long ago when it seems like last week?"

He lifted a crystal-framed photo from a nightstand and dusted the glass with his sleeve. "Like the Ruth of the Bible, my wife was persevering and had a heart that God must have filled daily. She went to sleep forever, here in this bed."

"Prior to my Ruth using this bed, another one as dear to me rested here and then slept forever. It was my mother. The woman you know as Priscilla ended her days here. She was an amazing woman, and I am proud to be her son."

He put a handkerchief to his mouth and coughed lightly. Then, he smiled. "I could speak to you in praise of her for many days. She was a woman of beauty, strength, courage, and vision."

A somber look hardened his face. "You wonder why she ended up with Reggie MacDonald. Many asked how that could happen. I struggled to understand it for most of my life. When she came here, we discussed many things. Now, I see her decision as one of courage and not foolishness."

Rennie sensed his anguish. "I made decisions out of what I thought was love or passion that I later regretted. At the time I made them, I was doing the best I could do. They felt right at the time."

"Thank you for that thought, dear. I do not think she ever loved Reggie. I doubt she could have loved a man who was a living testament to a world she despised. She thought he was strong, and that meant survival and possibly hope. In her heart, she knew she could not respect him. Ultimately, his death gave her the freedom to grow into a new life that was more fitting for her mind and heart. I am eternally grateful that she had that opportunity."

"Professor, tell us more," Angie said.

He leaned back in his chair. "My mother had only one true love in her life, except for her children, of course, and that was a young professor from America."

Angie placed her hand over her eyes and took a deep breath.

"It is a sad love story. I was so appreciative of what you said about his feelings. Until that moment, I didn't know his true feelings. I only knew my mother's love for him and her belief in his love for her."

"After he died on that tragic night, she had nowhere to turn. Her heart was in ruins. There was chaos at the museum, and rumors of all kinds. Reggie stepped in, and out of desperation, she accepted his rescue. When she was here with me, she revealed the story."

Rennie struggled to set aside her confused emotions and her

eagerness for the facts. "Please tell us what you know about the last days of Matthias."

Matthew rested his elbows on the arms of the chair. He stared at a map on the wall. "A problem developed at the museum. My mother said Matthias seemed to be in a different, serene place. It bothered her. She thought it might be from his plans to return home and his hopes and expectations that she would join him. That was her plan as well."

He grinned and shook his head. "One day, a police matter occurred regarding some shipments of precious artifacts and possible thievery. A fellow named Mort was their chief suspect. The authorities needed Matthias' assistance in prosecuting the case."

Rennie interrupted him. "Did they suspect Matthias?"

"Goodness, no."

"So, did Mort kill him?" Angie blurted out.

"I don't think old Mort could have done that. He was quite smitten by my mother and felt protective of her. He would not have murdered the man whom he knew was my mother's love. For an unknown reason, Matthias left the museum during an afternoon break in work, and he never returned. My mother learned later that Professor Justus went to his flat and from there, he went to the town home of a Lady."

"Was that Lady Jane Sotterfeld-Gris?" Rennie asked in a dry, interview tone.

"Yes, it was. You ladies did a remarkable job with your research. He went to see Jane, as she preferred we speak of her. She related that Matthias had come to tell of a discovery he had made and he needed to entrust it to her. With her at that moment was a church official—"

"Reverend Worthy?" Rennie interrupted again.

"Yes, Worthy was there. According to Jane, the presence of Reverend Worthy chilled the revelations that Matthias wished to share with her. From there, we could only surmise how he ended up being murdered."

"Professor," Rennie said carefully, "how is it you came to know Lady Jane and had what seems to have been a familiar relationship?"

"That is another interesting story. Perhaps we may get to that. There is so much to tell, but it is getting late. Do you want to continue?"

Angie blurted out, "Yes!"

"Very well then, I will share with you the stories my mother told me in her last months here. I believe she told them to me with relief as well as joy. Hearing it all was a blessing to me beyond measure."

"When I was a boy, Reggie regarded me as a project to turn into a man like himself. He took me to events that grown men should not see. He told me life was brutal and the sooner I saw it that way, the more likely I would survive. We saw men fight in the streets, men stealing and doing all forms of evil things."

"I'm sorry," Rennie whispered.

"I was repulsed by it all, and he knew it. He became even more determined to form me into that ugly sort of manhood. My mother objected mightily, and he answered her reproaches in his usual, hurtful manner. She did her best to protect me from his influence as well as guide me to another path. In my teen years, he was finished with me. He said I had enough education and it was time to get out and make my way like a man."

"How old were you then?" Rennie asked.

"I was fourteen. My mother and I had secretly and almost desperately spent years in special studies in the arts, history, and basic curricula. So, I was years ahead of others in my school. It wasn't the education that bothered him."

"It was the competition," Angie said.

"Exactly, my dear. But I later learned from my mother it was far more than me."

Rennie impatiently tapped her knee. "You referred to Lady Jane as Jane."

"Yes, we did. Unknown to everyone, she and my mother were secret friends. I later learned why. But this is where it may be interesting for you ladies. I had been away at a marvelous school on scholarship for about a year when I learned of Reggie's death. I came home to console my mother and my sister, but there was little need for that. As Mary may have said, Reggie had been very abusive to them. In fact, he died after an episode in which he terrorized them."

The old man took a deep breath. "As my mother finally told me, Reggie was found one evening mistreating my sister. My mother became enraged, and he laughed at her. That was the night she told him that I was not his son."

Both women gasped.

"Yes, quite a surprise for him as well. He taunted her and insulted her, denying what he had heard. Then she told him the truth. I am the son of Matthias Justus."

Rennie was so stunned she felt weak.

"That is why, when my father, Matthias, was murdered, my mother needed to be sheltered in marriage. If her pregnancy had become known to those at the museum and she was not married, she would have been immediately discharged. We would have had a future more bleak than one with Reggie."

"As it turned out, once she knew her condition, it was at a time when Reggie pursued her. They were quickly married to his delight and he believed that I was the product of their matrimony; until that night."

Matthew's expression became intense. He looked down at the comforter on the bed. "When she was here, she said Reggie became enraged when she told him the truth. He beat her. Then he went to a local pub and arrogantly told those around him what he had done to her. Mort, my mother's old friend from the museum stood nearby. The man had always loved her and knew he could never have her. Hearing what Reggie had done, Mort followed him from the pub and ran a blade into each of his kidneys. Neighbors told my mother that Reggie crawled for nearly a block as people he had treated badly laughed at him. It is quite sad, really."

Matthew closed his eyes, resting. Rennie felt exhausted.

Slowly, a smile came to his face. "So, the man you see before you is the son of the man you have studied with such profound attention. Mother revealed all this to Jane in an incidental meeting when I was a young lad. Jane had a genuine fondness for my father, so that connection bonded her with mother as secret friends until Reggie died. Jane gave me the scholarship when Reggie tossed me from the house."

Matthew's eyes sparkled. "Jane knew that my mother and Matthias were a perfect match. Jane was a special person in many ways. It was her generosity that enabled me to attend college. She often attended my special events with my mother, as if we were family. She hired my mother to serve in a position in her foundation, allowing my mother to blossom and finally achieve the life she hoped for."

Angie rubbed her temples and squinted. "Who were the women that came to Iowa?"

"Jane attended the funeral and made the arrangements. After Reggie died, she provided the funds for mother and me to visit Iowa to see my father's college and his grave."

Matthew swallowed hard. "I believe that trip inspired me to travel and investigate. I have wanted to return to Iowa, but I do not see that now."

Angie replied, "If you can make it to Beirut, you can get to Iowa."

"Maybe so. I'll forever be grateful to Jane for the trip to Iowa. The death of her husband was sad and bizarre. She became fearful after that, surrounding herself with protective people. She even had someone watch after my mother until she came to live with me."

Rennie stood and stretched. "I'm sorry, I need to move. This story is simply amazing. I just cannot take it all in."

Matthew rubbed his face. "I understand. Frankly, I'm also weary. There is one key event that you want to know and need to know. Mother told me in her last weeks how my father Matthias died."

His shoulders slumped forward, and he stroked his beard. "Mother said that on the night she and Reggie had their big, last argument, he told her he had run into Matthias on the street near her house. My father had gone to see Jane about some urgent matter and was on his way to mother's place. In his typical way, Reggie and his fellow toughs accosted Matthias and told him to stay away from my mother. He didn't have a chance. Reggie put a knife into him and threw him into the river. I'm sorry. I believe it is the true and final account."

Rennie glared at him. "Reggie," she hissed.

Matthew stood. "Will you both be available tomorrow? It would be most pleasing if we could meet again for brunch and continue. I feel I've found long lost family from America."

"That's a good idea," Angie suggested. "We could get the rest we need, process all of this, and get a fresh start tomorrow. How soon could we meet, professor?"

"I am a bit weary from my recent trip. If we could meet tomorrow morning at nine thirty, we can continue to share some stories. I would dearly appreciate hearing more from you."

"Okay, deal," Rennie said. "You let us know where, then we need to get back to our hotel."

Matthew wrote a restaurant's name and address on a slip of paper and gave it to Rennie. As he called for a cab, she opened the front door and peered into the night. She remembered the threats she had faced in pursuing this story of Professor Justus. Out there in the darkness, she imagined another Reggie, waiting to kill. Anger and determination moved her out the door to another day.

London, UK

VIII - 2

The lobby of the hotel was calm and felt empty. Rennie sat in a floral upholstered chair near the windows opening to a courtyard in the rear of the property. Her arms were loosely draped over the wide, stuffed arms of the chair. The morning sun poured onto her as a warm embrace. She looked at her watch. It read 8:32. She turned her head to see Angie come down the last steps.

Angie collapsed into a similar chair nearby. "I feel drained, and yet, I am so eager to see Matthew again."

"I feel the same way, I wish we had a few more days here. I have so much affection for that old man. Somehow, we need to get him to Iowa for a visit." She imagined Professor MacDonald walking across campus at Simpson College, honoring his father's memory.

"Rennie, what you have done is amazing. Our visit with Professor MacDonald has given him a chance for real peace with his past. It has also cleared the record of the life of Professor Justus. You and I are changed, too. That's a big result for some little assignment you took on."

"Thanks. I know those things are probably true. There remains the unfinished business with the letters. Professor MacDonald didn't say anything about them. I don't know how to bring them up."

"I know." Angie sat up straight. "Either they ended up in Reggie's filthy hands or went floating down the river. Either way, they're gone. It's an unbelievable loss."

"It's too hard to accept. They've been safeguarded through

history for a purpose. I've tried to consider all the options, and I can't come up with anything. It's the classic struggle between good and evil, and evil is winning."

Angie blushed. "I think not. We must put the good versus evil thing into some perspective. You know I'm a procedure type of person. The whole universe is very orderly, but people are the wild card in the system."

Rennie gave a thumbs-up sign.

"I'm not exactly a faith driven person," Angie added, "but I know the world is a temporary place. So, what happens here and with the letters, isn't the whole ball game. On balance, we have a massive amount of good prevailing."

Angie got up and walked to the windows. She folded her arms and stared outside.

"They say we shouldn't hide the light of our spirit under a basket. Sometimes though, I'd like to take that light, whack a few people in the head, and drag them out of the dark."

Rennie eased out of her chair and joined Angie at the window.

"I don't know. People of peace are a distinct minority. I'm not sure that hitting the bad guys with anything will make a difference. Besides, the hitting thing may not be in the procedure manual."

Angie leaned against the window frame and gazed at the flowers and manicured hedges.

Rennie poked her in the shoulder. "Listen, crazy librarian, humanity can't get beyond a 51 to 49 good to evil ratio, if it's that good. In fact, it's probably 80-20, bad to good. Finding and revealing the letters from Jesus might have helped those odds by enlightening a few more people."

Angie pointed her finger at Rennie's nose. "Are you done with all this rambling metaphor stuff? Those letters are important, and we need to find out what happened to them."

Angie took a breath and stepped back. "Maybe I'm speaking

as a professional in library and archival science. Being orderly, doing the right thing, is big for me. I like the whole idea of grace, but I'm a technical, practical person."

"We are different Angie, and your fixation on procedures sometimes makes me crazy. But I also look for some sense of justice. At least I used to. It was part of the energy I put into every article I wrote. I don't know where I'm at with that, now."

They stood awkwardly looking into the garden area. Rennie had felt good about what they accomplished in London, but she wondered if her responsibility for the story was bigger than she knew.

Finally, she said, "We'd better get on our toes. We have our meeting with Matthew."

"Yeah, I'm not clear on what else we need to ask him. He really laid out the whole story last night. I still can't believe it. I think it's a miracle how he grew up in that bizarre household, saw what he saw, was treated like dirt, and he became such a teddy bear. He's a brilliant guy and is so gentle and positive. Sure, he's got great genes, but even they can be wounded."

Rennie grabbed her bag and swung it over her shoulder. "Let's go."

Angie caught up with her in a few steps. "Let's be sure to talk to Matthew about Mary. He should go see her. If that relationship could be healed, that would be a blessing for both of them."

"You're right. He's probably the only family she has. I got the impression last night that he sees her more as a distant relative."

Rennie stopped and grabbed Angie's arm.

"Before we go out, we have to remember there might be someone out there, tracking us. We don't know what they want, but it's connected with Professor Justus and with what he found. I've been thinking about this. They must think we have an idea where the letters are and they are after them, too. This is about the letters."

They cautiously left the hotel and proceeded down the sidewalk. They looked in the windows of stores and observed what people were wearing and how they wore their hair. All the while alert to everyone in the area. Soon, they relaxed and were giggling and whispering as schoolgirls.

Angie pointed at a cab. They waved and yelled together at it, and then laughed even more as they ran down the street to get in.

London, UK

VIII - 3

They arrived at the restaurant on Euston Road and realized they were ten minutes early for their meeting with Matthew. Enjoying the new day, they strolled down the block to enjoy a closer view of the classic, elegant St. Pancras Station.

"It looks more like a palace than a train station," exclaimed Angie.

"People sure know how to do things right over here."

Continuing down the street toward the new British Library, they forgot the possible danger around them. Angie noticed the professor. "Hey, Professor MacDonald!" she shouted and hurried to meet him. She put her arm through his and clung to him. He displayed a toothy smile.

Inside the restaurant, Matthew greeted the manager warmly. She said she was happy to see him and asked about his trip as the party was ushered to a table near the front window. The ambiance was friendly and quiet.

Slipping onto her chair, Rennie beamed, "I'm so happy to see you. It was only last night when we were together, but everything feels so different now."

Angie agreed. "Not only that, I've decided to adopt you. I never knew my grandparents because they were gone when I was little, and you're too old to marry."

"I must say, I am at once humbled with compliment and wounded with disappointment," he replied laughing.

The server took their orders and returned with a teapot and cups with saucers as the party chatted about the day. They poured their tea, stirred, and tasted it while enjoying the comfort of their fellowship.

"Dear ladies, when you left my home last evening, I rested better than I can remember. You have helped me begin to find a deeper peace than I already enjoyed. For that, I thank you." Matthew raised his cup as a toast to the two young women.

Rennie tapped her cup against his. "We need to thank you. You've enabled us to bring closure on most of this beautiful but sad story that we've struggled with for the past two weeks. Without you, we would've been left with uncertainty and no ending. You're the beginning of a new chapter in the lives of Matthias and Priscilla's love, the new hope. That reminds me of something he wrote in his journal. He mentioned that his deceased wife's name was Hope."

Matthew sighed. "Tell me please, more about him, his wife, and his family."

"The simple story is that Matthias was an Iowa farm boy. We can only guess at the deeper, complex story. He came from a small town. He had a good mind and a great heart. From what he put in his journals, and that is all I have, he was proud of his parents. His father was an inventive fellow, worked at farming and in construction, and died in a mining accident. His mother died in the flu pandemic."

Rennie related what she knew and was surprised with her comfortable and complete awareness of the man's life.

"He was gifted in old languages and wrote articles about ancient times in the Middle East and Bible related matters. He knew Latin, Hebrew, Aramaic, and Greek. He came here for a temporary assignment at the British Museum to get away, to see something different. Of course, as we all know, he found new love."

"And," Matthew added, "he did something about it! Oh, sorry."

The women teased him.

"There is one other thing," Rennie added. "A big thing. Matthias found something while he was working in the collection."

"What was that?" Matthew asked.

Angie and Rennie glanced at each other. Rennie continued, "Well, he found some documents that relate to an early Christian period. I think they were letters. Could that have happened, professor? I hate to be terribly ignorant, but did they write letters back then?"

"Of course. I don't know what era you speak of, but the record is replete with documents going back two millennia before Christ. It was common for people throughout ancient times to write on ostraka, or pot sherds, on clay and wooden tablets, on animal skins, and of course on papyrus. Correspondence included personal letters, business transactions, and everyday issues as we have now. Among the Jews, boys were expected to read the Torah to grow into adulthood."

Matthew looked thoughtful for a moment. "What Matthias came across may have struck his fancy, given his language skills and appreciation for history. We've hardly scratched the surface in examining what we already hold in our institutions. Was he a man of faith? Did he speak of that?"

"Oh, yes." Rennie again glanced at Angie. "I think his faith shifted from intellectual to personal while he was here."

"I imagine that could happen, especially if he found new love." Matthew was interrupted when the server brought their food. "Ladies, I'd like to know more about each of you. Tell me about yourself, Angie. I think of Angel when I see you."

"Well, that would be accurate, but everyone says 'Angie.' I'm not that interesting. I'm a librarian, after all. I've lived a fairly normal life. I'm not married. I was in a relationship that was just going along. It's on hold right now. The only outside interests I have are digital photography."

Matthew grinned. "So, you're a creative technician."

"I don't know how creative my work is. I play with setting up Web sites for students and friends. I find the Internet and the wealth of information on it to be extraordinary. The fact that it's 99 percent free, except for the service provider, is a gift beyond measure to people with inquiring minds. I only wish it could be accessible to more people."

Angie paused, "Okay, Rennie, your turn."

Rennie feigned surprise. "Sorry, I've been a little distracted by something." Rennie stared at the large window exposing the street.

Matthew and Angie turned to see what caught her attention.

"What is it?" Matthew asked.

"Some guy has walked past the window a couple of times. Each time, he casually looked in as though he isn't interested, but at the same time, I think he is. There's just something in my gut. Hey, there he is again!"

Matthew and Angie spun around to see the suspect.

Rennie stood up, and as she did, the man looked in the window and saw her. He raced out of view.

Rennie hurried to the door.

"Rennie, wait. Don't." Angie called to her.

Reaching the door, she hesitated. Then, she burst out onto the sidewalk and yelled to the man, who was near the end of the block. "Hey there!"

He didn't stop.

Rennie glanced inside and then back at the man. He reached the corner and disappeared past the building.

Rennie was breathing heavily when she returned to the table. Her mind was racing, and her stomach churned with anger.

"Who do you think that was?" Matthew asked her.

"I don't know. We've garnered the attention of someone rather shy." Rennie tried to grin. "I'm sure it's nothing. He probably saw a couple of hot, American chicks and thought we'd ask him to join us if he walked past enough times."

No one spoke for a moment.

"I'm sorry to get weird on you. Where were we?" Rennie pretended to relax.

Angie glanced out the window and responded, "Matthew asked about us, and it's your turn."

"Oh, that's right. Being a reporter, I don't give information. I only ask questions. Just kidding. Well, I'm inclined to evaluate how information relates to bigger issues. When I think of how I approach things, it's from a macro or systems perspective. That probably gets me into trouble. I tend to see activities or relationships that convey more meaning to me than to others, like seeing suspicious pedestrians."

They all laughed.

"Well, someone needs to see the big picture," Matthew added.

Rennie stared out the window. "Seeing situations from the systems view points out how individual actions can skew the results of a process. Sometimes that can be intentional and even corrupt. A person who is focused on a specific task may not recognize, that doing one thing affects the outcome of the larger process. A good reporter sees how one person or one decision affects many others."

Matthew replied, "Taking your perceptions to a more personal level, would you say you may be inclined to see the right and wrong in issues, more than other reporters might see them?"

Rennie grinned at Angie and then Matthew. "Have you two been talking about me? I doubt many people in the whole media system care about right and wrong. They get hung up on the so-called objectivity of our job. Taking a critical view of some issue forces one to the fringe of the industry. Except for government, the media is the only entity that can affect society on a community or even national scale. Doing that is actually our responsibility."

"So, where does that leave you? It seems you have a heart for what is right and not just for facts barren of life." Matthew stroked his beard and studied her.

"Good question. It's something every person of conscience in every profession must deal with. I'm sure Matthias felt that. If we don't have a conscience and a sense of purpose of what to do with it, the very few who have a position of any kind will prevail. That's probably what brought me to London."

Rennie studied Matthew. "We'd love to know more about you."

"Ha, this old man can bore you for hours. But then, there may be some surprises in store."

PART NINE

London, UK

IX - 1

"Judy, get Sfumato on the phone, now!" Seth Galila screamed to his assistant.

"Yes sir, right away," she replied as she hurried to her desk. "Mr. Galila, it's probably very early in the morning in California," she said fearfully.

"Do you think I care?" he roared. "Get him, now! Idiot," he said quietly. "I know what time it is there."

He paced across his office and studied the morning traffic filling the road outside his window. His fury made his teeth chatter.

"Judy," he yelled again. "Get Daniel in here!"

"Yes, sir," she muttered. "There is no answer at Mr. Sfumato's number."

He strode to her office door and gazed at her. "Did you dial the right number, Judy?" he asked with bittersweet sarcasm.

"I'm certain I did. I'll try again, sir."

"Please do, Judy. I have the feeling that a man of Sfumato's status might have a messaging service." He flexed his fists.

Galila paced across his office. Stuffing his hands into his pockets, he kicked one heel into the thick green carpet as he turned to glare at his assistant's office door.

Judy called out to let him know she had a connection with the elusive phone in California. "The recording is running," she added.

Galila grabbed the phone from his desk and sneered. "Hello,

dear friend. I regret the timing of this call, but I especially regret that I cannot at this moment let you know personally that you had better get your people out of London. It is not a safe city."

The tone of his voice shifted from snide to anger. "I will not tolerate you or your people getting in the way of my business!"

He slammed down the phone and pushed it aside. "Where's Daniel?" he shouted.

A few minutes later, Judy let him know that Daniel was on his way into the building.

When the man arrived, he carefully took a step into the office.

Galila stepped away from the window where he had been in deep thought and pointed at a chair in front of the desk.

Daniel hesitated for a moment before going to the chair and sitting.

Galila turned again to face the window. "So, it is my understanding that your people were unable to perform their duties. Is that correct?"

"Our man at the hotel tried to do —"

"He didn't do his job!" Galila screamed.

"Sir, you are right, but he was going to until they got to him," Daniel quickly added.

"Tell me exactly what that means."

"Well, when the ladies were at their meeting, my man was prepared to enter their rooms and do his research. Two fellows showed up in the hallway outside the rooms, introduced themselves as hotel security, and had him come with them. They took him down a stairwell, into the alley and forced him into an awaiting van. He didn't have a chance."

Galila strolled toward the nervous man and snarled. "My, it certainly is lucky he didn't run into the ladies, isn't it? They might have really roughed him up!"

"They secured his hands and put a bag over his head, sir.

When they let him out, he was on the edge of the city. They told him it would be best for his health if he found another job."

Daniel looked down at his hands in his lap. "I don't think we expected this."

"What I didn't expect Daniel is that you would hire idiots. So, what happened to the other two?"

"Basically, the same thing; two men quietly met each man individually and took them away. It would not have been a time or place to resist. We want to maintain a low profile, I believe."

Galila smoothly moved to the side of his desk and sat on the edge. "Do we know who these people are, Daniel?"

"At this point, all we know is they are very skilled and determined. It would fit with the methods of the one in California." After a pause, he added, "And, they are inclined to use something other than stones."

"My friend," Galila said softly, "I recommend the stone for only the special people. You know I prefer a sliver of stainless steel applied to the hearts and minds of others." With that, he sniffed and gently slid off the desk. Galila brushed his pant leg and stepped around to his chair.

"How would you like us to proceed?" Daniel asked.

"Until I speak with our interference in California, simply watch the ladies. Know everything about what they do. However, the moment they appear to have what they are looking for, do not be deterred again. Finish them!"

"What if they just leave?"

"Send someone reliable to follow them. At this point, we cannot assume they know nothing. There is a reason they came here."

"Send someone to America?"

Galila grinned. "Absolutely. My dear, courageous mother sent our defenders of faith to places in Europe and even to Egypt. No effort is too great to protect the church from the passions of individual glory seekers."

"One other thing Daniel, send your people to visit the home of Professor MacDonald. I don't care if he's at home at the time or not. He may not know what we are after, but we must determine if he has the letters or knows of them. In the past, we assumed he was as much an ignorant peasant as was his father. It is time we review the situation again. Take care of this immediately. Don't let your people be distracted this time. If they are, they'll deal with me."

The man arose quietly and slipped out of the office. Galila didn't bother to watch him leave.

London, UK

IX - 2

Matthew finished his remaining food and thought for a moment.

"It always amazed me when my colleagues would be covered with the dust of history at some dig site, holding in their hands what may be artifacts five millennia in age, and the mindset of these colleagues was cold and intellectual. They may as well be actuaries or bureaucrats who simply move numbers or push papers."

"So, they're focused on process and not substance?" Angie asked.

"Exactly. This is not to say they don't do their work very well. They seem to have little passion for the discovery. My breath has often been pulled from me upon finding a simple pot or uncovering part of an ancient wall. There is a powerful connection between my work and me. I am an old man, but that does not mean I am empty of passion."

His eyes became intense. "Rennie, I am compelled to do what I believe is good and right, and I think we know the challenges that come from that drive when one works in any organization."

Angie held up her cup. "I for one understand the distinction between just doing a project and being committed to it, especially now."

"Ah, yes," Matthew responded. "Universities offer no relief from the tension between mindless functioning and doing the right thing. For people who care, the dilemma is deciding what and when we do something about it."

"Matthew," Rennie asked, "have we placed more value on

doing and being productive in modern Western society than we have on the moral qualities of what we do?"

"It isn't particularly modern. In the time of Jesus, the Pharisees pronounced as good those who closely obeyed their laws. The world of power is still Pharisaical in structure. If the laws of those in power are followed, one is a good person. Unfortunately, those laws have more to do with maintaining societies that are in opposition to what Jesus taught us."

Rennie snorted. "It's easy to see how that message creates conflicts. I'm experiencing a conflict at my paper right now. There's a story I believe is important, but the top brass don't want to hear about it. I know it's the right thing to do."

Matthew nodded. "I understand. If we follow Jesus in trying to do the right thing, we put ourselves on a different path than that of the world and its leaders. That's very hard to deal with."

Rennie was annoyed. "But we're pursuing Matthias's story because we think it is the right thing to do. Is that wrong?"

"My dear, I believe you are here today because of your heart and not some duty. Am I right? And, the time will come when you must take a stand on this story."

Rennie laid her hand on his and grinned. "Okay, you got me there."

Matthew pointed at the window. "Is that the man who walked by earlier?"

Angie and Rennie swiveled in time to see the man hurry past the window and disappear.

Rennie slapped the table. "I don't know who that guy is, but he sure knows how to tick me off."

A single eyebrow rose on Matthew's forehead. "I think I should go check on this fellow."

Rennie glared at the window, fighting the desire to go to it and look for the man. Instead, she said to Matthew, "No, it's okay."

The old man's face displayed a tired sadness. "I believe I am consuming your entire day when you have much more to do. Is there anything else I can help with at this point?"

Angie touched Matthew's jacket sleeve. "Matthew, you have been an enormous help to us, some we may not even know of."

"Dear ladies, there's one additional piece of information that I must share with you. It's not public but is known to key people. It's something I did, perhaps out of selfishness or pride."

"Matthew," Rennie responded, "you've shared enough. You don't need to say more."

"You might be pleased to know this. After my dear wife passed on, I decided to make a big change — specifically, I changed my name."

Rennie blinked with confusion.

"As I related last night, Reggie MacDonald was not my father. Carrying his name as mine for so many years and knowing that truth left within me a boil I could no longer ignore but had to resolve. After my dear Ruth was gone, I had my last name legally changed from MacDonald to Justus. I am Matthew Justus, son of Matthias."

Rennie looked at Angie and erupted into laughter. "That's wonderful! It's perfect! Your father would be so proud. Angie, I can't get over this. Everything has come together, and it's all good."

"Well," he continued, "some of my colleagues at the museum know and were pleased. Some in my family were not. All have kept the MacDonald name except for my grandson David. When I changed my name to Justus, he did the same. He's an independent fellow and quite brilliant; a physicist and rather gifted in ancient Greek and other languages. I was privileged to have him join me on several expeditions when he was a boy. That sparked his interest in the ancient world."

"My gosh," Angie gasped, "this is all so much and so quick.

Matthew Justus. I like the sound of that."

Rennie lifted her water glass. "Here's to Professor Matthew Justus, son of Professor Matthias Justus! Wow, I like the sound of that."

"Thank you. See what your shrewd interrogation techniques have done."

"Matthew, I have a question," Angie said. "This goes back to something Matthias wrote about. Huh, I guess I could say 'your father' wrote about. Cool. He referred to a box he found at the museum, and I believe he mentioned it may have been from Antioch. How could we follow up on that?"

"Yes, I could help with that. I'm familiar with the staff of the Department of Ancient Near East at the museum. The Assistant Keeper for Syria and Palestine is a very good fellow and a professional friend. His name is Donald Abramson. He is brilliant and helpful, self-taught in many aspects of the work. Another colleague and old friend is Professor Alistair Snapper. Either will be helpful."

Matthew noticed the remaining customers were leaving. "As I mentioned when we met last evening, the excavation I came from was in Turkey, not far from where Antioch was located. I was at the Jerablus Tahtani site and had planned to move on to the work either at Sidon, Lebanon or at Capernaum. The latter site is not one sponsored by the British Museum, but they have welcomed my assistance. I could follow up to see what the museum may have on artifacts from Antioch, but I'm not aware of anything found in Antioch like that."

Rennie sighed, "Professor, from my reading of his journals, I do not think the item was found in Antioch, but rather was sent from there and found in Egypt."

"That explains it. A great deal is still being found in Egypt itself. A substantial number of manuscripts were found recently in a Coptic monastery there. They dated to around the seventh century from what I recall. I think it was at Deir al-Surian. The history of the Coptic Church dates back almost to the original disciples of Christ and the founders of Christian thinking. The Apostle Mark went to Alexandria to help spread the word there, and he died there at the hands of the Romans."

"So, could he have brought to Egypt something from Antioch?" Rennie asked.

"Indeed, he not only could have, he probably brought and later received much from the other followers. Their nature was to write to each other for encouragement and for clarification of ideas. Just look at the letters of Paul to churches all across the area, from Rome to Ephesus. The New Testament books were written outside of what we call the Holy Land. In fact, after the temple in Jerusalem was destroyed in the year 70, the area of what is now Israel and Palestine was not safe for Jews or Christians."

Rennie pushed dishes away from her. "So, what was going on with the churches in Antioch and in Ephesus?"

"Those, of course, were among the first churches, along with Alexandria. The Christians in Antioch were the first to carry the name of 'Christian' and Ephesus soon followed. It was also in Antioch that the document we know as 'Q' may have been written and subsequently used as the basis for the Gospel books by Matthew and Mark. By the way, the Gospel writer Mark is a different one from the disciple we know as Mark; perhaps, John Mark who was an associate of Paul."

Rennie breathlessly asked, "So, the Apostle Matthew and this other Mark may have jointly assembled their recollections of the ministry and then individually wrote their books? And, might Luke have spoken with Mary to write his text?"

"You pose an interesting approach. I'm not sure I've heard it put that way. There is no question of the coordinated development of the Gospels, except for the Book of John. What you suggest is certainly possible. It would have been a natural process for the aging disciples to get together and share their remembrances in trying to write the complete story of Jesus."

Rennie ran her fingers through her hair. She glanced at Angie. "We've got to get those journals into the hands of Matthew or someone. It's all we've got."

"Matthew, I'm sorry for the intrigue, if that's the right term, but we need to review some things and get back with you. Could you come to Des Moines?"

"It's possible, but I would appreciate knowing more about what concerns you. I have other travel coming up. Perhaps, I could get a sponsor to send me to your college."

"That's a great idea." Angie responded. "I'm sure we could get some funding to bring you to Simpson. I'll get on it as soon as we return."

Rennie felt an inner coldness. Quietly, she asked, "Matthew, is there any record of Jesus writing letters?"

His eyes flashed. He responded in a flat, careful tone. "I am not aware of any such writing. Obviously, he was capable of it." He paused and studied Rennie. "Tell me why you ask."

Her large eyebrows moved with her thoughts. "It seems he would've done that."

Matthew's expression didn't change. His eyes met hers in a challenge for truth.

He responded, "He may well have written letters. Who knows what lies on the secured shelves of the Vatican library, or goes unnoticed in any other archives."

Everyone stewed in an uncomfortable silence. When the server returned with the bill, Rennie immediately grabbed it and playfully tapped Matthew's hand as he reached for it.

Angie asked, "When do we leave tomorrow? I'm not sure if we'll see Matthew again."

Rennie sorted through her British currency. "I think our

flight is around noon. That means we'll have to be on the way to the airport by about nine or so. We get back to Des Moines around six or seven in the evening. This is probably it for us, here."

Matthew cleared his throat. "I would love to see you again, so let's plan on another time somewhere."

Leaving the restaurant, Rennie took a tentative step out the door. She scanned the vicinity, feeling eager to confront her stalking enemy. She remained tense as Matthew and Angie joined her. For an awkward moment, no one said anything.

Matthew stepped in closely to the two women. "I don't know the purpose of your adventure, but I'm grateful to have been part of it. I thank God for you. I'll encourage you with this thought. Whenever you are unsure of what to do next, focus on whose you are. It is easy to think of who we are and what we do. But, if you remember whose you are, you will know the right thing to do."

"Oh, I like that," Angie cooed.

Matthew laid his hand on her shoulder. "You may feel like you're alone in doing what you believe to be right, but you are part of a community with the same mission. You are part of a community of people who are humble to the One whose will is at work. Placing what must be done in that framework may take the burden off of your shoulders."

Angie gave Matthew a warm embrace. "God loves you so much," she whispered in his ear. Then, she released him a little and looked at him with their noses nearly touching. "And I do, too."

Rennie reached in as they slipped apart so she could also give Matthew a hug. After a strong embrace, she kissed his cheek. Then she said, "I could marry an older man. Do you think we might be able to stay in touch?"

They snorted their amusement. He looked down for a moment as he removed a white handkerchief from his pocket and touched beneath his nose.

"Oh dear," he said, briefly looking away. "This goodbye is difficult. I feel as though my family is going away. I hope you can come back to meet my children and grandchildren."

Angie stepped up. "Would you do me a favor? It would fill my heart up knowing that you and Mary could find a way to renew your relationship. She needs you, Matthew. You'll be a wonderful blessing to her."

Matthew removed his glasses and wiped his eyes. Then he reached out and held Angie. He stepped back and looked at both women. "I'm not sure about marriage, but I would be interested in adopting both of you."

They shared another laugh, another hug, and then said they would see each other again. As they walked away, Rennie and Angie in one direction and Matthew in the other, they turned to look back several times and waved.

Matthew reached the corner and stood for a moment before proceeding. He threw a kiss when the women looked back one last time. Matthew bowed slightly, turned, and disappeared behind the building. The women continued down the street, quiet for nearly a block.

Finally, Rennie asked, "What should we do now? I need to stop thinking."

Angie stopped. "I know. Let's take a tour. You know, get on a bus and let them take us around. It would be mindless, and it's about time we got a break. Besides, tomorrow morning we're out of here. I'm sure the hotel can set us up with something."

"Girl, you're so right." Rennie held up her hand and Angie slapped it. She placed her arm through Angie's and lurched ahead. "Let's go, partner."

Across the street, a man watched them. He slipped a cell phone from his pocket, touched a few buttons, and placed it to his ear.

London, UK

IX - 3

Rennie's tired eyes tracked massive aircraft rolling down runways and up to the wings of the airport terminal. The mixed exhaustion of insights, confusion, and lack of sleep she felt were aggravated by the noise of a crowded passenger waiting area. She needed to go home and was eager to board the next plane.

She had the answers to most of her questions about Matthias. The absence of information about the letters from Jesus weighed her down more than physical depletion.

Rennie glanced at Angie in a plastic chair near the gate. She was amused seeing Angie's head bob to the hidden rhythms of music pumped through earphones. She drifted over to an adjacent seat and fell into it, stretching out her legs.

Angie removed the plugs from her ears. "How you doing? That was fun yesterday. We got pretty silly on that tour bus."

"Yeah, we did. You held up your image as the wild librarian. It was nice to take a break from all the seriousness. I never got a sense of anyone following us, either."

"Me neither. I'm glad we treated ourselves to a good dinner, too." Angie yawned. "Are you okay? You're looking a little wasted."

"I'm okay. You know us old women can't carry on like you young chicks." Rennie rubbed her eyes. "I guess I've been thoughtful of all that's gone on here. It was only a few days, but it seems longer. I also can't get Matthew out of my mind. What a life."

"Yeah, and what a sweetie. It would've been nice to see him this morning. I hope we can get him to Iowa to look at those journals." Angie turned off her phone and put it in her purse. "Have you thought about the letters?"

"That's all I can do. Everything else is a distraction from thinking about them. It would seem that the culmination of Matthias' journey here was for Matthew to come into the world instead of revealing the letters. That's wonderful, but at what expense? The letters are gone. Matthias finds them and then loses them and his life."

"Yeah, it's hard to understand."

"Then, there's the issue of someone tracking us, or me. What's that all about? They're gone, so they must've figured out we don't know anything."

"Have you thought about your story, yet? What're you going to write?"

"I've been thinking about it. The challenge is what do I say about the letters? Isn't that what changed everything? If Matthias hadn't freaked about the police issue at the museum and then raced over to ol' Lady Jane's house and on to Priscilla's, he wouldn't have been killed. They would've gone to Iowa and lived a pleasant life and might have been famous in disclosing the letters. Just think, Matthew would have been an Iowan."

"He sure would've stood out with that English accent."

They laughed and wearily got up when they heard the announcement for the departure of their flight.

As they gathered their things and prepared to board the aircraft, Rennie touched Angie's shoulder. "I just want to say thank you for all the help and energy you put into this. I couldn't have done it without you."

"Well, Matthew reminded us that we are not alone in this world, and I'm glad we're on the same team."

Too many weary hours later, a flight attendant announced

their approach to Chicago. Rennie laid her pen on her notebook and stretched her tired fingers.

Angie awoke. "How's it going with the article?"

Rennie added a couple of words and closed the book. "Okay. It's a good start, and I think the paper will run it. I'm not backing off the letters. They are a key part of the story, a key part of history. The fact they aren't around is irrelevant. This is big and people have to know about it. It's really why Matthias died, and I think it's why he was supposed to go to London. I'm laying it all out."

Angie drew in a deep breath. "Good for you. Trust yourself and go with it."

At 7:04 p.m. their flight arrived in Des Moines from Chicago. They trudged quietly up the concourse from the gate. Nothing was said as they waited for their luggage to arrive on the baggage carousel. Occasionally, they shared a grimace of weariness. After jerking their luggage off the conveyor belt, they walked together to the exit. Only once did Rennie think about looking around to see if anyone of concern was nearby.

"Angie, you drove and it isn't necessary to give me a ride home. A cab will get me there and save you an hour in getting to bed. Is it all right with you if we split up, now?"

"Not a problem. As you say, there's no need to keep us out of our beds for another minute. I feel like someone dipped my body in formaldehyde or something. I can hardly move."

"My body is telling me it's three in the morning. Let's meet for dinner, tomorrow. I must get into work as soon as possible to see what's going on. Bud will be rampaging. It'll be good to reconnect at the end of our first day home. Are you sure you'll be okay?"

"Yeah, let's get out of here. Let the adventure continue! Woo!" Angie punched her fist in the air.

Rennie snorted a tired laugh and waved to an awaiting cab. Collapsing onto the stained upholstery of the cab's back seat, she realized she was home, but it would be a different place. She was about to make it all different, and she was committed.

PART TEN

Des Moines, Iowa

X - 1

The hard buzz of an alarm clock jarred Rennie's senses. One eye glared at the wall. Her other eye was buried in her pillow. She fumbled for the snooze button, managing to quiet the noise for six minutes. The alarm repeated its call two more times until she groaned her way out of bed. She stumbled into her suitcase and across the clothing she had been wearing on the return trip from London.

Half-way down the stairs, she paused and sat down. She ran her fingers through her hair and yawned before struggling her way to the kitchen. She made coffee, checked her e-mail, and prepared for a new day; perhaps, a new life. With breakfast and familiar surroundings, her energy quickly returned.

By nine, Rennie felt she was nearly back in business. Then, she realized her days in England were almost a distant memory. She wandered to the couch and dropped onto it. She looked up at the ceiling and asked, "What am I supposed to do with this?"

Her head jerked forward, and she snatched from the coffee table a note pad. She scribbled her thoughts until she identified two pages of tasks. The phone rang. She was confused for a moment before hurrying across the room to pull it from her purse.

"Hi Rennie, this is Roger," said the voice. "So, you're back."

"Yeah, I got in last night. It was exhausting; good, but exhausting. How's Balderdash?"

"He's fine, except for my keeping him in the microwave all week. No, he's okay."

Rennie snorted a laugh. "Thanks, I appreciate your watching him. Should I come over now to get him?"

"If you like. You had a good time? You okay?"

"I'm fine. Just a little tired. Thanks."

Rennie hung up and called her office number to retrieve messages. After jotting down a note about each phone call, she called Bud. She got his voice mail and left a message:

"Hey, it's your favorite wayward reporter. I'm back and I've got a great story; maybe historic. I'll be in a little later today. Thanks again. It was a good trip. No, an important trip. See you soon."

Rennie dialed Angie's home number. When she got the answering machine, she started to leave a message but was interrupted when Angie came on the line.

"How you doing?" Rennie asked.

"Not bad, considering I don't know where I am, and I feel like I walked home instead of drove. How about you?"

"Okay, I guess. I've had some trouble getting my bearings. Once I made my to-do list, I felt better."

"Ah yes, the to-dos. Have you decided which ones are in line with your purpose of being on Earth?" Angie laughed.

"Oh, don't start with me. I'll get hit in the face with this sense of purpose thing when I walk into my boss's office. If I survive, I'll call you. Do you want to come over for dinner tonight? I'll probably get take-out, maybe Thai. How's that for you? We need to review all this."

"Good for me," Angie responded. "See you then. Oh, Rennie?"

"Yeah."

"Be careful. We're back in the world."

Rennie didn't know what to say at first. "We can do this. See you tonight."

She put the phone down on the table and stood for a moment gazing out the window. Angie's last comment stayed in her ears.

She took a deep breath and headed out the back door. She enjoyed the short stroll across her backyard and past the garden to Roger's house. The morning sun felt warm and clean. The lawn was a cushion of living comfort.

Roger peered through the screen door and greeted her. He had Balderdash in his arms. "It's about time. He's been nothing but trouble," Roger grumbled. Then, he smiled. "Good to see you. The trip was okay, huh?"

"Yeah, it was pretty good. I got to see some places on the last day. The rest of the time it was all business. How are you doing?"

"Great! I figure any day I can get up is a victory. Would you like to come in and see my new computer? I got it at a garage sale and put in some new memory, a new modem, and a new DVD read-write drive. New computers don't have those, you know. It'll run rings around whatever you've got."

Rennie grinned as she took Balderdash in her arms. "Roger, you are an interesting old man. Maybe another time. I've got to get into work. If I don't come home tonight, it's because they killed me."

"Right, like they'd do that. You're the best thing that old rag of a paper has going for it. Do they ever hire real reporters anymore? You take it easy. Don't try to fix the whole world on your first day back."

Rennie waved and started across the lawn. Roger yelled, "Maybe, you can just fix Iowa. That will be a start!"

Without turning around, she waved again.

Twenty minutes later, she realized she was in her car, driving on the right side of the road and on the way to work. It had been less than a week, but it seemed as though she was seeing and experiencing her environment in a new way. Rennie felt less involved with driving the car and with the space through which she moved. She was more observer and less participant. There was a tangible sense of peace in the air.

Arriving at her desk, Rennie remembered when she was last there. Instead of a being focused on her assignments, she was now detached from the pressures that used to drive her ahead. She had the same interest in all the messages and memos stacked on her desk, but her intensity had been replaced with a kind of joy. Her connection with that desk reunited her with Matthias, and the discovery of the letters.

A few co-workers greeted her as they passed by her cubicle. Dave, a young reporter, stopped and suggested in a conspiratorial way that it might be best if she see Bud right away. As Dave moved on, he glanced back at Rennie. She knew something was different.

When she arrived in Bud's office, he was talking on the phone, bent over, looking into a cardboard box full of files.

"I don't know," he yelled into the receiver. "How should I know? All they send me are kids! They've written a few term papers and edited their school paper so now they're journalists. We hire them at minimum wage and say we're the guardians of the press. Okay, I'll find out!"

He sat up and slammed the phone down. Rennie was already sitting in front of his desk.

"So, welcome home. Nice of you to stop by. Anything I can do for you, ma'am?"

"Bud, you need a break. When will you do that?"

"When they put me in a box and haul me away. Then, you can have my job. Are you really back to work or are you just stopping in to see what working people do in the daytime?"

"I'm here to get back at it. As I mentioned in my message, this story may be historic."

Bud jumped up. "Historic! Stop the presses!" He waved his arms in the air. "Wait, I'll call the President; no, maybe the Queen. That's who you went to see, wasn't it?"

Rennie sat peacefully. "Will you sit down and cool off? I don't want to get sprayed when your blood vessels burst all over."

She leaned forward and put her hands on his desk. "Listen, I don't want to see them take you out of here in a box, or even in a straight jacket. You deserve something better. Can you let go for a little bit, please?"

He fell into his chair, resting his arms on his belly. He took a deep breath. "So, they're right. You want me out of here."

"Hey, if I wanted that, I'd encourage you to continue this crazy behavior you're living."

"Look who's talking! You are suddenly the maharishi of Des Moines. What's next, chanting and wearing robes? Rennie, I'd like to have my reporter back? Do you know where they put her? You're a pretty good double, but I need the real thing. I think I liked the angry one better. This paper has a need for material, and I'd like to get her back to produce it."

"You have her, chief, and she'll give you better stuff than ever. Just wait. Tomorrow night, I'll file a draft that'll knock your socks off."

She got up and glided toward the door.

He growled, "Great. Just make it about something other than how pleasant it is that we have air. Oh, and now that you're back, maybe our publisher will stop asking about you."

She blew him a kiss, and as she walked past his glass wall, she dragged her fingertips lightly along the glass. He crunched some paper into a ball and threw it at her.

Easing into her chair, she swiveled back and forth. She stared at her phone, then grabbed it and looked through the contact list. Finding what she wanted, she made a call.

"Hello, this is Rennie Haran from the *Record*. I'm calling for Mrs. Knoche. Is she there? Yes, I'll wait." She leaned back and smiled.

"Hi, thank you, same here. I'm delighted to let you know that what I learned about Professor Justus is nothing but the best news. I met his son. Yes, he has a son. You'd love him. He's not only a real English gentleman, he is a gentle man, and quite a scholar, too. Simpson can be proud of Professor Matthias Justus. I'll tell you the whole story sometime. Thanks, Mrs. Knoche. Bye."

Rennie reviewed her messages. She spread out four of them and began to make calls. As she handled the phone, she wrote notes and occasionally grinned or waved at people passing by her cubicle. By 1:00 o'clock, she realized she had nearly caught up with the backlog. She stretched, picked up her bag, and started down the hallway between the cubicles. As she did, one of the assistants caught up with her.

"Hey, Rennie! How're you doing? Were you away?"

"Hi, Sandy. Yes, I was out of town for a few days. How are you?"

"Good, thanks. You seem a little different, kind of happy or something. Is there anything, you know, anything you'd like to share?"

"No, not really. Nothing new. How about you?"

"Me? Nothing new. Same old, same old. Well, see you later."

As Rennie left the sprawling office area, she looked back and saw Sandy talking to another assistant, shrugging her shoulders and shaking her head. Rennie was amused and cruised out the door to lunch.

When she returned, she created a new file on her computer for short summary statements on her story, based on what she had written in her notebook. In an hour, she laid out three pages of double-spaced notes, rearranged many of them, and printed her list. She sent the file to herself by email.

She rested against the back of the chair and closed her eyes for a satisfying minute. Yawning deeply, she knew it was time to leave. She shook her head, blinked rapidly, and took a deep breath. "Okay, let's go," she said.

Striding down the hallway, she winked and nodded at people

along the way to the main entrance, leaving many with confused looks.

As she settled into her car, she opened the sunroof and delighted in the sun on her face. Easing into traffic, Rennie sensed that her smile seemed to control the traffic around her. This day was surprisingly easy.

She stopped at her favorite Thai food restaurant and ordered two meals. While waiting, she received a call from Angie.

"Hi, how are things at the library? Me, too. I could have fallen asleep at my desk a little while ago. It was okay. In fact, I'm feeling so at peace and yet more productive. It's weird, really. I'm picking up dinner now, so if you like, you can come over earlier. I can't believe how wiped out I am. I'll see you later."

Rennie paid for the food and visited briefly with the hostess about her children. Unlike her previous visits, the young Asian woman seemed to be warmly engaging. Rennie was surprised but pleased as she left the restaurant.

Driving home, she began to think of Matthew and their conversation in the restaurant in London. It seemed so long ago that it may have been nothing more than a wonderful dream.

Turning into her driveway, she noticed her neighbor Cathy trimming a bush near the sidewalk. They waved at each other, and Cathy walked over to her car when she parked.

"It's so nice to see you again. Did you have a good journey?"

Rennie removed from the back seat the plastic bag with containers for dinner.

"Hi Cathy, yes I did, thank you. It was good in every way. I've been thinking about it now and then, and it's almost hard to believe it was real. How have you been?"

"Fine, fine dear. We didn't get any rain while you were gone. The weather has been just perfect, and I've been well, too. I'm certainly blessed."

"That's wonderful. I think I realize more than ever before

what that means. I'll see you later."

"Oh, by the way, dear," Cathy began and then stopped.

Rennie turned back and waited.

"Well, last week, you might remember that I thought you had your house for sale." Cathy looked past her neighbor with a sense of embarrassment.

"Yes, Cathy," Rennie replied in a more serious tone.

"I must have been mistaken, and I'm sorry. After you were gone, I didn't see anyone come around. Silly me!"

Cathy flipped her hands in the air as though she was batting bugs away from her face.

Rennie lost her breath for a moment. Finally, she said, "It's nothing, Cathy."

She hurried to the porch and into her home. Before closing the door, she glanced down the street. Rennie took the food into the kitchen and placed the containers in the oven. Then, she returned and locked the front door. She kicked off her shoes and stretched out on the couch. Balderdash came over and repeatedly meowed to her.

"Hey buddy, how are you? Come here. Come see me."

The cat carefully jumped onto the cushion and slowly walked up on her to lay down. Gently, he kneaded her belly and began to purr. Rennie was soon asleep.

An hour later, the phone rang. Rennie struggled to get up and Balderdash leaped off her, over the back of the couch. She sat up and tried to sort out where she was. The phone continued to ring until she reached it.

"Hello?"

"Hi, this is Angie. What's up?"

"I'm not sure. I fell asleep. What time is it?"

"It's a little after four thirty. I've been wiped out, too. I wondered if I should bring over a bottle of wine or something."

"Gosh, no. If I have a glass of wine, you'll find me face down in Thai noodles. But, bring it if you like."

Angie laughed. "I'm in the same boat. I'll pass on that. I'll bring some hot tea, instead."

"Terrific idea. Come whenever. Bye."

Rennie went into the kitchen and washed her face at the sink. She opened the refrigerator and removed a jug of iced tea, poured a full glass, and drank it down. She poured another and stepped onto the back porch for fresh air. It was a beautiful summer afternoon. She sat down on the wooden stairs and observed the world around her.

Her mind drifted over the story of Matthias and Priscilla, her trip to London, and her new and serene perception of life.

A sense of urgency struck her when one question lodged behind her eyes, "What do I do with this?"

She went back inside, found her bag, and thought of the notes she sent to herself. She logged into her computer with renewed focus. After opening the new file on her story, she saved it in a new file and reviewed the notes.

Her mind raced with the implications the story could bring to Simpson, to her paper, to the worlds of archeology and religion, and to the hearts of anyone who learns what Matthias found. Her lips became a thin, hard line on her face as her intensity grew. She opened a new page and began to write.

An hour later, Rennie heard someone walk onto her front porch. She stopped typing and sat quietly, listening. There was a knock on the door, but she didn't move. Another knock sounded.

Des Moines, IA

X - 2

"Hello, Rennie, it's Angie! Are you there?" Angie knocked again on Rennie's front door.

Rennie pushed back from the table and hurried to the door. "Hi, come in."

"Are you okay? What happened?" Angie asked as she entered the house.

"Why? What do you mean?"

"You look so serious. I thought something must have happened."

"No, nothing. Well, I'm working on the story. Have you given any more thought to it; I mean, to everything?"

"Yes, about every third moment. There's something else I've noticed. It seems like I just look at things a little differently."

"I know," Rennie replied. "My perspective is different."

Rennie led the way into the living room. They found opposite corners of the couch as if they were soft places of refuge.

Rennie held a pillow on her lap. "I feel a separation from the world. It's odd but comforting in some way."

"Exactly." Angie said in a hushed but excited voice. "Everyone around me seems to be so intense while I feel at peace. It is a strange detachment, but I like it."

She looked around. "Hey, you've got a nice place here. I noticed it a little when I came by to pick you up. It feels comfortable."

"Thanks. The home is one of those oldies but goodies. I like the wide, dark wood trim and wood floors. It could use some updating, especially the bathrooms and kitchen, but I'm used to it. Are you hungry yet?"

"I've been so tired, it's hard to know if I'm hungry, but I could eat. How about you?"

Rennie set aside the pillow. "Come on, you can help me in the kitchen. We'll get it together in there and eat at the dining room table."

"Where's the kitty?" Angie asked.

"Balderdash is probably in his afternoon position, lying on his back catching some rays in the front window upstairs. I liked the fact that Matthew had a cat when he was a kid. People need pets, especially in tough times."

"I agree. Who took care of Balderdash while we were gone?"

"My neighbor, Roger. He lives in the house behind me. He's great; an old widower, and he likes to come off real crusty, but he's all heart. By the way, did you bring tea?"

"Well, sort of. I forgot to brew it, so all I've got is a pocket full of tea bags. It's good stuff, though."

"That's fine. There's a tea pot in that cupboard and the cups are up there."

As Rennie retrieved the food packages from of the oven and warmed them in the microwave, Angie prepared the tea and helped set out plates and silverware. They worked with quiet, diligent grace. Rennie turned on the audio system and selected a few old CD's to play as Angie set the table.

As Rennie returned to the kitchen, she turned on the light in the dining room.

"Is it okay with you if we share the meals? We could set out the boxes and just take from each."

"Great idea. I'm suddenly hungry."

Once they were settled in the dining room Angie scooped up food and filled her plate. Then she noticed that Rennie was quiet and looking down. "What's up?" she asked.

Rennie looked into the distance.

"I don't have to go too deeply to bring up Matthias' words in discovering the letters."

She shivered with emotion.

"Just think, he held in his hands and read letters written by Jesus. I cannot get that out of my mind. He held them in his hands. What did they say? And, what if people could read them! What would that do for people who are looking for something or someone to believe in?" Rennie paused, breathless.

Angie put down her fork.

"That would be incredible if they had survived, if someone could share them with the world. But they're gone, Rennie. People can still read what He said. That's what the Bible is all about. It's the biggest selling book in the world."

"You're right. Besides, it's faith that's important, and that's in the unseen."

Angie eagerly began to eat and talk at the same time.

"The difficulty that people have with reading about Him is they are put off by the institution of the church and dogma. They can't get through to Jesus. Having a few letters from Him would be incredible, and I'm sure they would make a difference to countless lives."

Rennie nodded her head as she ate.

"I know. I guess it's just the combination of a loss of the letters and Matthias dying for nothing that stings."

The next twenty minutes were spent in dining pleasure, with modest small talk. As they finished, each slowed to a stop. They looked at each other and laughed.

"Would it be okay if I just slept here, in this chair, tonight? I don't think I can get up!" Angie giggled.

"I feel the same way. I might crawl over to the couch and crash there. Let's get this stuff into the kitchen before we fall asleep right here."

They cleared the table and rinsed the dishes, leaving them

in the sink. Angie refreshed her tea with the remainder from the pot. Rennie got a glass of ice water. Then, they settled in the quiet peace of the living room.

As Angie's gaze drifted around the room, she noticed something. She leaned forward.

"What is that?" Her face became intense. "Rennie, what is that?"

Angie stood up and pointed at the bookcase.

Rennie was surprised and confused.

"What? What are you looking at?"

She looked in the direction of Angie's pointed finger. Suddenly, Rennie jumped up, spilling her water.

"Oh my gosh!"

She turned to Angie, whose gaze was fixed on the object.

"Oh my gosh. I totally forgot about that! Angie, I'm sorry. I can explain."

Angie responded with unexpected ferocity, "Tell me. Tell me why that is here."

"Oh, no. I'm not sure. I can tell you how it got here, but I can't tell you why. I totally forgot about it."

Rennie walked to the bookcase and picked up the metal, lunch tin from Matthias' attaché case. She carried it to Angie who stared at it.

"That is from my archives, Rennie. I am responsible for this. Why is it here? You did not ask me to take it," Angie said with teeth set.

"I know. I know. I'm sorry. I don't know why I did it. On that last day at the library, I was putting everything away, and I had this out. I thought it was too bad that I had not gotten to read the letters Matthias sent home. I just mindlessly put it into the box you brought for me, along with my files and notes. I felt uncomfortable about it at the time, and well, I'm sorry. It was mindless."

Angie glared at Rennie and then the box.

"Did you take anything else?"

"No."

Angie was breathing hard.

"Darn it, Rennie! What were you thinking? This is so wrong. How can you put me in this position?"

Rennie's pained expression seemed to keep her from speaking.

Finally, she simply blurted, "Angie, I'm sorry. It was stupid. I don't know. What should I do?"

The word "nothing," slipped from Angie's lips. "I'd better get this back to the library."

"Angie, I'm sorry. I meant no harm. It happened. I wouldn't get you in trouble for anything. Please forgive me."

They both took deep breaths. Angie took the box in her hands and looked at the scrawled note under the wrapped cords. "Letters home," she quietly read.

She sat down again on the couch, still looking at the box. Rennie's breathing was shallow.

Finally, Angie looked up. "I guess I'm responsible now. Do you think we should open it at this point?"

Rennie dropped to her knees next to the coffee table and put her hand on Angie's arm. "Angie, I'm sorry. I would never put you in jeopardy. You do what you think is okay."

"I will." Angie carefully examined the box. "Do you have a knife so the Director of Archives can officially open this precious lunch box?"

"Yes, I'll get one." Rennie got up and grabbed a scissors from her desk. She looked back. "What about gloves?"

Angie looked at the box. "It's okay at this point. We can open it. If there's something inside we need to examine, we'll wait for gloves."

"Just one more thing," Rennie added. She quickly locked the

front door and pulled down the shades on all the windows.

Resting the box in her lap, Angie clipped the cords and set aside the note. She paused, "I hope he didn't leave any fruit or meat in here."

They laughed and relaxed for a moment.

Angie put the cords on the table and struggled briefly with the cover. With a final, firm push, it popped off. A puzzled look went across her face as she studied the cover sheet. It was a hastily written note and appeared to be Matthias' writing. Beneath it, there was a linen material surrounding the contents. She cautiously lifted and opened the note.

Her eyes met Rennie's. "Well, here we go." She began to read.

"I only have a few moments. I don't know why the police want to question me. I have done nothing wrong. The letters, by the most precious hand of all time, are safe. I must take my transcripts to Lady Jane. She will understand the glory of what has happened. The wonder and power of this discovery! With endless joy, Priscilla and I will live in our love and know firsthand of God's love. I must hurry and let the unfolding begin! Thanks be to God! By His very hand, my life is new!"

Rennie and Angie shared a look of concern. Rennie's heart raced with anxiety and confusion.

Angie set the box and the note on the table and hesitated. She studied the linen, and then glanced again at Rennie. With delicate fingertips and hesitation, she grasped one corner of the material and gave it a gentle pull. She tried another corner and then another. Finally, the third corner slipped slowly upward. Using just her fingernail tips, Angie drew up the linen along the side of the box. Her eyes focused like lasers on every detail beneath them.

As Angie lifted the material aside, Rennie struggled to

determine what she was seeing. There appeared to be heavy parchment within the linen covering.

Rennie's eyes dashed from the box to Angie and back. Her breathing was shallow and difficult.

"I wish I had my gloves," Angie finally said, and attempted to smile.

"Let me see what I can find. Oh, wait! I've got a pair of dress gloves that I wore at my high school prom. I'm sure they're cotton."

Rennie ran up the stairs as Angie quietly sat before the mystery on the table. Rennie returned holding a pair of dark green, forearm length gloves. "You might imagine, I've not had many opportunities to wear these."

"Let me see. They might work. I think it's okay if I briefly see what we have here. We just won't handle anything too much."

Angie put on the gloves, then cautiously slipped a finger between the box wall and the parchment. Slowly, she lifted it, tilting it in the box. "It's heavy."

As one end came up, she placed two fingers under the linen material that was wrapped under the package. They both attempted to smile but glared at what Angie held.

"Well," Angie said with difficulty, "let's see what's inside."

She laid the package on the table, being sure to place the linen wrapping between the table surface and the parchment. Angie gently rolled the package up on its side.

Rennie clasped her hands. "Wait a minute. I'll get some fresh, clean cloth to put on the table."

She ran up the stairs and came back with a white cotton sheet.

Angie lifted the linen from the box as Rennie spread the folded sheet on the table and Angie held the parchment. Rennie knelt down by the table.

Angie rolled the package over, revealing the folds underneath. She hesitated and took a breath. Slowly, she lifted two of the folds. The parchment seemed to be nearly stuck to another layer of linen between the sheets. With delicate persistence, she pulled open the first layer. She blinked her wide eyes and held her breath. From what she could see around the folded sheets still within the linen wrapping, the writing of the first page lying under the package appeared to be a blurry scrawl.

Rennie tried to focus on the words she could see. She looked at Angie who also appeared to be confused.

Angie removed the remaining package from the box and set it on the cloth. She stared at the document lying before her. The question, "is this parchment or papyrus or what?" slipped from her lips.

Suddenly, her mouth dropped open and her eyes grew large. She looked at Rennie in panic. Rennie looked back at her, and then rose up a little to look at the document.

"Oh, my God! Oh, dear God!" Angie gasped. She looked down at the revealed page and at the still-wrapped package. She stared at Rennie, who was stunned and confused.

"This is it. This is it," Angie stuttered. "These are not Matthias' letters home. They are, oh dear God, they are the letters from Jesus!"

Rennie's mouth opened. She fell back against the chair behind her. She stared at the simple materials lying on her table. "Oh, my God." she muttered.

Des Moines, IA

X - 3

Rennie and Angie stood in the dining room staring into the living room at the tin box and its package of holy documents. Slowly, they sank into chairs at the dining table.

"I don't believe this," Rennie finally said. "It's too much. Angie, what're we doing?"

Angie didn't respond.

Rennie reached across the table and touched Angie's arm. "We need to call Matthew. We need to get him here, now."

Angie's face expressed dull shock. "What do we do with this?" she whispered. "Rennie, I'm not worthy of dealing with this. I'm not worthy. I should not be in this house. What is going on here?"

"I don't know. All I can think of is we must get Matthew here. This is too big for us. It's as though we are pieces of a puzzle coming together."

Angie again shook her head and gazed into the living room. "I've got to put that all back together. Somehow, the box was sufficiently sealed to protect the documents."

She turned to Rennie. "What do I do with them? Take them to the library? I'm not sure that's a good idea. We can't just leave the box sitting around."

Angie studied her fingertips. "Do you realize I touched it? I touched what He touched with His hands."

Rennie checked her watch. "What time is it in London? I guess it would be after midnight. We need to call Matthew about two or three in the morning, our time. That will be like eight or nine for him. I don't know if I can sit here until then with that box."

Angie got up from the chair. She approached the table and knelt next to it. She closed her eyes and opened her hands in front of herself. Her lips moved for a few moments. She leaned over and looked at the open letter.

Looking back at Rennie, she said, "This must be Aramaic. Just think, Jesus sat in front of this and wrote these words."

Rennie came to the couch and stood quietly. She leaned over and considered the lettering and the texture of the document.

"It's too amazing to take in. I wonder which letter this is. You know, not all the letters were from Jesus. One was from Mary and one was from Matthew. You know, the biblical one."

Angie grinned. "That's right. Do you have a basement in this house?"

"Yeah, and a fruit cellar. Why?"

"For now, I think we need to keep the box here. There's no telling what might happen if news of this got out and it was at the school. I think it would be best to keep it in a dark, cool place."

"How about the refrigerator?"

"That's probably a little too cool. Well, here we go. Oh, Lord, forgive me for touching this. Guide my hands." Angie took a deep breath and began the process of returning the documents to the exact, linen-wrapped package it had been.

Rennie gently held the box after Angie had the package ready for placement inside it.

Angie shook her hands. "Okay, here goes." She raised the package with a delicate touch and placed it in the old tin box.

Rennie noticed Matthias's note. "Should this go in, too?"

"Yes. It all must be the way it was. Remember what Matthew said about archeological discoveries? Anything related to the artifact must be kept with it. That reminds me. I wonder if I need to get his journals out of storage and bring them here."

"Angie, I just had a crazy thought."

"What's that?"

"When Matthias found these documents at the museum, he probably took them away in this box - his lunch box. He didn't mean to steal them. He just wanted to look at them."

"Yeah, so?"

"I did the same thing. I took them from the library, in his lunch box, just to look at them. Isn't that a strange coincidence?"

Angie took a deep breath after she firmly shut the lid on the box. "Rennie, there is so much coincidence in this whole deal. I don't see how it can all be coincidence, at this point. If you have some strong rubber bands, let's put them around the box to replace the cord he used. I put the cords inside."

Rennie removed from a desk drawer several rubber bands.

Angie reverently lifted and held the tin container as Rennie strapped on the bands. For a moment, they breathlessly regarded the awesome possession.

Embracing the box, Angie placed an arm around Rennie. "I need to hold you for a moment. I'm overwhelmed."

"Me, too. Let's take it downstairs and find a hiding place for it. If someone broke in, they wouldn't notice the box down there."

Angie followed Rennie through the kitchen to a door opening to the stairway to the cellar. Rennie flipped a switch that illuminated a single light bulb at the foot of the stairs.

Stepping down the old stairs, every creak and shift of the wooden steps was amplified by the significance of their mission. When they reached the bottom, Rennie turned to the right and tugged open an old door. A small storage area behind it offered six dusty wooden shelves holding a variety of bottled goods and spider web-covered items.

Rennie placed the tin box behind a couple of old glass milk bottles.

As she was about to close the door, Angie stepped forward. "Wait. The box is too clean." Angie scooped dust off the floor and another shelf into her hand and blew it onto the box. She then blew on the floor and the shelf to blur the places where she took the dust.

"Wow," Rennie exclaimed. "You're good. You could advise those TV crime scene shows."

"Let's hope there was no need for all this intrigue. I'd like to return to being a boring librarian."

"I'm not sure you do. I've seen another side of you. Let's get upstairs and brew some tea."

By 8:20 p.m., they had a cup of tea and were quickly tiring. They checked their various phones and services for messages. Rennie noted several callers did not leave messages.

Rennie rubbed her eyes and crumbled into a chair. "Hey, how about if I make a bed for you on the couch? I don't have an extra bed in the house, but I've crashed there many times and it works. We shouldn't split up right now. I've got some old, cut off sweats or something you can wear."

Angie yawned. "Thanks. It's so hard to think straight right now. I need to turn in."

"Me, too. We'll regroup in the morning. There's a half bath over there. We can take turns using the shower tomorrow. All I know is I've got to get to bed."

The corners of Angie's mouth tucked into a grin. "You sold me. Just put out some sheets or whatever for the couch and I'll take care of that. Do you plan to set an alarm so we can call Matthew in the early hours?"

"Good thinking. I'll do that right now. Now, you need to turn in. I'll bring down the sheets."

In fifteen minutes, the lights were off, and the house was quiet.

At 7:15 a.m., Rennie stepped into the shower. Although tired, her mind was racing. She was eager for the day. Fifteen minutes

later, she wrapped a towel around her hair and came down the stairs. She saw Angie untangling herself from the sheets on the couch.

"Hey, sunshine."

Angie groaned. "Is that coffee I smell?"

"Yep, let's get some."

Rennie glanced at Angie, amused with her shuffling away from the couch.

As Angie rubbed her eyes, she poured a cup of coffee and took a banana off the rack. She pulled out one of the two chairs at the small, kitchen table and fell into it.

Rennie took the lid off a yogurt container and ate from it. "You were snoozing pretty well on that couch. Did it work out alright?"

"Terrific. I went out like somebody flipped the switch. But I'm having a little difficulty getting my bearings. Did I dream all that went on last night?"

Rennie leaned against the counter. She closed her bathrobe more tightly and pushed on the towel wrapped around her hair. "I've been wondering the same thing. I'm almost afraid of going downstairs and looking in the pantry."

She set aside the yogurt and poured a cup of coffee. "I called Matthew about two this morning. I didn't get him at first, so I left a message. I tried again and got him. I told him we had found something from Matthias' things and that we need him to come immediately."

She blew on her coffee. "He didn't say anything for a bit, so I just waited. He seemed distant or guarded. Finally, he said he would come if we thought it was that urgent. I told him it was so important we want him here today, and we would arrange his ticket from here if necessary. Something was different. He was different."

Angie looked concerned. "So, is he coming? Come on partner,

what's the story?"

Rennie hurried to the table and sat down. "Okay, he's coming. He gets on a flight at 4:00 o'clock his time, that's just a couple of hours from now, and he gets into Chicago about six tonight. He'll be here about nine. Of course, considering O'Hare, who knows what his connection will be like. We've got to get ready, not just to meet him at the airport, but what on Earth do we tell him?"

"Rennie?"

"What?"

"I'm so excited, I need to use your bathroom."

Rennie laughed. "Well, do your thing and get back here. We're going to be busy girls today. Hey, did you call in sick for today?"

"Oh, my gosh. I'll do that in a minute."

Rennie unlocked the door and tentatively stepped onto the front porch to get her morning paper. She saw Cathy next door and they waved at each other. As she looked around the neighborhood, it seemed as though nothing had changed, and yet everything had changed. It was a beautiful day, but she sensed a shifting of massive forces around her.

She returned inside with the paper, tossing it on a table. She turned on her computer.

Angie hurried in. "I've decided to go to the library, clear up a few things, and get the journals. Matthew will not only need them, he will treasure them. It's the closest he'll ever be to Matthias."

"That's a great idea."

"Are you going to work? What are you doing about your story and what will you say about the letters?"

"The situation has changed. I've only thought a little about that, and it may not be a big change in the story. I was going to talk about the letters anyway. Now, we know they exist. I intend to address the facts directly and let the results happen. We cannot step back from this, Angie. We've been handed an extraordinary gift to the world."

"That's an understatement."

"You bet. I'll finish the story this morning and turn it in after lunch. An open question is, do I say where they are or do I have to make them available? Who keeps them, Angie?"

"I was thinking about that. Who can be trusted to keep them? Maybe, Matthew will know, considering his knowledge of the profession and the whole political environment of these types of things."

Rennie studied her coffee. "I think for now, we shouldn't tell anyone. They stay in the box. We still don't know who was watching me or why. What do you think?"

"It's going to be tough to act like nothing has happened. I agree with you, though. When Matthew gets here, he can help us decide what to do with the letters. This will be the biggest news in his life."

"Good plan. I'll call my boss and tell him the story is in the works. That'll appease him for a few hours."

Rennie's voice lowered into a heavy whisper. "As of last night, all my priorities have been swept away. I wish I had felt this clear earlier in life. I'm not sure of the details, but my energy for doing this is abundant."

Angie's eyes narrowed. "Handling this will not be easy. We're changing and we'll face a hostile world. Revealing letters from Jesus will shock most people. But, I'm ready for it. There is something empowering in seizing one's destiny."

Angie grinned. "For now, I guess I'd better seize the shower."

"It's all yours. I'm going to work on the story. Things have changed."

Angie ran up the stairs. Rennie ate breakfast and got dressed. She called Bud and left a message for him.

Forty minutes later, Angie came downstairs and found

Rennie at her computer, intently writing her story. "How's it going?"

"It's good. Better than I expected. I'm keeping it tight. A few minutes ago, I sensed something odd. It was as though I was getting in the way of what was supposed to be written. I was over analyzing the issues. When I let go and allowed it to flow, it felt good. What are you up to?"

"I think I'm ready to rejoin the world." Angie laughed. "It's funny how good I feel. Do you feel it? The things that used to seem so important are now trivial. I can still live my life, but now I will live it better. When should we meet up again? Do you want me to come here?"

"Yeah, if that's okay with you. We'll go from here to the airport to pick up Matthew. I'm not sure where he might feel comfortable staying. He's welcome here. I don't want to stick him in some hotel. The old guy should be with friends."

"He could stay with me, too. Let's think about it and talk later. Well, here we go. God bless."

Angie hugged Rennie and breezed out the front door. She paused on the lawn, waved at Rennie, and jogged to her car. Rennie stayed at the computer but listened to Angie's car starting and leaving.

"Here we go," she whispered.

By noon, Rennie had rewritten her story. After fixing a snack, she turned on some music and settled into a chair at the kitchen table. She felt totally refreshed. She put her feet up on the other chair and enjoyed the peaceful view out the kitchen window as she ate. A warm, fresh breeze came through the window screen and caressed her face. A deep breath was followed by a yawn.

She awakened with startling confusion at the sound of a dog barking in a nearby yard. Rennie checked her watch. It was 12:40 p.m. She hurried into the living room to retrieve her story.

She eagerly read every word as though she had never seen

the text. When she finished, her energy and clarity had returned.

She called Angie. "So, how's the wild librarian doing?" Rennie asked.

"Less wild and more focused today. How about you?"

"I passed out in a quiet moment, but I'm fine and back in action. I read my draft story again and it's good. I'm going in now to present it to Bud."

"Do you think he'll have any problems with it?"

Rennie thought for a moment.

"In the past, he'd give me a hard time on some things, but pretty much rolled over with only modest changes. But he's been acting really nervous. It's like he's threatened by something. I need to prepare for this more than I normally do. Did you get the journals?"

"What journals?"

"The ones Matthias … Okay. Forget it."

Rennie realized that Angie might be concerned someone may be listening to them.

"When can you be here? We need to visit before Matthew gets here."

"How about six o'clock? I was thinking that since you got dinner last night, I'll bring something tonight."

"Sounds good. Angie, I'm feeling anxious. Say a prayer for me."

"You're covered. Maybe you should say one just before you see him."

Rennie grinned. "You're the best. From the mouths of babes, as they say. See you tonight."

Rennie dashed upstairs and prepared for the office. When she returned downstairs, she felt the need to do something she rarely did. She closed and locked all the windows and doors. Standing in the front doorway before walking out, she scanned the interior of her home. She shivered. The tin box in the basement was more vividly present than anything else in the house.

She was so focused thinking about her story, she didn't notice the drive to the office. Striding down the hallway in her office building, she walked as though she were marching into battle. Her gaze was steady. She gave a slight wave to people who greeted her as they passed. When she reached her desk, she immediately went to work saving her story file to the computer and then reviewing the text.

She decided that she would see Bud before sending it to him. Rennie grabbed the folded pages from her notebook. She stood and looked in the direction of Bud's office. She paused and put her hand over her face for a quiet moment. Then, she stepped out of her cubicle and marched away to find Bud.

He was just returning to his office when she arrived at his door. "Rennie, nice of you to stop this year. Mind if we visit for a moment before you go away again?" Bud gestured a welcome into his office, but his face showed no delight.

"What's going on, Bud?" Rennie asked as she sat in the guest chair at his desk.

He grabbed the back of the chair next to hers and snapped it around to face her. He sat down. He looked detached and serious.

"Let's stop the game playing. This is a business and we have to produce. The old days are gone. We adapt or we die like the dinosaurs."

Rennie was surprised with her sense of calm. She saw the intensity that oozed from his pores.

"What you are talking about? What are the games, and what is it you need?"

His face reddened and he clasped his hands. "It's not what I need. It's what the people who run this place want. You prance around here talking about the significance of what we do. You proclaim, 'We're journalists. We must live up to our profound standards of truth and justice.' Where do you get that garbage? This is a business and 99 percent of the people who get our product don't care about truth and justice. They want the Sunday funnies, local and national gossip, television listings, and the classifieds so they can sell their junk. That's it. That's what we do. We maximize revenue and minimize cost and risk. It is that simple."

"Bud, am I not producing for you? Do you want to fire me, or do you want me to do other things? What do you want?"

Bud rubbed his face and looked around. He took a deep breath. "Look, we're going through changes here. They've been going on for some time and you haven't been paying attention. The truth is, I wasn't paying attention. You and I are among the few who believe we're journalists or were."

Bud leaned forward. "They're snapping my chain, Rennie. Now and then we can do a meaningful story to remind ourselves of our trade and let the public think we're still looking out for them. But our real job is to produce earnings, just like any other business."

"Hello in there. Is Bud around? I'd like to speak with him please." She observed panic on his face.

"Bud listen, I'm sorry you have so much pressure on you. You know I'll protect your backside. You want pulp? I can dish it out, baby."

Bud looked down, "Listen kid, I don't know if I can protect you. I value you more than just about anyone, but they can swoop into anyplace now and pull the cord on anyone."

"Who are we talking about? Has someone threatened me? I told you about that guy."

"I'm talking about the ownership; whoever they happen to be today. I don't think they're after you, but we're in a different business, today. Listen, I'm blowing off steam and you're the only person I can do this with."

"Bud, I've learned over the past week that the world is a dark and dangerous place. Our job is to be who we were made to be and do what we were made to do in spite of the world. We must not give in to the powers that want to manipulate us. Having integrity is being the special person God made and not the one the world wants you to be."

He sat up. "What are you talking about?"

"Bud, here's the question. Are you happier being someone other than the authentic person you are? I don't believe anyone is. Being yourself gives peace and joy. Any other way is painful."

He stared at her. "Don't you see the problem here? Don't you see the clash between you, and this organization? Rennie, wake up."

"Bud, the clash is you trying to be someone you're not."

"Rennie, we need to adapt to a new world. Okay?"

She smiled. "Fine. We're on the threshold of a new world. Do you want to know my story about Professor Matthias Justus of Simpson College?"

He relaxed. "Do I have a choice?"

Rennie's voice was nearly a whisper. "This story may be one of the most powerful that will ever come from this or any other newspaper. It may have more impact on the personal lives of the people who read or even hear of it than anything else in their lives."

He pushed back against his chair. His hand gripped the cushioned arm. "What are you talking about?"

"Here it is. Three simple pages of the greatest story ever told. Well, maybe the second greatest."

She handed him the sheets of paper. "This story reveals the truth of the murder of Matthias Justus when he was in London. It unlocks the extraordinary discovery of the greatest archeological discovery known to humanity, found by Professor Justus. The story confirms that Jesus lived and offers his own words on his mission for humanity. How about that?"

His mouth opened slightly, but he said nothing. He blinked

but didn't move.

"Bud, I see this as a three-part story. The first part is about Matthias. The second part is about his discovery, which is a bundle of personal letters written by Jesus. The third part may be the most powerful. It's what happens to people after reading the first two parts. What do you think?"

He got up from the guest chair and walked to the chair behind his desk. He looked down and seemed to be uneasy. Putting his hands on the high back of the chair he said, "You must either want me dead or you want me committed to some looney bin. I must have heard you wrong because what I heard is simply crazy."

"Bud, it's incredible. You cannot believe what I have been through in discovering all this."

He turned the chair and collapsed into it. As it rotated, he looked at Rennie as if in a daze. "Have you totally flipped out? This professor found letters written by Jesus? What proof do you have? Why has no one else ever heard of this? I don't know if you've gone crazy or I have in listening to you."

"The story is absolutely true. Read it yourself. The story's in your hands, and when the world reads it, everything will be different."

"Don't you get it, Rennie? People don't want life to be different. They struggle to keep what they have." He shook the papers in his hands. "I don't have a clue what you are talking about with this fantasy about letters from Jesus. Do you know what you are saying? Did you not hear what I was saying just minutes ago?"

"I heard every word, and you heard mine. It's real. Jesus is real. His letters are real. His mission was real. People need to know that."

He had a painful look on his face.

"Bud, do yourself a favor. Go for a walk. Cool down and get

back to the real you. Then come back here and read my story. I'll be at my desk."

"Rennie, just go to your desk. Leave me alone so I can rejoin the real world."

His head fell back against the chair.

"Take a break, Bud. You'll need it. This exhausted me when I first realized what I found. Since then, I have been getting in touch with that peace all people search for. It changes everything. I want you to have it, too. Take a break, and then read the story."

He closed his eyes and waved her to leave.

She got up from the chair and placed her hands on his desk. "Bud, the story is true. Once you take that in, life will have a different meaning. It's where you really belong and can live out your true purpose."

"Rennie, leave. Go."

She reached over and patted his hand. "Big things are about to happen my friend."

Des Moines, Iowa
Offices of the *Des Moines Record*

X - 4

Rennie checked her meeting schedule and finished reviewing her new email. She enjoyed the fresh perspective she found in her cubicle. Even the typical mid-afternoon lethargy passed by without stopping her. Her phone rang.

"Hi, Rennie, this is Floyd in Information Systems. I need to give you a heads up. I'm going to shut down your connection for a little bit. I'm doing a system recovery."

"Okay. How soon?"

"As soon as possible. Could you close whatever you are in so I can take care of this?"

"Sure. Could I have just a minute or two? Do I need to call you when I'm out?"

"No, I'll see when you're down. You won't be able to get back in for a while. Sorry."

"How long will this take? I've got some critical stuff to finish up."

"I don't know. It depends on what's found in the system."

Rennie listened very carefully and did not respond. This did not sound right. Floyd's voice sounded nervous. She sensed darker strategies at work.

"So, if you could finish up, I'll get going with this."

"Floyd, what's this about? What's really going on?"

"What do you mean? I said what we're doing."

"How big of a system shut down is this? How many others will be affected?"

"Not many. I need to do this now, so if you could close up, we can get started."

"Okay, I'll take care of it. I'll be a minute. Let me know when I'm up again."

Rennie stared at her computer screen. She opened her e-mail file and forwarded to herself her new and old messages from the past week. She opened her recent documents file and copied everything onto a flash drive. Then, she did a screen shot of her list of email messages and printed it. A message appeared on the screen advising her to shut down immediately. Another message appeared, and then her computer went dead.

Rennie stood up and surveyed the people in the cubicles around her. Everyone was busy and their computers were on. She walked toward Bud's office and observed that everyone had functioning computer monitors. One of the department's administrative assistants came by.

"Steve, do you know of any computer system problems, or shutdowns?"

"Not that I'm aware of."

"Do you know where Bud is?"

"No, he left about an hour ago. You might try his cell phone."

"Thanks."

Rennie hurried to her cubicle. She tried to start her computer. It was still dead. She found Bud's cell phone number and called it. She left a message.

She dialed Angie's office number. "Hi, I didn't expect to get you. How you doing?"

"Good, thanks. This is a better day. I retrieved the books, and I'll bring them over tonight. Did you hear anything from Matthew?"

"No. He's probably over the Atlantic right now." Rennie glanced to the side. Quietly, she said, "I need to talk with you, but I'm not sure what it is. I think there's something going on here. I talked with Bud this morning about the story and he kind of freaked. I gave him my copy of the story but didn't hear anything from him. Now, he's gone. Also, a few minutes ago, someone from IT called and said they had to shut down my computer. He didn't give me a good explanation. I've checked around. No one else is down. Something's going on."

Angie gasped. "I should have called you."

"Why? What happened?"

"Some guy called from the paper. He had a weasel kind of voice. He said his name was Terry. He said he was a fact checker and he wanted to double-check a few things."

"Like what? They don't do that on my stories. It's rarely done."

"It seemed innocent, and I was going to call you. Then, I was called into a meeting and just got out of it when you called. What's that about?"

"What did he ask? What did you tell him?"

"His questions seemed harmless enough. He asked about the archived materials for Matthias, and I confirmed we still had them in reserve. I'm so glad I got the journals. He asked about the letters, but he came at those very indirectly. I'm sure he wanted to know where they were. Naturally, I acted ignorant and innocent. This scares me. So, they've shut you off the system?"

"Yeah."

"Rennie, we've been given a mission. This will work out."

"Angie, I can't help but think that Matthias said the same thing, and he was killed. The dark world is very powerful."

"And it gains power when we operate on its terms. Center yourself. Find that peace we found."

"Amen, sister. Sorry, I had to say that. Angie, I feel like I'm gearing up for whatever we may have to face, and I've got to say I like it. We need to be very careful, at least until we sort out what's going on. That includes phone calls and email. Can you move the journals to a safe place? It might be best to give their whereabouts deniability."

"I will. We also have to think about Matthew. If things start to get sticky, we may need to protect him. Rennie, I don't like this."

"Me neither. Good thought about Matthew. Okay, we need to think big picture and tactically at the same time. I have to find Bud, then I'll call you back. Good luck."

"You, too."

Rennie grabbed her water bottle and drank it down. She got up to refill it at a water fountain when an admin came to her.

"I got a message that Katherine wants to see you. They want you up there right away."

A cold chill went down her spine. "What for? Who told you that?"

"Hey, don't shoot the messenger! Her secretary called and said she tried to reach you and your phone was busy. So, she said I should tell you. Hey, it's the eighth floor. When the boss calls, you jump. Maybe you won the Pulitzer or something."

Rennie's mind raced as he disappeared down a hall. She sat down and took a deep breath then another. She closed her eyes.

Okay, review. They knew I was on my phone. How did they know that? Did they hear me talk to Angie? What do I need to do? Whatever happens, I do what I need to do. Be peace. Breathe.

Rennie put a hand over her face. When she finished, she stood, grinned with determination, grabbed her notebook and water bottle, and headed for the elevator.

She got off the elevator on the eighth floor, introduced herself to the receptionist, and asked where the rest room was located. She needed a moment to settle her emotions. When she returned, Bud was standing by the reception desk.

"Bud, what's going on? They say I'm up for a Pulitzer."

An awkward smile creased his face. "What? I don't know. Who knows? I guess we need to go in there."

"Before we do, you owe me at least a ten-second explanation. I'm not going anywhere until I get it."

"I don't know what's going on. This is way over me. All I did was share with the chain of command the gist of your story. It went up fast." Bud stroked his thin hair. "I don't know what happened next. Come on. They're waiting."

He did a quick pivot and went into the publisher's office.

Bud sat in a chair away from the desk area. Katherine was standing in front of her desk, speaking with a man in a tailored suit. Rennie glanced around at the luxurious suite and the view of the city.

Katherine smiled and held out her hand as she stepped toward Rennie. "Rennie, I am so delighted to finally meet you. Your work is highly regarded here. I am glad you are on our team." She turned toward the man. "Do you know Larry? Larry, this is Rennie Haran."

Rennie shook the man's hand and looked him in the eye. She carefully managed her breathing.

The publisher gestured to a burgundy leather guest chair. "Please come and sit down. Bud said you're working on a new story. It sounds very exciting. I'd like to know more."

Katherine stepped around her massive desk and sat in a high-back, black leather chair outlined with brass rivets. Larry sat in a chair off one corner of the desk. The expression on his face was pleasant but unreadable. Rennie glanced at Bud. He strained a smile.

Rennie eased into the chair. "I am delighted to meet you Katherine. It must be very challenging to be the publisher of a paper like this."

"It is, yes. It is also very worthwhile when one thinks of the responsibilities we carry. Without the people's right to know, our society is threatened. Don't you think?"

Rennie grinned when she thought of Bud's tirade earlier in

the day. She was certain the pressure he was under came from this office. It had nothing to do with noble platitudes.

"That's what we like to think, ma'am. May I ask a question?"

Katherine smiled and glanced at Larry. Rennie noticed their connection. "Of course. We expect questions from our best reporter."

"I just wondered if you read the copy I gave to Bud, and what you think of it."

"I'm glad you asked. That's why I wanted to visit with you. The story is most impressive; historic really. It certainly would put the *Record* into a remarkable position. We wondered if you have fully checked it out. The profound nature of the story begs the question."

Rennie relaxed. "Before I answer that, may I ask another quick question?"

Everyone's eyes quickly looked at everyone else. Katherine's smile slid away. She nodded.

"My computer is down right now. I wondered if that might be related to this."

Katherine's nostrils slightly flared. "We will look into that. I don't keep track of those things."

Bud stood. "If you don't need me, I should go back downstairs."

"Fine, Bud, thank you," Katherine replied without looking at him.

He offered a faint smile to Rennie and left the office, closing the door behind him.

Katherine shifted in her chair. "So, please tell us about this discovery by the professor. Very sad, him getting killed and all that. To the point, have you seen these letters? Do you know what they say?"

Rennie's lips lifted into a soft grin. Her mind was clearer than ever. "You ask a good question, ma'am. Did you read the story?"

Katherine tried to disguise her annoyance with Rennie. "I can say I looked at it."

"Well, in there I mentioned how the letters were found at the British Museum, in London. I went there and was fortunate to meet a distinguished fellow who is the son of Professor Justus. He told me the story he was told of the Professor's death."

"So, the letters were lost or stolen, or were they recovered?"

Rennie felt cornered. She leaned forward. "It turned out he had not taken the letters with him. They remained in his room in London."

"That is all very interesting, but my question was whether or not you have seen the letters. I think verification of this fact is fairly important here."

"Yes ma'am, it is and, I intend to get that verification."

"Are the letters in your possession?"

"No, ma'am, they are not. I contacted someone in London who was going to try to get his hands on them and when available, authenticate them." Rennie smiled. "He has outstanding credentials and connections with the British Museum."

"So, your contact in London has them?"

"My source in London will arrange everything."

"I hear you use the word 'source.' Is that for a reason?"

"Well, we know the importance of those in this business. I'm sure you appreciate that. Given the importance of this discovery, this is an obvious situation where confidentiality is paramount."

"Even from your own people?"

Rennie again remembered to manage her breathing. "We all know that managing our sources protects the team."

She controlled her desire to laugh. "By the way, could you arrange for my computer to get going again? Obviously, it's important for me to get some things done here."

Katherine stared at her.

Rennie turned to the quiet man in the chair. "Larry, are you with the *Record?*"

Katherine gave a subtle nod in his direction. "I am not with the *Record.* My firm is retained by the company for advice and assistance in special situations."

"I'm not clear on who you are, Larry. As Katherine said, this is a very important situation. I like to know who is on the team."

"Of course, I'm sorry my role wasn't explained. I'm outside legal counsel for the *Record.*"

Rennie shifted toward Katherine. "I knew we had legal staff. I didn't know we retained outside counsel as well. Very interesting."

"Your cooperation with Larry will be most appreciated. It will serve the company well."

"Certainly. Larry, call me anytime I can help. Should I clear things through Larry before going to Bud?"

Katherine's lips twitched. "No, you work with Bud as you always have. We don't want to hinder proven success, do we?"

"No, ma'am. May I get back downstairs now? I need to see if my computer is up."

"Of course. Thank you for bringing your wonderful story to us. Many would never have gotten this far with it. Please keep us up to date. By the way, the interest in those letters is higher than you may think."

"I think the interest in these letters is higher than anyone in this world can understand," Rennie replied.

Katherine slowly stood and placed her knuckles on the desk. "If you have the letters, they need to go into the right hands. It's best you do not underestimate the situation or overestimate yourself."

Her icy stare didn't intimidate Rennie. "There are people who should have them, and it's time to not play games. Deliver them to me, and I will see they are properly handled."

Rennie arose from her chair without looking away from her powerful boss. "Where do you see this going?"

"That's not easy to say. Would you like to know your future?" the publisher responded with a modestly disguised sneer.

"Katherine, if one is right with God, they know their future. Do you know yours?"

"I may have some knowledge of your future."

"It is said, the future is where the dust will blow. We all are dust. But I know the wind."

Katherine looked confused.

Rennie pivoted to Larry and offered her hand. He hesitated, got up, and shook her hand.

She walked with casual grace out of the office without looking back. Riding the elevator down to the seventh floor, she raced to an empty desk to call Angie. Her cell phone number responded with a voice message. She hung up and looked at her watch. It was 4:28 p.m.

Where is she?

Rennie didn't know what to do. She dialed her home phone number and listened to a new message. It was from Angie.

"Hey partner, I'm taking off early. I figured it might be a late night again, so I'm going home to take a nap. Could we meet at your place at seven? We can go over some ideas before going to the airport to pick up Matthew. See you then."

Rennie returned to her cubicle and found her computer was on. Someone had not only started it, but it was online. She called Floyd in IT. His voice mail took the call. She hung up hard.

She did a quick review of her files to see if anything was different. She had so many folders and documents it was difficult to remember what should be where. Giving up on that, she got into her e-mail to check for messages. Something looked wrong.

She found the screen print of new messages. It indicated that three messages were no longer there. She found them in the old message file. Someone had gone through her e-mail. She jumped up so fast her chair slammed into the cubicle wall. A man working a few spaces away stood up, looked over the wall, and saw the fury in her face. He quickly sat down.

She logged off her computer, looked around her space to see if anything had been moved, and then left the office. As she walked through the parking ramp to her car, she thought about her e-mail and the vulnerability of her communications. Her cell phone and computer belonged to the newspaper. If people wanted to, they could probably also get into her home phone and the computer there. It was time for a new perspective and attitude.

On the way home, Rennie stopped at a traffic signal in front of a consumer electronics store. She cranked the steering wheel around and raced into the parking lot. She went straight to the cell phone section of the store and inquired about various plans. Leaving the store, Rennie had two new cell phones and monthly service on a "family share" plan. She felt empowered with the thought of being a step ahead of whoever might intrude on their mission.

Rennie returned home and welcomed a greeting from Balderdash. He purred loudly, arched his back, and brushed against a corner of the wall. She laid down her bag and hurried through the house opening windows to release the contained warmth of a summer day. She kicked off her shoes, tossing them under a table.

She considered how to accommodate Matthew for the evening and beyond. Running upstairs, she surveyed the small rooms. She leaned against the doorjamb and wondered where he would feel most comfortable. Glancing at her suitcase and clothing on the floor, she returned downstairs with a sense of urgency.

PART ELEVEN

Des Moines, Iowa

XI - 1

Angie approached Rennie's porch and noticed a note taped to the front door inviting her in. She stepped inside and called out, "Hey Rennie. Are you here?"

"Yeah, come on up. I'm fixing the bedroom for Matthew."

Angie greeted Balderdash and went up the stairs. Entering the bedroom, she saw Rennie smoothing the comforter on the bed. Towels were piled up on a dresser.

"Very nice," Angie said, "the place looks great. Is someone special coming?" She laughed.

Rennie was in no mood for joking around. She shook her head "no" and put her finger to her lips. She waved for Angie to follow her.

Rennie picked up the bag of cell phones and went down to the kitchen. She closed the swinging kitchen door behind them and shut the window. She turned up the volume on a CD player and turned on the sink faucet.

Angie looked confused and whispered, "What's up? What happened at your office and with your computer?"

Rennie was intent and strong. "I know this seems odd. We need to be very careful. My meeting at the office raised red flags like crazy. I met the publisher. No one meets her unless it is very good or very bad. I'd like to think our story is on the good side, but she didn't give me that impression."

Rennie's voice softened. "Angie, it was all very sinister. She wanted the letters, and earlier, the IT guy in our office called

342

me. He said they were doing a routine system check. But my computer was the only one shut down and someone checked my e-mail. I didn't have time to see what else they did."

"Oh, my gosh," Angie whispered, "they don't trust you. Or, maybe they aren't to be trusted."

Rennie took a deep breath. "Angie, in my meeting with her, I was so at peace. It was amazing. I asked the right questions, and I think I said the right things. This transformation we've been going through is wonderful. I feel empowered."

"Me, too. I have this sense of separation from the world, like a visitor."

"Right. Me, too. I need you to keep me on track. All things are new now."

She turned up the water faucet to create additional ambient noise.

"There's something we need to do. Until this gets sorted out and we know the letters are safe, we must be careful with our communications with each other."

"I don't understand."

"People have followed us Angie, they broke into my house, and I think they're now monitoring our communications. They want the letters. To keep ahead of them, I got a couple of new cell phones."

She opened the bag from the store. "We should use these only to talk with each and with no one else. If we call anyone else, they'll get our numbers and make the phones less secure."

"I can't believe it, but you're right."

"The letters are too important for any mistakes. We don't know who's after them and what they'll do."

"I agree. What about Matthew? He'll be in soon. Have you figured out what we should say?"

"We need to lay the whole situation out for him. We've got to trust him. What do you think?"

343

"Absolutely. I don't think it's a coincidence that Matthew is part of this. We're now a three-person team."

Rennie nodded. "We still need to decide on where and how he reads and reviews everything. Where are the journals, by the way?"

"I left them in the car."

Rennie felt a moment of panic.

"Just kidding. I'm not that dumb. I set them on a stand in the entry when I came in. They're wrapped in some textbook covers I got from school. Pretty good, huh?"

Rennie hurried out of the kitchen and found the journals. She opened each one and fanned the pages. Then she looked around the room trying to decide where to hide them.

"What's up?" Angie asked.

Rennie whispered, "I'm just thinking about where to hide these. I've never dealt with this kind of thing before. We need to step back and relax a little."

"I just thought of something. Do we need to go into the kitchen?"

They returned to the kitchen, and Angie suggested a plan. Rennie agreed and removed a roll of aluminum foil from a cabinet. She wrapped each of the journals in foil and then bound each again in plastic wrap.

"Now, where can they go?" Angie asked.

"I've got an old freezer downstairs and I'll put them in there. It's not likely that someone would look there. Is that okay? Will the cold damage them?"

"Is the freezer on? Is there food in there?"

"No to both. I've not used it for a while."

"If it's not too cold or hot inside then no, and not with the foil on them and with this type of paper. A little cold is not a problem, but any humidity would not be good for the paper. This is okay for a few days."

Rennie took the wrapped journals downstairs and returned a few minutes later.

"Angie, did you bring any food?"

"No, sorry. I was focused on the," her voice softened, "the journals. How about if we go out for something on the way to the airport? We have time."

"Fine with me. Are you ready? It could get strange."

"I'm beginning to like strange. Let's get food and then Matthew."

Rennie hurried through the house and made sure all doors and windows were locked. She pulled down the window shades and turned on two lights. When they went out the front door, she locked it, and paused to look around the neighborhood. It seemed quiet. Rennie made sure her car was locked.

They got into Angie's car and slowly drove away. As they did, Rennie looked out the back window. A dark sedan about a hundred feet down the street came out of a parking space and drove past her house. It slowed down, and then it picked up speed as it followed them from a distance. Two blocks later, the car turned and disappeared.

They stopped to eat at a chain restaurant and didn't discuss anything but the fun parts of their trip to London. Their laughter felt good. A reminder tone on Rennie's phone triggered a change in attitude. They said nothing as they put together some money, paid the bill, and returned to Angie's car.

She parked in the ramp next to the airport terminal then walked to where schedules for arriving flights were displayed. Matthew's flight number was indicated to be on time and arriving within minutes. They found two seats together in the waiting area.

"Rennie, I hope Matthew can handle it."

"What, the flight? He's a veteran of travel."

"No, the discovery. He's an old guy. His ticker may not be

strong enough." Angie tapped her chest. "Wouldn't it be awful if Matthew died as a result of the letters just as Matthew did?"

Rennie rolled her eyes and responded with a soft tone, "We simply need to present it to him gently. First, give him the journals. Get him started in the one toward the end where Matthias talks about finding the letters. Then, when Matthew knows of that, we tell him we found them or what we think might be them. He has to review them to see what we found. We don't really know what's in that box. It's like my editor always says, we need verification."

"Look, people are coming down the escalator. I wonder if they were on his plane."

They tried to see Matthew down the concourse. Rennie looked around at the others who waited. She noticed a young man sitting in the most remote chair from the walkway where passengers would pass by. He didn't seem to be anxious or look toward the escalator. Rennie glanced in his direction several times but never directly at him.

Several dozen passengers walked by and were greeted with affection by those awaiting them. Rennie and Angie shared their excitement, anticipating Matthew's arrival. Rennie looked again in the direction of the young man. He continued to read a magazine and paid little attention to the arriving passengers.

Angie grabbed Rennie's arm and said in a hushed voice, "There he is."

When Matthew saw them, he grinned and gave a subtle wave. Reaching the bottom of the escalator, he stepped to the side.

"Hello Angie."

She hugged him.

When Rennie embraced him, she caught a glimpse of the young man looking with indifference at the greeting line for the passengers.

"Thank you for coming, Matthew," Rennie said. "We're so happy to see you again. Let's get your luggage, then we'll get you home so you can rest. Are you hungry?"

"Not at all, my dear. I lose my appetite when I travel long distances."

Angie put her arm through his and drew him toward the baggage claim area. They engaged in small talk, but Rennie kept watch in her peripheral vision for the young man. As they made the turn to go to baggage claim, the man got up, left the arrival area, and went out of the terminal.

When Matthew excused himself to use the men's room, Rennie pulled Angie's arm and moved close to the wall.

"We're being followed. There was a guy sitting with all of us waiting for the arriving passengers." Rennie looked around. "He didn't greet anyone, but the moment Matthew arrived, he got up and left. He's probably outside waiting for us to take Matthew home."

Her voice fell to a whisper. "What do we do?"

Angie looked stunned.

"What guy?" She looked around. "Are you sure?"

"Absolutely. We've got to be extra careful."

"Okay, if you're right, then whoever they are knows Matthew is here. They may or may not know who he is. If we act like we're afraid or concerned, we lose the edge. We need them to think we don't know they are there."

"This might have something to do with my meeting with Katherine and my computer being checked out. I know now I've been watched since this assignment began. You're right though, we have to act like we're oblivious to them. Hey, here he comes."

Matthew buttoned his brown tweed sport coat as he strolled up the hallway. "Ladies, it is delight for this old man to find himself in the company of you two lovely ladies again. Now that I am refreshed and, on the ground, I look forward to hearing what wonders you have discovered that require such urgent involvement of one like me."

Angie put her hand on his shoulder. "Maybe, we just wanted to show you off to our friends."

Rennie felt a growing sense of urgency. "Matthew, despite what my teasing friend here has to say, this is a mission of great importance. When we get back to the house, we can fill you in on some of the details. You can rest up tonight so your gifts can be put to work tomorrow. How's that sound?"

"Brilliant. I look forward to the adventure. Let's get my bag and be off."

Most of the passengers had already taken their luggage, so Matthew's bag was easy to find on the carousel. Rennie pulled it off the conveyor with a determined lift.

"I'll get my car and pick you guys up," Angie offered.

"I think we should all go to the car together," Rennie responded. She looked at Matthew. "It's late, and it's not too far."

Matthew nodded. "Then let us all go together. It will give me a chance to begin my tour of Des Moines, Iowa."

Once in the car, Rennie's eyes tracked every shadow, while her smile never dimmed. Matthew rode in the front seat with Angie. Rennie sat in the back, watching to see if any cars were following them.

When they arrived at her home, Rennie hurried from the car and opened the front door. She turned on the porch light and welcomed her special guest.

They briefly toured the house as Rennie turned on lights. She made tea and put the pot and cups on the dining room table with a few cookies. They settled into chairs and relaxed. Rennie got up and turned on music that was louder than what one might have for dinner conversation. Angie moved her chair close to Matthew.

She cleared her throat. "Matthew, it's hard to know where

to begin. You know some of the basic information. There is a very important additional item." Her voice softened. "We discovered it when we returned. It was the discovery that your father had made."

Matthew's expression did not change.

Rennie slipped forward in her chair. "We found something in the archived materials here that was overlooked. We happened to open a sealed box and found something remarkable. We aren't sure what it is or how special it may be, and that's why you are needed. I think you should review Matthias's journals to read his own words of his discovery. Then you can look at what we found and see if you think it's the same thing. How does that sound to you?"

"It sounds rather mysterious. I am intrigued. Whatever the treasure may be, I'm not sure it will equal this opportunity for me to review my father's written words."

"Matthew," Angie interjected, "believe me, it will more than equal your father's written words."

Rennie asked Matthew, "Could we begin in the morning? We're all tired and can start fresh then."

"Very well. As of tomorrow, we will begin to unfold the answers to your concerns."

Rennie grinned. "You don't know how close you are to the truth. Angie, can you stay, too? I can set you up here on the couch. I'll sleep on a cot I used for camping trips. Matthew, let me show you to your room."

With cordial wishes for good sleep and the lights off, they all settled in for rest and renewal. Rennie eased herself off the cot and checked to ensure the doors were locked. As she passed by a window, she peeked into the night past the drawn shade. The faint light of a cell phone was on in a car about two houses away. She held her breath wondering who they were and what they wanted.

Des Moines, IA
Rennie's Home

XI - 2

A sound in the kitchen awakened Angie. Light of a new morning slipped around the window shades. She was immediately alert but didn't move. The kitchen door creaked as it slowly opened. Angie's heart rate rose to a rapid thump in her chest. She quickly sat up and looked over the back of the couch just as Matthew stepped from the kitchen.

He was startled and jumped, spilling hot tea on his hand. He set the cup on the dining table and hurried into the kitchen.

Angie leaped off the couch and ran to the kitchen. "I am so sorry. I didn't know it was you. I heard a noise and wasn't sure who or what was in the house. Are you okay?"

"Yes, yes dear, it is not the first time I have worn my drink. Really, do not worry yourself."

A puzzled look appeared on his face.

She looked down at the oversized gray t-shirt and floral boxer shorts she had worn to bed.

"I'm sorry Angel, or Angie, I don't think I should see you this way."

He looked away to tend to his hand.

"Oh, that's okay. It's just what I wear to bed. Excuse me, I need to run upstairs for a moment."

As Angie tiptoed out of the kitchen, she noticed Rennie sitting upright in the cot.

Angie waved and whispered, "It's okay. It's Matthew."

Rennie got up and shook her head, throwing her hair about and letting it settle. She rubbed her face as she walked into the kitchen.

Matthew opened the door and stopped when he saw her. "I must say, this is the busiest morning of interaction with young ladies that I can remember. And particularly, ladies attired in such interesting ways."

He looked at the floor as he eased past her.

Rennie put her hands on her hips. "Hey, what's wrong with running shorts and a t-shirt? One thing you need to learn around here," she said with mock seriousness, "is that you never cross me before I have coffee. Understood?"

Matthew gave a slight bow and covered his eyes with one hand. Then, he chuckled. "So, am I to understand that the standard evening wear for women in America is a sport shirt and men's underwear?"

Rennie pointed at him. "Consider yourself warned, mister."

He carried his cup and saucer into the living room, set the saucer and cup on a coffee table, walked to a window, and pulled the bottom of the shade, allowing it to slowly rise up.

"Don't, wait!" Rennie yelled as she stepped out of the kitchen.

Matthew released the shade string, causing it to spin to the top of the window. He grasped at the cord hanging from it, missing the string several times.

"Matthew, I'm sorry. It's okay. I've been a little on edge for a couple of days. It's fine."

"It's no trouble to close the shade. I can get it."

"No, it's fine. Please leave it open."

She returned to the kitchen. He regressed to a chair and cautiously drank his tea.

Angie came down the stairs. "You people are sure noisy in the morning."

"It's my fault," responded Matthew. "I promise I will not move again."

Angie collapsed on the couch. "Did you get enough sleep? It's only six o'clock."

"Yes, dear, I did. My body clock tells me it's much later. I will adjust soon. Actually, I laid awake when I first woke up and have been wondering about the great mystery that beckoned me on this trip. When do I learn of it?"

Angie glanced toward the kitchen door. She stood and stretched. "I think it's time. If it's okay with you, let's have some breakfast first. Rennie and I will get cleaned up, and then we'll lay it all out for you. I'm glad you're here, Matthew. This is a golden moment."

As Rennie approached, Angie whispered to her, "I told him you and I need to get ready and we all need to eat. Then it's time we give him everything."

"One question, ladies," Matthew inquired. "Is there anything I should not be doing while you are in preparation?" He grinned.

Rennie said he could feel free to look around and might enjoy the rocker on the front porch. Then, she dashed upstairs to get ready.

Within an hour, the ladies were ready for the day, breakfast was ready, and Matthew was called to the table.

As they ate, Matthew gazed at his new friends.

"Thank you for your warm welcome. The informality with which I am accepted makes me feel more like family than a distant visitor. And, this feast must be intended for more than just the three of us."

Rennie put her paper napkin to her mouth and laughed. "If you only knew how badly we eat around here, you would understand how rare this breakfast really is."

"And, how welcome!" Angie added. "I didn't realize how hungry I am."

Another minute of enjoyable, quiet eating passed by. Rennie finally decided to tell Matthew why he was called. "I think it's time we got into it. The reason you are here."

She glanced at her audio system. She excused herself from the table and got the remote control. She turned on some classical music and raised the volume.

Rennie spoke in a soft voice. "While you were on the front porch this morning, I got out a few books that we would like you to read. They are Matthias's journals. For now, there is only one part, the last part, of the last book that we would like you to review. It is the denouement, as one might say, to Matthias' time in London. It's his description of his discovery, and if it moves you as it did us, you will see the significance of your being here."

Rennie glanced at Angie and leaned toward Matthew. She whispered, "There is another aspect to this situation that is important for you to know. We may be watched or listened to. I believe we have been watched and we must be careful."

He stopped eating and studied her with a cool seriousness she had not seen before. He said nothing but appeared to wait for more information.

"Since I filed my draft story with my paper about Matthias and what he found, something has been going on behind the scenes. I don't think it's friendly."

He put down his utensils. His voice dropped to a low, airless tone. "If what you have found and reported is as significant as you suggest, it will be of no surprise that dark forces have become active. I have seen it before. There is a tenuous understanding between the worlds of science and greed, when it comes to the ancient world. One must be ever vigilant. I suggest we enjoy this wonderful beginning to our day and then begin."

He gave a quick grin and nod, followed with attending to his eager appetite.

They finished the meal in focused silence. Then they met in the kitchen. Rennie ran water in the sink to create background noise. She unwrapped the journals.

"I placed a bookmark in this one, where I recommend you

begin your reading. The section will not take long. You are welcome to go back farther if you wish. Matthias was a good writer.
You might feel more depth to his words than we did, since it's the
first time you will hear from him. Take as long as you need. We
called in to our offices to let them know we'll be in later. Matthew,
we plan to be here with you until you get through this journal.
After that, we can plan the day."

He took a deep breath. "There may be no adequate way to
express my appreciation for what we are doing here. Where would
you like me to pursue this?"

He looked at the journal and stroked its cover.

"There's a spare room upstairs that's set up for you. It has a
desk and a chair. The lighting is good. If you need anything, just
let us know."

Matthew stepped closer to them and whispered with a sly
grin, "All will be well." He left the kitchen and proceeded up the
stairs.

Rennie listened to him walk across the wooden floor, open
and close the old door, and slide the chair back from the desk.

"How do you think he'll respond?" Angie asked.

"There's no way to know. It's too much to comprehend. I'm
still not in touch with it. I hope he'll be okay."

"Rennie, do you think we're being watched? Is there someone
out there?" Angie tilted her head toward the window.

"Yes. I don't know their agenda. It's important we continue
to appear to not know they are there. At the same time, we've got
to safeguard what we have here."

"Are we going to leave him alone? I know I've got to go to
work this morning."

"I do too, and I've thought about that. My neighbor Roger
will work with us. He lives behind me. We'll sneak Matthew
there without anyone seeing him. The backyard is well shielded
by a fence and bushes in the front and on the sides."

Rennie's eyes danced with excitement. "I'll call Roger using my new phone. We can be invisible to anyone trying to break into our lines of communication."

"Good. While you do that, could I use your computer to check my e-mail?"

"Sure, go ahead."

Rennie turned off the water flowing from the kitchen faucet. She followed Angie out but went upstairs with a careful effort to not make any noise on the stairway.

As she finished getting ready for work, she heard a gasp from Matthew's workroom. His chair could be heard moving on the floor. She leaned into the hallway and could hear him pacing across the small room.

Rennie returned downstairs and called Roger. She explained the situation and that Matthew needed a quiet place to do some research while she was at work. Roger said he welcomed the company. She said she would let him know when they had worked out the details.

Rennie heard another gasp from upstairs, as Angie was about to leave.

Angie ran half-way up the stairs. She hurried back down. "We have to see if he's alright."

"Why don't you go up?"

Angie quietly moved up the stairway. Her hand formed around the top post of the banister, levering her slowly into the upper hall. Rennie remained at the foot of the stairs, silently watching.

Angie called out Matthew's name. "Do you need anything?"

"Some water would be welcome."

She didn't move and hardly breathed. Then she returned to the top of the stairs and whispered down to Rennie, "He needs some water."

Rennie hurried into the kitchen, promptly delivering a

plastic tumbler of water and ice. Angie met her on the stairway then looked at her watch and grimaced.

"I need to leave. Can you take over?"

"Sure. Let me know what else he needs."

Angie delivered the water and came down the stairs. She looked shaken. Rennie put an arm over her shoulder and walked her into the kitchen.

Angie turned on the faucet. "He said he doesn't need anything. Something is touching him deeply. He's at the discovery of the letter from Mary and from Matthew."

"So, he isn't to where Matthias mentions the letters from Jesus, yet?"

"No. The journal itself is quite a shock for him. It might be best if you go up and sit in the hallway. I've got to go. If I don't show up at the library, things could get ugly for me. I've had some odd contacts with my boss."

"Then you'd better go. I'll let you know what happens here. Remember to use the new phone. We've got to be safe now. God bless you," she whispered.

"And, you too."

Rennie escorted her to the front door. She looked out the small window before opening the door.

"Be safe," she said. "And try to be natural."

"Yes, Mother."

She laughed as her steps took her swiftly across the yard to her car. She waved as she drove away.

Rennie closed the front door but stood for a short time, looking out the window at the cars in the street and a few people walking down the sidewalk. She breathed a deep sigh.

Des Moines, IA
Rennie's Home

XI - 3

Remembering the box hidden downstairs, Rennie locked the front door and hurried to a closet to find a canvas bag. She took a few steps up the stairway and listened for any sounds of Matthew. Then, bag in hand, she hurried through the kitchen and went down the basement stairs into the darkness. In the limited light from a small window, Rennie went to the storeroom and opened the door. Her hand knocked a jar off the shelf, but she caught it as it fell. She took a deep breath and looked around.

Taking the box with the letters, she put it into the bag, and blew hard on the dusty shelves. Then she closed the door again.

She heard the basement door open. She spun around, grasping the bag in both hands.

"Hello!" Matthew's voice called out.

Rennie breathed again. "I'm down here!" she shouted. As she ran up the stairs, she stopped and clasped her hand over her mouth.

"That was stupid," she whispered. Rennie met Matthew in the kitchen.

"How's it going? Did you need something?"

She set the bag on the counter and turned on the water faucet.

Matthew eased himself onto a stool. "I never expected I would know him so intimately. It's an intellectually and personally inspiring experience. I see now what you meant when you said I needed to be rested and prepared."

"How far along are you?"

"It is difficult to know where to begin. In a short time, I've listened to the voice of my father and become aware of the personal intensity of his life. I'm aware of his finding certain precious letters that indicate a most remarkable origin."

"Did you read the results of his translations?"

"No, but the box from which they came is indeed a wonderful find, a clue to a wondrous history. Antioch was a hotbed of early church formative efforts. The same is true for Alexandria, which sustained some of the most articulate early Christian voices."

He relaxed with a great sigh. "After a short break here, I am eager to finish the journal."

"Well, that might be a while. When you finish this part of the journal, you may be compelled to pursue something new and more profound."

"Really?"

"Since I need to get into my office for a bit, I've arranged for you to continue your studies next door at my neighbor's place. He's a great guy. His name is Roger, and he's kind of a tough old Norwegian, but he's as good as a person can be. I told him you needed some private space to work on a special project while you're here. He'd like the company, so I'll call him now. I hope that's okay."

"I'd be perfectly fine here, but if in your wisdom I need to be elsewhere, I trust your judgment. I'm sure Roger and I will get along fine."

Matthew slipped off the stool and looked out the window to the backyard. "There's something I haven't told you."

Matthew's weary eyes narrowed so the puffy lids nearly closed together. His lips became thin.

"A dramatic event occurred on the day we met at the restaurant. When I returned to my home, I discovered that vandals had ransacked the place. Given that we were together for less than two hours, there must have been at least three or four people moving very fast. It was shocking. I fear what they would have done if I had been at home."

Rennie rested her hands on his shoulders. His body sagged under the weight of the memory.

He looked past her and struggled as moisture glistened in the lashes of one eye. "Receiving your call to come to Iowa was a wonderful opportunity to escape the violation of my space. I called a few friends who promptly came to my rescue that day. They cleaned and straightened everything immediately, but I must admit I needed to get away."

"I'm so sorry. I feel responsible. There is so much you need to know. Your life will be changed when you hear everything."

"Thank you for trusting me with the truth. I place myself in your hands for how this is to proceed. If you think I should spend some time with your neighbor, then that is where I will be. Let us begin the grand finale."

Matthew gave her a light kiss on her cheek.

"I'll be working on my computer for a few minutes and will make a few calls. If you need me, just stomp on the floor. Whatever happens, please know it's okay."

Matthew started up the stairs and gave a little salute. She laughed.

As Rennie headed to the computer, her new cell phone rang. "Hello? Angie?"

"Did he read it all yet?"

"No, he didn't get to the revelation near the end. He took a break, but he's back upstairs now. Angie, you will not believe this. After we met him for lunch in London, he discovered that people had ransacked his house. He's really wounded by it."

"How sad. That does it. Whoever did it must have seen us with him and figured he must know what we know. My gosh, they might have thought he had the letters. What are we going to do?"

"At this point, we've got to keep moving forward. For the moment, we're alright. Let's not forget our mission."

"Fine, but a strange thing happened at school. I've been called to the office of the Vice President of Business. It's very odd. I don't know what's up."

"Stay focused, but relaxed. We've done nothing wrong, but I think wrong is trying to force its way into this situation. Maybe it's something simple. You might have won an award or something."

"Yeah, right." Angie's deep breath could be heard on the phone. "I like the idea of these phones, Rennie. Good call. I'll let you know what happens."

"Angie, do me a favor? Don't go and hit anyone in the head with your lamp of truth."

"Got'cha. No whacking. Be safe."

Rennie settled into her chair, logged on to her computer, and found the story file. She read with a discerning eye every facet of her historic report.

Twenty-five minutes later, she realized that she had not heard anything from upstairs since Matthew went up there. She sat back to listen for any noise. There was nothing. She grabbed her cell phone and approached the stairway.

When she started up the stairs, Matthew appeared on the next level and beckoned her to join him. She hurried up. Tears poured from his eyes. His lips quivered. She wrapped her arms around him.

"It's okay."

They slowly sank to the floor where he sat like a large child. He buried his face in his hands. "You were right. It is too profound for words. How glorious a find. How wonderful that he could have held such a treasure. He read them, Rennie, the very words! Whatever became of it all?"

"This is where it gets really amazing," she whispered. "I

think I may have them."

He looked up at her with shock.

"Quite by accident, I might have ended up with them. That's why you're here. You're the only person with the talents we could trust. You can look at them, translate them, verify them. Then we need you to help us decide what to do."

"You have them?" he whispered.

She nodded. Taking his arm, they went down the stairs. She walked him through the kitchen and turned on the faucet again. She pulled down the window shade. Rennie opened the canvas bag and removed the tin box wrapped with rubber bands.

Matthew gave her a perplexed look. "Is that —?"

"This was Matthias' lunch box. It must be what he used to secret the treasure from the museum."

"How ironic." Matthew grinned. "There is an old find in Egypt called Oxyrhynchus that yielded hundreds of quality documents. Those who discovered them ended up using biscuit tins like this to deliver them out of the country."

"I think the box in which Matthias found these came from Oxyrhynchus."

"Rennie, is what is in this humble box what I think it is?"

"I believe so. Matthew, I think we all came together for this, to find this and reveal it."

"Do others know of this? People at your newspaper?"

"Yes," she said. "That's why we must be careful. That's why Roger's place is perfect for doing your analysis. No one will see you go over there, and Roger will keep you safe. I can reach him on his phone when I need him. Are you ready?"

"This may be what I have been prepared for through my entire life. In my heart, I know I am unworthy to touch what may be in this box. But I will do this in honor of my father."

His eyes twinkled as he looked at the box in his hands. "Call Roger. I need to get to work."

Des Moines, IA
Offices of the *Des Moines Record*

XI - 4

Rennie strode through the newsroom and headed straight toward Bud's office. She didn't stop at her cubicle first or notice that no one greeted her as she passed by. As she neared his office, she stopped. His room was dark, and the door was closed. She had never seen it that way in seven years. She felt confused and looked for help.

"Hey Molly," she called to a woman several cubicles away. "Where's Bud?"

Molly seemed to be focused on something.

"I don't know. Strange, huh? Check with Sherry over there."

Rennie hustled over to a confident, peaceful woman who was reviewing a document. "What's the deal with Bud? Is he all right?"

The woman glanced at his office. "I'm not sure. We got a call from the eighth floor saying he wouldn't be in today. Someone tried his house, but there was no answer. Katherine's secretary said he was okay. He told her he was taking your advice and knew that you would do the right thing. Some say you know what's going on. Why do you think he isn't in?"

Rennie's face showed nothing. "I don't know. But I'm glad he's taking care of himself. If you hear from him, tell him he knows who loves him."

Back in her cubicle, her desk phone indicated she had a message. She eased into her chair and stared at the phone for a moment before picking up the receiver. The message was from Will, down in the vault.

"Hey, this is Will. You asked me about some Simpson prof from back in the twenties. Don't say anything about this to anyone, but a guy I never heard of called me wanting similar information. He asked if I gave you any information, and if so, what. I asked him who he was, but he said if I had any questions, I should call the eighth floor. What's going on? Be sure to delete this message. Be safe, girl!"

Rennie continued to hold the phone to her ear. "Okay," she said quietly.

She pushed the message delete button on the phone and hung up. She took her new cell phone out of her bag, but then stood up and looked across the newsroom.

She grabbed her bag and headed across the office to the small conference room in the opposite corner. Her new cell phone rang. Rennie smoothly but quickly entered the conference room and closed the door. "What's up?"

Angie spoke in a hushed voice. "I just got out of my meeting. Someone called the school. You were right on target. They said some alumni or donor had made certain inquiries about the archives and how we manage things. It seemed innocent at first, until they asked about Matthias and his records. They had pulled the in-out records. They wanted to know if we have anything from the archives. I didn't lie, but I did mislead them. Is that okay?"

"We can't let them in on anything, yet. Matthew has to do his work."

"What happened this morning? What was his reaction?"

"It hit him. He's a tough, smart cookie, but he was over-whelmed. I took him to Roger's place. Roger set him up in a good room, with privacy, layout space. Where are you now?"

"I'm in my car. Are you at work?"

"Yeah, and it's spooky. Bud is gone. Nobody knows what's up. I found out someone is on my trail at the paper. We've got to try to act natural and not arouse suspicion. Matthew needs the time."

"Where is this going, Rennie?"

"I'm one of the pawns. All we can do is what we're called to do. What is important now is disclosing those letters. I don't see my story running at this point."

"I've got to get back. Be careful."

The moment Rennie hung up her phone, it rang again.

"Hi, this is Roger. Is that you?"

"Yes, what's happening?"

"Matthew's working away, I guess. But there's something odd going on here."

Rennie's mouth went dry. "What's odd?"

"Do you have cable at your place?"

"Yeah, why?"

"Have you had problems with it?"

"No. What's happening?"

"Well, there are a few guys in your backyard. They drove up in what looks like a repair van and they're wearing hardhats. Two of them have some kind of detection devices and they're walking along the property line. The other guy was up on the back porch. Hold on. I don't see the one that was on the porch. Rennie, I'm going over there. There's something wrong here."

"Wait, Roger. Don't do that. I'll call the cops. Please, just take care of Matthew."

There was a long silence. He finally responded. "Okay kid, whatever you say. I don't know what's going on, but you be safe."

"I will, thanks. Please keep Matthew there."

Rennie dialed 911 on her new cell phone but stopped. It occurred to her the 911 operator would identify her new number. She ended the call and picked up the receiver of the conference room phone. She dialed out and then the number for the police dispatcher.

"Hi, this is Rennie Haran from the *Record*. I've just received information that someone may be breaking into a house. Can you send someone over there right away?"

She gave them the address information and her business cell phone number. When she hung up, she sat down and gazed at the empty white board on the wall. Her eyes flowed across the board as if she was reading a diagram.

Her phone rang. "It's me again. I was watching those guys. All of a sudden, one of them put his hand to his ear and he called the others. They raced to the van and took off. I don't know where that third guy ever ended up, but he was with them. Hey, wait a minute. There's a police car coming into your drive. Did you call them?"

"Yes. Did the van get away?"

"It sure did, but not by much. Seems like they got tipped off."

"Is Matthew still okay?"

"Yeah, fine."

"You take care. Bye."

Rennie drifted back to her cubicle. Along the way, a thought came to her. *We've got to do this on our own.* She stopped and rubbed her temple. "How?" she whispered.

She logged on to the computer system and found the *Record's* intranet. She wondered if she could post her story of Matthias and the letters somewhere in the system to expose it to a large number of people. After reviewing several pages, she picked up her phone and called a friend in the advertising department.

"Bob, this is Rennie. It's been awhile. Say, I've got a quick question. You know how popular blogs are, especially for sharing information. I wondered if we had any way of doing that on our intranet."

"Not yet? Yeah, progress happens when some people are pushed screaming into the future."

Anxiety suddenly pulsed through her. Her story was dormant. Her boss was gone. She couldn't trust the system or anyone in it. She needed to take action, and it was time to move ahead.

She logged off her computer and hustled out of the office ready for battle.

She was only a few feet from her car door when two men in dark suits got out of a nearby car and came toward her. She struggled to locate her car keys to jump into her car. When they were nearly there, she searched for the can of pepper spray in her bag.

"Miss Haran, may we speak with you for a moment?" one man called out. "Please Miss Haran, we're with the government."

Her breathing had left her for a moment. She felt cold but focused. "What do you want?" she asked in a hard tone. Her jaw locked her teeth together.

The men stopped near the end of her car. A stocky man in rumpled suit pants reached slowly into his coat and removed a wallet. He flipped it open, revealing a gold badge next to some kind of identification card.

Returning it to his pocket, he said, "Miss Haran, we are with the local office of the FBI. Information has come into our office from the Department of Homeland Security, and we would like to ask you a few questions. Would you come with us to our office?"

"Gentlemen," she said with confidence, "I'm a reporter, and the local stories I do have no connection with any threats to our national security, except —" she paused and smiled, "except for investigation opportunities I may have regarding elected officials."

The men glanced at each other and relaxed. They seemed safe. "We understand. Sometimes, information might come from unlikely situations and have an impact on much larger issues. As a good reporter, you recognize that. Would you come with us, please?"

"As a good reporter, which is what you said, I have some questions for you. You didn't allow me to see the identification card you briefly flashed, so I don't really know who you are. I'm always happy to help with law enforcement activities, as long as it doesn't compromise the media's protected interests."

She found her keys and unlocked her car. "What area of inquiry would you like to pursue? We can set a time for us to sit down, in the paper's offices over there or yours. Our corporate counsel may need to be informed first. So, gentlemen, how can this member of the press help you? What is the topic?"

The man in front took a noticeable breath. One eye twitched as he shifted his weight. He took a step toward Rennie. She crossed her arms and stared at him. "Miss Haran, this is not an appropriate place for us to discuss something this important. May we come by your house later today?"

"I'm sorry gentlemen, but I didn't get any names here."

He took a deeper breath. "I'm Agent Maxwell."

"Agent Maxwell, what's the topic?"

"Miss Haran, if you wish to make this difficult, we can pursue this at another time. Tell me what you know about a man from the UK by the name of Matthew MacDonald."

Rennie hoped she showed no emotion in response to the question. Her mind raced with ideas. "Matthew MacDonald?"

"We know you're acquainted."

"I do know someone by that name. A retired professor who is about eighty or ninety years old? Is he a threat to the security of the United States?"

"Sometimes people are not all they seem to be. Professor MacDonald has made frequent trips to the Middle East and even to Syria. Syria is on this nation's list of terrorist states."

Rennie couldn't contain a burst of laughter. "Are you serious, or do you have too much time on your hands?"

The man's face puffed with anger. "We never fool around with national security, Miss Haran. You can tell us what you know now, or we can pursue this in more formal ways."

"Let's do it more formally, gentlemen. I'd prefer to be better dressed when my newspaper hears about this. By the way, is it true that under the so-called Patriot Act, you can go into a person's house without a court order?"

"I'm here with just one question. Will you cooperate?"

"You and I are not in opposition. I encourage you though, to look carefully at why you've been sent to me. Consider who sent you. Who are you really serving?"

Rennie opened her car door, got in, and locked the doors. When she started the car, the men stepped behind an adjacent car to avoid her quick exit.

She drove fast but was not sure where to go. For six blocks, she glanced into her rear-view mirrors. She wove through the downtown area for fifteen minutes until she realized she needed to stop and make some decisions.

She swerved into the entrance of a City parking ramp and drove up two levels before stopping. Rennie got out of the car, leaving the engine running. She paced back and forth in the safe haven of concrete and steel, alert for any cars that followed her. None appeared.

Her heart pounded and her breathing quickened. She returned to the car and called Angie. The call went to voice mail. She sensed she was beginning to panic, so she took a few deep breaths and closed her eyes. When calm eased through her, she called Roger.

"Roger, I wondered how things were going."

"You sound a little frazzled. What's up?"

"I'm staying one step ahead of disaster right now. I am not sure what the next step is."

"I heard once that when you get into that spot, consider what you might tell someone else to do."

"You're probably right. I'm feeling a little alone right now."

"Are you alone, or are you just not with those who are with you?"

Rennie laughed. "Since when did you become the Zen master? Okay, I understand."

"Since you think I'm funny, I'll ask you another one. When are you ever really alone?"

"Maybe, I'm trying too hard. I'm not doing this for me, so it would seem the burden isn't mine either."

"There you go," he replied. "When you introduced me to Matthew, I could tell you were into something very big. Rennie, if you are following a call of some kind, it's like going downstream in a fast current. You don't have to row. But you have to steer. Try to enjoy the ride."

"Thanks. I got distracted by the water and the rocks."

"Stay focused on where you are going, not where you are."

"It's time I got back at it. Tell Matthew I'll be there soon. How is he?"

"I checked on him a little bit ago. He came to the door but wouldn't open it. He basically told me to take a hike."

A cold chill went through Rennie. She thought of what Agent Maxwell said about Matthew. She wondered who she could trust. "Roger, I wondered if I could park in your garage. Do you have room?"

"No problem. Should I get the door now?"

"No, I'll call you when I'm ten minutes away. You're the best."

"Well, you haven't gotten my bill, yet. See ya, kid."

Rennie called Angie, told her about meeting the FBI agents, and what Roger saw happen at her house.

"Oh, no. Did someone go in your house?"

"I don't know. My gosh, I don't remember if we left the journals upstairs. Angie, what do we do?"

"You and I need to get with Matthew and hear what he has to say about what is in that tin box. That determines how important this is. If those manuscripts are not what we thought, then some of the heat is off. Otherwise, we need to take decisive action."

"You're right. Roger said we could come to his house instead of mine. It's on a different street and they won't notice. How are you doing?"

"This has been an awkward time. Somebody from IT called a minute ago and said they need to work on the system, so I had to log off my computer."

"You know, that happened to me, yesterday. They want to know who you've been communicating with. They'll check your e-mail. Can you get back in and delete anything related to our project?"

"I'll see what I can do. Yes, I can still get back in."

"Print whatever you can, or send it to yourself, and then delete everything."

"Okay. I'll call you back when I'm done."

Des Moines, IA
Offices of the *Des Moines Record*

XI - 5

Rennie sat quietly in her car for a fresh perspective. With renewed focus, she left the parking ramp and stopped at a drive-up ATM machine. After withdrawing the maximum $300, she considered how to approach Roger's house without being seen. It wasn't going to be easy.

She turned into traffic and saw a police car approach from the opposite direction. The driver seemed to watch her as they passed. At the next corner, she turned, then turned again at the next light.

Taking side streets, Rennie worked her way to the baseball stadium. Attentive to everything around her, she crossed the bridge over the river and left the downtown area.

Her energy grew as she felt in touch with her purpose. It was even more fun to do in such a stealthy way. *Who would play me in the movie?* She wondered.

Two blocks from Roger's house, she slowed to an unobtrusive glide. As she approached the last stop sign before her turn, she noticed a vehicle half a block down the street. It looked like the van Roger had described that morning. She realized she forgot to call Roger to open his garage door.

She pulled over to the curb and grabbed her cell phone. "Roger, I'm almost there. I'm sorry I didn't give you more notice."

"It's good you called. Stay where you are right now."

"What do you mean?"

"I've been watching your place and the neighborhood from my second-floor windows. That van I saw this morning is on a side street leading to your house on the east side. There's a dark sedan on your street but to the west. It arrived a little over an hour ago, and it's still there."

"I'm parked on your street about three houses down."

"You're what? Stay there for now. I think they have someone in your house. If they happen to look at my place from yours, and if they see you come into my driveway, it could get difficult for everyone."

"What do you suggest? I need to see this through. Hold on, I have a call coming in."

She switched calls.

"Angie what's up?"

"I think I got everything wiped out."

"Good job. You won't believe this. I'm parked about three houses down from Roger's house and he says my place is being watched. Angie, we've got to get with Matthew, and do it now."

"I had an idea earlier. I have a place for us all to meet and stay if we have to. It's secluded, comfortable, and safe."

"Where?"

"Have you ever heard of Wesley Woods? It's a retreat center and camp for kids, just a few miles south of town."

"I know it. I did a story on a non-profit here in town. They took inner city kids out to that place."

"I know the director out there. I called him and he has a few open cabins. All I need to do is let him know and we have our pick."

"Angie, you've done it. That's exactly what we need. Let's meet there."

"Deal."

"Make the call and get us a place big enough for you and me, Roger, and Matthew."

"Consider it done."

"Angie, be safe, and don't go home. Assume they know your car."

"Got it. By the way, if you have any clothes at the cleaners, you might pick them up. You could need them."

"What a little conspiracy junkie you are. Thanks, see you soon."

Just as Rennie hung up, a dark sedan turned onto the street and slowly rolled toward her. She laid down across the seat of her car and heard it go by. She glanced in the window to see its reflection. When it passed, she got up and started her car.

She drove past Roger's house to the corner, turning away from the block their houses shared. She continued down two more quiet streets, and turned left, parking in the middle of the next block. She called Roger again. "Hey neighbor, we have a plan."

"It's about time."

"What's going on?"

"Matthew is ready to brief you. I'd like to know what he's been studying. He went through two tablets with notes. I've never seen a guy go from being full of energy to such spent, quiet peace, in such a short time."

"Roger, have you ever heard of Wesley Woods? It's a camp or retreat center located south of Des Moines."

"Sure, I take my RV there. Nice place."

"I didn't know you had a motorhome."

"Yeah, I keep it at a storage place."

"Tell me where you store it, and I'll meet you there. We can park our cars there, take the motorhome down to Wesley Woods, and no one will notice us. Pack up some food and some clothes, too."

Rennie jotted down the directions on the margin of her newspaper. A determined smile formed on her face.

After picking up clothes at the dry cleaners, she got food at a drive-through. She reached the storage facility in a few minutes. She wasn't sure what Roger's car looked like, so she parked in the middle of a small group of cars, turned off the engine, and waited.

At the far end of the lot, a large RV came around a corner and slowly rolled toward the parking lot. A small pickup truck followed it. Rennie saw Roger driving the RV. Then she realized Matthew was driving the truck.

She got out of her car and removed her dry cleaning, the food, and her other things. When the RV stopped, Roger opened his window and yelled, "Hey lady, you want a lift?"

Rennie hurried across the front of the motorhome and stepped in the open door.

"This is amazing. What's with Matthew driving that truck?"

"That's my truck. We couldn't leave it out back. What's with all the stuff? You moving in?"

"Wow, this is big enough to live in. I had no idea you were a road warrior."

"It's okay. She's only thirty-one feet, which is good enough for this ol' boy."

Matthew locked the truck and dashed over to the RV. He had a big smile. Rennie stepped outside and hugged him.

"Hey, big guy. It's good to see you." She looked into his eyes. "So, are they the letters Matthias said they were?"

Matthew's expression grew serious. "Dear friend, they are," he whispered.

Rennie's breath slipped away. She held him more tightly. "Let's get on board. We need to talk."

He nodded and motioned her to the door.

"Do we have all we need, at least for now?" Roger asked. "I'm getting this buggy on the road, and there's no stopping until we reach our destination."

"What's it going to be, thirty minutes?" Rennie pretended to complain.

"The peanut gallery can sit down now."

Matthew laughed. "So, how long have the two of you been married?"

Rennie glared at him pretending to be shocked. "You're in big trouble, now."

Roger waited as Rennie hung up her clothes and set aside her bag and other items. Matthew placed on the table a notebook, pens, and tablets from a leather attaché that Roger loaned to him.

Soon, they were on the road to the campground. Rennie sat next to Matthew at the table. "Where do we begin?"

Matthew adjusted the tablets and pens on the table. "I don't know what to say. The only way I have been able to proceed, after discovering the letters, opening them, and realizing what lay before me, has been to compartmentalize my emotions and the gravity of this treasure. Somehow, I set aside my heart, operating on intellect alone."

His right hand began to shake. They both noticed it.

"I'm sorry," he said. "I must be careful in getting in touch with all this."

Matthew opened his notepads. They revealed names, timelines, phrases in Aramaic, Latin, Greek, and a series of questions. "Based upon what was in his journals, —"

"Are they here," Rennie interrupted, "or were they left at the house?"

"I have them. Aside from the letters, those journals may be my greatest possessions. I hope to spend some meaningful time with them when this immediate excitement has waned."

"I hope you can. After I had read them, I felt I knew Matthias. You can be very proud of your heritage. Are the letters what he described?"

"Oh my, yes," Matthew said with energy. "My father did not have access to the latest information and reference texts, such as the Gnostic documents or the Qumran find. Even so, those documents help to place these letters in an appropriate structure. There is one item that father was a bit in error with. Perhaps out of an emotional reaction, I believe he referred to the apostle Mark, who was in Alexandria according to tradition. The date and unfortunate method of his death there is well known. But my father's journal refers to the gospel writer and the disciple Mark as the same. Scholars believe they were different people."

Matthew took a deep breath. "I could not help but think of the gospel of Thomas, one of the Gnostic books, when I read the letters from Jesus. All in all, except for carbon dating of the material and confirmation by more specialized experts, I must admit that these are the real thing."

Matthew's face expressed an innocent joy. "What is so extraordinary is that the letters also offer insight into where Jesus was and what He was doing in those missing years between twelve and thirty. This is going to take exhaustive study and deep reflection."

Rennie sat back; her arms folded against her chest. "So, what did you learn?"

Matthew briefly looked at his notes. "Jesus wasn't too specific, but He apparently traveled quite a bit. He taught, and what's interesting, in one letter, it seems that when He was young, He wasn't quite clear what His purpose was. It was later when that became real for Him."

Rennie was stunned. "So, just like the rest of us. That's incredible."

"I wouldn't go that far. The letter doesn't say that. His situation was definitely not like the rest of us. Consider who He was and the conflicts in that condition. He could have devoted Himself to goals such as conquering the world, healing people, or teaching divine wisdom. Instead, He did all three in a perfect and unlikely way."

"Could these have been faked in any way?" she asked in a whisper.

"I have considered that. If you found them in this box, and if he found them as he described in the journal, we must take it as leading to only one conclusion. Jesus was a fairly common name, and there may have been one by that name who wrote home while he was away, but with the surrounding letters from his mother and from one named Matthew, which by the way makes me most proud, prove that this is the one we know as Jesus Christ. It almost takes my breath away to say it."

"Hey, back there," Roger yelled. "I won't have anyone swearing in my house!"

"Settle down," Rennie shouted back. "We are talking about Him. We aren't using His name in vain."

Roger gave a thumbs-up signal and continued to drive. "We'll be there in a few minutes. Take a look at that corn out there, Matthew. Have you ever seen anything like it?"

Matthew moved to the seat next to Roger. "Brilliant, truly remarkable. The productivity of this land, its expanse, and its beauty is beyond measure. Is this what they call the 'food basket' of the country?"

"Bread-basket, my friend, but I like food basket better. Corn, soybeans, hogs, and much more comes out of this little state in sufficient levels to feed whole nations. This is God's country."

Matthew glanced back at Rennie.

"Yes, my friend, I believe we have found God in this country."

PART TWELVE

A Campground
Outside Indianola, IA

XII - 1

Roger jerked at the steering wheel as the motorhome lurched along the rough dirt road entering the campground. Matthew and Rennie held on to their chairs to keep from being thrown around. Rennie spotted Angie's car parked near some cabins about fifty yards away.

"Go over there, Roger," she directed.

"Aye, aye skipper," he answered with a salute.

"Park so people can't see her car from the road," Rennie suggested.

When they stopped, Angie came out of a cabin. She had an odd smile. "There must be a very good story that comes with all this," she said.

"There is," Rennie replied, "but let's get inside so we can discuss it more privately. We should bring everything in with us."

Everyone grabbed the things they needed from the RV and carried them into the cabin. Angie gave a brief tour of the layout. Everyone agreed that the two bedrooms and two bathrooms would serve them well. Rennie worried about Angie's car out front even though Roger's RV blocked it from view. She suggested that Angie move her car to a more distant and secluded place in the campground.

They settled into the cabin and Roger offered to go to a grocery store to pick up more food.

"That's a good suggestion, Roger," Rennie replied, "but you're owed a full explanation about what we're doing."

"No, you don't owe me anything."

"We not only owe you that, but we also need to discuss it and plan what's next."

Angie returned from moving her car, so they gathered around the dining table. Rennie felt the intense anticipation of explaining their situation.

She turned to Roger. "In the course of a routine story investigation, I came upon what might be one of the most historic discoveries known to humanity."

She felt a rush of emotion and swallowed. "Roger, we have found letters written by the hand of Jesus Christ. That is why Matthew is here."

Roger's face went pale. "Matthew is an expert in this area, and he has confirmed that Jesus appears to be the author. Yesterday, I submitted my story about this to the paper, with all the appropriate wiggle language about further testing and review. It has generated the specter of a threat that was unexpected but is very real."

Rennie looked at Angie and Matthew. "And very dangerous."

"What kind of threat?" Matthew asked.

Rennie wasn't sure what to say. She leaned on the table. "During my research on the story and before we came to London, I was warned that someone might harm me, and someone broke into my house. In London, I know people were tracking us there. Very strange things have occurred at my office and at Angie's since I made known what we discovered. It is clear this story is of great interest to some very powerful people. In fact, they may want me, and maybe Angie or you, out of the picture. Roger, you witnessed unusual behavior at my house just today."

Rennie took a sip of water. "Also, today several men who claimed to be with the FBI approached me and wanted me to go with them. They said it was about Matthew and his travels to the Middle East. But, I'm not sure what they wanted. This is a dangerous situation, and that's why we're out here. We have the letters with us. Whoever is after them is out there, and we must not only care for them, but make them known to the world."

Roger looked at the others. "I don't know what to say, but I'm grateful I'm here. Just tell me what I can do."

Rennie put her hand on his. "I'm sorry I got you into this."

"It's okay, neighbor. This might be the best opportunity in our lives to do something really important."

"Amen to that," Angie said. "Okay team, we're an odd bunch, but that's the way God puts things together. Let's get at it."

As they got up, Roger suggested that he stay there instead of going for more food. They agreed that was a good idea, so he went out to the RV to lock it up.

Matthew laid out his notepads on the table. Angie and Rennie sat in anxious silence. "Angie, I will soon retrieve the letters from the box. I said to Rennie the only way I've been able to review the letters has been to stay in the analytical aspect of my being. When I slipped for a moment into the more human part of me, my emotions ran away. So, please understand why I must try to be scholarly as opposed to the simple man that I am."

"Matthew, I don't know how anyone could possible deal with it differently and be functional. We all know we're dealing directly with the hand of God here."

"Precisely. That grants to us an awesome responsibility as well as privilege," he replied. "There is no doubt in my mind that there are people who are after these letters. There are countless stories of powerful people either wanting or fearing something as profound as these letters. Once the word gets out among them, the darkness in the human spirit can take over."

Rennie felt a surge of anger. "Darkness versus the light. I know what team I'm on. Let's decide where we go from here."

"Excellent." Matthew exclaimed. "Our mission appears to

have two aspects. One is to care for the letters. The second is to make them known to all people. Where shall we begin?"

The cabin door burst open, surprising them. Roger seemed perplexed as he entered. "What?"

Angie got up and rubbed her hands with excitement. "I'd like to play a role in the second part, the revelation of His words."

Rennie tapped Matthew's arm. "You know, you have to look out for the quiet ones. She's always coming up with a good idea while I'm sitting like a lump."

As they chuckled, Matthew offered a notepad and pen to Angie.

"Thanks, but I'm more of an electronics media type. If I could have an hour or so with the letters, with your assistance Matthew, I could get started on one approach to preserving and displaying the letters. Have you written out the translations?"

"Yes Angie, I have them in my notes."

"Good. I don't know what your handwriting looks like, so I'd like you to print your translation of each letter, one to a page. I'll set up in the girls' bedroom, over here. There is only a small window and it's up high on the wall. What will we do with them for the long term?"

Matthew scratched at his beard. "That is a critical question. They must be preserved in the proper environment with proper handling. We cannot stuff them back into a tin box whenever we wish to set them aside."

"What are our options?" Roger asked.

"They're not much different than they were for Matthias. Placing them in the hands of a museum or similar authority will generally relinquish any assurance they will be revealed. We cannot know, and we may never know if there have been similar finds in the many libraries and museums between Jerusalem and here. We know of some interesting discoveries just in the last few decades. The question remains however, what was found and not made known?"

Rennie nodded. "That's been my fear. If I had walked into my office with that tin box and just handed them over, or if Angie had turned them over to the college, there is no telling who would have them now. We like to assume the best."

Matthew replied, "Exactly, but the best rarely happens."

Rennie turned to Angie. "What's your plan for making the letters known?"

"It begins with digital photography. I brought my photography gear. I better get going." Angie hurried into the women's bedroom, closing the door behind her.

"Okay, I like that. Matthew, what can you do?"

"I need a bit of private time in the gentlemen's bedroom. I have an idea that needs to be pursued."

"Of course. Roger, how about you?"

"It's good I brought a magazine. I'll be the bus driver until you tell me what to do."

Rennie went to work organizing the kitchen and preparing the meal. Roger noticed it was getting dark outside, so he turned on a few lights. As he returned to his chair, he stopped and looked at the windows. He went to each one and pulled down the shades.

Twenty minutes later, Matthew and Angie left their rooms and joined the others in the dining room, as Roger helped Rennie set the table.

When they were ready to eat, they joined hands for a prayer.

Rennie pushed her fork into the food on her plate. "There's something about sharing food with friends that brings a sense of peace to a house."

"Good food," Roger said. "Say, Matthew, what is it about your work that keeps you going?"

"It's the questions. There will always be plenty of them as gifts from the intersection of history, archeology, and religion."

Matthew set down his utensils. "For example, Christians

tend to think the church they know is the one that grew up after the Ascension of Christ. The facts are quite different. The development of the new church was pushed by revolt and turbulence into regions away from the holy land. Ephesus, Antioch, and Alexandria became centers of the faith. The books we know as the gospels were likely written in these distant lands. Paul's letters were written in and sent to many points around the Mediterranean. Finding letters and documents that are directly related to Jesus and the early faith in places such as Egypt or elsewhere is to be expected."

"You mean, like the Gnostic Gospels?" Angie asked.

"Exactly, and more," Matthew responded. "The document known as the Secret Gospel of Mark became notorious in scholarly circles. A professor found a reference to it while rummaging about in a monastery. He actually found dozens of manuscripts."

Matthew seemed to look into the distant past, clearly excited with the thought. "Comments by Clement of Alexandria in the second century referred to this Gospel of Mark. Prior to him, Pantaenus was highly regarded and was probably a Hebrew who may have known some of the original twelve disciples. Before him was Philo, another great teacher and devoted to his Jewish heritage. Here you have a Jewish man, in Alexandria, who may have set the framework in place for the birthing of the Christian church. So, finding letters from Jesus in Egypt is reasonable. Someday, we might even find another letter from the Apostle Paul."

Rennie passed a dish of food to Roger. "There is so much about that time that is important and I'm ignorant of it. The idea of them writing letters is a surprise in itself."

Matthew chuckled. "You mentioned writing letters? The ancient Egyptians documented nearly everything in the administration of the kingdom, two thousand years before Christ. Before Abraham in old Mesopotamia, there were libraries with thousands of documents on everything from science to philosophy and law. The Weld Prism was a type of Genesis book containing a history of the world and it dates back to 2200 BCE. There are tens of thousands of documents that are far older than texts from the time of Jesus. Many are not even properly stored! In the 1990's, scholars studied papyrus fragments of documents that had been stored in common paper folders. They were found in the Berlin Egyptian Museum in the 1960's and weren't looked at for thirty years. It's called the Gospel of the Savior, and it dates to the second century. So, finding the letters of Jesus the way Matthias did is not a big surprise."

Roger pushed his empty plate away. "What about the Gospel of Thomas?"

Rennie and Angie looked at each other with raised eyebrows.

"What?" Roger expressed with mock shock. "Do you think I just grow weeds all day?"

Matthew was amused. "You are right on target. Some said Thomas was a late interpretation and blending of the canon Gospels, particularly since the order of sayings is entirely different. It's probably one of many documents shared among early churches."

Rennie sighed, "What are we supposed to make of all this?"

"The truest of all books or letters are the Gospels. They were written most closely to the time of Jesus, within a few decades of His ministry, and they were written by people who either knew Him directly or knew those who knew Him. Then you have Paul's letters, which were written before the Gospels. In addition, there are large numbers of original copies of our New Testament written in the early centuries."

Matthew stopped, and his face became pale.

Angie got up and went to him. "Are you alright? Do you need something?"

"I just realized I have the real letters. They are there, in that very room. I've been talking about this theory and that, this document and that. We can get up, walk in, and touch the real thing. Dear Lord, we must regain our senses and press ahead."

A Campground
Outside Indianola, IA

XII - 2

Everyone helped put away food and clean the area. They
gathered in the living room.

Rennie paced across the room. "Let's be clear, we are
in hiding, from a tangible threat out there." She pointed to the
window. "Angie, you said you had a plan. What is it?"

"I'm excited about this idea. I had it before I left work, so
I came here prepared. I play with website building and digital
photography. So, with Matthew's help, we lay out each of the letters. I take a high-quality digital image of each one, and then I
upload it onto a new website. We can also put up his translation
of each one. In that way, we get them out to the entire world all at
once. With the right links to some big sites, with loads of productive meta tags, and by putting referral messages onto targeted
blogs, we will get tons of people to the site. They can download
the images and there is no way it can be stopped. People will
comment and debate, comparing their ideas about the letters."

"Brilliant!" Matthew exclaimed.

"Excellent," Rennie added. "Can you do it from here or do
you need to go somewhere?"

"I'm all set. I brought my laptop, and I have my camera and
a monopod to provide a steady shot."

"Is the cabin wired with a phone line?" Rennie asked.

"Yup, it's in. I checked before selecting the cabin. It's too bad
we have to use dial-up versus cable. If I shoot the images at five
megs, they will take forever to upload."

"I've got cable at my house." Roger said. "But it means we

have to go back there."

Angie's eyes flashed with thought. "Well, that would get it done a lot faster. I don't know how to weigh the risk thing."

Rennie felt a rush of anxiety. "Will the photography be a problem for the letters?"

"There should be no need for a flash to take the photos and the documents are in extraordinary condition. After the photos, we must get them into the proper hands. I have an answer to that concern."

Matthew stood and began a slow stroll around the room. "When we first arrived, I retreated into the bedroom and used my cell phone to call an old friend at the British Museum, Donald Abramson. It was quite a shock for him considering the time in London at that moment was about two o'clock in the morning."

Rennie interrupted him. "Do we want them to back in the British Museum? Besides, how on Earth can we get them there? Time is of the essence."

"My friend Donald is a member of an ancient order known as the Knights Templar."

"Oh no," groaned Roger. "This sounds like a movie plot."

Matthew chuckled. "My friend, sometimes truth is stranger than fiction. The Order has existed for a thousand years. It's alive and well, scattered across the globe, and there are members here in the States."

"So, are we going to have knights in shining armor ride in and take the letters?" Roger asked.

"That would be dramatic and highly unlikely. Members of the Order are people like us, who share high ideals and a devotion to Christ. Their aim is to promote love, charity, respect, and of course, chivalry."

Rennie nudged Angie. "We need to meet a couple of these guys."

"I informed Donald of the situation we are in, describing the treasure as a relic of profound historical value to the faith. He mentioned he knew of people in Chicago and in Minneapolis, but we were not certain of the time requirements to drive those distances."

"Minneapolis is less than four hours away," Roger offered.

"Excellent," Matthew replied.

Rennie was skeptical. "So, how would this work?"

"Donald, representing the museum, and then the Order itself, would mutually be responsible for the security of the letters and for ensuring their proper and prompt disclosure and technical analyses. Since the museum is in a bit of a financial situation right now, Donald was delighted that such a find might renew the prospects for the institution."

"I'm with Rennie," Roger said. "Do you trust this guy?"

"Absolutely, sir. I've known him for several decades. His word is his honor, and it's part of his faith. For this situation, the Museum and the Order would have a symbiotic relationship in securing and revealing the letters. The specific nature of what is being transferred need not be known. They will simply be aware it is of profound importance to the faith. Now, we must await his call."

Angie washed her hands in the kitchen sink. "In the meantime, I need to get to work. Matthew, will you help me? If we all participate, it will go more quickly."

Everyone got up and followed Angie into one bedroom. Matthew went into the other bedroom and returned with his personal bag. It was made of heavy tapestry material with a leather handle. It bulged with a hard, rectangular object.

Angie had covered the small window with a double folded sheet. She spread another sheet onto one of the beds and moved a short bookcase up to the end of the same bed. She tilted her monopod against the bookcase and secured her camera to the top. Matthew removed the biscuit tin from his bag. He gently set it on

388

the bed sheet and stepped back.

"Should we say a prayer?" Angie whispered.

"I think we are the prayer," Roger answered.

Angie stepped to the side of the bed. "Matthew, you can place the letters down in consecutive order, with each letter followed by your translation notes."

"Good. I will need to look at each briefly. Before you are ready to shoot, let me review my notes."

A loud knock on the front door made everyone jump. There was another knock.

"I'll go," Rennie said.

"No, I'll go," Angie said. "They know me here." She marched out of the bedroom and closed the door behind her.

Rennie could hear the front door open and barely heard some conversation. Matthew's cell phone began to ring in the other bedroom. Rennie heard the front door slam shut, followed by Angie running into the other bedroom. A moment later, she entered the room with the phone to her ear.

"Thank you, sir, Matthew is right here." She offered the phone to Matthew. "It's Mr. Abramson."

"Donald, thank you for calling back. Can we do this? This treasure exceeds all others. Yes, the gift will be entirely anonymous. For now, no one must know from where or from whom it has reached your hands. I know it will come under harsh criticism without the origins being known. How it came to be will be laid out at the appropriate time. Donald, you and I will never touch such glorious treasure again. Would you hold for a moment?"

Rennie felt hot with doubt. She remembered her confrontation with Agent Maxwell and his concerns about Matthew.

"How will this work?" She glared at him.

"A gentleman of the Order is driving from the city of Rochester, Minnesota. He is familiar with Des Moines, but he needs directions to where we shall meet to deliver the package."

Roger, Angie, and Rennie huddled. Rennie debated several sites then they agreed on one. Roger stepped from the group. "There's a zoo on the south side of the city. Adjacent and to the south of that, there's a golf course. You'll meet in the parking lot of the golf course whenever he arrives. It's at the corner of County Line Road and Southwest Ninth Street."

Matthew repeated the instructions into the phone. He glanced at Rennie. "Donald, can he be entrusted with this package? Good. I look forward to seeing you soon back in London. God bless you, my friend."

Matthew slipped the phone into his coat pocket. "The gentleman who is coming will call my cell phone number when he is one hour away. That may be sooner than we expect, so we must get busy here."

"Before we continue, who was at the front door?" Roger asked Angie.

"It was just Rod, the camp manager. He wondered if we needed anything. He's okay."

"We can't be too careful right now," Roger said. "Matthew, what do we need to do?"

"I recommend I remove each document, lay it out where Angie needs it, and then after the photo is taken, either of you two can set out my translation and notes in the space where the document was located. Once they are all photographed to Angie's satisfaction, I will return them to the fold in the manner they had been stored."

Everyone agreed with some hesitation. Rennie looked at her fingers and then at the tin box.

Matthew offered another thought. "It's important that we recognize how we might react to what we are about to see and do. If you feel moved or possibly overcome, it's understandable. These are letters written by the hand of Jesus, as well as from his mother and Matthew. They are in Aramaic, so you will not casually read the text. This is the last time we will have the privilege to be this close to them. We are blessed beyond measure. Are you ready?"

Angie put a hand over her mouth. Rennie stared at the sheet lying on the bed. Roger seemed grim.

"Wait," Roger said. "No matter what happens from here on, I'm grateful for your bringing me into your confidence. This moment makes life worthwhile. I don't know what comes next, but I welcome it."

Rennie put her arm around his waist.

Angie breathed on her glasses and cleaned the lenses.

"Okay, team. Let's get at it."

A Campground
Outside Indianola, IA

XII - 3

Rennie thought she heard a noise behind the cabin. She lifted a corner of the sheet that covered the window to look into the dark woods.

"Darn, I can't see a thing out there."

Matthew moved the third letter of Christ from its position on the bed to allow Angie to photograph the translation and notes. "Angie, I'm grateful you brought the archive gloves. I was worried about my grimy hands touching these precious documents."

She had a gleeful look on her face as she helped direct the papers into place on the sheet. "I cannot believe these are letters from Jesus. He's here with us."

She grabbed the monopod and looked at the image on the back of the camera. "Just for reference, I'm shooting these at five megs. That'll deliver reasonable clarity for anyone who wants a closer look."

"How're you doing, Roger?" Rennie asked.

He didn't respond. She noticed the redness in his cheeks and nose. His face expressed a concentrated determination.

He took a deep breath. "I've been thinking about where we go from here. The file sizes she'll be putting up would take a full day on a dial up connection. We don't have the time. Angie and I will take the RV to my house to create the Web site and upload these images on my cable line. You and Matthew take Angie's car and meet the fellow from Minnesota to hand off the package."

Rennie nodded. "Great idea, Roger. If anyone is looking for us, they won't notice you. Whoever is searching for us is less likely to spot Angie's car."

Matthew moved the documents for the next photos. "Once the letters have been passed on and the Web site is on-line, I recommend we meet at Rennie's house. It's best to insulate Roger's residence for the time being."

"I can handle whatever they'd like to dish out," Roger said with energy.

Rennie grinned and pointed at him. "Remember, gently and humbly. That is a good idea, though. When you guys are done on the Web, we should be home already. Just call before you come over."

Peaceful energy flowed between them as they worked together with precision and grace. Forty minutes later, the photography was completed. Matthew folded the documents into place. Then he lifted the package, looking closely at the top layer. He raised it to his lips and kissed it.

His lips quivered and his eyes filled with tears. "I'm sorry. I could not resist. This is the closest I shall ever be to the physical presence of my Lord. I am so sorry." He began to openly weep. Tears formed in everyone's eyes.

Rennie raised her hand. "Holy, loving God, we humbly thank You for this opportunity to know Your presence in our lives and to try to serve You. Amen."

All said amen and shared hugs. A hard knock on the front door hit their senses. They looked at each other for a moment. Angie hurried to the door as the knock sounded again. Rennie ran to join her. Roger and Matthew closed the bedroom door.

Angie snapped open the dead bolt lock and eased open the door a few inches. She peered through the crack and saw a young man in a sweatshirt and jeans. She fully opened the door.

"Hi, Rod. Good to see you again."

He shifted his weight, looking uneasy. He glanced at Rennie but stared at Angie. "Angie, I got a strange call. It was a guy named Maxwell. He said he was with the FBI." Rod's face twitched and he jammed his hands into his pockets.

"He asked if I knew someone by the name of Rennie Haran. I told him no and asked why. He said he was just making inquiries. Do you know who this person is, and what's going on? I never got a call from the FBI before."

Rennie's nostrils flared. She stepped forward but Angie stopped her with a subtle touch.

"Yes, I know that person, but I don't know this fellow Maxwell. If I can tell you anything more, I'll let you know."

He glanced at both women and briefly into the cabin. "Well, okay. It seemed odd. Is there anything else you need tonight?"

"No, thanks. Our meeting is nearly over, so we'll probably leave soon. Sometimes, Bible studies can end more quickly than expected."

He smiled uneasily. "Well, yeah. You don't hear that too often! Like I said, if you need anything, let me know. Good night."

Rennie and Angie watched him walk into the night. He looked back and waved.

After they closed the door, Rennie was furious.

"Maxwell is the purported FBI guy who stopped me at my car. How the heck did he connect me to this place?"

Roger and Matthew came out of the bedroom, meeting the women in the living area.

Rennie became agitated. "That was the camp manager. He said he got a call from the guy who stopped me at my car. How did he track me out here?"

"That doesn't matter," Roger replied. "Now we know they think we might be here. It's good we're done with the photo work. Angie, you and I need to hit the road. You can work on your laptop in the motorhome while I get us back to my place. Rennie, you and Matthew take the box and get out of here. Just drive around if you have to. Make your connection with our knight in shining armor, and then we'll meet at your house. Okay?"

Rennie shook her fist. "No! I want —"

Matthew interrupted. "Roger is right. However, this came to be, we must proceed to the next step."

Rennie took a deep breath. A realization hit her. She hurried to her bag and removed her company cell phone.

"This might be it. These come with GPS that can be tracked. It rang a while ago and let's see. Yeah, some 'unavailable' number called. They called the phone and determined where it was."

Angie responded, "Rennie, it's all right. We're done here. Let's go."

Everyone packed up their belongings. Matthew bound up the biscuit tin and placed it in his tapestry bag. He removed from the bag Matthias's journals, placing in them his translations and notes. He then wrapped the journals in a dish towel and placed them into a plastic bag, then in a paper sack with a bag of chips, a loaf of bread, and some plastic utensils.

Angie was about to bring her car to the cabin when Rennie stopped her. She handed Angie the business cell phone.

"Here, I turned it on. When you get to your car, go a little into the woods and throw it as far as you can. If they're tracking its signal, it will be a little diversion for them."

They slapped hands in a high-five. Angie hurried out the door and Rennie continued to help pack up.

When they were ready to go, they shared hugs and got into the vehicles. Roger guided the RV down the dirt road and through the dark woods as Rennie followed in Angie's car.

Matthew clung to his bag as the car bumped along the road. "We may want to consider which route any authorities may take to this location. They may not recognize Angie's vehicle, but we must be cautious."

"Quite right, my friend. Unfortunately, there's only one road into the woods. We need to get to a county road as soon as possible. I wish we would hear from our Minnesota friend."

"I, as well. It's quite admirable that he has undertaken this cause without knowing any details. He is a true disciple."

They followed the motorhome through the night as dust from the dirt road floated across the car. Reaching the county road, Roger turned right and proceeded up the highway toward town. Rennie accelerated straight across the road, continuing away from the camp.

On the Road Home

XII - 4

Rennie opened her window, allowing the late-night air through the car. She leaned her elbow on the door, enjoying the wind in her hair. She checked the clock and noticed it was after ten.

"We should be hearing from that guy at any time. I'm concerned we don't have a backup plan."

"O ye of little faith," Matthew replied with a grin. "Once he calls, we will need to be at the appointed place within the hour."

"Not a problem. If I can get to the freeway, we can cruise along until we hear from him. We can be at the hand-off place in twenty minutes from wherever we are if we stay on the freeway. All he needs to do is give us that much notice."

Matthew relaxed his grip on the bag. "Have you thought about where you will go from here, I mean regarding your career? I am concerned that the newspaper you work for may feel awkward having you on staff when this is resolved."

"The way I see it now, one's career is an opportunity to express one's personal gifts. If one place doesn't allow that, you move to where you can. The main thing is to do what you were crafted to do."

Matthew watched the road ahead. "So, for what were you crafted?"

"I'm a little closer to understanding why I was put here. What we are to do doesn't have to be some great thing. It's okay to work on an assembly line if that's your calling. But, if you are an artist and you're twisting a bolt every thirty seconds on the line, you will kill the spirit you were given. People are terribly unhappy when they are working for things instead of living out their destiny."

"How will you live out your destiny when this is over?"

"I haven't had a chance to think of that. We've been a little busy. I seem to be a little more mission oriented than task-based. I think where I go will be revealed to me. Okay, here's the freeway coming up. It's time to fly!"

Tilting with the roll of the RV as it cruised down the highway, Angie worked away on her laptop. In a fluid motion, her fingers danced across the keyboard inputting information needed for the Web site. Roger turned on an old CD player. He occasionally checked the rearview mirrors for other vehicles.

As the motorhome approached the on-ramp to Highway 5, Roger squinted to see past the overpass, where several cars appeared to be moving quickly down the road. They were unusually close to one another.

"That's odd," he said.

"What's odd?" Angie asked, while she continued to type.

"It's odd that three cars are coming this way, all together, and at this hour of the night. Hang on. I'm taking the on-ramp. You'd better get down. They shouldn't see you if they can look in here."

Angie folded together the laptop and stretched out on the bench seat, holding the computer in her arms.

Just before the cars reached his position, Roger turned onto the access ramp to the highway. He accelerated and looked into the rearview mirrors.

"It looks like they slowed down a little, but I'm not sure. They aren't following us."

"Is it okay for me to continue?" Angie asked as she got up and reopened her laptop.

"Looks good. It was probably nothing. Our timing was lucky, though. We'll call this a short cut. How much longer do you need?"

"Not long, maybe fifteen minutes. When we get to your place, I'll have the bulk of the text and set up needed for the site. Then it's just a matter of filling in the blanks. Let me know when we're close."

Matthew's phone rang. He removed it from his coat pocket and put it to his ear.

Rennie felt renewed suspicion and urgency as she glanced at Matthew listening and responding to the call.

He turned and handed the phone to her. "His name is Dale and he needs directions."

"Hi, this is Rennie. I'm glad you're close. Are you at all familiar with the City of Des Moines? Good. I'll try to get you to the meeting location along a simple route."

Rennie provided him with the route to the designated meeting point. When she felt confident he knew where to go, she had a question for him. "One last thing before we meet. What will you do with this package? How do you intend to get it back there? I'd like to know the details."

Matthew motioned he wanted the phone.

"Hold on, Matthew wants to talk to you."

"Hello. I understand. It's not a problem. We look forward to seeing you soon. God be with you." Matthew put away the phone. "Rennie, it will be alright. We need to trust at this point."

She glanced at her companion, wondering if she trusted too much. "It's hard for me to let go of some things. That's one of my problems. I need to fix everything."

"It is a good burden to have, my dear. There are few like you, and the world needs many. You can trust this."

As they approached the turnoff to their meeting place,

Rennie suddenly became nervous. She checked her rearview mirrors and scanned the area, ducking her head back and forth.

"What's wrong?" Matthew asked.

"I just realized that if there was anyone looking for us back at the campground, they might come this way. This road also goes to the camp. What if they see us?"

"We have no choice, now. We must do what must be done. There are only a few minutes to our meeting time. Can you get there in time? He will not wait for more than a couple of minutes."

"Why, does he have other plans tonight? Sorry. It's up ahead. Do you have it ready? Say, are you giving him your personal bag?"

He held the tapestry bag in his arms and slid his fingertips across it. "Yes. It will be a privilege to know this was the transfer case. My father, Matthias, purchased this bag for my mother when they were on an outing. She always treasured it, and now the greatest treasure of all will be carried forth in it. I believe they would be pleased."

Rennie bit her lip and nodded. Then, she pointed. "Look, there's the parking lot. Do you see him? What's he driving? There he is, in the corner."

She turned off the road and drove across the lot, turning her lights out as she came close to the other vehicle. A man stepped out wearing khaki slacks and a Minnesota Golden Gophers t-shirt. Rennie stopped the car next to him.

"So, our white knight is a Gopher?" she said with a smile.

"He is this evening," he replied. "I'm Dale. I appreciate the call."

Matthew got out of the car and walked around it to shake hands with their contact. "Hello, I'm Matthew. I'm very pleased that you would assist us. Please tell any others who may be involved they will soon know how remarkable this venture is."

"It need not be remarkable, sir. It only needs to serve God. That's why I'm in the Order. I guarantee your package will reach its destination. I'll be leaving now. God's peace to you."

"And, God bless you, my friend," Matthew responded.

The man took the bag, got into his vehicle and drove to the parking lot exit. When he reached the road, he turned on his lights and accelerated up to speed.

Matthew tugged at his beard and looked down at Rennie through the driver's window. "That was a bit quick."

"Yeah, for me, too. I'm feeling a little empty." She looked at the road. "Matthew, did we accomplish anything?"

"That will depend upon Angie and Roger. I hope they arrived safely at his house."

"Let's get over there and see."

Matthew got into the car, and Rennie turned the car around. She stopped and stared out the window. He observed three cars stopping in the street and the entrance to the parking lot.

"How long have they been there?" he asked.

"They're just arriving. I hope they didn't see our buddy leave."

"I suggest you go straight to your house. Don't try to evade them."

Rennie winked at him and drove out of the parking lot past the cars. All three followed her home. When she turned into the driveway, the cars parked on the street one house away. No one got out of them.

Rennie and Matthew strolled to the house without looking toward the street. When she got to the front door, she discovered it was unlocked.

She looked at her key. "It seems whoever broke in couldn't bother with locking up when they left."

Rennie turned on lights as Matthew closed the window shades. She hurried to the back door to see if there were lights on in Roger's house. She saw one light on the second floor.

"Shall I make some tea?" Matthew called from the kitchen.

"Please do. I can't believe how good it feels to be home. Are those guys outside going to simply sit there? I don't get it."

"It's difficult to say. They may be awaiting orders. They obviously move very carefully."

Rennie got out her new cell phone and called Roger's number. The call went to voice mail. As Rennie began to leave a message, Roger answered.

"Hi there," he said.

"How's it going? Has Angie got the website up?"

"She's doing a great job. The basic structure is set up. She laid in the text she prepared as we drove up here. Now, it's taking some time to upload the images. Once that's done, it's show time."

"Our friends who have been on my tail found us. Luckily, it was just after we made the hand-off of the package. It's on the way. Three cars came up behind us and followed us home."

"What, three cars?"

"Why?"

"We saw them on our way back. They were flying down the road toward the campground. I turned onto the access ramp to Highway 5 just in time. They must have found you on their way back. Did you ask them if they found your phone?"

Rennie laughed. "I didn't get a chance, yet. They're still sitting out front."

"No kidding. What do you think we should do when we're done?"

"Call me. If I don't answer, stay there. Otherwise, we'll decide then."

"Okay, bye."

Matthew approached with a cup on a saucer. "Here you go, dear. I took the liberty to put out some sliced cheese with crackers. It would be good to refuel at this point. It may be a long evening."

HOME!

XII - 5

A loud knock on the front door startled them.

Anger rushed through Rennie. She shoved open the kitchen door.

Matthew placed a hand on her shoulder. "This is nearly finished. Let's not fall into their ways."

Her energy and emotion drove her forward. She jerked open the door. The two men she had met at her car were standing there. They said nothing.

"Agent Maxwell, I presume. Did you come back to lock my door?"

The men stepped aside to allow an older man to come forward from behind them. His manner was refined, and he wore finely tailored clothing.

"Miss Haran, it is time that we met. My name is Charles Sfumato. May we come in and visit for a moment?"

Rennie turned to see where Matthew was.

He came up behind her and said, "It's alright."

She motioned for the men to enter. The two "agents" stepped in, surveying the environment as they moved. Sfumato gracefully went to a chair in the living room and touched it, as if requesting permission to sit. Rennie nodded her approval.

Matthew appeared to be alert to every detail of the men. His eyes flashed from one to another but dwelled on the older man. He sat in a chair across from Sfumato, with a table between them. The two "agents" stood in opposite corners of the room with their hands clasped in front of them. Rennie stopped behind the couch, using it as a barrier between herself and Sfumato.

"Please Miss Haran, I will need to stand again if you do not sit with us. Please join us."

Matthew indicated his agreement.

When she sat down, she was surprised to feel confident and calm. "So, are you the local FBI boss, or are you a boss on the other side of the line?"

He tapped his fingertips together. "Miss Haran, I regret the unfortunate ruse that was presented to you by my associates. We eagerly wished to discuss with you the remarkable find you and the distinguished Professor MacDonald may have made. In such a situation, discretion is foremost. We obviously erred in the approach taken as we tried to maintain a low profile. You were quite effective at eluding our contacts."

His smile showed a hint of arrogance, yet respect.

"Am I supposed to know you mister? Who are you?"

"There is no particular reason why you would know me." He looked at Matthew. "But then, Professor MacDonald may be acquainted with my name."

Matthew's eyes sparkled. He turned to Rennie. "I can offer some small insights. Mr. Sfumato is a noted collector of antiquities. He is quite actively involved in all aspects of finding and collecting ancient artifacts, except of course, actually digging for them. You are from California, is it?"

"Quite right, Professor. My home and office are in San Francisco."

Matthew adjusted his glasses and his face became tight, almost pale. "There has been much talk in the professional world we share that the thousands of priceless items taken from the Baghdad Museum and other preserves of history found their way into private collections." His nostrils flared. "What do you know of this?"

Sfumato flicked a piece of lint off his pant leg. "That may undoubtedly happen. It is quite distressing what happened over there. My only wish is that the artifacts are safe."

"And, what was your role in that?" Matthew shot back.

Rennie interrupted the sudden tension between the men. "Excuse me. Mr. Sfumato, how did you become so quickly aware of any discoveries I may have happened upon?"

He tugged on a shirt sleeve and adjusted his cuff link. "In my business, it is important to have friends in many places. Even here in Iowa, I have a few valuable acquaintances. This assignment you have been on may have commenced from one of them. Your sudden journey to London suggested that something interesting may have arisen."

His eyes narrowed and his relaxed demeanor stiffened. "While you were in London, you were being watched, Miss Haran."

"I know that." She felt a renewal of her intensity.

"Perhaps, what I intended to say was that my people in London were watching over you. I believe you received an unexpected gift at your hotel one day."

Rennie grit her teeth. Before she could respond, Sfumato continued.

"The stone you received was not from my people. It came from a man who has an inordinate passion to keep holy treasures from reaching the populace. He is directly related to the story you have been pursuing."

A grin reappeared on Sfumato's face. "You see, there was a cleric who knew the Professor when he was in London. This fellow, —."

"Worthy," Rennie spit out.

Sfumato looked pleasantly surprised. "Yes, exactly," he purred. "The Reverend Worthy had a daughter to whom he apparently told the story of Professor Justus. Through marriage and political skills, she grew to be quite a commanding presence. She was more disciplined, shall we say, than her father."

Rennie felt calm and clever. "So, what about her, this

daughter."

"She developed something of an obsession with this story and passed the illness on to her son, Seth Galila. He became quite wealthy in the corporate legal field. More relevant to our interests, he became a serious problem to anyone interested in ancient treasures, particularly those with connections to Jewish or Christian matters. He is devoted to stopping any such artifact from becoming revealed and does so by obtaining and destroying them. He thinks of them as dangerous to Christian doctrine. His practices can be deadly."

"Mr. Galila's people somehow became aware of you. One of my people in London observed them following you. Miss Haran, at a certain point, your safety was questionable."

"I get the feeling Mr. Sfumato that you're suggesting you are on my side."

"Miss Haran, everyone is on their own side. That's how the world works. It just turned out that for a moment, my people were able to eliminate the threat you and your friend were facing in London. Without their actions, you might not be here today."

Sfumato's face was suddenly transformed into an almost child-like innocence. "What's more, the man sent two of his people here, following you on your return. Those men are now in police custody. It only took a call to certain Homeland Security people in Washington. Galila's men didn't get past Chicago," he exclaimed with pleasure.

Rennie relaxed into the couch. "So, why are you here?"

"Once information was made available regarding your possible success in finding the treasure, I immediately flew here. This business includes people in all strata of society. Some, like Galila can be dangerous. Wouldn't you agree, Professor? It is in your best interests that I arrived first. Someone more interested in the artifact and less interested in you might have handled this with less dexterity."

Matthew turned to Rennie. "That is true. As with all things, there is a light side and a dark. I'm just not sure on which side Mr. Sfumato wishes to be."

"Aptly put, Professor. Your frame of reference is not unexpected."

Sfumato rested his hands in his lap. He gave Rennie a sinister look. "Given the late hour and our journeys through the bucolic charm of Iowa, please update us regarding the status of your find."

Rennie didn't like his snide attitude. "I'm surprised you aren't up to date on that. Didn't your associate Agent Maxwell have a sufficient log of my calls, e-mail, and travel? Perhaps he missed some key information when he was in my house."

Sfumato glanced across the room at one of the men standing in a corner, then back at her. "I'm not in touch with all that goes on. I thought it would be best if we discussed this face to face. I'd like to know the nature of what you have found, where it may best be preserved, and how we can resolve these questions."

Rennie leaned forward. "Would you like to begin by seeing what it is that I found?"

His eyes brightened. "Yes, I would be most delighted to see your discovery. Is it here?"

"Yes. I keep it right here." Rennie patted the couch cushion.

He glanced at the cushion. "There is no need for sarcasm, miss." His voice rose in volume. "I am not here to wage some petty disagreement. I am a businessman who has a reputable role in preserving the ancient treasures of this world. Our time is valuable. The nature of what you may have found deserves the respect of considering all options in its preservation."

"What about its disclosure? How would you disclose its contents to the world?"

"We would consider that in due time. Once it is secure, properly reviewed, and in the right hands, we would make decisions as to any disclosure."

Rennie felt intense. "If I understand you correctly, and please feel free to chime in here Matthew, when you have this treasure securely in your collection, you will decide whether or not the contents or nature of the find is made known to others?"

"Miss Haran, with the most precious artifacts, one must always be cautious of revealing their existence. This is an unpredictable world. I must be blunt. We need to move forward. What is the price you wish to receive for your discovery?"

Rennie relaxed again. "Thanks for being direct. I regret I don't know your business. What's the value of something that is priceless?"

"I am always amused with that term. Somehow, people are always able to name their price. Their marriage, their home, their health, their dignity all has a price. So, what might be yours? What personal dreams can be fulfilled for you?"

Rennie enjoyed a deep breath. "Now you're talking my language. I can translate that back to you. Is that okay?"

"Absolutely, whatever helps us move ahead."

"Good. This is how I think of price. From my perspective, price is not something I get. It is the willing gift that I pay to honor God. There is no price too high for that. I regret I haven't come to know that sooner in life nor well enough even now. The treasure I have found is priceless, and that means I will give it to you for free."

Matthew's mouth dropped open. Sfumato appeared to be confused, looking quickly at Rennie and then Matthew.

"That would be most generous of you, Miss Haran. Are you serious?"

Rennie's telephone rang. "Excuse me, gentlemen." She hurried to answer it.

It was Roger. "We're done. Can we come over?"

"Wonderful. Please come."

Sfumato shifted in his chair and straightened his suit coat. His eyes darted around the room. "Are more guests coming, Miss Haran?"

"Just a couple of friends. One you may know. She's a wild librarian."

He looked at his watch. "It's nearly midnight. Perhaps, we should continue our discussion later this morning. I need to fly back very soon."

Rennie realized they had done all they could do. The package was on its way and the website was up. She returned to the couch.

"Mr. Sfumato, I apologize for my behavior tonight. Within the frame of reference you live in, people probably consider you an honorable man. This has been a challenging project and an emotional roller coaster of mythic proportions. If you want to see what we found, please wait for just a few minutes."

He took a noticeable breath and seemed to relax. "Thank you, and there is no need for apologies. Our own approach to this may have been less than appropriate. I hope we can move ahead in a positive tone."

Rennie stood up. "While we wait, how about if I get some snacks?"

She checked with the two men in the corners. They smiled awkwardly and declined.

Sfumato slipped forward in his chair. "That would be gracious of you. Would it be acceptable if Professor MacDonald and I chatted for a moment?"

Rennie nodded to Matthew. "To the degree you believe it appropriate, go ahead and describe what was found. Oh, and by the way Mr. Sfumato, the Professor's last name is actually 'Justus.'"

Matthew followed by Sfumato moved to the dining room table where their conversation was more private. Rennie observed them for a moment, then proceeded to the kitchen. Matthew's demeanor was cool and scholarly, but he became more animated and seemed to enjoy the discussion.

Rennie used her cell phone to make a brief phone call. Then she arranged cups, glasses and small plates on the kitchen table and was removing cheese and fruit from the refrigerator when Roger and Angie entered through the back door. Rennie whispered a brief explanation to them. They quickly helped her assemble the appetizers and placed them on trays. Her cell phone buzzed, and she answered the call. She listened for a minute and said, 'thank you.'

As they brought the items into the living and dining rooms, Rennie provided brief introductions of Angie and Roger.

Angie went to Rennie's computer, logged on to the internet, and found her new Web site. Roger prepared a dish of snacks, and with a glass of water, sat in a wing-back chair near the bookcase.

Rennie noticed the diplomatic guile of Sfumato disappeared as Matthew described what had been found and what was in the letters. Sfumato asked questions with the urgent, wide-eyed desire of a child anticipating Christmas.

Noticing the others were waiting, the two men stood and warmly shook hands. Sfumato expressed new vitality. He turned to Rennie. "Miss Haran, you and your team has undertaken an extraordinary task in a brilliant fashion. I congratulate your investigative diligence." He shook her hand with enthusiasm. "I would embrace you if I were not a gentleman."

"That's okay, shaking hands is fine. Please sit down and have something. Your associates are also welcome to sit. There's no danger here."

Rennie took a chair next to Matthew.

With some hesitation, Sfumato prompted his associates to join them at the dining table. Angie moved to the couch from the desk.

"Have you heard of anything like this before?" Rennie asked

Sfumato.

He swirled the tea in his cup. A slight smile emerged at the corners of his mouth. "For centuries, there have been rumors that such documents exist. Some suggested the Vatican's private libraries held remarkable texts. Others said the Antiquities Authority in Israel has much more from the Qumran discovery than the Dead Sea scrolls. There are also rumors of remarkable documents in the archives of the Topkapi Museum in Istanbul. And, you might imagine, since the 1920's, there were stories of a find at the British Museum. Efforts to clarify these were never successful."

He studied Rennie and Matthew for a moment. "People inquired as they could, but until now, the real story was unknown." A wistful smile appeared on his face. "Now, this special quest of mine is complete."

Deep calm filled Rennie. "I must be straight with you. We no longer have the letters. They are on the way to London. The British Museum has agreed to participate in securing the letters."

Sfumato blinked a few times. He glanced at Matthew as if expecting him to say something.

Rennie beamed from an inner joy. "Not only that, at this moment, people all over the world are now able to see the letters, and they can see them for free. We set up a website that displays the letters and translations of the letters. Angie has it over there if you want to check it out."

Angie went to the desk. Sfumato appeared to be confused. He looked at his men, as if in need of help. With the assistance of one man, he left his chair and joined Angie at the computer. He stared at the screen as she moved through the website pages. His face appeared pale and lifeless. His eyes reflected a flurry of thought.

"How could you do this?" he said in a weak exhale. "This is a disaster."

"We tend to think it is a triumph, sir," Angie said.

Sfumato glared at Matthew. "Who in London has the letters? You know I can find them."

"They're in good hands." Matthew replied.

The man pointed at Angie. "You may find that your school will have some serious questions for you regarding your management of its priceless assets. As for you Miss Haran, I believe your role in legitimate journalism may be over."

Rennie leaned forward, resting her elbows on the dining table. "Frankly, those concerns have meant little to us since we realized our mission. In fact, while I was in the kitchen earlier, I called my boss to let him know what was going on. He called our publisher, whom you may know."

She sensed how fragile Sfumato had become.

"Even at this late hour, he reached her, and he called me back. They look forward to seeing the information online. You see, the newspaper wanted the story, not the letters. The paper got what it wanted."

"And Simpson College," Angie's firm, clear voice cut through the air as she stood up. "Simpson College will be pleased to announce that priceless documents from the British Museum were found in its archives and that they have been returned to the museum."

She glared at Sfumato. "They might even send me to London for the announcement."

Sfumato staggered toward the front door. His men came to his side to support him. As one man opened the door, Rennie looked at the old man with compassion. She left the table and went to him.

"I want you to know this was not done against you but was done for truth."

"I don't understand, Miss Haran. Do you realize that without scholarly verification and support, the authenticity of the letters will remain in question?"

"It's not as important that the letters are verified as it is that the presence of Jesus is renewed in people's hearts and minds."

His head dropped, and his men helped him out of the house to a car. Another man got out of the car and opened a door for him.

Rennie and Roger followed onto the porch. As the car drove away, Rennie heaved a deep sigh and leaned against Roger.

Returning inside, Matthew greeted her with a warm hug.

"My dear," he said, "this is an historic moment. I thank God for you. Now, I need to make two telephone calls. One is to my friend Donald in London, to let him know what has transpired. The other will be to my sister, Mary. I would like to see if I might be able to visit her when I return. My grandson David might also find an interest in this. In fact, I'd like you to meet him."

Angie placed her arm around Matthew.

Rennie winked at her. "Hey, I didn't know about Simpson and that announcement."

"Well, they aren't aware of it either, at least right now."

Roger yawned and stretched. "Well, if you don't need the bus driver anymore, I'm going to turn in."

Rennie took his hand. "Thanks, good friend."

He squeezed her hand. "So, what are you going to do now?"

"Everything is so different. I think I'll go see my parents. There's a big gap between us that needs to be filled. I've had a taste of belonging and love. I want more, and I want to share it."

"Friends," Matthew said, "this old traveler needs to find a bed for a long, glorious rest. Rennie, in the morning, perhaps we can chat about what's next."

"Definitely. One item on my list is a return to London. The British Museum will be a place to start."

Acknowledgement

The interplay of characters with plot, scenes and subjects is a tapestry that each reader experiences in their own way, with personal attention to detail or as distant imagery. Some will wonder how one thread connects to another, while others sit back and enjoy the flow of colors across a full design.

It is this sparking of ideas into unknown realms of thought and feeling that makes writing a privilege and a responsibility to writers. The offering of a pathway into little worlds of discovery of the mind and soul is a profound opportunity.

It is my hope that all readers of literature in any form taste the words and run their fingers gently over the material that engages them so they too can become aware of the special moments that personally await them.

Reading is a unique experience, and you dear reader, are a unique person on the way to becoming even more interesting. Journey on.

Thank you for being and becoming, and for allowing this work to be part of that process.

https://rdHathaway.com
Twitter: @HathawayRd
Facebook: @R.D. Hathaway

Other Works by This Author

After *Secret Passages*, what happened next?

Hidden Passion by R.D. Hathaway

Join Rennie Haran again as her determination and courage drive her into the depths of a deadly adventure. *Hidden Passion* is a race-against-time thriller set in the mysterious world of tradition and ceremony of the Catholic Church. When a controversial secret is uncovered that has been hidden for millennia, unknown forces will stop at nothing to prevent the news getting out.

Made in the USA
Las Vegas, NV
07 December 2021

36492239R00233